MW01486739

MAD MICK

MADMICK

FRANKLIN HORTON

MASTERS OF MAYHEM

BOOK TWO IN THE MAD MICK SERIES

Copyright © 2019 by Franklin Horton

Cover by Deranged Doctor Design

Editing by Felicia Sullivan

ISBN: 9781795075213

All rights reserved.

No part of this book may be reproduced in any form or by any electronic or mechanical means, including information storage and retrieval systems, without written permission from the author, except for the use of brief quotations in a book review.

Created with Vellum

1

Bryan Padowicz sipped a cup of coffee and stared out the frosty window of his cabin. Beyond it, Douthat Lake held a crescent of floating leaves collected by the current and dropping over the rustic stone overflow a few at a time. Fall was deepening and Bryan would guess that most of the leaves had fallen off the trees by now. They would all be gone soon and a depressing winter would settle on them like bad news.

A ragtag assortment of dirty women dressed in ill-fitting clothes were making their way down a leafy walkway along the lake, heading to work on the crops. The group's winter food, their financial security, the very future of Bryan's noble project rested upon the fruits of those women's labor. As sad as it was, that handful of women represented nearly everything he had left of his prisoner workforce.

At one point he had forty to fifty women held at his farm, a former state park. He was planning to double that by this winter but nothing had gone as intended. The women, conniving witches to the very last one, had schemed and plotted, poisoning the men's clothes with some extract of poison ivy, driving the men nearly mad with itching. Some of the men tore at their flesh until it became infected and they had to be treated in the infirmary.

In the midst of their itching misery, when the men of Douthat Farms were distracted by their constant discomfort, the women turned on them with the tools of their labors. Hoes, shovels, mattocks, soup ladles, and laundry cudgels became weapons that battered and killed their guards. As a result, over half of Bryan's workforce of captive women escaped. A handful were shot and killed in the commotion. What remained were pitiful and downtrodden, demoralized waifs praying for their own deaths. Bryan had to admit it looked as if the collective efforts of these poor women and his remaining men would not be enough to carry this operation through the winter.

After the *rebellion,* as Bryan referred to it, he sent two dozen of his best men on a journey south to bring back more women. He didn't want women collected locally because he feared it might motivate the locals to turn on him. It had been several weeks and they had not returned. Bryan didn't have many more men to spare. He sent out the occasional rider when he could, looking for signs of his party, but they found nothing. Sometimes locals indicated they'd seen riders pass but no one knew what happened to them.

He didn't have enough men left to send out another raiding party. Although they needed more captives, he barely had enough men to run the day-to-day operations. Without labor, they were doomed. He wasn't sure what to do.

A couple of days ago he sent an emissary into a local town and managed to hire a couple of men. He'd always been reluctant to do that before, fearing that local men might reveal details of their operation. He didn't want the town to know he was raising drugs to sell. Nor did he want them to know he was using captive women to do it. In desperation, he hired two men, fed them, and put them on sentry duty, which required fewer skills than many of the other tasks.

The pair disappeared yesterday and took two more of the captive women with them. It was possible they would tell other folks about the slaves. It was yet one more thing to worry about. While Bryan still had dreams that his Douthat Farms estate could turn into a modern day Monticello and him a modern-day Thomas Jefferson, that hope faded more with each day.

He understood the lights would probably come back on one day soon and all of this would go away. The clock was ticking. He had to stake his claim and build a fortune before order was restored. People would trade their worthless cash, property, and more for the food he grew. When the lights came back on, all of that cash and property would make him a wealthy man, but without slave labor he would earn nothing. Loss hung over him like the darkness of an approaching storm.

Bryan finished his coffee, placed the mug on the empty kitchen countertop, and returned to the living room to stoke the fire. He dressed warmly for a morning outdoors, strapping on a Colt 1851 Navy revolver. It was an affectation he adopted because he never actually expected he would have to fire his weapons. They were show. Part of his costume. He wasn't even a very good shot.

He hung an AK-47 over his shoulder before stepping out the door. He hadn't even reached the edge of his porch when he saw a figure in work pants and a hoodie jogging toward him. It was Michael, who led the work crews that tended the greenhouses. When he saw Bryan, he raised a hand in greeting and slowed to a walk. He was still trying to catch his breath when he reached the base of the steps.

"This better not be bad news," Bryan said. "I have no more room in my soul for it."

Michael was still breathing too hard to talk but raised his eyes with a wary hesitation that could only mean he had nothing good to pass on. "The marijuana is gone," Michael gasped. "Somebody cut off the lock and ripped up all the plants. They took it all."

"There were over a hundred mature plants," Bryan said. "They got all of them?"

"There are footprints everywhere. There must have been a couple of people."

Bryan sighed. It had to be the local men they'd hired, the ones who just ran off with two of the women captives. The greenhouses were secluded, located inside old maintenance sheds used by the state park staff. The lights ran off solar equipment that Bryan had installed himself.

It wasn't likely someone just came across them. A few weeks ago he had guards on those greenhouses all night but he didn't have the men for that now. If they'd still been there, this never would have happened. Now he barely had enough men to keep the woodstoves in the greenhouses going.

"Are the poppies okay? The vegetables?" Bryan asked. There was a hint of desperation in his voice that almost embarrassed him. He needed some good news.

"I'm not sure," Michael replied. "I don't think so."

"They took those too?"

"Not exactly," Michael said. "Whoever stole the marijuana plants broke into the other greenhouses and trashed everything. Turned the plants over and hacked them up with machetes. Then they left the doors open so the temperature inside dropped into the twenties. I think everything they didn't damage is probably too shocked to survive."

Bryan stood there stoically, resisting the impulse to sling his AK into the yard, scream, and curse. He had been so close. Everything was nearly to the point of harvesting. He was angry and hurt on so many levels. Worse yet was the crumbling of his dreams before his very eyes. He'd grown marijuana for enough years that he was certain of his horticultural skills. He'd raised the marijuana to sell and trade for other goods. He raised the poppies for making opium to sell and trade.

For the people who didn't want drugs, he was raising enough food that he could support his own folks and still trade for other things they needed. Now he would be lucky if they had enough food on hand to make it through the winter themselves. He was nearly certain they didn't. His people would soon be reduced to scavenging like everyone else. How loyal would they be to him then? How dedicated would they remain to his vision, the birth of a magnificent estate that would enrich him and his family for generations, that would successfully support those who believed in him?

"Is there *anything* left?"

"The potatoes are probably still safe. We planted those in five-gallon buckets so I'm sure the soil protected them. There's a lot of them but I don't know if we can survive off them or not."

Bryan was crushed but continued to push his emotions inward. He needed to be a problem solver, a leader. People were depending on him. His descendants were depending on him. "Harvest all the potatoes. Store them in the root cellar."

Michael shifted uncomfortably. "The cellars were not completed. You put men on it just before the revolt but they only got a couple of days into it. All we have is a hole in the ground beside the dining hall. It's about the size of a large grave but has no roof and no door."

Bryan lowered his head to his chest and took a deep breath, speaking through gritted teeth. "Dig. The. Potatoes. Put them in. The dining hall. For now. Make sure it's warm enough that they don't *freeze*. Gather all the men. In the dining hall. I'll meet you there. In one hour."

Michael hurried off, anxious to escape the uncomfortable and disappointing line of inquiry. He was fully aware he'd delivered nothing but bad news. Most of the employees at Douthat Farms thought Bryan was eccentric but none of them made the mistake of thinking he was harmless. He made erratic decisions sometimes. Occasionally, people paid with their lives. Michael had stood in fear throughout that entire conversation, certain he was about to pay the ultimate price for a situation he'd played no part in.

Bryan spun stiffly on his heel and went back inside his cabin. He unslung his rifle, replacing it on the rack among the historical weapons he'd stolen from a nearby museum. He went to his desk and sagged into his antique chair, leaned back with his limbs splayed in all directions. He was very nearly a broken man. He felt the burden of a defeated general or the leader of a crime family as the Feds were closing in. How could he handle this?

He sprung to his feet and strode to an antique crystal decanter resting on a Queen Anne table. The claw-and-ball feet reminded him of his mission and his place in history, or rather the place he intended for himself in history. He removed the top from a Ravenscroft decanter and poured himself a tumbler of a 1988 Macallan single-malt Scotch. The sip turned into a hasty slug. It was an abomination to gulp such a fine liquor but it couldn't be helped.

He poured another and went to his desk, laying his head down on the bare wood. Was he done? Was this where he called it quits? Where he hung up his Jeffersonian ambitions and went home?

The founding fathers were not the type of men who gave up in the face of hardship and Bryan did not want to be that type of man either. He raised back up and sat with more authority, stiffened his spine, and picked up his tumbler of scotch. He could retake the reins of this team of horses at this very moment or he could let it run to its own destruction. Which would it be?

He sighed deeply and stood, removing his vintage leather belt with its Colt Navy revolver. He piled belt, holster, and revolver on his desk. Across the room, he selected a Colt 1911 .45 automatic from a wooden pistol rack. While perhaps not as modern as a Glock or a Sig, it gave him the ability to reload from magazines while still retaining a little more classical styling. He ejected the magazine and found it to be full. He replaced it in the handgun, cycled the slide, and made certain the safety was on. He tucked it into his belt and put three spare magazines into his vest pocket.

He hung the AK over his shoulder and returned to his porch. The cold air was sobering but he still felt a general state of numbness brought about by the drink, the ebbing adrenaline, and the fugue state of such a profound indecision. He wasn't certain how long he'd been inside thinking this over. Had it been just minutes or was it closer to an hour? Either way, he was back in the game now and the path forward was clear to him.

He descended the creaking porch steps and strode boldly toward the dining hall, his spine stiff with resolve and determination. He neared the building and saw the puff of wood smoke from the stone chimney. Just outside the dining hall was a wide porch with a plank bench filled with the remaining women captives, the main workforce of Douthat Farms. The men must have left them outside, unsure of what Bryan wanted to discuss with them.

Bryan stopped in front of the women and regarded them with no emotion. They were a haggard and sorry lot. Sadly, he could assign no blame for their appearance to anyone other than himself. It was his doing, his failure, staring him right back into his face. Only he could fix it. Only he could right the ship.

The Colt 1911 was in his hand before anyone even noticed. The shots rang loud in the silent valley. He shot three of the women in the head at point-blank range before any of the others even reacted. But now they knew what was coming. They could see it in his eyes and they scrambled to get away, screaming and crying.

It was a futile effort. They were lashed one to another like a string of packhorses. When the first fell dead, the remaining women found themselves anchored to the three dead bodies and could make no escape. The remaining women were not clean kills. They were struggling and flailing about, making it difficult for a headshot even at this close range. He fired center mass to disable them and then the pistol ran dry, the slide locking back.

He reloaded and picked up where he'd left off. When the last shot echoed to silence, Bryan's remaining captives lay dead, their blood running in thin rivulets down the gently sloped planks. It ran from the edge of the porch and into flower beds once perfectly appointed by a state botanist but now weedy, overgrown, and blood-soaked.

Bryan stared at his handiwork. He heard the creak of floorboards and turned to find his men standing behind him. When they heard his gunshots, they assumed the worst, rushing to his side with their guns out and ready for a fight. When they found him, discovered his deeds, they did not join but watched frozen and terrified.

Bryan smiled at his men. He felt reinvigorated, ready to reassume the mantle of leadership. It was a new day. It was a new era. Today, they rose from the ashes.

"We need to talk," he said. "Let's go inside."

2

The sun rose to a frosty morning on top of Jewell Ridge. While the temperature would probably hit the mid-fifties later, there was no ignoring that cooler days were upon them. Barb woke to a chilly bedroom, but the warmth of the main living area put a smile on her face. The heat of the fire and undercurrent of wood smoke in the air always meant comfort to her. Despite all the things that changed in her life—that changed in the world at large—the appreciation of a warm fire on a cold morning was like a universal truth, like a law of physics. It connected the twenty-first century man with first century man and beyond.

"Morning, sweetie."

Barb turned to smile at her father, feeling a twinge of pain in her chest, an injury from the kidnapping that was not completely healed yet. Her dad extended a mug to her.

"You can have this coffee," he said. "I'll make myself another."

She regarded the mug with its *Coffee Makes Me Poop* inscription and shook her head. "No thanks."

"What is it? I've not even had a sip from it."

"I can find my own mug."

Conor looked from his daughter to his mug and back. "But it's my favorite mug. To allow someone to use one of your most prized possessions is to bestow an honor upon them. I feel like you just kicked my honor in the begonias. Besides that, you picked this mug out."

"I picked it out because it's perfectly suited for you. It's not befitting of me."

"So you're too damn good to drink out of me mug?" Conor asked with dramatic flourish.

"You've obviously forgotten I'm a delicate feminine flower that drinks with my pinky extended and without slurping noises. I can find my own bleeding mug and make my own morning beverage, thank you."

Conor withdrew his arm and shielded his mug protectively. "Didn't want you using me mug anyway. I don't like it when my coffee smells like delicate feminine flowers."

Barb padded off toward the kitchen mumbling about the state of her dad's mental health. Conor smiled at her camouflage cargo pants, Wilson Combat t-shirt, and fuzzy pink house slippers.

"It be the lucky man that wins your hand one day, my daughter," Conor called out. "Though I'm certain he'll have to fight like hell to get it."

Barb stopped in the kitchen door. "What are you saying back there?" she asked, a note of both suspicion and warning in her voice.

"Nothing, my delicate feminine flower."

Barb gave him a withering look and continued on into the kitchen. Conor heard her shuffling mugs in the cabinet and then pouring a cup of coffee from the drip coffee maker. "Any thoughts on breakfast?" she asked. "I'm so hungry I could eat a goat."

"Glad to hear it. I was thinking eggs and goat sausage," Conor replied.

Barb returned to the living room with a cast-iron skillet and set it on the wood stove. "That was quick. You lay awake all night thinking about a plate of goat sausage and eggs?"

"No, but I did wake up to thinking about Bojangles again. I was imagining a ham biscuit, a sweet tea, and maybe a doughnut from Krispy Kreme for dessert."

"I'm not sure breakfast is a meal traditionally served with a dessert."

"Mine is," Conor responded. "Two chocolate glazed creampuffs. Not my fault you don't understand a good breakfast."

"You're a cruel bastard, bringing up the Krispy Kreme at a time like this."

"I've done worse."

"You know what sucks? I could probably figure out a way to make a chocolate glazed creampuff but *my* favorite doughnut is the toasted coconut. How far you think I'd have to go to find a coconut about now?"

Conor shrugged. "No idea."

"Me neither. I take it sleeping beauty is still out cold?"

"Yeah. The poor kid wouldn't have survived the winter without us, Barb. The thought of that boy trying to live in a mobile home with no heat and no food pains me to my very soul."

"There's people out there doing it right now," Barb pointed out. "We probably just don't know about them."

"We can't help all of them. I know that."

"If you can get your Mad Mick Militia together then maybe you can help a few more of them. Help them to help themselves, you know?"

Conor snorted. "Mad Mick Militia."

"That's what folks are calling it," Barb said. "They're saying that the double-M you've been carving into trees stands for Mad Mick, Mountain Militia, or Mick's Militia."

Conor laughed at this. "As long as they're talking, they're spreading the legend. That in itself carries some power."

Suddenly, an electronic trilling filled the air. A look of panic crossed Barb's face. Conor could see her mind racing through the possibilities–the motion detectors, the perimeter alarms.

"It's the satellite phone," Conor said, getting to his feet.

"Fuck," Barb muttered.

"Delicate feminine flowers don't talk that way," Conor said to her as he left the room, his voice lilting.

"The last bloody time that thing rang you ended up leaving to rescue a damsel in distress," Barb called after him. "Don't answer it!"

"I still have to see who it is." Conor opened the door to the ready room. He found the phone and checked the display.

"Fuck."

"Delicate flower," Barb reminded him, obviously eavesdropping.

Conor answered the call. "Hello." It was not a question. He knew who it was.

"Forty," said the voice on the other end. It was the challenge phrase.

The last challenge number they'd been using had been forty-eight. That meant Conor, when presented with the challenge, should respond with the appropriate number that, when added to the first, would add up to forty-eight.

"Eight," he responded.

There was a moment of silence that made Conor thing he'd responded incorrectly, then the voice came back, warmer this time. *"How's it going, Conor? World treating you alright?"*

"Such as it is," Conor replied. "About how you'd expect for the collapse of modern society."

The voice on the phone was Ricardo. For the last dozen years he'd been Conor's contact, handler, or boss, depending on the assignment. Conor still wasn't certain exactly who Ricardo worked for. He didn't know if he even had a single employer or was simply a contractor who aggregated specialized services for hire to government alphabet agencies. Either way, Ricardo was the man who put Conor in the machine shop on Jewell Ridge so Conor had an appreciation, if not fondness, for the man.

"Times may get worse before they get better, my friend," Ricardo said. *"Stay low and keep your friends and family close."*

"You're preaching to the choir," Conor said. "I've had a little experience in that department already." Conor had recently learned the lesson of letting his daughter stray too far from his sight and he wasn't sure how long it might be before he made that same mistake again. Hell, he may just put her on a leash and keep her within ten feet until order was restored to the world.

"Sorry to hear that."

There was a moment of silence before Conor broke it. "So, Ricardo, you just calling for a status update? Surely you don't have a project for me."

"You'd be surprised, Conor. Our world goes on. Sometimes it's easier to settle old scores when the world is distracted by chaos."

"So you're calling about a job?"

"No, a favor."

"Fuck me running," Conor swore. "I hope your expectations are low because I don't have a lot of capabilities at the moment."

"You're well positioned for this one," Ricardo said. *"I have an employee I'm trying to find temporary housing for."*

Conor was silent so Ricardo continued.

"He's a specialist like you. I had him overseas on an operation when the shit hit the fan. I'd forgotten about him, honestly. I'd assumed he was still operating and that I'd hear from him when the dust settled. Instead, he turns up here in the city and rings me up."

"Why can't you find some military base that will take him, or one of your training facilities? Surely there's somebody that can give this stray a home."

"This guy can't be seen. He's been some places and done some things. He's got plenty more dances on his dance card too, so I have to protect him. He's valuable."

"How valuable?"

"Valuable enough that you're the only *person stateside I would consider putting him with."*

Flattery didn't buy points with Conor. "Ricardo, resources are tight and they aren't being replenished. Our living arrangements are kind of Spartan and I expect them to get even worse if this keeps going on."

"You were well-positioned to weather this. I saw to that myself. Every-

thing you could possibly need. I know you have five years of provisions because I arranged the delivery myself."

"Those rations won't last five years with more people eating them," Conor said. "I hate to be a bastard about it but I will be. You know I don't like to say no to a favor, but I may have to say no to this one."

"He's a dad and he has his daughter with him. It's just the two of them."

"You're a prick," Conor said. "You did that on purpose, telling me it's a dad and daughter. You know that's a weakness of mine."

"He's also a doctor."

That got Conor's attention.

"That interest you?" Ricardo said, noting the silence.

"Perhaps. As long as he comes with supplies. I don't have enough medical gear to treat a group of any size."

"Conor, you know medical supplies are hard to get these days. It's sheer chaos out there. The supply chain is broken at every link."

"You haven't heard me out," Conor said. "If I take him in, he comes with his own firepower plus extra ammo for me, just for the inconvenience of having company in the house. He comes with surgical setups, a pharmacy, and his own fucking food. Can you do that?"

"Conor..." Ricardo said, his tone implying that Conor might be asking for just a little too much.

"That's the deal," Conor said. "Take it or leave it. You have five seconds."

"I'll take it," Ricardo said quickly.

"How you getting him here?"

"You have a landing pad, right? Big enough for a Chinook?"

"Affirmative," Conor said. "I have a massive paved parking lot with plenty of room for approach and take off. How the hell did you get a Chinook?"

"The chopper is leased. I've been on the phone all night trying to set this up. The bird is from a logging operation in Canada. The flight crew is G4 Securitas. I got a high-value contract to fly a container from Oak Ridge National

Laboratory and drop it on the deck of a research vessel anchored offshore. The chopper is supposed to deadhead out of Norfolk, Virginia, tomorrow and head west. It's going to fly right over you anyway. No one is going to bat an eye if it stops at your place to dump a shipping container and fast-rope off two people."

"Just remember that container of supplies. I don't care if the guy is a doc or not, if he shows up with no supplies, he'll be walking back to the coast."

"You're valuable to me, Conor. I wouldn't lie to you."

"Appreciate it, mate."

"Then expect this guy tomorrow. If for some reason he's not there by afternoon just assume there was a change in plans."

"This chap have a name?" Conor asked.

"I'll leave the introductions to him."

Conor was preparing to say he didn't like the sound of that when the call ended. Was there some reason he didn't want to give a name? Conor checked the battery life on the phone and decided to put it on the charger. He stepped out of the ready room, shutting the door behind him.

Barb was frying sausage and giving Conor a hard stare. "So what did you commit us to this time? I heard you in there folding like a warm tortilla."

Conor sighed. "If you heard me in there *committing*, then you should have also heard me in there *protesting*."

"So what won out? Your protests or his impassioned pleas?"

Conor didn't immediately answer. He was looking for an angle that might present him in a better light when Barb figured him out.

"I knew it!" she yelled. "He threw some kind of sob story at you, didn't he? What is it this time? You having to go rescue another damsel? Some other kind of mission? An operation? An *assassination*?"

Conor looked at the floor. "It was Ricardo. He had some special deep cover operator show up unexpectedly and he needs to store him on ice, somewhere he won't be seen. He thought of me and this place."

"Well this place isn't just you. It's me too, and now I have to take care of two middle-aged louts instead of one?"

"I don't think so," Conor said. "Part of the deal is he has to bring his own supplies. He also has his daughter with him and if he's loutish I assume that's her responsibility to tend to."

Barb was tight-lipped and growing angry. "All I can say is they better be able to take care of their fucking selves. My dance card is full."

Conor held a consoling hand in his daughter's direction. "Those are all things I've already said to Ricardo. He knows the score and he swore to me he'd make it worth it. I told him we needed extra supplies for our pain, suffering, and inconvenience. Did I mention this guy is a doctor?"

Until that moment, Barb had been furiously flipping sausages around her skillet with a metal spatula. She froze and looked at her father. "A doctor, you say?"

Conor nodded slowly, meeting his daughter's eye. "We could use a doctor, both for our own needs and for building goodwill in the community."

Barb shrugged. "Aside from the everyday hazards of just existing in the world right now, I guess there is the fact that you're quickly turning into a tottering and senile old man. Maybe, if we're lucky, the doctor will have a little experience in geriatric medicine."

"Maybe he has an obstetrics background in case you and Ragus tie the knot and start putting out little Conors," Conor fired back with a mischievous gleam in his eye.

Barb didn't miss a beat. "Or maybe he's a proctologist who can treat my asshole of a father."

Conor feigned pouting but hunger won him over. "Do you need me to mix up some eggs? I think there's some peppers, onions, and *maybe* a little feta in the refrigerator."

Barb didn't answer. The comment about Ragus and babies still had her festering like an angry bee. She wasn't done with him yet. "I don't know what kind of devious machinations are twirling about in your bowling ball head there, dear father, but I got no interest in the lad back there. Let's be clear about that. He's still a boy as far as I'm concerned and him fluttering about the place with those puppy dog eyes is far from enchanting. In fact, it's downright annoying. I'd throw his ass out if I thought he could survive the night but I'm not sure he could. A kitten would be better suited for survival."

Conor opened his mouth to make another comment. From the mischievous glimmer in his eyes, Barb knew it was not an apology but another jab. She'd had enough of him. In a preemptive strike she drew back and hurled her greasy spatula in his direction. Conor dodged to the left and the spatula bounced off the wall.

"Geez, Barb! You could addle an old man with a blow like that."

Barb retrieved her spatula and glared at Conor. "Let that be a lesson to you. Next time it might be something a wee bit heavier and a wee bit sharper."

3

"I'm pretty sure by now all you guys know I used to be a history professor."

Bryan sat in a chair at one end of the dining hall addressing his dwindling assembly. Rather than a charismatic speech from a leader of men, this felt more like a confession, like Bryan was new to Alcoholics Anonymous and was sharing his story.

"One of the aspects of history that has always interested me on a personal level is how family dynasties find their way to wealth and power during times of national strife. Whether it was the turmoil caused by Western expansion in the nineteenth century, or the global turmoil of the great world wars, or whether it is wealthy Russians who rose to power during the collapse of the Soviet Union, there have always been men who found avenues to success because they were willing to look beyond the darkness. Sometimes it's dumb luck, simply being in the right place at the right time. Sometimes it's because people understand there may only be brief windows in the span of your life where you have the potential to grasp opportunities. As I've said before, fortune favors the bold. If you hesitate, you lose out."

Bryan stood and took slow, measured steps to the dining hall window, looking out. His was a near mournful expression, a look of profound sorrow directed at something slipping away, or perhaps already lost.

"I envisioned good things for those of us who staked our claim at the ground level of this disaster. Some of you were there with me when we discussed these plans in the wake of the attacks. Others of you came in later, but I still want to think you believed in our mission too."

Bryan turned away from the window as if he could no longer bear what he saw out there. "You see, cash and personal property mean nothing to people now. They can't eat their silver and gold, their family heirlooms. They can't eat their stashes of paper money. They can't eat the deeds to their property. But if I can trade them things that they *can* eat for those things in which they see no value, if I can convince them to sign those things over to me for a couple of meals, then I will still own those assets when the world is set right again."

He sagged back into his chair at the front of the room and looked from face to face. He needed to know that he was reaching them, that they were connecting. "If our crops had matured I would have sent dozens of armed convoys out into the local community with eggs, jerky, potatoes, dried beans, and even marijuana and opium. What do you think people would trade for those things? If this disaster went on for a year, how many houses do you think we could own at the end of that year? How many trunks of cash would we have stored? How many sacks of gold jewelry and silver coins would we have?"

No one responded. The men were silent but enthralled. They saw his vision. They had experienced it in action. They had seen it come to fruition and then shatter like a beer bottle against a rock.

"I'm telling you this *not* because I think the opportunity is lost, but because I want you to know what is it stake here. We can still right this ship. Whatever happened to the men we sent out of here was a declaration of war on us. It was a declaration of war on the very dreams that you and I share. I will not let that stand. *We* cannot let that stand."

Bryan stood and his voice hardened. A fire was flickering to life inside him, an angry inferno that he wanted to spread from man to man across this room like a wind-driven brush fire. “When you leave this room today I want you to arm for war. Take your best weapons and gear. We’ll take a chuck wagon and pack horses with food, cooking gear, and more ammo. We will search until we figure out what has befallen our comrades. Along the way we will build an army and we will lay waste to anyone who stands in our way."

One of the men dared raise his hand. Bryan nodded at him to speak.

“How do we build an army? There are so few men out there willing to leave their families in these circumstances. Who do you think would be willing to come with us? Is there some incentive we’re offering?"

Bryan smiled. "Have you ever heard of the Shining Path?"

4

Conor stood in the yard enjoying the sun and raking leaves. Although his structures were fairly fire resistant, he was always concerned about leaves allowing fires to travel between the buildings on his property. He was pulling the leaves onto a dirty blue tarp when he heard the rhythmic *clop clop* of shod horses on the paved road.

In a flash, Conor dropped his rake and grabbed his rifle from where it was leaning against the building. He ducked behind a continuous mining machine parked nearby specifically for the purpose of providing cover. The machine was a remnant of the property's past. It was over a hundred tons of dense steel that could mine, scoop, and convey coal, all while being controlled remotely.

He opened up his rifle scope to provide the widest possible picture and monitored the road. Two riders came into sight. Neither looked familiar to him but they appeared comfortable, as if they knew the area. In fact, they rode right up to his gate and paused as if trying to figure out if anyone was home or not.

"Can I help you with something?" Conor called from cover.

The men startled at his voice, unaware they were under surveillance. When they finally located Conor behind the massive machine, his rifle scope trained on them, they were even more startled. No one liked being at the receiving end of a firearm.

"We're looking for Conor," said the older of the two men.

"Who's asking?"

"My name is Johnny Jacks. This is my son Jason."

Conor stood from behind his cover and slung the rifle over his shoulder. He walked to the eight-foot tall rolling gate and drew the string of keys from around his neck. He sorted, then found the correct key to open the padlock. When it was open, he dropped the chain and shoved the gate back on its rollers.

"I'm Conor," he said, extending a hand to the older man. "I believe I had the pleasure of meeting your wife."

Johnny swung off the back of his horse and walked around to take Conor's hand. The older man, tall with thick white hair, smiled warmly and shook Conor's hand. "You did. That was the day we were out trying to wrangle all our critters back home. It was a hell of a job. I apologize for just now getting back to you but we've been too busy to leave home. Then you have to worry about what might happen to your home when you're gone."

The younger man slid off his horse and joined them. He shook hands with Conor also. "I'm Jason Jacks. We heard you might be looking for some horses."

"I was," Conor said. "I'm actually flush with hooved beasts at the moment."

"You taking to riding those goats?" Jacks asked with a laugh, pointing at one of Conor's herd.

Conor shook his head. "No, to be honest there was some trouble. My daughter and some other women from the area were kidnapped. I went after them. By the time I got my daughter back I had more horses than I knew what to do with."

Johnny nodded, processing. "I heard a little about that. A friend of my wife's was taken. Glad to hear that you got them all back. If you don't mind me asking, how did you accomplish that?"

"He may not want to talk about it, Dad," Jason said.

"You don't know if you don't ask," Johnny replied.

"Hell hath no fury like a vengeful father," Conor said simply.

Johnny and Jason waited for more but there was nothing. When it was clear Conor wasn't going to elaborate, Johnny nodded with understanding.

"The only reason I was asking is that I have a few security concerns of my own," Johnny said.

"What kind?" Conor asked. "I'm in the early stages of forming a militia of sorts. After the kidnapping I thought it might be a good idea for the residents of this community to take a little more proactive approach to safeguarding it. It's purely voluntary, of course, but the idea is to demonstrate a presence that might act as a deterrent to anyone with bad intentions."

"My concerns are not necessarily about the bad intentioned," Johnny said. "I've got some strangers wanting to buy horses and I can't get a read on them. They were kind of shady but they haven't been threatening. They talk like they want to trade for the horses but I'm a little apprehensive about taking in goods that might have been stolen."

"Where does the trade stand?" Conor asked.

"They're supposed to swing by later this afternoon and make a final decision on how many they want. That's why I wanted to make sure you had horses before they cleaned me out."

Conor looked at his watch. "I need to grab a few things but how about I follow you to your house and meet these guys?"

Jason looked at his dad. "You think that's a good idea? It could make us look weak. Like we need backup."

"No shame in playing it safe," Conor said. "I'll just be upfront with them and explain that I heard they were from outside the area. I wanted to get some information on the kind of things they ran into on the road."

Johnny looked at his son. "No harm in that, is there?"

"Makes sense, I guess," Jason replied.

"Give me five minutes. I need to gear up and let my daughter know what's going on. I'll be right back. If you need to water your horses there's a trough over there. Just close the gate behind you."

Conor jogged to the main living quarters but slowed before he went inside. He didn't want to startle Barb by bursting through the door like a crazy man. He found her in the kitchen dehydrating what was probably the last green peppers and onions of the season. Their poor garden was now a tangled mess of dead and dying plants.

"Barb, sweetie, that Johnny Jacks fellow from across the ridge came by to see if I was interested in some horses."

Barb raised an eyebrow at him. "You told him no, right? I'm not sure we can feed all we have right now."

"I did, but he told me there's a group of strangers who want to trade him for some horses. He says he's not certain about these characters. I think they're making him a little edgy. I told him I'd come along, both as backup and to ask the strangers what they encountered on the road. It might also give me an opportunity to talk to him about our efforts to improve security in the area. He might have some ideas of how to better reach the people in his side of the county."

"You be careful," she warned.

Conor smiled. "You're starting to sound like me, daughter. All concerned about the bad shit waiting outside the gates."

Barb shrugged as if the comment required no explanation.

"And you, my girl, I prefer you not leave the compound until I'm back. Ragus is here with you. I know he's not nearly as capable as you are in a fight but he's a warm body that can hold a gun."

"I've got plenty here to keep me busy here. I've also got a long list for Ragus."

Conor smiled, sensing just how much Barb enjoyed bossing the boy around.

"What are you smiling at?" Barb asked.

"Nothing. I expect I'll be back tonight barring any crazy turn of events. If I'm not, don't come looking for me. I'll be fine."

With that, Conor was off to the ready room. Since he didn't expect this to be a long trip he didn't change his pants and shirt into the BDUs he'd worn when chasing down Barb. He did slip on the plate carrier with full plates, strap on his battle belt, and throw his Go Bag over his shoulder. Since he didn't know the odds of the situation he was walking into, he grabbed a .300 Blackout with burst-fire capability from the weapons rack. He checked that the suppressor was tightly threaded on, then switched the magazines on his plate carrier from 5.56 caliber to .300 Blackout. He did a quick double-check to confirm he had everything he needed. Only then did he slip out of the room and call a second goodbye to his daughter.

He locked the front door behind him, just as he did when Barb was a teenager and he was going out for a few minutes, a habit he had no intention of breaking. Conor jogged by the men at the trough. "I need to saddle my horse and I'll be right with you."

Johnny nodded and smiled. He seemed like a good bloke.

“Ragus!” Conor yelled, spotting the boy adding fresh bedding to the goat shed.

Ragus sprinted over while Conor threw a blanket and saddle onto his horse. It was the same one he'd been riding when he caught up with Barb and her kidnappers. He didn't know a lot about horses but he'd taken a shine to this one. The animal had behaved as well as he thought a horse could behave and somewhere on that trip the two developed a tolerance for each other.

“What is it?” Ragus asked.

Conor put his Go Bag behind the saddle and tied it on. “I'm going with Johnny Jacks and his son to his farm. I'll be most of the day and may not get back until late. If I don't make it home tonight, don't come looking for me. I'd also prefer you not leave the compound today. Barb's still not back to a hundred percent.”

“Got it,” Ragus said. “Be careful.”

“Always, my boy. Always,” Conor said, hopping on the horse and nudging it toward the trough.

When he reached the men, Johnny and Jason regarded him with curiosity and a touch of amusement.

"What is it? My fly unzipped?"

"You haven't been riding long, have you?" Jason asked.

Conor shook his head. "No. What gave it away?"

"If you don't mind, why don't you climb off that horse and let us show you how to saddle one right. It may save you a heap of aggravation one day. It also makes a long ride a lot easier on the horse," Johnny said.

Conor slid off the horse, gesturing that it was all theirs. The men efficiently removed all the tack then replaced it, explaining each step to Conor as they went. He hadn't realized how much he didn't know until seeing the more proficient horsemen demonstrate the proper way to do it all.

"I think your horse will like this better," Johnny said. "It may even keep you from falling off on a hard ride one day."

Conor was grateful for the lesson. There was no shame in being taught to do things the right way, whether it was shooting, fighting, or saddling a horse. No one came into the world knowing everything. Throwing a wrench into the whole matter was the fact that skills that were important a year ago were vastly different from the skills that were important now. Having the right knowledge was always like trying to hit a moving target.

The men saddled up and rode out the gate, Ragus locking it behind them.

“I was noticing all the squirrels up here,” Johnny said. “You ever eat them?”

“Can’t say I have,” Conor admitted.

“When I was a boy, there were a lot of foreigners that showed up in the coal camps because of all the jobs. Hungarians, Italians, and even Irishmen like yourself. My dad had this Hungarian friend he invited over for supper one night. He came with his wife and a couple of kids and we had a big time. I remember this man’s wife asking what the meat was that we were eating because it wasn’t familiar to her. My mom explained it was squirrel.

“‘What is *squirrel*?’ the Hungarian woman asked in her rudimentary English. My mom told her they were small and furry, with long tails, and that you see them hopping around in the yard, climbing trees and fence posts. She said they were good eating.

“‘Very good,’ the woman told my mom. So a couple of weeks pass, then the Hungarian couple invites all of us over to their house for supper. We go and they have this big spread of food. Some of it was cooked in ways we weren't used to seeing so it was a big deal. They had Hungarian dishes and this fancy stew that everybody loved. It was pretty good. So my mother compliments the woman on the stew and asks her what it was made with.

"'It is squirrel,' the woman told my mom with great pride, and said she caught it herself. My mom asked her how she got it.

"'I go outside with rifle because I see squirrel hopping around all over the place,' the woman told my mom. She said when it saw her, it climbed up on a fencepost and looked right at her. It made a 'squirrel sound' at her and she shot it.

"They kind of chatter sometimes, my mom said.

"'No chatter sound,' the lady told her, the '*Meeeeoooowww* sound.'

"It was then we realized we'd eaten cat stew," Johnny said. "None of us dared look at each other. We didn't know what to say."

"How did it taste?" Conor asked.

"Not like squirrel," Johnny replied. "It was good until we found out what it was. We were raised to be polite so no one said anything about it but we puked our guts out on the way home. Even my poor mother threw up cat meat in the weeds."

5

The morning after so abruptly terminating the employment of his slave labor force, Bryan Padowicz and what was left of his army departed Douthat Farms. Most of the men rode horseback, armed with a plethora of scavenged weapons. A covered wagon brought up the rear, stolen from the display at a feed store. Bryan rode in the lead but it was not with the bearing of a general setting out on a glorious campaign. His was the slump-shouldered posture of a bankrupt businessman closing the door on his dreams.

Bryan had a master plan for this place. In fact, he'd stolen a wall map of the entire park from the ranger's office and sketched his master plan directly upon it. As he left his farm, bruised but hopefully not broken, only Bryan saw the ghosts of those unattained dreams. There was the hydroelectric station he envisioned at the edge of the lake. There was the cluster of larger, better-built green houses with natural irrigation, wood heat, and solar lighting that could provide his whole organization with fresh food for themselves and for local commerce.

There was the permaculture area where they would cultivate fruit and nut trees that would feed them year after year with minimal labor. There were the dormitories he would have built for their workers and the jail he would have constructed for those who refused to get with the program. For more egregious felons, there would be a gallows. For minor offenses, such as fraternizing with the prisoners or drunkenness, there would be a set of wooden stocks where the prisoner could be locked neck and wrists on public display. There, he or she would be subject to the ridicule and physical abuse of their peers.

At the exit to the camp, where visitors were greeted by the same type of welcome sign that adorned every state park in the Virginia system, Bryan had envisioned a more grandiose display. He wanted tall stone towers with guard posts atop them. There would be a heavy wooden gate with wrought iron strap hinges befitting a medieval village. A sign above the door would read Douthat Farms.

When he passed that welcome sign for what might have been the last time, Bryan released a sigh so deep he was certain a part of his soul divested his body and rode away upon his exhalation. In releasing that sigh, he also released himself from his mourning. He would not allow himself the distraction beyond this point in the journey. He would either come back stronger, a leader with a larger army and the labor he needed, or he would die gloriously charging into battle.

Though he had not considered it until this point, it occurred to him there even existed a third option, that he might take the land of his enemies and rebuild his vision elsewhere, rechristening it with the new name. With his skills, with his vision, he could do that. After all, flexibility and adapting to the current conditions was the basis of his entire philosophy.

Barely three miles from the front gate, Bryan and his party encountered their first strangers. They appeared to be a local family, standing on the riverbank, trying to catch their dinner. A line of fishing poles ran along the bank, laying in the forked crotch of sticks stabbed into the sandy soil. A man and woman in their fifties had been watching the tips of the poles for any movement until they heard the approaching riders. Now the couple watched Bryan and his men with the same wary anticipation with which they observed their fishing poles.

Two teenage boys of high school age were digging in the bank with sharp sticks, searching for worms and anything else they might use for bait. They too were frozen in their labors, watching the riders as the riders watched them. Bryan broke from his procession and rode closer.

There was nowhere for the family to hide, nowhere to run. Perhaps they were armed, but in the face of greater odds did not tip their hand. Bryan addressed the woman as she was the only one not directly impacted by his actions. He was not searching for women on this day. He spent no time preparing a formal recruitment speech. He would speak from the heart and hope his enthusiasm made people eager to be part of his crusade.

"Pardon me, miss, but may I trouble you on a matter of grave importance? My compatriots and I are on a quest of epic proportions. Unfortunately, our force has been decimated by a conspiracy of circumstances beyond our control. Our success is only guaranteed by restocking the coffers and replacing what has been lost. I was hoping I could relieve you of your manpower."

The man at her side was overweight and garbed in a massive pair of bibbed overalls that gaped at his sides. He leaned forward and spat between his feet. “If your fancy words are a way of asking for our boys, you ain’t taking them. Having their help around the house is about the only thing helping us get by."

Bryan smiled in a way that belied the little tolerance he had for people who told him *no* in any form or fashion. "Sir, I was not addressing you, but I do believe you may have misunderstood me. My recruitment efforts were not just directed toward the younger and more physically fit members of your party. At this point in our journey, my standards are so broad as to include someone like yourself who has long since moved beyond your optimal fighting weight. Even taking that into consideration, you are still a warm body who could sit atop a horse and wield a firearm. As such, you are of use to me. All I require from you is a yes or no answer as to whether you are up for the task or not."

The man’s expression curled into a wary snarl. "*Hell* no."

Bryan sighed. "Very well then." He promptly drew his Colt 1911 and shot the man dead center of his sternum.

The man toppled, fell, and twitched amidst audible gasps from the remaining members of his family. They rushed to his side but got not a single word from the blood-flecked lips of the dying man. In seconds he was gone. Clutching his warm body, all eyes moved back to Bryan.

Bryan smiled. "As you may have surmised by this point in our interaction, there is but one chance. Survival depends on your immediate answer and that this answer be to my liking. I'll give you one more chance and ask again. Might I take leave of your manpower?"

With that request hanging in the air, Bryan moved the pistol toward the older of the two boys.

"Take them! Take them!" the woman bellowed and sobbed, collapsing onto her dead husband.

Bryan knew what she was thinking, that she could not watch another loved one die. Her grief meant nothing to him but her cooperation did. Bryan holstered the pistol. "Very well then. Glad to see you figured out the rules."

The woman rose and hugged her children, both of them larger than her, nearly as large as grown men. "Go with this man. Don't give him any reason to kill you. I love you very much and we'll see each other again. I know it. Now don't you cry. Just do what he tells you."

The admonition that the boys not cry was futile. Sobbing, the boys hugged their mother tightly.

Bryan rolled his eyes. "I don't have all day. Let's keep the theatrics to a minimum." He turned back to his men. "Double them up on one of the spare horses."

The woman shoved her children away from her. The two boys held onto each other as they rushed by Bryan in pure desperation. They were at an awkward age where they shunned affection and contact, especially with a sibling. In the wake of their trauma, they reverted to the support of the only thing they had. They helped each other mount the unsaddled horse, the older taking up the reins.

A gruff command and a boot applied to their horse's rear flank got them moving and the group departed. They watched their mother until the trees formed a wall between them. Their last glance of her captured her collapsing anew across the chest of her fallen husband. Then it was just the boys again, suddenly part of a new world they didn't even know of until a few minutes ago. They looked around desperately but there was no support and no comfort to be found.

At the front of the procession, Bryan addressed a man named Nathan. He'd filled in a lot of the leadership gaps created by the absence of Top Cat and Lester. "You ever hear of the Shining Path?"

"Only when you mentioned them in the dining hall." Nathan hadn't been comfortable with Bryan since the murder of the women, but he thought it an inopportune moment to bring that up considering the amount of killing the normally docile Bryan had been moved to commit recently.

"Sendero Luminoso," Bryan said. "They were a guerilla movement in Peru with hardcore traditional communist ideals. They were known for their brutality. The thing I remember about them is that they would go into villages to recruit with the simple philosophy of *join or die*. You got one chance. If you refused, you were killed. Even though the Shining Path has been crushed for the most part, that one technique always stuck with me."

When Bryan said nothing else the silence became awkward and Nathan felt pressured to speak. "It works, I guess."

Bryan looked at Nathan with cold eyes. Nathan could see madness swirling in them like cream stirred into coffee. "How could it not? With that technique, we shall build an army."

Nathan thought of all the people he would likely see killed. He had been a graduate student in agriculture. He planned on getting a job on a large farm after college and living the pastoral life of a man who worked the land on a daily basis. However, he'd been sucked into Bryan's vision. For now, the world offered him no better options.

But could he stomach the killing?

6

With the three men being newly acquainted Conor, Jason, and Johnny went through bursts of conversation on the trip to the Jacks' farm. They talked of general matters until they reached a point in their travels where the trees opened an incredible vista before them and all fell silent in appreciation. With the breathtaking beauty of the view came an awareness that settled on all three men equally. Whether it was the phenomenon known as seasonal affective disorder, brought about by the shortening days, or whether it was just the sense that these three men knew what the coming months might bring, the lighthearted conversation ended abruptly, like music when the stylus was swept from a phonograph. It was amazing how an incredible view could force you to realize just how small you were in the scheme of things and turn your focus inward.

"So have you guys heard of my efforts to organize people into some sort of defense?" Conor asked.

"Some," Johnny replied.

Sensing an affinity with this older man, Conor adopted the approach of pointing out what he suspected were similarities in their way of thinking. "I've worked by myself most of my life. I've kept to myself and taken care my own business. My plan was to deal with this whole collapse situation in the same way. My daughter and I would keep to ourselves and stay close to home. We hoped if we didn't mess with anybody that nobody would mess with us."

"That was our plan too," Jason said. "So far we're only batting about fifty percent with that system. We never look for trouble but it still finds us. People are stealing our shit. Some of our neighbors have even reported finding strangers in their houses and barns. My dad was always against carrying guns around inside the house but we've taken to doing that now. We don't see a choice."

"Minding my own business, or at least the business of my daughter and myself, has not worked well for us either. My daughter was just walking down the road to her friend's house when she was taken. She's pretty capable too. She's a fighter. Had the odds not been so against her she could probably have taken her attackers. The point is that the whole mess happened because we let bad people get too close."

"I understand wanting to organize the community but it's a hard time to ask much of people," Johnny said. "People are starving. A lot of them are anyway. They barely have the energy to scavenge for food. We can't exactly be asking them to patrol the countryside."

"I understand that," Conor said. "About all we've done so far is conduct a little psychological warfare. The battle to get those women back was brutal and I'm hoping word of it spread. My people and some of the others have also been systematically carving a double 'M' into trees throughout the area. The hope is to eventually associate that symbol with the violence that took place in the battle to get my daughter home. When people see the double 'M' mark I want them to know that area is patrolled by the Mad Mick. I'm hoping there might be a deterrent effect."

"The Mad Mick?" Johnny asked. "That's what you call yourself?"

Conor shook his head. "My coworkers started it. Either way, the name stuck. At least in certain circles."

"I thought you were a machinist," Jason said.

"I am," Conor replied.

"You have a lot of guns for machinist," Jason said. "If you don't mind me saying so."

Conor laughed. "Maybe you just don't know the right machinists, my friend. Now tell me about these visitors you had."

WHEN THE THREE reached Johnny's farm, the horse buyers had not arrived yet. Both Johnny and Jason's wives were holed up in the main house, sitting by the windows with guns to watch for any visitors. The first thing Johnny did was wave his hat toward the house and let them know he was back.

"I hope your wife is watching, Jason," Johnny said. "I'm not sure your mother can tell one man from another at this distance. I love her dearly but both her eyesight and her aim are poor."

With time on their hands while they waited for the buyers, Johnny and Jason showed Conor around the main areas of the farm.

"How many acres do you have?" Conor asked.

"Over three hundred total. A lot of it's straight up and down. We keep the trees cut back, which is quite a bit of work, but it keeps the land fit for grazing. There are a couple of decent fields for hay or corn."

"You have cattle and horses grazing it now?" Conor asked.

"We used to. Now it's a gamble to let any stock out of your sight," Jason said. "The fields near the house are mostly eaten down so if we keep stock close we have to supplement them with hay. We don't want to do that because we're trying to save what little hay we have for winter. The distant fields have more grass left but we've lost cattle in those fields because we can't watch them as close. Dad is against it but I'm considering taking them to the far pastures and—"

Johnny's dog suddenly went ballistic and bolted from where the men were talking.

“Must be company,” Johnny said, heading back to his horse. “We better go. I don't want anybody to get nervous and shoot him."

Johnny was already riding off in pursuit of the dog before Jason and Conor remounted their horses.

After Jason rode off to join his father, Conor paused, lagging behind to double-check that his primary weapon was ready. He did so then slung it over his back. He didn't want to look threatening, like he was brandishing the weapon, but with it on his back he could maneuver it into action quickly if needed. He performed the same check with his handgun before nudging his horse and joining the other men.

His delay made him the last to arrive at the party. By the time he reached the gathering in the driveway, Johnny and Jason were already engaged in conversation with a force of nearly two-dozen strangers. Johnny was speaking with a man who must've been a leader, or at least the spokesman, of that group. The man was heavily muscled and even in the cool weather wore a T-shirt that revealed extensive tattooing.

Conor paid close attention to the tattoos. People often gave away a lot of information with their ink. Sometimes it told the story of imprisonment, military service, or gang affiliation. Nothing in those tattoos revealed anything to Conor at first glance. When he raised his eyes to the man's face he found the man staring at him just as intently.

"I'm sorry if we left you the impression you needed backup, Mr. Jacks," the man said, his comment directed more at Conor than Johnny.

"Conor isn't backup," Johnny said. "We don’t require backup. He's a neighbor who was interested in hearing any news of the world that you may bring with you."

Conor nodded at the man, a greeting intended to defuse the tension that had obviously been dialed up a notch by his appearance and by the tactical gear he wore. "My name is Conor Maguire. I live down the road. Just thought it might be nice to know what is waiting for us out there in the world. We don't get much traffic in these parts. Don’t get a lot of information."

"I'm Wayne," the stranger replied. "I’m not sure how much useful information we have. We’ve travelled a long way and we’ve seen a few things."

"If you don't mind me asking, where did you travel from?" Conor asked.

"Detroit area."

Jason let out a low whistle. "That's a long damn trip."

"An ugly one as well, I'm sure," Conor added. "Detroit can be rough in the best of times."

"And it's far from the best of times," Wayne said.

"You come all that way on horses?” Conor asked.

Wayne shook his head. “We had a convoy of vehicles with enough fuel to get us this far. Now we’ve drained the last can and can’t find anymore.”

“That’s about the state of things,” Conor said. “No one around here can get any either.”

“That’s why we’re buying horses,” Wayne said. “We were lucky to come across Johnny. He’s apparently known around these parts as the guy to get horses from.”

Conor held up a hand. "Well, don't let me get in the way of your business. I just wanted to hear if you had any news."

Wayne nodded. "No, and I've got a lot of men tied up here that could be useful back at camp. I probably need to get this taken care of and get back to things.”

With no role in the horse trading, Conor hung back a polite distance while Johnny, Jason, and Wayne negotiated. From behind reflective sunglasses, he spent his time assessing the other members of Wayne’s party, certain they were doing the same with him. His initial effort was aimed at determining what type of relationship existed between these men. If he could figure that out he might get a better handle on whether they posed a threat to his community or not. Were they coworkers? Members of the same gang? Neighbors? A bowling club?

In his line of work, Conor had traveled around the world and seen street gangs in all their various iterations. He'd seen American street gangs, gangs in Central and South America, Asian thugs in Thailand, and brutal Russian gangs that he hoped to never cross paths with again. These guys didn't give him that type of vibe. They were clearly not a biker gang. Bikers practically wore uniforms and were easily identifiable. There were no visible indications they shared a similar military history or other type of fraternity.

There was certainly no rule that men only traveled with men like themselves, but it was human nature in tough times to look for the support of those with whom you could share some sort of bond. Unless a person was completely stranded alone on the highway and forced to team up with strangers, he'd be likely to find friends or family he felt safe with. Knowing what bonded these men would help Conor understand them and understand their motivations.

When they agreed upon a price, Jason and several men from the group of strangers rode to a nearby pasture to cut the horses from the herd. Wayne gestured at a man in his crew who held a string of pack horses. He led those horses forward while Johnny slid from his and joined Wayne on the ground. The pair opened saddle bags and examined the goods inside.

Johnny and Wayne dickered for a little while longer, then finally shook hands. Wayne directed his man to follow Johnny up to the house to drop off the trade goods. That left Wayne and Conor alone there in the driveway.

After regarding each other in silence for a moment, Wayne nodded toward Conor's gear. "You look like a prepared guy, Conor. You think you're ready for whatever the hell is going on now?"

Conor understood that the comment wasn't a challenge but more of a probe. "Every man has a past, Wayne. My past required planning and organization. It required being prepared."

"What kind of past was that?" Wayne asked, his face smile indicating that he knew just how pointed a question that was but he was still going to ask it anyway.

"Some might call it a sordid past."

Wayne realized this was a dead-end line of questioning. Conor wasn't going to tell him anything. "Gotcha. If you told me, you'd have to kill me, right?"

"Something like that," Conor agreed, his tone leaving a lot of latitude in how the comment might be interpreted. He could have been joking but he could also have been acknowledging that killing was an option still on the table. "As long as we're asking questions, do you care to share anything about your own recent past? I'm pretty damn good at reading people but I have not nailed you guys down yet."

Wayne replied with the same slight smile he'd given Conor a moment ago. "You know, if I told you I'd have to kill you."

Wayne arched uncomfortably as if experiencing a twinge in his back. He did a few stretches, trying to work the kinks out. Conor studied the man's clothes carefully and saw a clue at the corner of the man's right jeans pocket. The top edge of the pocket was frayed threadbare in a wide strip. Conor knew exactly what caused that.

"Construction, right?"

Wayne looked up suddenly and eyed Conor suspiciously. "What makes you think that?"

Conor pointed at the jeans pocket. "Tape measure."

Wayne looked down at the place his jeans had worn from wearing a tape measure clipped to the pocket and laughed. "Every damn pair of jeans I've got looks like these."

"Travel will be a lot slower with horses. If you don't mind me asking, are you guys moving on or thinking about holing up here for the winter?"

Wayne stiffened in a way that demonstrated the question touched a nerve. "I guess that's something I'm not prepared to discuss right now. It's dangerous to share too much with people you don't really know."

"Fair enough," Conor said. "It just pays to know who's in the neighborhood."

Wayne regarded Conor warily. "Is this where the sheriff tells me to get out of town?"

Conor shook his head. "Not at all. I'm not sure people would describe me as the sheriff anyway. I was never cut out for that line of work. Law enforcement always had too many rules for my liking. It's in my nature to go a little unhinged at times and they frown upon that."

Wayne didn't have an opportunity to respond to that. Conversation was interrupted by the sound of approaching horses. Johnny was leading the pack. At his side was the man with the pack horses. Behind them was Jason, then the rest of Wayne's men riding either the horses they'd come with or the new ones they traded for. As that group rode past the men assembled in the driveway, they gave no friendly departing wave as would have been customary in this part of the country. Heads forward, they rode on past.

Wayne remounted his horse and nudged it closer to Johnny's. He extended a hand, exercising a bit more civility than the rest of his group. "Nice doing business with you, Mr. Jacks. I expect we'll be seeing each other again sometime. You and the family stay safe."

Johnny shook the man's hand. "Thanks. I hope your people stay safe too."

Wayne looked at Conor and gave him a wary nod. "Something tells me I'll be seeing you again."

Conor replied with a nod. Wayne spun his horse and galloped off to catch his crew.

"First people I ever met from Michigan," Jason remarked.

"What you think?" Johnny said.

"Bunch of pricks."

Johnny laughed but Conor was still focused intently on the men riding away, wondering if Wayne was correct in his assessment that the two men would meet again.

"Conor, you interested in sticking around for dinner?" Johnny asked.

" I appreciate the offer but I've got my daughter and a boy to take care of. I want to get back to them before it gets too late."

"How about a shot of liquor for the road? I've got a few Mason jars aging in the rafters of the barn."

"Thanks, but I don't drink. I would like to ask you a question before I go. I was going to ask you on the ride over but it slipped my mind."

"What's that?" Johnny asked.

"I've got the word spreading to people on my side of the mountain about everyone working together to keep things safer. I don't know any folks over on this side of the mountain. Any idea how I might be able to see if people are interested?"

Johnny scratched his chin while he pondered.

"Reverend White's church maybe," Jason mentioned. "There's people there every day."

Johnny waved a finger in exclamation. "That's right! He's operating the only organized event taking place in this little valley. Matter of fact, they've got a never-ending pot of soup. They started it about a week or two after the disaster. Folks add new stuff every day and anybody in the community that wants to can come by for a bowl in the evening. You have to bring your own cup and folks who are able bring a contribution to add to the pot."

"You know these folks?" Conor asked.

Johnny and Jason both nodded, and Jason said, "Small place. We all know each other."

"I might like to drop in on the Reverend White. Would you folks mind going with me? He might be more trusting if I have a familiar face with me."

"Tomorrow would be a good day," Johnny said. "They actually have a sermon tomorrow so there'll be a good turnout."

"What time would be good?"

"Maybe three in the afternoon," Johnny said, looking at his son for confirmation. "They've moved the service up since people are walking and not everyone has batteries for flashlights, and it's getting dark earlier. They'll have the sermon and then everyone will eat before heading home."

"What time would we need to leave here?" Conor asked.

"Be here around 2:30 and that should give us plenty of time," Johnny said.

"The whole family go?" Conor asked.

Johnny shook his head. "Can't leave the house empty. Someone has to stand guard. Small community but it has its rogues."

"I'll see you gentlemen tomorrow," Conor said. He gave a wave and nudged his horse into a trot.

7

Barb was working on a new chicken house. The day had warmed to the point she was shedding layers, though still breaking a sweat. She decided to stop for a drink of water and maybe a snack. She found Ragus in the kitchen making himself a sandwich.

"Whatcha having and where's mine?" she asked.

Ragus built a sandwich with the same intense look of concentration she saw on her dad's face when he was constructing one. "One of those fancy sandwiches your dad is always going on about. Thin sliced goat with goat cheese and a pickle on flatbread."

Barb nodded. "My dad does love his food. He calls that one the Goato Cubano."

"I never had goat before moving in with you guys. It's good. Can I make you one? I've got all the stuff out already."

"No, but thanks. I'm going for canned tuna. I'm suddenly starving."

"You must have the metabolism of a teenage boy," Ragus said. "You eat nearly as much as I do."

Barb cocked her head at him. "Listen, kid, when you start training as hard as I do every day you'll have room to talk. You try one of my workouts and your arms will be shaking so hard you won't even be able to hold that Goato Cubano to your lips."

Surprising Barb, he shot back, "I might like to take you up on that sometime. After seeing you in action I've realized it might do me some good to learn some of the things you know. I used to be a wrestler but it's nothing like the way you fight."

"Grappling is just one tool in the tool belt, Ragus. When it's all you have, it's like trying to fix every problem with a set of pliers. Learning multiple martial arts gives you more to draw on. Jujitsu, Krav Maga, and Tae Kwon Do give you other tools to use."

Ragus finished the construction of his sandwich, folding the flatbread over with the same precision one might use when carefully placing a processor into a motherboard. He dusted his hands off, then took his sandwich to the table. He sat down, admiring his sandwich again before raising his eyes to Barb. "I'm serious. You were impressive."

They had not discussed the kidnapping and rescue, especially just between the two of them. Most of what had been discussed on the trip home was Conor asking questions and them providing answers. The whole experience made Barb uncomfortable on several different levels, not least of which was that she now felt obligated to the boy in front of her. It was a position she didn't like to be in. He'd risked his life to come after her.

"Look, I've been meaning to bring that up. I appreciate you coming after me. I honestly do. I know I can be a bitch sometimes. I've never said it but I appreciate it. You didn't have to do it. With all the times I've smarted off to you and given you shit about things, I'd have completely understood if you just turned away from the whole mess with the kidnappers."

Ragus flattened his sandwich beneath his palm, trying to keep the whole conglomeration together and reduce it to a size that would fit his mouth. When he was done, he looked up at her. "There was no choice. I had to do it. How could I live with myself?"

His response made Barb feel like she owed him an explanation for why she treated him the way she did. She could be a hard person but she didn't like to leave things unsaid. She understood the fragility of life better than some.

"The reason I've always treated you like I do is because I know you've had a little crush on me and I was trying to discourage it in the best way I knew how. I don't have a lot of experience with men. Or *boys*. I was trying to be a bitch so you would quit chasing after me."

Ragus raised an eyebrow at Barb over a mouthful of sandwich. "Really?" The expression on his face was one of amusement.

She shrugged. "What?"

Ragus set his sandwich down and wiped his mouth. "You honestly think I did all that for you? Seriously?"

She looked at him as if he'd gone mad. "Of course you did. I *know* that's why you came after me. I could see it in your eyes every time you looked at me. Why else would you have risked your life like that?"

"For your dad." He said it like it was the most obvious thing in the world.

Barb was floored. "My dad?"

"Barb, I want us to be friends and get along. But I tried to rescue you for your dad. He saved my life by taking me in. As far as you are concerned, I know you're a bad ass and all, but you're just not my type of girl. It's nothing personal, and I still hope we can be friends."

"Friends?" Barb asked, her mouth nearly agape. She made a *harrumph* sound, and spun on her heel to leave. "I've got work to do."

"That is what you wanted, right?" Ragus called after her. "Friends?"

She didn't answer him and it made Ragus smile. She was right. As much as he worshipped Conor, he *had* pursued Barb because he had a crush on her. He knew the age difference between them was significant to her. She saw him as a young kid, but it wasn't that much of a difference, only a couple of years. He'd had time to think about this, and he'd arrived at some epiphanies.

He knew that some women, when pursued, behaved like prey. It was their instinct to flee. Sometimes it was subconscious, a purely instinctual reaction, but at other times it was more contrived and done to see if the man pursued. In one of their more personal conversations Conor pointed out that his daughter was not like most girls. If Ragus pursued Barb and she fled, it was most likely so she could circle around behind him and snap his neck. Conor warned that he should never expect her to behave in the manner of girls her own age. Her life experiences had just been too different. She was her own unique creature.

Ragus made the decision that he would not humiliate himself further by chasing her around and nipping at her heels like a puppy. In fact, he decided he would do much more than give her space. He decided with much glee that he would pretend as if the whole thing was in her head. He wanted to see how she would react if he started moving *away* from her instead of *toward* her. He'd been waiting for the opportunity to broach the topic and it had finally come. She'd even been the one to bring it up. While he didn't want to jump to conclusions about the effect this conversation might have on her, he was certain that what he'd said was provoking a reaction. She was questioning her instincts now, and that was exactly where he wanted her.

It was the most conniving and manipulative thing he'd ever done in his short life and he was quite proud of himself.

8

The next morning Conor was drinking his coffee and considering his breakfast options when something got his attention. It took him a moment to process that it was both a sound and a feeling. His body pulsed while his ears registered the sound of rotors.

Chopper.

Already dressed for the day he walked back into the kitchen and set his coffee mug back on the counter. "Guests are here!"

Neither Ragus nor Barb had stirred yet and they needed to be up for this. Not just for the spectacle, either. You never knew if things were exactly what they were promised to be. You always had to be ready for things to slip sideways. Being ready meant being armed.

Conor pulled on a fleece jacket, grabbed a gun belt from a hook by the door, and took it out onto the porch with him, strapping it on. Not only was there the concern that the chopper might be bringing someone or something other than what he agreed to, there was also the concern that the noise of the chopper might bring folks toward his compound. They might assume the chopper was dropping off supplies they could steal. Anything out of the ordinary was a chance for the world to screw you. Conor had learned that long ago.

When the Chinook came into sight Conor let out a low whistle. Since moving to this compound deep in the Virginia hills, he couldn't recall the number of times choppers had landed on his property. In fact, it had become sort of a routine occurrence around the place. Sometimes it was commercial jet helicopters bringing in supplies or picking up completed projects Conor had whipped up for a job. Other times it was an Apache or Blackhawk dropping off someone that Conor needed to train on a special weapon he'd put together.

With all those landings he'd never hosted anything like the behemoth that he saw chugging over the trees. This was a massive cargo chopper with twin rotors, capable of transporting people or suspending loads beneath it. The ungainly craft looked more like a submarine than something you'd see suspended in the air.

Conor reached back into the house and grabbed a pair of sunglasses from the table by the door. Although not safety glasses, they would still protect his eyes from dust and debris churned up by the rotor wash. He jogged to the flat employee parking lot off to one side of the facility, waving his arms until he was certain he had the pilot's attention.

The chopper squared off with him and approached to a distance of around fifty yards. Conor's body was jostled by the turbulence created by the massive craft. His clothes flapped and he had to slap a hand onto his head to keep his hat from sailing off. A conex shipping container hung beneath the chopper, suspended by four steel cables. Knowing the chopper would have to drop its load before it could discharge any passengers, Conor was prepared to guide the chopper to drop the box and then direct it a short distance away for the landing, but that wasn't what happened.

The chopper descended gently and lowered the shipping container to the pavement with impressive precision. Conor was fairly sure that if there was a bottle of champagne sitting on a table inside it would not have been disturbed during the placement of the box. When the pilot was certain the container was safely on the ground he gave himself a little slack and then dropped the cables. Conor had a clear view of the cockpit and was certain the pilot could see him. He directed the pilot to the left for the landing but the pilot ignored him with a little wave, banking off to the right, and disappearing over the tree line.

Conor was confused. Ricardo hadn't said anything about there being a gear drop prior to the passengers arriving. He made it sound like this was a one-shot opportunity to get these folks aboard a transport that just happened to be coming this way. That made sense. Conor watched the skies frequently and there was very little air traffic moving.

"Where's the people?"

Conor jumped at the voice, turning to find Barb and Ragus standing behind him. He hadn't heard their approach. He shrugged and took a couple of steps toward the container, looking for any markings or perhaps even a message that would communicate the plan to him. What he did not expect was a loud bang on the door of the container. It came from inside.

He reacted by drawing his pistol. He wasn't about to shoot at the container itself. He knew he could damage it with a rifle, he'd done it before, but he'd never fired on a container with a handgun. He didn't have enough information to open fire on it at this point anyway but he wanted to be ready. There was still the lingering concern that it could be full of hostiles ready to burst out the door and open fire on them.

With that thought moving to the forefront of his mind, Conor was preparing to retreat and direct his family back toward the house when a muffled voice came from the container. Besides the thick steel walls, these containers had gaskets around the door to prevent rodents and weather from infiltrating them. The effect was such that the voice inside sounded as if it was coming through a damaged audio speaker. He only managed to decipher a single word from the garbled speech.

Mick.

With his handgun still at the ready, Conor approached the container and placed his head to the door. “Hello?"

There was a voice again. "Is that the Mad Mick?"

The voice was still muffled but Conor was certain he'd heard every word this time. Whoever was in that container knew about the Mad Mick. Were the visitors he was expecting *inside* the container?

It made sense in some ways. Maybe the pilot was uncertain as to whether to trust that Conor indeed had a landing pad capable of handling his craft. Also, by carrying the passengers in the container he could discharge them without landing, saving time. Conex boxes typically had to be opened from the outside so it was up to Conor to let them out.

"Back up!" he directed Barb and Ragus. "Put yourselves back around that corner until we know who's in here."

Conor took one hand from the grip of his gun and approached the latch. He took a deep breath and unhooked it. There was a heavy clanking sound that echoed inside the box. He backed away slowly, pulling open the heavy steel door and shielding his body with it.

He immediately noticed that the furthermost three-quarters of the container were packed solid with gear held back by a sturdy cargo net. The remaining quarter of the container, the end closest Conor, held two recliners strapped down to the deck with cargo straps. A passenger sat in each recliner with the cargo strap running across their lap like a seatbelt. The man in one recliner had a rifle in his hand, apparently having used the butt to bang against the door and attract Conor's attention.

Reacting to the sight of the gun, Conor leveled his weapon on the man holding it, then recognized him. "Fuck me," he muttered, pointing the pistol away from the man and turning away in disgust.

The man in the recliner smiled broadly. "Don't run away now. It's a pleasure to see you too, Sunshine. I don't think you've met my daughter. This is Shannon."

Conor turned back to find an attractive young woman, perhaps in her late teens, waving shyly to him. When there were no gunshots and Conor let down his guard, Barb and Ragus took it as a cue it was safe for them to approach. They reached the container about the time that Conor whipped his knife from his belt. It was a razor sharp Donnie Dunn custom. The knife was stout enough that Conor could have cut a man-sized hole in the side of the container with it if he wanted to.

He waded in and approached the strapped down man. He observed that neither passenger was able to reach the release handle. Apparently neither had the foresight to bring a knife. Poor planning on their part.

Seeing Conor approach, wielding the sharp weapon, the man suddenly looked scared. He threw up his hands. "Look, I'm sorry about Helsinki. We're cool, right?"

"We're far from cool, my friend," Conor growled. He lowered the wicked blade toward the man's groin and then lunged with it, stopping the tip less than an inch from the bound man's crotch. The man lurched and his body tightened with fear. He did not dare breathe. With a flick of the blade, Conor severed the taught cargo strap, freeing the man, then cut free his daughter, though in a significantly less threatening manner.

The man laughed nervously. "You about had me there, Conor, old buddy. For a minute I thought you might be holding a grudge."

"I am."

Feeling emboldened at not having been castrated, the man looked around Conor to Barb and Ragus standing by the door. "Those your kids?"

"You could say that," Conor replied. "That's my daughter Barb. The young man is Ragus. He's family too, but a newer acquisition."

"Barb..." the man replied as if the name stirred a memory from deep in the recesses in his mind. "She's grown."

"Have I met you?" Barb asked, struggling to recall the face.

The man shook his head. "No, but I've seen your picture. Seen several, in fact, but you were much, much younger."

"Dad, who is this?" Barb asked.

Conor turned to Barb with a look of exasperation in his eyes. "It's Doc Marty."

"*The* Doc Marty?"

Conor nodded as if he were once again the recipient of fate's cruelty. "The one and only."

Barb cackled. "This is rich. Oh, this should be good." Addressing Ragus she said, "I don't know what went on between these two but I know it wasn't good. We'll see some sparks."

"So you all know this guy?" Ragus asked.

"Oh, your friend the Mick here knows me well," Doc Marty said. "We've run many operations together over the years."

Conor shot the man a bitter look. "If Ricardo had told me it was you, I would have said no."

Doc Marty shrugged. "We expected that. That's why he left out some of the pertinent details. I knew exactly how to make the offer tempting—mention I had a daughter and that I was a doctor."

"Except you're not really a doctor. You're a dentist." Conor knew that was a sore spot with a man and he jabbed right for it.

"Dentists *are* doctors," Doc Marty said, taking offense to the comment. "People address us as 'doctor.' We know the basics. We can save a life."

"A good dentist might be able to but you're not even that good of a dentist. Not even second-rate, but some even lower tier."

Doc Marty stood. "There's plenty of time to argue about that later. Are you going to allow me to stay or not? I brought all the things you requested from Ricardo. Everything you requested as payment for room and board is strapped onto a single pallet with your name on it. We brought our own food and supplies, and a ton of medicine and medical gear. We won't be any trouble to you at all. That's a promise."

"How long?" Conor asked.

"How long are we staying?"

"Yeah."

Doc Marty cast a glance at his daughter. "That's hard to say. We have no itinerary. We have nowhere else to be. We may be here a while. If you take us in, you do so with the understanding that we could be here until this mess blows over."

"*If* it blows over," Barb said. "No guarantee of that."

"The rest of the world hasn't gone to shit with us," Doc Marty said. "Things will level out eventually. When that happens, Shannon and I will clear out to our next area of operation."

"If you live that long," Conor said. "I have a long memory and I hold grudges."

9

The sun hadn't yet risen when Bryan Padowicz awoke at a highway rest area along the interstate. His men had taken shelter beneath metal canopies suspended over picnic tables. They'd kept watch all night, a single man that rotated out every two hours. Seeing Bryan stir, the guard nodded good morning at him. Bryan didn't acknowledge the greeting.

After obtaining the first two recruits for his army, teenage boys who had been fishing with their family, Bryan's team found no one else until the end of the day. They were looking for a place to spend the night when a campfire at the rest area drew their attention. Bryan left his entourage behind and rode forward with one other man, where he found a group of truck drivers who had been living at the rest area since the collapse.

One of the truckers had been delivering palletized canned goods between a distribution warehouse and a chain of grocery stores. As long as they could keep the cans from freezing over the winter they could potentially have years of food for a group their size. The truckers had been living comfortably out of those pallets of food since the collapse.

Like a lot of truckers, they traveled armed for their own safety and had been successful in fending off anyone trying to approach the rest area. Upon seeing Bryan and his rider approach, the truckers stood and raised weapons. Bryan raised his hands and prompted his companion to do the same.

"This here rest area is taken," one of the truckers barked. "Move along or we'll shoot."

"I don't want anything but information," Bryan said. "I'm looking for some missing men."

"There's going to be two more men missing if you all don't get the hell out of here," the trucker said.

"How many men you looking for?" one of the other truckers asked.

"Around two dozen. They would have come this way on horse-back, leading a string of pack horses. We have a farm up the road a good bit. Those men left out of there a couple of weeks ago and haven't come back."

The truckers looked at each other and exchanged some low words Bryan couldn't hear. Finally, one of the men spoke up.

"We seen some fellers like that, but like you said, it's been a couple weeks ago. They went by here and never said a word to us. They ain't come back this way either. We'd have noticed."

It was news Bryan had expected. Whatever had happened to them had happened further away than this. "May I approach your fire?"

"What for?" one of the truckers grumbled.

"I'd like to speak to you for a moment."

The truckers conferred with each other but it did not appear there was a consensus. Low voices argued.

"Alright, you can come over here, but if you try anything funny we'll kill you without so much as a warning. If you got any doubts as to my sincerity, you go to the far side the road and look over the bank. You'll find the remains of men who didn't take us seriously."

Bryan found it significant that these men had not moved on. When the collapse stuck the truckers at this rest area, they had remained. Did it mean these misplaced and lost stragglers had nowhere to go? Did they have no families or homes or people waiting on them elsewhere in the world? If that was the case, perhaps that created an opening for him, a starting point around which to form an invitation to join his crusade.

"Why haven't you folks moved on? Most people stuck along the highways had somewhere else they needed to be. I think you're the only folks I've seen that approached the situation with the attitude that where they landed was as good a spot as any and they might as well stay there."

"Maybe that's none of your business," said a freckled, red-haired woman in a down jacket.

"I'm not prying for information. It wasn't even a question. But I take your remaining here to mean that you must have food and water available to you. Clearly you're surviving somehow. Would you continue to choose mere subsistence and survival if someone came along and offered you the opportunity to thrive in this environment? To build a new life for yourself that could offer rewards that continued to benefit you even after the world righted itself?"

The group looked skeptical. They looked from one to another with tired expressions. The man spoke like an infomercial. Bryan could tell that some would prefer to just kill him, get him out of the way, and get back to their evening.

"Sounds like a load of bullshit to me," one of the men spoke up. "This is just another asshole trying to talk us out of our food. I'd just as soon kill him as listen to him talk."

Bryan nodded, conceding the point. "That's fair and I understand your reaction. You don't have to take my word for it. I've got a group of men back there waiting on the road. Any one of them could tell you we had a good thing going on. We have a farm in the mountains. Thousands of acres. Bringing our vision to life took a lot of warm bodies, so I sent a group of men out to recruit more women to work on the farm. Those men haven't come back. I've been forced to take what men I have left and head out on a mission to find them. We plan to either return and rebuild our camp, or find a new place that's even better. I can't do it without more men, so our current mission is not just one of recovery but one of recruitment."

"What's in it for us?" asked a bearded trucker in an army field jacket. He held a shotgun across the front of his body, his finger resting right on the trigger. "Is this about building something nice for *you* or something nice for all of us? Because I'm not sure why I would want to help you. You're a bit mouthy."

Bryan cocked his head and held out a finger as if he were lecturing a group of students. "I'll be honest with you. Most of what I have to offer is a lot of hard work in the beginning. We have greenhouses for growing crops year round, all of it powered by solar energy and wood heat. We had crops on the way, nearly ready to harvest, but we were attacked and our crops were destroyed because I didn't have enough men available to guard the place. I had a plan for raising enough food to sell to local communities. Every man who comes with me is entitled to a share. This is not an operation for families. I'm looking for individual men willing to work hard and able to make tough decisions. I'm looking for men who are up for being wealthy when the world gets back to normal. Any of this sound appealing to you guys or should I just ride on out of here?"

The oldest of the truckers, painfully thin and wearing a cowboy hat, shook his head and spat on the ground. "I ain't a bit interested in traipsing around the country. I got bad legs from sitting in that truck all these years. My blood pressure is high and my heart don't do what it's supposed to half the time. I'm just going to sit this one out, boys. If you want to go, you're welcome to it. I'll be fine right here."

"What about us?" the red-headed woman asked.

Bryan shook his head. "I got no place for women. They don't do anything but stir up trouble."

The old man cackled like Bryan had just stirred a hornet's nest.

The woman looked offended. "You're lucky I don't blow your damn head off. What kind of sexist bullshit is that? I can do anything a man can do. Ask any of these guys."

"I don't give a shit what you can do," Bryan said. "The rules are different now in that there are no rules. A man can be as sexist or racist, as biased and bigoted as he wants. Of course, that comes with the risk that someone who doesn't care for your attitude might kill you."

That comment was a bad choice on Bryan's part. The woman drew a large revolver and leveled it at Bryan's chest. "My thoughts exactly. I'm one of those people who don't care for your attitude and I'm fixing to kill you."

The bearded trucker gestured at the pistol-wielding woman. "Hold on just one second, Carrie." He addressed Bryan. "Your offer is intriguing. I'm used to life on the road and I'm getting a little restless being stuck here in one place for so long. I can't speak for these other guys but I'm sure some of them probably feel the same. But if we go, she goes."

Bryan studied the bearded trucker, then moved his eyes back to the redhead. "Can you make tough calls? I can't take people who are going to get all soft over spilling a little blood."

The woman returned the gun to her pocket. "When I was twelve, I killed my daddy for beating my mother. He didn't think I'd do it but I got the last laugh. How's that for making a tough call?"

Bryan conceded the point. "Welcome to the team."

The red-headed trucker turned to the other woman in the group, fiftyish and overweight. "You going with us?"

The woman shook her head and looked at the older, scrawny trucker. "Nah, I'm staying with Bert. You all go on without us."

"Then let's split this food up tonight," the bearded trucker said. "Everyone will need as much as they can carry. We'll leave the rest in your care, Bert. I hope if this endeavor doesn't work out, we can come back and join you."

The old trucker smiled. "I was a hundred and eight pounds last time I weighed. I ain't sure I've lost any weight but I sure as hell haven't gained any. I ain't likely to take a notion to plump up and eat it all."

The bearded trucker nodded at his buddy. "If you do take a notion, have at it. You could use more meat on your bones."

By daylight, breakfast was cooking and men were packing gear. The truckers contributed some canned sausage, canned gravy, and powdered milk to the breakfast. Everyone ate well enough that they questioned the ability of the horses to even carry them.

The work of packing continued through the meal. Bryan had spare horses and tack but they had more canned food than even the chuck wagon could carry. They needed more saddle bags. The bearded man, whom they now knew as Zach, walked the parking lot of the rest area until he found a Subaru with aftermarket seat covers. He peeled them off to find that they were basically nothing more than two stretchy sacks. When bound together at the top, they could hang over a horse's back just like saddle bags.

When Zach was able to make his set work, everyone else went on a search for more seat covers. They used their knives to remove the seat belts from cars, the strong webbing making a good material for strapping the seat covers together. Each set of bags was filled with an assortment of canned food from the grocery truck. Human nature was such that they overfilled the bags and there was concern that they might break from the weight or slow the horses.

"That's my problem," Zach said. "If they break, we'll fix them."

"Good enough," Bryan said. "But let's be clear that there's only one leader on this journey. By agreeing to be part of it, you also agree that I am in charge. The final decisions are mine. The penalty for not following orders is death."

The mood of the group changed at hearing that. It broke the sense of camaraderie with the suddenness of an icy plunge into a river. All of Bryan's existing party knew the rules. The new people, the truckers, understood that Bryan was serious and intense but perhaps hadn't grasped *how* serious and intense.

"Can you live with that?" Bryan asked. "Now is the time to decide."

Zach threw a look at his companions, the four men and one woman who chose to join him. They exchanged looks and subtle nods. They wanted the change. They wanted the opportunity. Though they'd all been equals at the rest area, it seemed they were making Zach the leader of their small group, or at least appointing him as the intermediary between them and Bryan's group.

"We're in," Zach said. "We understand."

Bryan smiled. "Good. Welcome aboard. Let's ride."

The truckers waved back at Bert and his female companion.

"You think he can defend that place?" Bryan asked Zach. "I'm sure it was easier with the rest of you there. More guns and manpower."

"It's a risk," Zach said. "He's mean enough, but with just two of them it will be hard to post a guard every night. They won't want to do that. They'll get slack about security. Hard to say how long they'll make it. They might still be here if we pass back through and they might not."

"He's not fit for travel?"

"Nah, got health problems. He was fine in a truck but he couldn't handle what we're setting out on. We'd end up leaving him on the side of the road somewhere. It's best he stay where he's got resources."

Bryan nodded. "There's something else I want to make you aware of. If we find that my men were killed, I'm going to track down the people that did it and lay waste to them. I'm building an army for that purpose. Some of my recruitment techniques may seem harsh but that's how it is. I'll ask that you just go with the flow."

Zach was silent for a moment, the only sound that of creaking leather and clattering hooves. "We're big boys, he said eventually. "If we find it not to our liking, we'll pack our toys and go home."

"Fair enough," Bryan said, not sure if he would allow them to leave or not. It was one thing to keep scared boys from running off. It was quite another to attempt to keep men onboard that weren't scared to fight back. He would have to consider his moves carefully. Each day was a new adventure.

"I'm going to fall back and talk to my own people," Zach said. "I don't want them to think that joining up with you guys was all about me. I don't need them getting the wrong idea."

Bryan didn't respond. His mind was elsewhere. As Zach dropped off and waited for his own crew, Bryan's mind kept returning to the truckload of food and the frail couple guarding it. If they ended up returning to Douthat Farms, that food could provide a good safety net. He'd glimpsed the interior of the trailer. It was forty-two feet deep and the truckers had only eaten their way back a few feet. That food could last him a long time. It would be a shame to let it fall into the wrong hands.

10

Conor settled Doc Marty and Shannon in a secondary office building he'd set up exactly for this purpose. He called it "the bunkhouse." Over the years he'd lived on the compound, this was where he put up work-related guests. Although he didn't get many visitors, there were times he built some specialized device and the operator running it required training that only Conor, the designer and builder, could provide.

The bunkhouse was not quite so elaborate as Conor's own living quarters. There was a basic solar system that stored power in an array of marine batteries and powered twelve-volt lighting throughout the small building. There were no receptacles and no inverter to provide AC power.

As a former office building, there was a lobby with a waiting room that was barely larger than the tiny offices. Conor set up the living room with a compact wood stove he'd picked up locally. There was a bathroom, a kitchenette, and a half-dozen offices that had been converted to bedrooms. Three offices were empty for folks who brought their own cots. The other three had built-in bunk beds that allowed four people to cram into each room. Some of the bunks had mattresses, others did not. Conor picked them up when he saw them available at yard sales, as long as they didn't have those billowy yellow blooms of urine stains. The bathroom and the kitchen had running water from an elevated tank nearby. There was no hot water, nor did any of the appliances in the kitchen work without grid power.

After the quick tour, Doc Marty did not seem concerned. If Shannon was flipping out, she hid it well. Conor had known Doc for years and knew the man had seen much worse conditions. In fact, the two of them had shared worse conditions on numerous occasions. The bunkhouse beat muddy jungle, caves, spider and snake infested drain pipes, and any number of shitty conditions the two had seen over the years.

Despite that bond, Conor was still pissed at the man. Had Shannon not been with him Conor might have made him sleep in the shipping container or one of the unheated shop buildings. They had been close friends at one point, their friendship forged by hardship, dangerous conditions, and the type of operations that men were never free to speak of in general company. Then Helsinki happened.

"It won't be so bad after we move our stuff in," Doc Marty told his daughter. "We'll get those recliners in here, set up our bedrooms, and we'll be fine.

Shannon didn't look so certain but understood that this was the situation, for better or worse.

"We'll even volunteer the lout there to help you carry gear," Barb said, gesturing to Ragus.

Ragus wasn't aware that Barb was referring to him as *the lout* but quickly figured it out. He gave Barb an angry glare, then looked at Doc Marty and Shannon with a wide smile. "I'd be glad to." He shot Barb a look of smug satisfaction, wanting her to be aware that he was a nicer person than she and willing to help out a couple of folks in need.

Barb returned a *whatever* look.

"I'll go ahead and get those recliners," Ragus said.

Doc Marty touched his daughter's shoulder. "How about you give the lad a hand."

Shannon smiled at Ragus. "Sure."

When Ragus and Shannon left the room Doc Marty asked Conor, "So how do we prepare meals here?"

"This kitchen isn't set up for cooking while the grid is down, unless you use the top of the woodstove. Besides, it's a more efficient use of resources to cook our meals together. There's less wasted food that way and we tie up fewer people in the kitchen."

"Excellent," Doc Marty replied. "That's sound planning."

Barb cleared her throat. "That doesn't mean we're taking you to raise. It means we all contribute to the pot. We all take a turn at the labor. We all damn sure take turns at the cleanup."

"That's completely understood," the Doc said, then to Conor, "Your daughter clearly gets her...efficiency in planning...from you."

Barb laughed. "It's fine if you think I'm a rude bitch. I'm just making certain we're all on the same page. The room and board don't come with a serving wench."

Doc Marty laughed. "I like you. Your honesty is refreshing. You seem to be a lot more fun to work with than your dad."

Barb barely curled the end of her mouth. It wasn't even a smile. "You've just barely met me. We'll see if you feel the same if we have to winter together. You may be ready to hike out of here in waist-deep snow just to get away from me."

Conor looked at his daughter. "Let's you and I go whip up a big breakfast. I'm afraid you're scaring the poor man. We'll leave Ragus to help the Doc and Shannon unpack."

Barb shrugged indifferently. "I like scaring men."

Conor took his daughter by the arm and led her out of the room.

The group filed out the door of the bunkhouse, the Doc breaking off toward the shipping container. Ragus and Shannon were already coming toward them. Ragus had a recliner balanced on his head while Shannon carried two suitcase-sized pelican cases.

Doc Marty spun and jogged back to the bunkhouse door, swinging it open to help Ragus negotiate the recliner through the door.

"I'm not sure what I think about that man," Barb said once they were out of earshot. “Especially since there are gaps in my information.”

“I've known him eighteen years or so," Conor said. "My opinion of him ebbs and flows."

"Do you think he’s a security risk? Is it safe to even have him here?"

Conor shook his head adamantly. "No, Barb, he's solid. He’s a team player but a bit of a cowboy sometimes. We have a difference in styles. I'm a machinist at heart and I do everything with the machinist’s attention to precision and detail. Doc Marty...well, I don't know what you’d call his style. He gets his jobs done at any and all cost. Some of them are ridiculously complicated and incredibly dangerous."

“I don’t particularly like the idea of folks that get the job done at all cost. That sounds a little reckless. And what the hell happened in Helsinki?"

"Nothing I want to talk about right now."

"That bad?"

"It’s a sore spot."

"That bastard put you in danger?"

Conor shook his head.

"Did he blow an operation?"

"No, he just crossed the line and I'm not ready to talk about it yet."

Barb threw up her hands in surrender. "Fine, fine."

"His daughter seems nice," Conor said. "Maybe you ladies will hit it off?"

Barb made a sound of indifference. "We'll see. I’ve been known to scare women as badly as I scare men."

"If nothing else, maybe Ragus will take to her and give you some breathing room," Conor said. "I'm sure that would be a relief to you. Right?"

"Of course it would."

Doc Marty, Shannon, and Ragus unloaded the basics out of the shipping container, meaning only the gear they needed to get by or anything that might be damaged by freezing temperatures. All of the extra stuff remained in the shipping container since it was the only secure storage Doc Marty had at this point. At Conor's insistence, they unloaded the pallet of gear Ricardo sent with Doc Marty as rent. Conor wanted those items under his control as soon as possible so there was no room for a misunderstanding.

The pallet included an assortment of batteries, five thousand rounds of 9mm, and ten thousand rounds of 5.56. The remainder of the pallet designated for Conor was filled with cases of MREs, with the exception of two unmarked plastic pelican cases. Those cases were padlocked and Doc Marty hadn't been told what they contained. He was, however, intrigued by the smile they brought to Conor's face.

When everything that had to be unloaded had been, Doc Marty padlocked the container and slipped one key in his pocket, giving the other to Shannon. He noticed Ragus watching him.

"No offense, son," Doc Marty said. "I just don't know the neighborhood yet."

"No offense taken," Ragus said. "Conor has been broken into before. That's how we met. He caught me in his chicken house."

Both Doc Marty and Shannon looked at him with surprise.

"It's okay," Ragus assured them. "It's a long story. We worked through it."

Ragus was saved from further explanation by Barb calling them to breakfast. The three joined Barb and Conor in the main living quarters.

"Oh my God," Shannon said. "That smells amazing."

Conor gestured to a counter filled with fried ham, biscuits, eggs, and local honey. "Dig in."

While Shannon filled a plate, Doc Marty's eyes roamed, checking out the place Conor called home.

"So this is where they stuck you?"

"This is where I *asked* to be," Conor clarified. "I found this place myself and was going to buy it with my own money but you know how that works. Ricardo likes to get you on the hook. He, and whoever he works for, likes to keep you in a position of owing them. They like to keep you feeling obligated."

Doc Marty shrugged. "Sometimes it works to our advantage. I'm not complaining. They paid off my dental school. They paid for Shannon's private school. They've set me up with dental practices in some of the most beautiful places in the world."

"But there's a catch," Conor said. "Everywhere you end up has some benefit to them. Every practice you've ever had was there for a particular reason. For a particular client or a particular job. How did you feel when you got the call that it was time for you to move, that your practice was going to be disassembled overnight, and all records destroyed? I couldn't live like that."

“Sometimes that sucked,” Marty admitted. “But it was the nature of the job.”

“That's why I preferred my role better. I wasn't interested in putting down roots particularly but I didn't like the idea of having to move around a lot. I wanted to be able to set up a shop the way I liked it. I wanted to live the way I wanted. I wanted to be out in the country.”

“So you built this fortress of solitude?”

“I did.”

Doc Marty grew serious. "Would you change it? If you could go back in time, would you say no to those men who turned up at your door? Would you give up the excitement and the experiences to work as a welder in a small shop somewhere?"

Conor considered the notion. "I was raised to make the best of whatever situation I found myself in. I've enjoyed this but I would have found a way to enjoy whatever I ended up doing. But as farmers are fond of saying, I've already hoed my row.”

“What the hell does that mean?” Barb asked.

“It means things are what they are and there's no changing any of it at this point,” Ragus replied. “That right?”

Conor nodded.

"Are you still working?" Doc Marty asked. "Have you had any assignments since the shit hit the fan?"

"Not until Ricardo called me about you. I assumed everything was on hold."

"I thought we were friends," Marty said with mock offense. "You consider this work?"

Conor said nothing but shot Doc Marty a nasty look.

“The world isn’t on hold,” Doc Marty continued. “This disaster is localized to the U.S. and some aid is moving in. If anything, I would say our kind of business has picked up. What better time to make big political moves than in times of chaos and upheaval? People with grudges are settling scores like crazy. They have a little window where murders won’t receive much investigation or media attention so some people are trying to take maximum advantage of that.”

Conor looked pensive and returned to an earlier comment. "Just so you know, we *were* friends. After Helsinki I put you in that *to be determined* category. You’re on probationary status.”

“So you’re back on that again? I thought we were talking about business. That was a special situation. The job demanded fast action and my options were limited. It was an emergency.”

“I have to say, the more I hear about Helsinki, the more intrigued I get. It’s not often I see my dad acting this way. Whatever happened clearly pissed him off,” Barb said.

“I'm done talking about it at this time," Conor said.

“Spoil his breakfast and you pay all day,” Barb warned the group.

"Fair enough," Doc Marty said. "We'll just put that little episode behind us then."

That comment brought a devious cackle from Conor. "You’ll wish it was behind us. You best sleep with your door locked in case I dwell on the past a little too much one night and feel a sudden urge to settle old scores."

"So what do we do around here for entertainment?" Shannon asked, anxious to defuse the tension in the room.

Barb raised an eyebrow and looked at Shannon as if it were the dumbest question she’d ever heard in her life. "Uh, we try to survive."

Shannon swallowed, admonished. “Sorry I asked.”

Barb still focused on Shannon with a withering look but the younger girl didn’t appear put off by it.

"Seriously, Marty, have you been so out of touch that you have no idea how hard times have been for folks in the U.S.?" Conor asked.

"Between us, I was on assignment in Dubai up until a few days ago. Shannon was with me and I had a dental practice there. We’d been there three years.”

"And you came back here?" Barb asked. "Why?"

Doc Marty shrugged. "I knew there'd been a disaster but I figured things would be back up and running soon. My operation in Dubai was running its course and we had to get out of there.”

"Nobody at any of the American bases told you that you shouldn't come back home yet?" Conor asked.

Doc Marty shook his head. "You know how it is when we show up on bases. We’re invisible. Nobody asks us questions. Nobody meets our eyes. They see our paperwork and suddenly we’re invisible. The only people who spoke to us were the ones responsible for getting us on our flights and making sure we buckled up. Nobody else even acknowledged our existence.”

“It was kind of creepy,” Shannon admitted.

Ragus looked at her sympathetically. Barb noticed it and rolled her eyes skyward.

“If you’re through eating, we’ve wasted enough time jawing,” Barb said. “Cooks don’t clean. That’s one of our rules around here. So one of you jokers who didn’t help with the cooking can roll up your sleeves and do the dishes. There’s water heating on the stove. That’s how we usually do it.”

“I’d be glad to,” Shannon said.

“I’ll give you a hand,” Ragus said.

Barb tightened her mouth. She had no patience for his obvious efforts at spending time with the new girl. Did the boy know how ridiculous he was acting? Conor watched her and smiled, wiping it quickly from his face when she nearly caught him.

“What are you doing today, Gramps?” Barb asked him.

Conor looked offended. "Your dear old dad is going to inventory the contents of the pallet of supplies we just got, then I'm going to stow everything where it goes. After that, I'm heading to Johnny Jacks' place. They're going to introduce me to a local minister who's running a soup kitchen. It might be a way to get some outreach about our effort to organize a defensive perimeter."

"You turning into a community organizer?" Doc Marty asked.

"Bite my ass, Doc. More like a recruiter."

11

Conor rode alone to Johnny Jacks' house. Both Barb and Ragus offered to go with him but he was already going to have Johnny and Jason in tow when he got to the church. He didn't want to present an overwhelming or menacing presence to the folks he was trying to befriend. The ride over the mountain was uneventful, little different from when he took the same trip a day earlier. He found Johnny and Jason ready to go, waiting in the barn and doing busy work while they waited on him. Johnny was repairing a saddle. Jason was crafting a rifle scabbard from an old pair of leather chaps.

"Ready to go?" Conor asked, not even dismounting his horse.

The two men nodded and went outside to where their saddled horses were tied off to a corral of red metal panels.

"How was the night?" Conor asked. "Any trouble?"

Johnny shrugged. Something seemed to be bothering him.

"Coyote problems," Jason said. "We lost a foal and a couple of lambs."

"Got traps out?"

"Don't have any of the right size," Johnny said. "We have some smaller ones for rats and some live traps I've used for coons."

"I'd set snares," Conor said. "Find where they're entering your pasture, create a choke point, and put in a couple of snares."

"We'll try that," Jason said.

"I can show you some tricks," Conor said. "I've learned from some of the best."

They rode for nearly an hour, following a paved road which itself followed a wide, shallow river. Fallen leaves were everywhere, already beginning to turn to the leafy confetti produced by trampling feet, giving the air a particular smell, earthy, that combined with the smell of river silt. The men made small talk about the community and the folks who lived there. Johnny shared the adventures of men long dead and pointed out the locations of events long forgotten by all but a few. Even without knowing the area, Conor appreciated the stories, enjoying the window into the past.

Homes in this isolated community were mostly distant from each other. Occasionally, there would be a family enclave where relations settled together, crowding homes into tight proximity to each other, sharing roads, yards, and drama. Wood smoke hung in the air and was visible rolling from the chimneys of some of the homes. Unlike other areas Conor had seen, this community seemed to be alive. People had not been driven out nor died yet of starvation and disease. It boded well for these folks. Maybe they were hardier than most, made durable by the challenge of daily life in such an isolated area.

They passed a single country store that had not escaped destruction. It had been ransacked and burned. The fact that some in this community might be working together to save lives should not be misinterpreted. These hill people, denizens of dark, remote hollows in steep, unwelcoming mountains, were much like Conor's own people back home. They had their habits and traditions. They had their *ways*. Sometimes those ways included burning down things that didn't belong to them. It didn't make all of them bad but it did mean that badness existed among them. It was something Conor and the people who lived here needed to remain aware of.

Pastor White's church stood at the intersection of two roads and two bodies of water. The road from Jewell Ridge joined the road to

Pilgrims Knob at that location and Hell Creek joined the Dismal River. The church could have chosen from any number of names but settled for some reason on the Hell Creek Assembly of God. Perhaps they felt that including Hell in the name of their church lent a degree of provenance to their name, as if they were fighting on the very front lines of salvation in the war between good and evil.

If they were indeed perched on the cusp of Hell, they had been there for some time. The church was a sagging and obtuse building that inferred a log structure later covered with plank siding. Inevitably, as the logs rotted and lost their structural integrity, only the planks held them in place, like wooden splints supporting a limb determined to remain broken. With each passing year, gravity tugged at the logs. One day the congregation would have no choice but to surrender the fight and rebuild. For now the structure stood, a relic of a day without power and indoor plumbing, restored again to the type of world in which it had entered, like an old man returning to his hometown to die.

A picnic shelter stood across the road from the church, overlooking the river. The shelter was of more recent construction and even without sides was likely a more substantial structure than the church itself. Folks sat at picnic tables eating soup from mugs or bowls. Other folks were still straggling in, carrying their bowls, spoons, and bibles. Despite the times and the hardship, these folks dressed for the evening. It was not suits and ties, but clean white shirts with long buttoned sleeves for the men, long dresses and wide hair bows for the women.

Most of these folks arrived on foot and Johnny's group drew some attention for their horses. Conor was pleased to see that the pastor's flock was not made up entirely of sheep. There were guns present, leaning against tables or worn on the belts of the faithful. That was an encouraging sight. These men would not go down without a fight.

Johnny spotted a man ladling out soup and threw a hand up to him. "Pastor White!"

The pastor turned his ladle over to the woman beside him and wiped his hands with a dishtowel. He stalked toward Johnny in long, lurching steps. It was the gait of hill people, men and women who grew up having to walk wherever they wanted to go. The pastor had his hand extended and a smile on his face before be even reached the visitors.

"Brother Jacks! How are you?"

Johnny took the hand and shook it vigorously. "I'm good, Pastor White. You remember my son Jason?"

The minister nodded in Jason's direction and reached to shake his hand. "Jason."

Johnny gestured toward Conor. "I know you've not met this fellow before. This is Conor Maguire. He runs a machine shop on top of Jewell Ridge."

Pastor White studied Conor for a moment. "I'm good with faces but I don't recall seeing him before." He extended a hand and shook with Conor. "It's good to meet you. If you're a friend to this family that tells me all I need to know."

Conor nodded. "Same here, Pastor. It's good to meet you."

"You here for the sermon, Johnny? Haven't seen you in the soup line before."

"No," Johnny said with a shake of his head. "Not that I wouldn't enjoy hearing you preach. I wanted to introduce you to Conor. We also brought some canned goods for the pot."

Jason extended two jars of pork his mother had canned the previous year. The minster took them gratefully, catching the eye of the woman he'd turned his ladle over to and raising the jars to show her.

"The pickings getting slim?" Conor asked.

Pastor White nodded. "Times are hard and people are seeing the back of their pantries. That's never a good thing."

"I brought a few items too," Conor said, retrieving two cans of corn and two cans of chicken from his pack.

"Thank you much, friend. Meat is scarce," the pastor said, relieving Conor of the cans and handing them off to the approaching woman. She wasted no time adding them to the pot.

"I'll not waste your time," Conor said. "I can tell you're a busy man, already making a valiant effort to help your community. That's what I'm here about."

"Can we take a seat?" the pastor asked. "I've already stood long enough my bones are protesting."

"By all means," Johnny said. "Which way?"

Pastor White pointed toward a line of plank benches looking out onto the river. It was an area that the church had once maintained for the benefit of its congregation. From there a person could sit and watch the Dismal River flow over the rocks, watch the herons wade the shallows, and reflect on life. The men took seats on the benches, sitting close enough that they could converse with a degree of confidentiality.

Conor wasted no time getting to the point. "I don't know if you've heard any of the stories, but my daughter was recently kidnapped. She wasn't the only one. There was a group of men from outside the area who kidnapped several local women. They were taking them further north to use as slave labor. Fortunately, I got word of what happened and was able to pursue them."

"I heard of some kidnapped women being returned home," Pastor White said, searching for the details in the whorls of his memory. "Did the men that did this face justice?"

Conor didn't miss a beat. "I sent every man to the Lord, Pastor. I trust He took care of that."

Pastor White nodded in understanding. He made no comment. He had no idea what to say and how to respond to such a brazen comment. Since he answered his calling, he'd counseled young couples on how to tell their parents that they'd conceived a child out of wedlock. He'd listened to young men who confessed to stealing and robbing to pay for an addiction. He'd accompanied a young man to the jailhouse to turn himself in after killing someone in a hit-and-run accident. He'd gone to innumerable homes to console the bereaved. Never had he experienced a man telling him in such a matter-of-fact way that he'd dispatched a whole party of wrongdoers and sent them to meet their maker.

"Are you at peace with what you've done?" Pastor White asked.

"I don't present myself as a model of righteousness, Pastor. My ideas of right and wrong may be different than most but I aim to leave the world a better place when I depart it. I assume I'll answer for my methods at that time."

The Pastor nodded, having nothing to add to that. "We all will."

"Pastor, I tried to keep to myself up there on the ridge. My daughter and I stayed close to home and we left other people to their own business. We didn't look for trouble. At the same time, we didn't make enough of an effort to keep trouble away from our door. While I was trying to get my daughter home, not knowing if she was living or dead, I had a lot of time to think about things." Conor looked Pastor White in the eyes. "I realized that I couldn't let evil get that close to us again. If I wanted to keep my home safe, keep my community safe, we had to draw a line in the sand and dare bad men to cross it."

"Are you talking about something you will be doing or something you want everyone to be part of?" Pastor White asked.

"One man cannot do it," Conor said. "A community can."

Pastor White cocked his head to the side and looked doubtful. "Times are hard. People are having trouble taking care of themselves. I think getting them to do any kind of neighborhood watch is going to be a hard sell."

"I thought the same thing," Johnny said. "But Conor is right. We need to know who is in the area. We need a way to pass the word. We need some planning and organization. I traded off a bunch of horses to a group of strangers just yesterday. They showed up at the house and said someone told them I might have horses to sell. There were a lot of them. If they had bad intentions we wouldn't be having this conversation right now. They could have killed me and taken what they wanted."

"I used to have this nickname," Conor said. "People I worked with called me the Mad Mick because I was Irish and I could get a little crazy sometimes."

"Like when you killed those kidnappers?" Pastor White asked.

Conor nodded eagerly. "Yeah, exactly like that. So on my side of the ridge we've been carving a MM symbol on the trees as a way to mark a territory. We've even put some signs up that say: *This area protected by the Mad Mick*. The idea is that eventually we may be able to scare people away. If we build a legend around that MM symbol it will make people wary of crossing into territory protected by the Mad Mick. If the legend carries enough weight, the bad people may decide to move on to easier pickings."

"Sounds like there ain't much to make up about it," the Pastor said. "Sounds like the truth should serve as an adequate cautionary tale for anyone determined to mess with you."

"It's not about me," Conor said. "It's about the community as a group building a legend that deters people with bad intentions."

"What are you wanting from me and my people?" Pastor White asked.

"Mr. Jacks told me what you were doing here and I've seen it with my own eyes. You have folks coming through here every day. You're feeding people and giving them hope. Maybe a good starting point is to just tell people to keep their eyes open. If they see strangers or anything that feels out of place, they tell you. You see about getting the word to Johnny or Jason here, then they can get word to me. I think building our network is the place to start. If we can get that working for us, then we'll work toward improving security for everyone."

Pastor White nodded. "That doesn't sound too bad. If you ask for something small, folks won't feel like you're asking too much. Then if they see a benefit from it, we can ask for more."

"That the same approach you use here, Pastor?" Johnny asked.

Pastor White smiled. "Maybe."

The sound of raised voices led all the men to turn toward the picnic shelter. The woman operating the ladle was speaking loudly to a young man. He was giving it back to her just as loudly.

"Looks like Sister Betty is having a little trouble," Pastor White said. "I better help her out." There was nothing in his demeanor to indicate that he was intimidated by the challenge. Whatever it was, he was certain he could handle it. He smiled and rose from the bench, the rest of the group standing as he left to watch what was taking place.

Knowing these kinds of situations had a way of accelerating out of control quickly—one minute people were arguing, the next they were dying—Conor hopped the bench and approached the picnic shelter. He wanted to be in a position to act if the situation merited it. From where he stood, he could see all the players.

"Everyone knows the rules," Sister Betty explained to Pastor White. "They're right there on the sign. Bring a cup or a bowl and get it filled once a day. They're trying to cheat the rules."

The group she was accusing of cheating was three men and one woman, all younger than Conor but with that dried-up look that came from long-term meth use. Conor hadn't seen any indications they were high but the ingredients to make meth were still readily available. It was likely there were several meth labs currently producing product in the area. Drugs were one of the commodities that seemed to be apocalypse-proof. The drug trade was always part of the black market in war zones and disasters, even when every other legitimate business had pulled up stakes.

"What have you folks done to rile Sister Betty up so much?" Pastor White asked in a friendly, folksy tone.

One of the men nodded toward the sign tacked up on the post. "The sign says we can bring a bowl. We each brought a bowl."

He was a scrawny guy with dark skin, straight black hair, and a patchy attempt at a beard. He looked like the kind of guy that carried around a general anger that he dispersed in small doses to everyone he encountered during the day. Conor didn't like men like that, the kind who didn't understand the connection between their actions and the way the world treated them. They were always full of blame, victimized by everything and everyone.

"Show them your bowls!" Betty demanded, spitting mad.

Each of the four held a bowl out, all large mixing or serving bowls. Between the four of them, they would completely empty the church's soup pot if their bowls were filled.

Pastor White shook his head playfully, like he'd caught a group of kids trying to sneak cigarettes. Conor almost wondered if he was going to threaten to call their parents. It seemed to Conor that Pastor White was living in the 1950s while these characters were living in the present day. Did the pastor understood how the rules had changed? Did he know that shaming didn't work with the shameless?

"You fellers didn't really think that was going to work, did you? We fill those bowls and we won't have any for anyone else," the pastor said. "That wouldn't be right, would it?"

"We don't have no other bowls," the woman said.

"Yeah, these are the only bowls we got," one of the men piped in.

"Sorry," Pastor White said. "Not doing it."

"You got other bowls?" the woman asked.

"We do have a few Styrofoam bowls left," Sister Betty said. "I guess we could give them one of those or maybe just give them a single scoop in their big bowls."

The pastor shook his head and held a hand up to silence Betty. "Nope. They don't get anything today. Let this be a lesson to you folks. You come back with a mug or a proper soup bowl tomorrow and we might be able to help you out. Today, I'm afraid I'm going to have to send you home empty-handed."

"That's not fair," scraggly beard said. "At least put a dipper in each bowl, like she said."

"I offered that once before," Betty said. "You wouldn't take it. You demanded I fill that big bowl up and you were downright hateful about it."

"Bitch!" the woman yelled.

"Hey!" Pastor White yelled. "We don't use that language here. You all can leave now."

The scraggly bearded man whipped out a pocket pistol and stuck it in the pastor's face. "You're the one about to learn a lesson. You're fixing to learn that there are people you shouldn't mess with. We're taking all your damn soup and anything else we want to take. There's not a thing you can do about it."

Conor saw one of the pastor's congregation gradually reaching for a rifle. He walked forward and rested a hand on the man's shoulder.

Startled, the man looked up at Conor, who shook his head at him. He would handle this.

Conor's movement was detected by the man with the gun and he whipped his head around. The scraggly bearded man took in Conor, his gear, and his clothing. "What the fuck are you?"

Conor moved forward, one step at a time, not rushing, not threatening. "I'm one of those people you were just talking about. The kind you shouldn't mess with. That man you have a gun on, the pastor, he's a good man. He saves people."

Conor took another step, closing in, just feet away from the man now. "I'm the opposite. I'm a bad man. In fact, someone once called me an angel of death. Can you believe that? Ask yourself what I must have done that someone would want to call me that." Conor gave a little laugh and a shake of his head, as it was the most absurd thing he'd ever heard.

The bearded man sneered. "Old bastard like you? The angel of death?"

"That's right," Conor said. He was within reach of the man now.

The pastor stood frozen, his eyes moving from the gun in his face to the man wielding it. "He's a killer, boy. He sends men to Hell. You going to make him send you today?"

The scraggly man took his eyes off Conor and returned them to Pastor White, preparing a response. Not a single word made it out of his mouth before Conor swept and trapped the man's gun arm. He jammed a finger behind the trigger so it couldn't be depressed, then snapped the man's wrist and peeled the gun free. The man screamed and cradled his arm. He tried to jerk away but Conor locked an arm around his neck, using him as a shield. He leveled the gun on the next man in line, another of the Mixing Bowl Gang.

"Your call, Pastor White," Conor said. "Am I filling Hell's waiting room today or do they get a second chance?"

The pastor cleared his throat, trying to regain his composure. He pointed angrily at the man Conor was restraining. "We're about forgiveness here but don't confuse that for weakness, boy. I'm going to ask that man to let you go and then I'm going to ask my congregation to pray for you. I'll respectfully ask that you don't darken our doorstep again. Our charity only extends so far. We prepare food for the righteous, not the wicked."

Conor shoved the injured man into his companions, taking advantage of the commotion to whip his own handgun up. He couldn't even be sure that the one he'd snatched from the punk's hand was functional. By the time the scraggly bearded man returned his glare to Conor, he found himself staring down a longer barrel.

"You can go now," Conor said. "And before you decide to screw up this second chance you've been given, take a look around you."

The four miscreants did as they were told, scanning the rest of the crowd. They found at least half the congregation was armed and all the guns were aimed at them.

"Go *now*," Conor repeated.

The group backed out of the shelter and toward the road, all the guns following them. As they turned their backs and hurried away, they were further pursued by the rising voice of Pastor White reciting scripture and praying for their souls.

Conor holstered his pistol. "I hope I didn't overstep my bounds. I didn't want to see any of you good folks get hurt."

Pastor White laughed nervously. "You can see that my flock is willing to defend itself."

The significance of the word choice was not lost on Conor. "I see that. Perhaps with a little training we could even sharpen your flock up a little bit and teach them to work together. A group of armed folks is more effective working as a single unit than as a mob of angry villagers."

"How about you come back to our church next week and I'll let folks know you're coming? If they want to hear what you have to say, they'll be here."

"That the soonest?" Conor asked.

Pastor White shrugged. "The folks of this church have been breaking bread on this same day of the week since before electricity came through, since before the train tracks and the coal mines. I ain't sure it's something I'm willing to take upon myself to change."

"Understood," Conor said. From the dump pouch on his battle belt, a kind of catch-all bag, he removed the thug's pistol. He ejected the mag, cleared the chamber, and confirmed the trigger function. He reloaded the pistol and handed it to the pastor.

"I'm covered," the Pastor said, raising the shiny grip of a revolver from his pocket. "However, I'm sure there's folks here in need of a handgun."

Conor extended a hand. "Good to meet you, Pastor White. I'll be seeing you again next week."

The pastor shook Conor's hand. "Thanks for visiting with us."

12

The clatter of hooves riding behind Bryan was now a larger chorus than it had been when he started out. He turned in the saddle and regarded his army with satisfaction. What had once been a handful of men was now nearly fifty. After bringing on Zach and his trucker buddies, they found a few more clusters of folks. Recruitment worked nearly the same in every case. Bryan made a brief pitch, killed the people who said no, and the rest of the men or boys reluctantly joined his force.

Bryan wasn't sure how it was going to go the first time Zach saw this in action. The man was a strong-willed thinker and more of a leader than he was letting on. That had the potential to be either good or bad for Bryan. The man could turn into an asset who could rise to help him run his military machine or he might attempt to subvert it and overthrow Bryan. Only time would tell. He needed leaders, though. He couldn't weed the man out just because he might be a risk. If he started eliminating people on that criteria be would soon be riding alone.

The truckers made no comment at seeing Bryan's Shining Path recruitment methods. In fact, when Bryan pulled the trigger on his first victim after bringing them onboard, he turned to catch the expression on each of those truckers. They were blank, impassive, revealing nothing of what was being processed internally. Bryan knew that group had killed before to protect what they had at the rest area. Maybe they understood that killing was just part of the new normal. It had replaced "unfriending" on social media.

They entered a river valley where God had apparently reached down and pinched the terrain a little tighter. The mountains were steeper and the space between them narrowed. While the mountains were not rocky cliffs, nor were they the type of mountains a person could hike up. They were unwelcoming and impassable by any means other than the labyrinth of sketchy roads. Four lanes filled the bottom of the valley with room for a row of businesses on each side. Anything else was pushed onto the low slopes.

The smell of smoke filled the valley. To Bryan, that meant the possibility of more warm bodies to fill empty saddles. When he hit what seemed to be a more densely populated area, where perhaps a dozen houses and mobile homes were within sight, Bryan halted to develop a strategy. Would he go house to house or would he call everyone out to line up before him? What if they didn't come? Were there enough people here to fight against his growing army? He certainly didn't want to lose any of his fresh recruits.

Pondering this, he heard the clink of glass hitting a rock and noticed a child sitting in a debris pile near the road. It looked like a fire pit, with trash protruding from the ashes. The boy was blond, with a ruddy pink face. He couldn't have even been five years old. He wore an oversized pink coat. His face, hands, and clothing were filthy from playing in the ashes. He had a rock in his hand, pecking at a scorched bottle like he was trying to break it.

Bryan closed the forty feet between him and the boy. His army stayed in place. The child didn't move when Bryan's large horse towered over him, puffing breathy clouds into the cold morning air.

"I expect your mother is going to spank you for getting so filthy," Bryan said.

The boy had no reaction, looking at Bryan as he spoke, then

returning to his bottle. He renewed pecking at the bottle with the rock, the sound ringing through the leafless trees.

"That bottle breaks, you might cut yourself," Bryan tried.

The boy responded in the same manner. He looked at Bryan with icy blue eyes set deep in cheeks pink from the cold, black from ash, but said not a word.

Bryan sighed. "Anybody else live here?"

The boy didn't look up this time, bored with Bryan and his pointless questions. *Clink, clink, clink, clink.*

"Hellooooooo!" Bryan roared.

The volume of Bryan's outburst startled the child. He dropped the rock and clenched his grubby hands into fists.

Bryan scanned the surrounding homes, watching for any movement. In a moment, a door opened and a woman burst out, hastily wrapping a blanket around her shoulders against the cold morning. She was wearing house slippers and ran to close the distance between her and her child. She was breathing hard by the time she snatched up her child. The blanket fell to the ground and she struggled to balance the child while picking it back up.

"You should keep a better eye on your baby," Bryan said. "In normal times, Social Services would be paying you a visit. That would be an improvement over what might happen these days."

The woman was too thin, with streaky blonde hair. She was only wearing a tank top and sweats beneath the blanket. She was chilled in the morning air, her skin like a plucked chicken. Her fiery eyes made clear that she had a lot to say but she had the brains to know this wasn't the time to say it.

Bryan studied her from the saddle, enjoying the intimidating height difference that being on horseback created. "These days people might take a child. Had we been of a mind to do so, you wouldn't have even known he was gone. By the end of the day, he might have been roasting over a spit. That is, if we were the kind of people prone to such depravity."

He smiled at her, a gesture intended to let her know that she had no way of knowing what kind of people they were. Maybe they were cannibals. Maybe they were child eaters. Maybe they were worse. He would let her wonder about that.

"What do you want?" she asked. "We got nothing left to take. If that's what you're here for, you're shit out of luck."

"My objective is information," Bryan said, his tone that of a man presenting himself at a reception desk. He was concise, all business.

"About what?"

"My companions and I are searching for a number of men missing from our group. We believe they may have gone this way a few weeks ago. It would have been a large number of men on horseback. They may have made inquiries for food and assistance along the way."

"You mean they robbed people," the woman clarified. "You can't hide behind those fancy words. I know what you're saying."

Bryan took a deep breath and eased it back out. "The laws that govern society and social interactions are different now."

"There you go with the fancy words again. What you mean is there is no law anymore," the woman said bitterly.

Bryan smiled. "Precisely. If you wish to benefit from the new paradigm, you should better position yourself to take advantage of it."

"You mean I should build an army like you? I should go around stealing off poor people who can't defend themselves?"

"That's one way," Bryan said. "Another option would be to seek employment with a larger, more established group. For your labor you would receive food and protection. Keep in mind that I'm not extending that offer to you now. At this point, you would simply be a burden on us in our travels. But once we find the answers we are seeking, the odds are good that we'll be returning this way. As we do, we'll be rebuilding our labor force. Women such as yourself—strong, fit, able—will be of use to us. You have some time to think about it."

"No thanks," the woman spat. "I don't need any time to think about it. I'm not interesting in being someone's slave."

Bryan was impressed by her quick grasp of the situation. He gave her a tight smile. "When and if the offer is presented, declining it may not be an option. We take what we want and no one stops us."

"Someone did," the woman shot back with an irritating tone of satisfaction.

Bryan raised an eyebrow. "Excuse me?"

"Someone stopped you."

"What do you mean by that?"

She threw her head in the direction Bryan was headed, the direction of the town they'd not yet entered. "Those guys you were asking about, they went through here all right. They tried to come back through our town, but they didn't make it. Someone stopped them. And all those women they had with them were set free. They went back home." She waggled her head as she spoke in a smug manner.

It was too much for Bryan. He leapt off his horse and charged the woman, knocking the child from her arms. He grabbed the woman by her shirt and slung her down in the ash pit. A cloud of dust rose as he slammed her to the ground. She screamed, her face screwing up in pain as the trash beneath the ashes scraped and gouged at her. Broken glass. Lids hacked from tin cans with pocket knives. Crushed beer and soda cans.

His face in hers, Bryan snarled, "What the fuck do you know about my men?"

Spit sprayed in the woman's face. She flinched against it, against the violence she expected to follow it. She didn't look so smug now.

"What do you know about my men?" Bryan repeated, slower this time. "You have five seconds or I kill your child in front of you."

"Just like you said," the woman replied, her voice quavering. "They came through here the first time and stole from people. They said they were on a mission to find women to work on their farm. On their way back, they made it as far as the bridge in town. Then something happened."

"What *happened*?" Bryan shouted, as angry as he'd ever been. His composure, his poise, his careful diction, all of it was gone. He was a snarling beast. "Did folks organize against them? Did your little town decide to ambush them to protect trash like you? To keep you from getting carried off to work at my farm?"

"No! It wasn't us that attacked them. It wasn't local people at all."

"Then who was it?"

The woman shook her head violently. "I don't know! I don't know!"

"Then what happened? Tell me everything!"

"We heard there was a big group coming into town. Everyone was scared because of what those men told us the first time they passed through. We all went back up in the hills and hid. Everyone in town did the same thing. We could see the fires where they were camping around the river bridge. Then all hell broke loose. Shooting. Screaming. More fires."

"If it wasn't your people, who was it?"

She shook her head again, urgent, desperate. "I don't know. We couldn't see. It was dark and we were up too high to see clearly."

Bryan shoved the woman down hard and released her. He stood and straightened his clothes. "We're going into town to see for ourselves."

Bryan mounted his horse and the woman struggled to her feet. She'd lost a shoe and blood streaked her filthy back.

"Things better be like you said," Bryan spat. "If it's not, we're coming back for you."

"Maybe I won't be here," the woman said defiantly, unable to restrain her tongue.

Bryan yanked his pistol from his belt. The woman grabbed up her son and began running awkwardly to her home, the other house slipper flying free. Bryan wasn't a good shot, but when the gun boomed she fell. She tumbled, falling on her son. The boy cried but the woman didn't move again.

The horse beneath him whinnied and shifted. Bryan spun it hard and faced his army. He studied their faces. If there was any reaction, any disagreement to what he'd done, they hid it.

"Be on guard!" he shouted. "We're close!"

Bryan kicked his horse to a gallop and tore off in the direction of town. Wisdom might have dictated a slower pace, one that granted the ability to more carefully probe for an ambush, but he rode with a singular determination. While some in his army were aware of the danger of riding so blindly into unknown territory, they were also afraid of the consequences of falling behind so irrational and impulsive a leader. Better to rush into the unknown than suffer at the hand of the known.

A quarter hour of hard riding brought Bryan to the immense steel bridge crossing one of the biggest rivers in the state. Four lanes of traffic could travel the bridge in better times. In its current state it was impassible. Abandoned vehicles were strewn at the approach to the bridge and on the bridge itself. They lay asunder and without orientation, as if tossed like dice by the hand of a bored mountain god. Some were burned, some had bullet holes, others had doors open and their contents strung out onto the road like the entrails of a shattered pumpkin.

Bryan slowed at the bridge, still not seeing anything that gave evidence his missing men had died here. So much of the highway system looked like a battlefield anymore that it was hard to recognize those places which had actually earned the title through spilled blood. His men caught up with him and he raised a hand to stop them. The group did as instructed, their excited horses stamping shod feet and snorting. The horses read the mood and anxiety of the group as a whole, their eyes rolling and wide, their heads slinging and pitching.

Bryan moved forward alone, forced to kick his horse into overcoming its hesitancy. Maybe it sensed what its rider could not yet see. Bryan studied an overturned van without stopping. He moved onto the bridge itself, the sound of the river louder in his ears, and found a car with all of its windows shot out. In this time of deprivation and shortage, men did not shoot this many rounds for entertainment. There were dozens of holes in this car alone.

Leaves carpeted the bridge, damp and brown, clinging to the ground and muffling the steps of the horse. They packed windblown against the rotting body of a saddled horse. The saddle was unfastened as if someone had tried to steal it but had been unable to free it from beneath the carcass. Just beyond it was the first human body. Those items of clothing not damaged and gore-encrusted had been stripped from the body. The man lay shirtless and waxen, a portion of his face crushed inward by a devastating blow that, to the extent of Bryan's knowledge, could have come either from bullet or bludgeon.

Other odd bits of gear lay scattered around the bridge. It looked like the aftermath of an outdoor music festival where all that remained was trash and lost clothing. The lighter items had blown to the side and gathered in piles that mixed with more leaves. Further on he began to find shell casings. There were pistols of all calibers, rifles, and shotguns.

Bryan slipped from his horse, dizzied by the ruin and annihilation that surrounded him. There were more dead horses and more dead men. The men lay in the awkward attitudes in which they died or the even more awkward postures in which desperate ghouls positioned them as they ransacked the bodies. Bryan did not know enough about horses or their gear to tell one from the other. They could have been Douthat Farms animals or perhaps not.

Soon after finding the second dead horse, he found the first man he recognized.

He couldn't remember the man's name but had seen him around Douthat Farms on a daily basis. He had a good attitude and seemed appreciative of the opportunity he'd been given. He had some mechanical aptitude and was often seen working on the mechanical systems of the farm, running water lines, installing solar panels, or making repairs.

The man was stripped of all gear and clothing. His neck was a black and brown encrustation of dense gore. His throat had been cut or ripped out with an edged weapon. His bare body was covered in bite marks from predation. Crows had dug at eyes and anus. Rats favored lips and fingers. What remained had taken on the sallow yellow tone of a scrap of fat ignored in a dog's bowl.

The carnage only increased as Bryan walked further, giving more evidence to what had taken place here. This was indeed a battlefield. Shell casings rang as he kicked them or rolled beneath his feet when he stepped on them. There were many more dead bodies. He hadn't counted them all but it looked as if it was roughly equivalent to the force he sent out.

This was likely all his men and they were all dead. He would have his men take an exact count later. It left him with a sick feeling, unrelated to what he saw but closely bound to the blow dealt him by this loss. It had been one thing to imagine that he'd lost such a number of his men. It was quite another to have his worst fears actualized and decaying in front of his very eyes.

He finally found Top Cat and Lester, his former lieutenants, amidst the carnage of burned vehicles and more stripped corpses. Some of the dead appeared fortunate enough to have died neatly from bullet wounds. Others had died ugly deaths, their corpses beaten, battered, and bruised. Some were cut, a few hacked to death.

There were no weapons or gear left to recover. Bryan could not say if the men who killed his force took their weapons or if they were looted by local folks in the aftermath. It was significant to him that there were no dead women among the bodies at all. Whatever happened here was undoubtedly chaotic but there was no evidence that any prisoners at all had been killed.

Bryan wondered about that. Had Top Cat stolen some women whose families organized a pursuit? It was possible, but to kill *every single man* he'd sent out? That was either the result of incredible odds or the product of a very diligent and determined pursuer.

Rage surged in Bryan like a volcano bursting and pouring its fire upon the land. He screamed long and loud. His horse spooked, pulling away from him and running back toward the rest of his men. He kept yelling until his voice filled the gorge like fog and wound its way into the creases of distant hollows. He only stopped when his voice failed him.

In that sudden quiet, he heard the shifting of a horse behind him. He found Zach standing there watching him, his face not giving any hint of how he felt about Bryan's outburst. That little thing somehow impressed Bryan, even in the strangeness of the moment.

"Anything I can do?" Zach asked.

Bryan cleared his throat. He tried to speak and it took a few tries to find his voice again. "Can you organize a search to make sure we find all the bodies? I need a count."

"You want a number or you want the bodies piled up?"

"No need to handle the bodies," Bryan said. "That may be a little too much for folks. Just get a count."

~

It was only as the body count neared completion and people began to think about the next meal that someone noticed the horse-drawn wagon carrying their supplies had not caught up with the rest of the group. It had been with them when Bryan shot the woman. When the men surged off in pursuit of Bryan, they all assumed it was behind them and would catch up. It never did.

When someone finally noticed, word spread among the men. No one wanted to tell Bryan about it because he seemed wound a little tight today. When Zach heard what was being discussed by the men, he relayed the news to Bryan. He didn't have the same fear of him that the former Douthat Farms employees had, nor was he as terrified as those recruited through Bryan's Shining Path "join or die" technique.

"Take a half-dozen men, damn it!" Bryan shouted. "That wagon has all our food and a lot of our gear. Find it!"

Zach grabbed two of his trucker buddies, a man named Andre and the redheaded woman, Carrie. He singled out three other men simply by proximity and the fact they were already mounted on horses.

"You three! Come on!"

The group shot away from the bridge at full gallop, hooves clattering and riders shouting to urge their horses onward. They made the ride at a faster pace than earlier but it still took them a full ten minutes to return to where they'd left the wagon. They found the driver sprawled like a starfish at the side of the road. He'd seemingly stopped to take a piss, as indicated by his exposed manhood and the bloom of wet pavement spreading out from his body, a mixture of both blood and urine.

"Shit," Zach mumbled upon seeing the man. He checked his surroundings and saw no sign of the wagon. "Spread out. Look for tracks."

After a few minutes of frantic searching, Carrie shook her head in frustration. "There ain't nothing here."

Zach pointed a finger up the road, the bearing from which they'd come earlier in the day. The group galloped off in that direction.

"They've got a head start but they can't make good time in that wagon," Zach said. "If they're still on the road, we'll catch them."

They rode for a few minutes, searching the shoulders for any clues the wagon may have strayed, but keeping mostly to the pavement.

"There!" said one of Bryan's men, pointing at a set of ruts in the soft soil of a puddle. "They turned off here." Without waiting on anyone to join him, he headed off in that direction, following what might have been a driveway or a logging road. It was hard to tell in its current overgrown state.

"Careful!" Zach called. He turned to Carrie. "Son of a bitch is going to get himself killed riding off like that."

"I smell smoke," Carrie said.

"We've smelled smoke all day," Zach said. "It's cold and people don't have anything else. It's probably some poor guy burning his coffee table to keep warm."

After a few twists and turns on the unkempt mountain lane, the riders found the wagon abandoned and fully-engulfed in flames. Every mind in the group reverberated with profanity but no one said a word. There was nothing to say that would change the outcome.

"Looks like they cut the horses loose and loaded them with the stolen gear," Zach said.

"There's a trail going up the hillside," came the eager voice of the man who'd gone up by himself. "We should go after them."

"I ain't so sure it's a good idea to charge up through there," Zach said. "Whoever stole this shit is local. They know the area. We ain't got a chance in hell of catching them on their own turf."

"Bullshit," the man snarled. "I ain't going back to Bryan and saying I wasn't man enough to go after them."

"Suit yourself," Zach said, motioning toward the trail. "I didn't take you to raise. You can do whatever the hell you want to do."

Suddenly free to act of his own accord, the man looked uncertain. "Is anyone going with me?"

Only one man accepted the challenge, another of Bryan's Douthat crew. The men regarded each other, hardened their resolve, and took off. The first man unholstered his gun, kicked his horse, and let out a whoop as he raced up the hill. He ducked branches and held on tight as his horse knitted its way among the dense trees. The second rider mimicked the first, not wishing to appear inadequate in the face of the challenge.

A gunshot rang out and the leading man fell like he'd been clotheslined by a tree branch. His horse, smarter than its rider, rotated on the steep hill and bolted back down. There were more shots and the second rider cried out, clasping his arm. He reined his horse, twisted it back around, and was heading back down when a second round caught him. It hit him in the back but pierced entirely through his core, staining the front of his denim jacket with a swell of crimson. He tumbled from the saddle and rolled beneath his horse, getting stomped multiple times as the horse tried to escape him.

"Fuck!" Carrie shouted.

The remaining horses skittered nervously, alarmed by the shots and the panic of their rider-less brethren. Zach surged forward, intent on snatching up the reins of the stray horses, when divots of earth exploded in front of him. He flinched, reflexively throwing up an arm in front of his face. His horse reared, jerked, and bolted back down the overgrown road from which they came. Zach was holding onto the saddle horn for dear life, unable to rein in the horse or attempt to steer it.

There were more shots and Zach glanced behind him to see his companions riding hell-bent to escape the gunfire. Knowing there was no longer any hope of recovering the wagon or any of its contents, Zach gave up trying to slow the horse. The shooting stopped as they all retreated. The gunfire hadn't been about killing them. It had been about discouraging pursuit.

It worked.

When they reached the rest of their group at the bridge, Bryan reacted in just the manner they anticipated. After a short tirade, he mounted his horse and returned to the burning wagon with the full support of his army. They charged the hillside, determined to find their property and the men responsible for taking it but there was no one remaining. Whoever had burned the wagon and fired at Zach's party was gone now. The tracks showed each of the loaded horses headed off in separate directions.

Bryan was intent on splitting his group and trailing each set of tracks but Zach talked him down.

"These men know the hills," Zach said. "They'll lead us into places where we can't defend ourselves and pick us off one by one. All your men will die, their horses and guns stolen. You've worked too hard to build this army to lose it now. I wouldn't focus on what you've lost. I'd focus on replacing and rebuilding."

Bryan considered the trucker's words. As much as it pained him to accept the man's insights, he understood he was probably correct. They did not have the manpower to fight these people in their back hollows and on their ridgetops. He promised himself that he would, however, return to this place when he had an adequate force. He would set fires and scorch this entire region from the face of the Earth. Then, as the ashes settled on him with the lightness of rain, he would have the last laugh.

13

Barb was not excited about making the flyers.

"We have a printer," she complained. "Print the damn things."

"We've got the one ink cartridge that's in the printer and that's all," Conor said. "I don't want to use it all up on flyers. On the other hand, I have stacks of Sharpie markers and a plethora of free labor. You all can make the flyers by hand."

"You need the ink for printing coloring sheets to keep you entertained this winter?" Barb asked. "You going to sit in your jammies, nibble your crayons, and color pictures of dinosaurs?"

"Maybe," Conor said. "But remember if I go soft in the noggin that you're the one who has to keep up with me."

"I'll keep you in the chicken house," Barb threatened. "It's not like I can be turned in to Adult Protective Services anymore. I'll charge the neighbors a buck each to gawp at you and poke you with sticks."

Conor shook his head and sighed. "You can't be my real daughter. If you were, you'd be sweet like your dear old dad."

She raised an eyebrow at him, finding such utter bullshit unworthy of response. They both knew she was just like him.

Conor smiled at her. "Just make the flyers. You know what to say, right?"

Barb groaned but nodded. "Yes."

"Get Ragus and Shannon to help you," Conor instructed. "Maybe if you spend some time hanging around the good kids it will rub off on you."

"You're in danger of getting hurt, old man. Your time would be better spent changing your diaper or touching up your gray hair with one of those Sharpie markers you have such an abundance of. You better get out of here while you can still walk."

Conor hugged his daughter. "I love you too."

She elbowed him in the ribs and shoved him away.

"I'm going," he said. He pushed out the door into the cool morning and went toward the bunkhouse where Doc Marty and Shannon were staying. Smoke chugged from the chimney pipe jutting out the side of the building. He banged on the door.

Doc Marty answered the door in cargo pants and a Hawaiian shirt. "Jesus, Doc, you can't get any more stereotypical than that. Classic spook uniform. Since you already have the cheesy mustache, all you're missing is the aviator shades."

Without a word, Doc Marty slipped his fingers into his shirt pocket and came out with a set of Ray-Ban aviator glasses. He slipped them on his face and regarded Conor.

"That's the look. They teach you that in spook school?"

Doc Marty replaced the glasses in his pocket. "You probably had the same classes I did."

Conor shook his head. "I don't think so. While you were taking tradecraft classes I was learning the dark arts. You were learning how to seduce old dowagers for intel. I was learning how to kill folks with a strand of spaghetti and a roll of toilet paper."

Doc Marty nodded. "Ah, yeah, I didn't have much of that, but I'd love to hear about that technique."

"If I told you, I'd have to kill you."

"Of course you would," Doc Marty replied.

"I need you take a ride with me today. Hang some signs. Learn the country. Ride the fences, so to speak," Conor said.

The Doc threw a look back over his shoulder. "What about Shannon?"

"I've got plans for her. She'll be working with Barb and Ragus to write up some flyers I'm going to hand out to the local folks."

"Write up? Don't you have a printer?"

Conor frowned. "I'm a cheap bastard, okay? I'm not wasting what might be my last ink cartridge on a bunch of recruitment flyers."

"Got it," Doc said. "What do I need?"

"Body armor if you got it. See me if you don't. Primary and secondary weapons, basic field loadout, and warm clothes."

"I'm a dentist. My basic loadout is a white jacket, a pick, and little mirror."

Conor smiled. "Then bring your pick and little fucking mirror. If shit goes down, you can take the lead while I watch."

"Point taken. When we leaving?"

Conor looked at his watch. "Fifteen minutes."

"Guess I better be finding my little mirror then," Doc Marty said. "Shannon and I will be over at your place in a few minutes."

~

IT WAS ten minutes before Doc Marty and his daughter showed up at Conor's place. Ragus brought two saddled horses around and helped Conor tie an awkward bundle of signs onto each of them. Conor gave Doc Marty a quick glance.

"Glad to see you dressed like an operator again," Conor said. "I was afraid you'd forgotten how."

Doc sniffed his jacket. "A little musty. Haven't had it on in a while."

"Still know your way around guns or do we need to do a refresher?" Conor asked, his tone both sarcastic and provoking.

"I remember the basics," Doc said. "Ricardo made sure I still got my trainings and range time in."

Conor made a sound of uncertainty. "We'll see."

"Are you going to need those weapons?" Shannon asked. "Is it safe to be going out there?"

"We're trying to make it safer," Conor assured her. "Better to be armed and not need the firepower than to need it and not have it. Bad things can happen so stay ready all the time. You may even want to consider wearing a weapon inside the fence. We've never had an incident here at the compound but that's not to say it couldn't happen. These are unpredictable days."

"I'll be fine, baby," Doc Marty said, giving his daughter a quick hug.

"She won't have time to be worried about you," Barb said. "We get to make flyers." She said it with a lilting, syrupy voice, then shot Conor a sarcastic look.

"Are you sure I can't go with you?" Ragus asked.

Conor started to respond but Barb cut him off. "If I'm making flyers, *you're* making flyers."

Conor turned to Doc Marty then gestured at the horse. "Can you get on the damn thing or do I need to fetch a ladder?"

Doc Marty gave a smug look, then efficiently mounted the horse. In fact, he did so with an ease that Conor envied. "A patient of mine in Dubai had a horse farm. We rode a lot."

"Horse farm in *Dubai*," Conor mocked. "Some of us were out here trying to fight the good fight. Nice of you to make sure the Middle Eastern elite were able to maintain their winning smiles."

"There was more to it than that," Doc Marty said.

"I can hardly wait to hear about it."

The pair said their good-byes and Conor continued to shout last minute instructions the entire time he was riding away.

"If you don't quit barking I'm turning the hose on you," Barb finally said.

"Fine," Conor muttered, riding out the gate.

Ragus locked it behind him. "Parents are gone. Party!" That earned him a sharp glance from both Conor and Barb. The word *party* was not in either of their vocabularies. It made him wish he was going with the guys and not stuck behind.

~

THE MEN WERE RIDING WEST, in the general direction of Johnny Jacks' house and Pastor White's church. Conor had placed his double M marks on a lot of trees and fences to the east but not so much in this direction. Today's goal was to change that. To put up a few signs and increase his presence in hopes it might encourage the locals to see a benefit in banding together for security.

"So what were you doing in Dubai?"

"I had a dental practice," Doc Marty said. "It was a pretty plush gig."

"I have no doubt. Haven't all your assignments been plush gigs?"

"Not all of them. In fact, those you and I went on together were guaranteed to never be plush gigs. This one was risky. I was concerned for Shannon much of the time. My patients were some of the richest and most powerful people in that region of the world. If I'd been found out there's no doubt that the two of us would have died ugly deaths."

"What was there to find out? What did they have you doing?"

"Ricardo set me up in a dental practice in a very exclusive neighborhood. The office was posh in a way that would appeal to wealthy, powerful folks. There was no waiting. I scheduled one client at a time and they were treated in the manner they expected from the moment they arrived."

"What was the point of that? Trying to develop assets?"

Doc Marty laughed. "Nothing that crude. This was way more evolved than that. Some of the science guys came up with a technique that allowed me to cause cavities."

"Cause cavities? That's every dentist's fucking dream, bunch of cruel bastards."

Doc Marty nodded. "It served a purpose."

"How fast did the cavities form?"

"Not fast enough to raise suspicion but over a matter of weeks. It involved applying an acid to the tooth while I was doing a cleaning, then sealing it beneath a polymer layer. The polymer kept the acid in contact with the tooth but prevented it from causing any collateral damage inside the mouth. Over a couple of weeks the polymer would wear away and the acid would be neutralized. People would notice the crater forming on their tooth when their tongue hit it. Then they'd come see me for a filling."

"What's the point of that?" Conor asked. "You trying to choke off the funding of terror networks by compromising their oral health?"

Doc Marty chuckled. "Always the smartass, aren't you?"

Conor shrugged, guilty as charged.

"You'd be totally jealous of this gear but the tech guys and I developed tracking devices that fit inside a human tooth. When I'm filling the tooth, I implant the device. Over a three year period I probably did about fifty or sixty of them."

"How can you make a transmitter that small with any range to it?" Conor asked. "There's no antenna."

"Simple. It doesn't have to reach any further than the target's phone. It makes an invisible, untraceable connection via Bluetooth technology, allowing us to track them."

"Pretty damn smart," Conor acknowledged.

"It was a sophisticated operation. I'm sure it cost a fortune but Ricardo said the intel was useful. I never knew why they chose the targets they did. I joined the best clubs, ate at the best restaurants, and built social connections with wealthy residents and travelers. Ricardo would send me a dossier, then I did my job, inserting myself into the target's life and luring them to my practice."

Conor snorted. "You'll have a job to do here too, but it won't be quite as glamorous as Dubai. No fancy restaurants, no indoor ski resorts, no shopping."

They rode in silence for a few moments, the only sound the clatter of hooves and the occasional gusts of cold fall wind whipping through bare trees.

Doc Marty chuckled, still thinking about the luxury of Dubai. "Yeah, this is a far cry from Dubai but it already feels like home."

"That's quite the experience for Shannon, getting to live all around the world. I'm sure she enjoyed it."

Doc Marty shrugged in a manner that indicated he wasn't so certain he agreed with that.

"You missed home?" Conor asked.

Doc Marty nodded. "Maybe you had the right idea here, old buddy. Keep a foot in the business, in operator life, but have a place stateside to lay your head. This has to be more relaxing than wondering if the door is going to burst open in the middle of the night. Wondering if you and your daughter are going to end up in someone's basement with hoods over your head."

"Eh, the place has its moments, though it's not as relaxing now as it used to be. I guess I'm like me mum. I never had trouble making decisions. I'm not the kind to second-guess everything I do. When I accepted Ricardo's offer all those years ago, I knew what I wanted from it. I knew it was a deal with the devil but I went in with both eyes open. I have no complaints. I've milked it for all it's worth. I've done well for them, they've done well for me."

"Maybe I'm different, or it's just old age, but I've been second-guessing my life a lot lately. I've been wondering if I made the right call. Maybe I should have turned Ricardo down. What values have I passed on to my daughter? What kind of childhood did I give her? My situation was a lot like yours. Shannon grew up without a mother and I think that's why you and I always hit it off. I wonder if she wouldn't have been better off with another family. Another dad."

Conor dismissed that with a toss of his head and a string of profanity. "That shit doesn't keep me up at night. You had to do something with your life. Everyone does. You did what you did and I did what I did. It was all we knew to do at the time. It's too late in the game for me to change strategies. I'm not about to become a phlebotomist, a petroleum engineer, or a golf cart salesman. I am what I am and I own every fucking inch of it. No regrets. No apologies."

There was a stirring in the leaves somewhere far to the left of them. Conor dropped a hand to the grip of his M4 but the bounding steps told him it was a deer. He listened until he was certain there was nothing else then nudged his horse back into motion.

"I know you saw more violence than I did," Doc Marty said. "It's clear in the way you react to things. We've all killed. We've all had those moments in the field where we did shit we have to live with forever. I'm sure you did more of it just by nature of the kind of assignments you got. Your job was killing, or helping others do it. You're okay with all that? It doesn't keep you up at night?"

Conor shook his head. "There's work and there's the rest of your life. I keep them separate and I sleep like a fucking baby."

"I wish I could say the same," Doc Marty said. "I can't."

Conor snorted. "You're growing into a whiny bastard in your old age, Doc. You may have heard this from me before but I'm getting older too, and I'm prone to repeating myself. I'm tired of all this complaining and indecision that people go on about anymore. They have way more opportunities than any generation before them and all they can do is bitch and moan. When I was a kid in Ireland, people had fewer paths available to them but everybody had a role and every role was valued. I'm sure it was that way here at the time too. It was a different age. But you had the tinker, the butcher, the paperboy, the junkman, the carpenter—all these bloody professions—and those people were proud of what they did. They held their fucking heads up. Hell, even the town drunk and the town whore served a purpose because they could be used as bad examples. They were cautionary tales about not living up to your potential. But me? I prefer to live with boldness and certainty. I drive looking ahead and not in the rearview mirror."

Doc Marty laughed at Conor's tirade but at the same time he was listening. After his laughter died away he processed those words for a long time. He tossed the words about in his head like a thoughtful writer twirling a pen in his fingers.

"Tell me something, Conor. In a world of teachers, town drunks, and all the little roles that people fill in society, where do men like you and I fit in? I've always seen myself as a dentist but lately I feel like I'm fooling myself. I'm not so sure if I'm a dentist or an angel of death pretending to be a dentist. What are you?"

There was no hesitation in Conor's voice at all. He knew the answer.

"Some days I'm the tinker. Some days I'm the bloody fucking butcher."

14

Men shifted nervously from foot to foot. Restless horses were tied to everything a rein could be wrapped around, whether it was a bridge railing or a car mirror. Bryan stood on the hood of a white Mercedes convertible, his muddy feet caked with gravel that screeched as it dug into the pristine paint. He was lost in thought, mired in the convolutions of his own mind. His army surrounded him, waiting expectantly, knowing that he was preparing to speak to them but uncertain how long it might take him to find his bearings. They were prepared to wait. They had nothing else.

From his vantage point on the car Bryan could see the dead, decomposing, and desiccated remainder of the army he had sent off from Douthat Farms. It had just been a few weeks ago but seemed so much more distant in time. In his attempt to grasp at the waning dream of Douthat Farms, he launched his current mission, which held promise until today. Now he had lost more men and much of their supplies. He was fully aware of what his troops were probably thinking. They were most certainly ready to revolt or to simply fade off into the mountains like the men who stole their wagon. This was a pivotal moment. This was where he won them or lost them.

Bryan cleared his throat and held up a hand to get the men's attention, though he already had it. None were even speaking between themselves. He raised his head dramatically and looked through the crowd, engaging the eyes of each man. This was between him and each of them. It was a pact.

"First, I want to apologize to you for being an inferior leader at times. I know you question the decisions I make. I know many of you are here against your will. Some of you even witnessed family members dying at my hand as I callously stole you without concern for whether I won your hearts and minds. That was naïve and short-sighted. I humble myself before you today asking your forgiveness, for a second chance at finishing what we so valiantly commenced."

Bryan swept his arms and gestured at the bridge they stood on. "It's fitting that we stand where we do. This very bridge represents both a physical and metaphorical crossing point. We will step off this bridge in a few minutes and it will be a new day for this effort. For this *army*. On one side of this bridge, the side we just came from, is who we used to be. When we step off it, we step off as something different. We step off it as new men. As men bound together with a single vision and a solitary purpose."

Bryan stopped. He took a sip of water from a bottle and looked around. They were still his. "I'm sure you all know that in losing the wagon we lost all the food, except for what you carried on yourselves to eat on the trail. We lost the tents, the tarps, and many of you lost your sleeping gear. Somewhere men are going through our gear and celebrating their bounty. They are laughing at our loss and the injustice they served upon us. We could go after them but I could lose more of you. We're not doing that. We will take our vengeance in a different manner."

Bryan pointed across the bridge, to the town they had not yet entered. "I don't know exactly what's over there, but it's yours." He gestured at his men as if he were displaying a buffet spread before them.

"You enter that town as an army and you take what you want. You take guns. You take food. You take anything we might need. If anyone challenges you, you have my blessing to kill them. When you're certain you've cleared a house, you may burn it. I ask that you remember one thing. When you came into this army, whether you came of your own volition or whether I persuaded you under duress, whether you were volunteer or conscript, know that you are from this point forward all *equal* soldiers in my army. What you take today is yours to keep. It is only a taste of the personal wealth and riches that will be yours at the end of this campaign if you continue to ride with me."

Bryan gesticulated at the town again, stabbing his finger furiously. "That right there is the point where our new life starts. Wherever we go, whenever people fail to give us the respect we deserve, it is to that town right there that we will point. It will not be Douthat Farms upon which we build our future. We will build it on the ashes of *today*."

Bryan looked from man to man again, making sure they understood. Within that glance was a covenant, a promise that he wanted each man to recognize was directed toward him individually. When his eyes left the last man, Bryan swept an arm toward the town like he was welcoming an old friend into his home.

“All yours, boys. Go get’em.”

15

When Conor and Doc Marty reached the valley bottom on the west side of Jewell Ridge they placed the first of their signs. Conor nailed it to a tree where anyone travelling on the road would be likely to see it. He'd constructed a stencil so that he could make each sign with spray paint instead of having to hand letter it. The sign read *This Community Protected By* and below that was a picture of a shamrock with the letters "MM" inside it.

"The Mad Mick?" Doc Marty asked.

Conor nodded. "If strangers think an area is protected by a crazy man you'd think that might have a bit of a deterrent effect. Eventually, if locals will accept a little organization and agree to take part in the effort, my hope is that MM will come to stand for Mountain Militia."

"Or Masters of Mayhem," Doc Marty said, running other possibilities through his head.

Conor smiled. "I like that. Has a ring to it."

"I figured you might," Doc Marty said. "The Mad Mick wasn't the only name you had in the business. Sometimes it was the Master of Mayhem."

"Nobody ever told me about that one. It's a shame. I'd have worn it proudly."

"I think you scared most people. They were afraid to point out they had nicknames for you. They were worried about what might happen to them. Like poking the bear or something."

Conor smiled innocently. "What? Angel like me? Bollocks."

Conor regarded his handiwork then remounted his horse. There were more signs to put up. He also had the stencil and some spray paint with him so he could apply the same message to wrecked cars, bridges, road signs, or anything else he damn well pleased. They got moving and Conor kept his hatchet at hand. At frequent intervals, when a prominent and highly visible tree presented itself, Conor walked his horse up to it and hacked his MM symbol into it.

"More Masters of Mayhem?" Doc Marty asked.

Conor nodded. "It's simple but should convey the message. I have people all over the area doing this as well. The idea is to make the mark so prevalent that people won't be able to miss it. I've also encouraged people to spread an embellished version of what happened when we rescued Barb. I'm hoping the legend and the mark can work together to create a deterrent. It's in the early stages but that's the plan. Maybe psych out the enemy before we have to draw blood."

"I'd be glad to provide a testimonial for anyone uncertain of whether you're truly a crazy bastard," Doc Marty offered.

"I'll take that under consideration."

"How much longer we doing this? I'm not used to riding a horse. This saddle is getting the best of me."

Conor wouldn't admit that his first trip on horseback had been painful too. He still held a grudge over Helsinki and wasn't about to have any sympathy for Doc Marty until he had the opportunity to exact some revenge. Maybe then they could start over and be real friends again. For now, the specter of that night in Helsinki overshadowed everything.

"A few more stops. I'm giving some of these signs to my friend Johnny Jacks for he and his son to put up around the community. They know the area better. Other than that, all you and I are responsible for is carving MM symbols wherever we think they'd be seen."

"Then lead the way but next time remind me to bring a pillow."

Conor frowned. "You do know, don't you, that any impression you're a badass pretty much goes out the window if you're so tender you have to ride around on a pillow."

"Let me worry about my own public relations."

~

JOHNNY'S HOUSE was several miles from the base of the ridge. They rode along a scenic river where blue herons squawked with the abrasive cry of movie pterodactyls as they took flight. They saw a bear drinking on the opposite shore of the river, but it startled when it caught sight of the riders and disappeared into the underbrush. They passed a local high school, long shut down, and turned into a community center, where the residents voted and the elderly fought over bingo games. They passed timeworn stores closed for decades and so engulfed by kudzu that they were only visible in winter when their framework protruded from the web of bare vines.

They turned at an intersection and, as they rode, the narrow river bottom opened up into land better suited for agriculture. It was ridiculously steep but there were some pastures created by hills that rolled gently at the top instead of terminating in knife-edge ridges. It was a rare mercy granted to the gritty folks who built a life in these confined valleys, allowing a determined farmer to graze, raise tobacco, and squeeze a few bales of hay out of the unforgiving landscape. It was a severe environment, ill-suited for those afraid to lift a finger or break a sweat.

"That's his farm there," Conor said as a twist in the road opened a partial vista before them. In summer they would not have been able to see the farm from this distance. Without leaves, the well-ordered farm stood out in stark contrast to the wilds that bordered it.

It took them nearly forty more minutes to reach the farm, following roads that curved like an injured snake, rising and falling like corrugated tin. The bright red gate that greeted visitors was usually closed but stood open. Conor paused there and held an arm up to Doc Marty.

"There's a dog. He usually sounds the alarm when folks show up."

The absence of the dog, the open gate, were setting off alarms for Conor. He didn't know Johnny Jacks well but he'd seen enough to understand the man was a creature of habit. Like Conor himself, he did things a particular way *every* time. Conor understood that meticulousness and he'd noticed it in everything the man did. People like that didn't leave gates open.

He scanned the visible areas of the farm, the barn, and the house. He was startled by a burst of movement to his right and Doc Marty shot off, galloping clumsily.

"What the fuck?" Conor mumbled.

He wanted to call after the man but didn't want to attract any more attention than they may already be drawing. They had no clue what was going on here but Doc Marty was no idiot. If he took off, there was a reason.

Conor kicked his horse into a run and soon caught sight of what drew Doc Marty's attention. It was a body.

A *moving* body.

Doc Marty dismounted by the barn, nearly falling in the process, and fought to untie his pack from behind the saddle. He was dropping down by the body when Conor reached him. He was by Doc Marty's side in a second, rifle at the ready. He studied the bloody face, the saturated clothing, and the full head of white hair.

"That's Johnny Jacks," Conor said. "Is he still alive?"

"I saw him move," Doc Marty said, ripping Johnny's shirt open. "He's still alive but he's shot all to hell."

"Damn it!" Conor spat. "Do what you can. I need to secure the scene."

Conor broke the cover of the barn, crouched low, and sprinted for the house. He flattened himself against the wall, circling it first. Listening. Watching.

He found blood on the back steps, drops and rivulets splattered on the concrete. There was no body visible. It could be victim blood or attacker blood. It could be Johnny's blood because he'd damn well lost enough of it.

Inside the house, Conor found Johnny's wife dead on the couch. She'd been shot at close range. One bullet passed through her hand before striking her in the chest and a second caught her in the neck. Blood drenched the couch. There were bloody boot prints all over the spotless oak floors but there was no telling whose blood it was. There seemed to be plenty to go around.

He stalked out the back door, angry and disgusted. There was no sign of Jason, nor of his wife. It occurred to Conor that she may be hiding. He called out to her.

"Hello! My name is Conor! I'm a friend. I was here with Johnny and Jason when the men came to buy horses. If you're hiding here, I can take you to safety. I can help you."

There was no answer. Conor gave the house a cursory search, checking the closets and all the other places he thought a young woman may hide in an emergency. He doubled back to each door and checked the bloody footprints a second time. He found none that seemed to be the size of a woman's foot. That told him nothing. She might have run out before the chaos, before the blood was flowing. She may have escaped out a window.

She may have been carried out over an attacker's shoulder.

Conor shook the thought from his head. He was no stranger to death and gore but he'd liked this man and his family. He saw Johnny as someone he could depend on in the future. Someone with skills, good advice, and wisdom tempered by years of life experience. He didn't know if the man would live or die but the best thing he could do for him now was to figure out what happened to his family.

He made several loops around the house, increasingly wider, looking for blood, bodies, or any signs. From the corner of his eye, Conor could see Doc Marty working furiously on the bleeding man. At times he slumped, a posture of futility and impotence, the posture of a man whose best efforts were just not good enough, then he'd find the strength to dive back in. Conor couldn't focus on that now. He had to find Jason and his wife. They could still be alive somewhere, though Conor had no reason to hold out hope for that.

Returning to the barn, he found Jason lying in a muddy drainage ditch. Conor jumped into the ditch, setting his rifle on the ground beside him. He dropped a hand to the man's neck and found a pulse. He slid his hand under the smaller man's armpits and wrestled him out of the ditch.

Conor was no medic but he knew the basics of combat lifesaving, the shit they teach you in hopes you can keep yourself or a teammate alive until help arrives. He straightened Jason out and gave him a cursory examination. He thought he'd been shot in the head at first because there was so much blood. It turned out that a flap of his scalp had peeled from what must have been a wicked blow to the head.

He checked the airway and found a mouthful of shattered teeth behind smashed lips. Conor raked a finger through Jason's mouth and scooped out the chips of his teeth and a clot of blood that could have run down from his broken nose. Jason coughed. Conor got to his feet and slung his weapon back around his neck. He took the man's arm and dragged him to the front of the barn.

"Fuck, another one?" Doc Marty asked. "I'm not sure I can do anything with this one."

"You got this," Conor said. "How can I help?"

Doc Marty wiped his forehead with a bloody sleeve. He'd gloved up and spread his trauma kit beside him. He was pouring sweat. "I have tourniquets on to stop the bleeding. Most of the gunshots were peripheral. There's one to his left side that's still bleeding a little. I'm going to have to dig in and get that bullet out. If it's nicked anything serious, he's fucked. I'm not a surgeon."

"You're doing fine."

"It's not fine!" Doc Marty shouted. "I can't leave the tourniquets on forever. I'm going to have to loosen them one by one and deal with the bleeding. If he's lost too much, he's pretty well screwed. I haven't even had a chance to check out the other guy. Who knows what he needs at this point?"

"What can I do?"

"You really want to know?" Doc Marty asked, taking his eyes from Johnny for the first time. "Help me get him in the house, then you get back to the compound and bring us some gear. I have a field surgical kit. I'll need antibiotics and IV setups."

"I thought you weren't a surgeon?"

"I'm about to learn," Doc Marty replied.

They moved Johnny first since his condition was the most delicate. They put him in his own bed. Conor was glad the man was unconscious and didn't have to see his wife's body in such an unbecoming condition.

"Where do you want Jason?" Conor asked.

"Let's put him in the same bed. I can't be running back and forth all over the house."

The men hustled outside and quickly carried Jason in, laying him in the bed by his dad.

"They did a number on this poor boy," Doc Marty said.

Conor didn't reply. He was disgusted by the situation. It was probably over something as simple as livestock. This sweet family of four had been attacked for a few cows and horses.

"Welcome home, Doc. This is the kind of shit we've been dealing with since things went south."

Doc Marty shook his head in disgust. "Where's the aid? Where's the rebuilding? Where's the fucking government?"

"It's not here," Conor replied. "Been a while since you've been in the shit, hasn't it?"

"Been a while since I've had to step over a dead body if that's what you're asking," Doc Marty said. "I assume whoever did this probably won't be caught?"

Conor looked around at the beautiful farm. He couldn't help but remember how positive this family had been even in the face of disaster. Sure, Johnny was aggravated about people trying to steal livestock but he seemed to be the kind of man who approached each day with a decent attitude, regardless of what lay before him. Most days Conor considered himself to be that kind of man as well.

"I'll catch them," Conor said. "I think I know where to start. When I find them, I'll set an example. The Mad Mick will earn his name again."

16

Barb, Shannon, and Ragus sat around the kitchen table with a stack of paper and permanent markers looking like a group of children coloring pictures for their parents. The radio on the counter crackled and Barb heard her name gasped in a desperate tone that terrified her to her core. She shot to her feet, knocking over her chair, and clutched the radio.

"Dad? What's wrong?"

"I'm fine," Conor said. *"I've been trying to get you on the radio but it's been hard to get a signal. Can you hear me clearly?"*

"Yes."

"I'm going to give you a set of instructions and I want them written down, okay?"

Barb gestured at Ragus. He nodded, pulling a blank sheet of paper in front of him and waiting.

"We're ready," she said.

"I need three horses saddled and ready to go. I'll be there in about thirty minutes. I want them ready when I get there. One is for you, Barb. The other for Shannon."

"Why?"

"No talk," Conor replied. *"Just listen. I need Shannon to get in her*

dad's gear and get a field surgical kit, IV antibiotics, and his emergency medical bag. I need that strapped onto one of the horses and ready to go."

"Is my dad okay?" Shannon shrieked, standing up from the table, closing in on hysteria with astonishing speed.

"Shannon is concerned about her father," Barb relayed, not taking her eyes off the girl. She intentionally did not ask if he was dead or injured.

"He's fine. We have other injured."

Shannon settled back down into her seat, breathing hard, but her panic subsiding. Ragus reached over and put an arm around her. Barb rolled her eyes.

"You still receiving me?" Conor asked.

"Loud and clear," Barb said. "Keep going."

"I need you and Shannon both dressed and geared up. We'll talk weapons when I get there."

"What about me?" Ragus asked.

"Ragus, too?" Barb relayed into the radio.

"No," Conor said. *"We'll discuss when I get there. Over and out."*

Barb replaced the radio on the counter. She looked at her wide-eyed companions and clapped her hands to break their trance. "You heard him. Let's get cracking. There's shit to be done."

~

THEY WERE ANXIOUSLY AWAITING Conor when he galloped through the gate, his horse sweating and frothing. The light of day was already fading but there was enough that the three folks waiting on him could see his blood-stained clothing.

"Where's my dad?" Shannon asked. "You promise that's not his blood?"

Conor strode toward her and placed a hand on each shoulder, looking her in the eyes. "Your dad is fine. We found a family that's been attacked. The two men are severely injured. One woman is dead, the other missing. Your dad is doing all he can to try and save the injured men but he doesn't have all of the supplies he needs. Did you guys do what I asked?"

"We did," Barb replied.

"Why am I not going?" Ragus asked.

"This is not up for argument or debate. Here's the assignments. Shannon, you're going with us to assist your dad on medical. He's overwhelmed and needs someone he can work with at his side."

Conor could see a look of fear flash across her face, uncertainty at what lay ahead of her. He suspected she'd never been in circumstances like this before. This was where they all, including Shannon herself, would find out what she was made of.

"Ragus, I need you to guard the compound. Johnny Jacks' house was hit. It looks like a robbery. I'm afraid to leave the compound unattended. I need on you on active defense. While I'm gearing up, I want Barb to set you up with an M1A with a night vision scope. We're going to put glint tape on our gear so watch for that. You see that reflection, do *not* shoot. Got it?"

Ragus nodded. If he was pissed at not being able to go on the mission, he choked it down. Conor was pleased with that. It was a sign of maturity. The boy was beginning to understand that every role was important to the success of an operation.

"What about me?" Barb asked.

"Set Ragus up with the rifle I mentioned. Make sure Shannon is squared away with a primary and secondary weapon. Girl, do you have personal weapons?"

Shannon nodded.

"You know how to run them?"

"Yes."

"Then get a rifle and pistol. A dozen spare mags for the rifle and a half-dozen for the pistol."

"Got it."

Conor took a deep breath. "Barb, once we have Shannon and the med gear delivered to Johnny's farm, you and I are going to run a little recon operation."

Barb raised a questioning eyebrow.

"I may know who did this," Conor said. "I don't want to point any fingers too soon but I was over there when Johnny sold some horses to a group of strangers. He was a bit anxious about meeting up with them because there were a lot of them and they weren't from around here. He wanted backup and I was glad to provide it. Those guys didn't set off my radar when I met them but they definitely weren't friendly."

"You think they decided to come back for more horses?" Barb asked.

"Or they decided they needed some cattle to feed their families."

"You sure these are the right people?" Barb asked.

"I honestly don't know but it's the only place I know to start looking," Conor said. "There's a girl missing. Johnny's daughter-in-law. She could be lying dead some place and we just haven't found her yet."

"Or they could have her," Barb finished.

Conor met his daughter's eye, leaving unsaid that she knew what that was like. She did know and she didn't want any other young woman to have to go through that. The part she'd never told anyone was that she wasn't done yet taking vengeance on men who stole women.

"Gear up appropriately," Conor said. "Close quarters weapons, rations, helmet with night vision, and body armor. Soup with all the fixings."

Barb spun and jogged off.

"We leave in fifteen minutes," Conor called after her.

~

THE NIGHT WAS cold with a damp wind that foreshadowed ugly weather. There were few stars visible with the naked eye. Conor was pleased to find that Doc Marty had included night vision and bump helmets in the equipment he brought with him. That meant they'd be able to travel without headlamps. Conor always hated moving in the night with a light on his head, feeling like it presented a glowing target to anyone wanting to put a bullet in him. He had a good night vision for himself and for Barb but those two sets were their only wearable night vision. Everything else was built into a rifle scope, like the one Barb had set Ragus up with.

"This is a little weird," Shannon said, uncomfortable at being on the back of the trotting horse with her perspective altered by the night vision.

"You get used to it," Conor said.

"Or you fall, busting both your ass and gear you can't replace," Barb added.

"Thanks for the encouragement," Shannon replied.

Barb grinned. "Not a problem."

The ride seemed to take forever. Conor pressed them to move quickly but he was afraid to go too fast. It was unfamiliar road to the girls and slick with a heavy dew. The horses had slipped several times just to remind him of the possibility. Eventually they reached the bottom of the ridge and sometime after that they turned off onto Johnny's road.

Conor had closed the gate when he left. He awkwardly opened it from horseback, finding the move to not be as easy as it seemed in the movies. He prompted Barb and Shannon to ride through and then he closed it.

"Does Marty have a radio?" Barb asked.

"No, we only took one with us," Conor said. "We didn't plan to separate."

"Did you arrange a signal?"

"No. I just told him I'd holler out as I approached."

Barb shook her head, finding the move awkward with the heavy helmet and goggles. "Couple of big time operators, aren't you?"

Conor ignored her, urging his horse into a run. The girls fell in behind him. At the house he dismounted and tied his horse off to the porch rail.

"Doc, it's me. Don't shoot. I have Shannon and Barb with me."

There was a sharp flicker of light inside, probably from a headlamp.

"Make sure your night vision is turned off," Conor ordered.

Barb and Shannon turned their switches and Conor swung his up out of the way. In a moment the front door swung open and Doc Marty stepped out. Shannon ran to him and wrapped her arms around him. From over her shoulder, the dentist glared at Conor.

"You had to bring her into this mess?"

"I needed someone to go with me and someone to help you. Would you rather I left her there alone at the compound with no way to communicate with us?"

"She'd have been safe," Doc said angrily.

"I'd have been terrified," Shannon replied. "I was already scared to death when Conor came back alone covered in blood. I thought something happened to you."

Doc Marty still looked unhappy about the situation. "There's nothing to be done about it now. You all get in here and help me get this gear set up."

They worked together to get the medical gear off Shannon's horse and into the house. Doc Marty tore into it immediately, sorting through vials of medications, pulling out some and tossing others back.

"How are they doing?" Conor asked.

Doc Marty shrugged. "They're both still alive. Jason regained consciousness long enough to throw up some blood and some teeth. I think he's got a concussion and I'm going to have to put a lot of stitches in him. His mouth is a wreck. I've got Johnny's bleeding stopped but I need to make sure he doesn't have any bullets still in him. He'll start bleeding again when I start poking around. Hopefully I can get him stabilized now that I have some supplies."

"What do you want me to do?" Shannon asked.

Doc Marty looked at his daughter very seriously. "These men are in awful shape. If it's too much for you, just say so."

"I want to help."

"All right. Then let's get these supplies in there where they're close at hand. I need to get an IV in the older man and I'll inject some pain meds in the younger man. Then we're going to check for bullets and sew up some wounds."

Shannon nodded, trying to reassure her father. "I can do it, Dad."

"I know you can, Shannon," Conor said. "You're tougher than you think you are. Do you still have the radio I gave you?"

Shannon nodded, checking a pocket on her vest. "Right here."

"Good," Conor said. "Barb and I are going to look for Jason's wife. When we make it back, which may after daylight tomorrow, we'll radio you. You guys stay here, keep a lookout. Stay alert in case those people come back to steal more than livestock."

Shannon's eyes got wide, previously unaware that this was even a possibility.

"You keep your gun handy at all times," her dad said. "Do not take it off. Do you have a round chambered?"

Shannon nodded. "Always."

"Good girl."

"Maybe you should get some blankets and make some blackout curtains," Barb suggested. "Then you don't have to worry about the light drawing attention."

"Good call," Doc Marty said. "We'll do that."

"We're out of here," Conor said. "You guys be careful."

"You be careful, too," Doc Marty said. "You're the ones heading into danger."

"I'm not worried," Conor said. "I have Barb with me. It's the other guys who should be worried."

17

Conor had no way of knowing exactly where Wayne and his men were camping. He hadn't asked and they hadn't offered, though he had an idea of where to start. The men said they'd come south from Detroit. In these mountains, roads were difficult to build so there weren't very many of them. Often they were just railroad beds where the tracks and ties had been pulled up. Many of the bridges and tunnels were still single lanes installed by the railroad in the early 20th century.

That limited the options. There was only one main road that came through the area from Detroit. Likewise, there was only one path between Johnny's house and that road. The odds told him that somewhere along that road, or not far off it, he'd find Wayne's camp. With those men not knowing the area, it was unlikely they'd stray too far away from the main thoroughfare.

There was a freedom in travelling at night that Conor didn't feel during the day. In the world of light, he was always worried about who watched from the shadows or if anyone had him in the crosshairs of their rifle scope. At night that was absent. There were so few people with night vision that he felt comfortable traveling down the middle of the road with his horse at a trot. If there were people lying in wait, ready to hit him and Barb with spotlights, it was likely he would see them first. They could either take cover or eliminate the threat.

They passed deer grazing the grassy shoulders and in the yards of dark homes. They saw raccoons tottering and scavenging. Though they never made an appearance, the pair heard the unsettling howl of coyotes resounding from the high ridges in the sparsely-populated area. In the best of times, residents of these mountain communities were an hour away from a grocery store, fast food, or a doctor. Homes were crowded in clusters on the rare pockets of inhabitable land, but those clusters could be miles apart.

Conor held out a hand, urging Barb to stop. "According to the GPS, the intersection we're approaching is about two miles from the highway. I expect those guys will be somewhere in the next two miles. There were a lot of them so I expect they'll either be occupying a large field, like a park, or more likely a building with enough room for them."

"Are these switched-on folks?"

"They had weapons but I didn't get a look at any other gear. I would assume they're shooters with no training or tactical experience. I doubt they have night vision or thermal but don't rely on that."

Barb double-checked her weapons, confirmed by feel that her weapon had a round in the chamber, and ejected her mag to confirm, again by feel, that it was full, then checked her handgun. She and Conor were both carrying suppressed .300 Blackouts so they could share mags if they had to.

"Single file from here on out," Conor said, checking his weapons also.

He moved forward and Barb fell in behind him. They passed a hydraulic repair shop and saw no indications of activity there. Just beyond it was a small cluster of houses and the smell of wood smoke. They came upon an automotive repair shop located in a cinderblock building that likely dated back to the 1940s, an antique Pepsi ad painted on its side. The rusting shells of disused vehicles were pushed back into the hillside, slowly being raked into the earth by fingers of kudzu.

Conor held out his hand again and stopped his horse. He slid out of the saddle and led his horse back to Barb. He gestured at her to move off the road. Only then did he speak.

"There's trash everywhere up ahead, scattered all over the road. It's not a sure thing but it's the only evidence I've seen so far that we may be approaching a camp. Let's stash these horses and move forward on foot."

Barb slid off her own horse, and she and Conor led them into the tall weeds off the shoulder of the road, tying them to the low branches of a poplar tree.

"Hopefully they'll stay quiet," Barb whispered.

Conor nodded. "A group this size may have a sentry or two. Our first task is to locate the sentry and take him quietly. We bring him back to this point and question him about the missing girl."

"What if he won't talk?" Barb asked.

"He'll talk."

"What if he denies it?"

"We play it by ear," Conor said. "Just follow my lead."

They slipped back onto the road and moved forward, stepping around anything in their path that would make noise. They went forty feet, reaching the point where Conor first noticed an increase in roadside trash. The smell of wood smoke was strong here but it was hard to tell where it was coming from in the dark. Likewise, it was hard to judge distance by smell. The stronger smell could be because they were closer to the source or could simply be because of a shift in the wind. It was unreliable information.

They came upon more reliable information shortly. In the distance they saw another block building, firelight flickering from the recesses of a rusty metal drum. Trash was everywhere.

Conor touched Barb lightly on the shoulder. "That's the volunteer fire hall. It's marked on my map."

"If they're staying there, where are the horses?" Barb whispered.

"Maybe they're around back so they're not visible from the road."

"Makes sense. They may have a sentry on them. That would be one of the most valuable assets they have."

"There's one up front somewhere," Conor said. "That fire is probably for warming hands, not creating a cozy atmosphere." He brought out a pair of binoculars and viewed them through his night vision.

"Anything?"

"Not yet." Conor continued to scan. There were empty folding chairs all over the parking lot and several van seats used as couches. There was a big fire pit at the epicenter of the parking lot and picnic tables had been dragged nearby. "This has to be them."

"Have you checked for people inside the vehicles?" Barb said. "That red van and the one that looks like a paramedic truck?"

Conor adjusted his view. "Good call, girlie. There's a man planted in the front seat of that van."

"Window up?"

"Yes," Conor said. "I can see the reflection of the fire off the window."

"Shit. That makes things harder."

"No kidding. Now I've got to yank open a door and hope it's not locked."

"I'm not comfortable with that plan," Barb said.

"You got a better idea?"

"Yeah, lure him out into the open."

"What's your plan?" Conor asked.

"I lose the tactical gear and stagger out of the darkness like I'm drunk. I don't have a coat on and I'm trying to get home. I see the barrel and stop to warm up by the fire for a second."

Conor was contorting his mouth, wrestling the idea around in his head. "I'm none too happy with your plan. It's risky."

"It will work though, won't it?"

"Probably."

"Once he comes out and starts talking to me I'll act like I'm nervous. I'll walk off into the darkness. Maybe trip and fall. He'll probably come help me up. Then I wrap him up like a fucking pretzel until he submits."

"Do you even need me here or should I just pack my shit and go home?"

"Before I choke him out, you step out of the darkness and put a gun to his head. Then we walk him to a more secluded location and you can do your interrogation while I gear back up."

"I don't like it."

Barb was already stripping off her gear. She shed the helmet, the plate carrier, and the rifle dangling from the sling. She unfastened her battle belt and lay it across the rest of the pile. She shoved her pistol into her waistband and covered it with an untucked shirt. She lost her gloves and anything else that might throw up a red flag. "How do I look?"

"Like a lost kid."

Barb smiled. "Perfect."

Then she was off, heading like a moth toward the flame before Conor could remind her to be careful or issue any more instructions, although that did nothing to stop him from repeating those warnings to himself. He settled into a comfortable shooting position where he had an unobstructed view of the front of the building. The Eotech optic on his .300 had a night vision setting that allowed him to view a targeting dot that would not interfere with his NVD.

He could barely breathe as he watched his precious daughter walk into harm's way. He kicked himself for not having talked her out of it. He should have put himself out there. He'd had luck before adopting the persona of an Irish traveler stranded in the U.S. by the terror attacks. It was too late now. She was out there. The operation was underway. All he could do was try to keep her safe.

~

BARB DIDN'T DRINK. She'd never been drunk in her life but she'd seen drunks on TV and in the movies. She'd also seen drunks in the streets when she'd visited cities with her father. She had no trouble adopting the staggering gait of a woman drunk or impaired by drugs. She walked out of the night and by the parking lot, hesitating at the sight of the fire in the barrel. She hugged herself as if she were trying to stave off the cold night.

She ignored the man in the van, acting as if she didn't see him, but watching from the corner of her eye. She caught him making a few subtle movements. She suspected he was readying a weapon. She went right to the fire, holding her hands over it, moving as close to it as she could, trying to absorb every bit of heat it offered. The night was indeed cold so it required no acting on her part to appreciate the heat offered by the fire.

There was a metallic click behind her, the door latch on the van opening, and she pretended to be startled by the sound. The man was opening the door slowly, perhaps to avoid making any noise that would wake the folks inside. He had a shotgun pointed at her but his expression was more curious than concerned.

"Can I help you?" he asked.

She focused on slurring, willing her tongue to not cooperate with her attempts to speak. "I'm sorry. I didn't know I was bothering anybody. I was just so cold."

The man looked away from her, out into the night. "Are you by yourself?"

She nodded, performing the motion in an exaggerated manner, as if it took great concentration. "Yeah. The people I'm staying with pissed me off. We were getting fucked up and things got a little out of hand. I got mad and left. I guess I went too far away and now I'm trying to get home and it's dark and it's cold." When she was done, she gave a big sigh, as if the speech took great effort. Then she forced another shiver and hugged herself.

"It's dangerous out there," the man said. "You shouldn't be out there wandering around. You pass out and you'll freeze to death."

"Tell me about it," she said. "Or some wild animal could eat me. That's why I need to get home."

The man was easing the barrel of the gun away from her. He looked more concerned than predatory. She'd been fully prepared for some man ready to take advantage of a drunk girl showing up at his camp in the middle of the night. That wasn't what she was getting. She'd have to go easy on him when this got physical. She'd have to remind herself not to twist his bloody head off.

"You need to get out of here," he said. "I can't allow you to stay. My instructions are to turn away anyone who approaches our camp."

Barb looked at him as if she couldn't focus. She nodded again, then saluted. "Yes sir. I understand. I have to get home. Thanks for letting me borrow your heat."

The man smiled. "No problem. Now get out of here and be careful."

She staggered away again with an ungainly stride. She turned to salute him again, then intentionally allowed her feet to tangle, causing her to fall to the ground. As expected, the man rushed to her. She struggled to sit up and he crouched in front of her, setting the shotgun on the ground.

She smiled at him, then her arms and legs fired out. Before he even knew what was happening, she had him tightly wrapped up in an uma plata, a shoulder lock she'd learned in Brazilian jujitsu. Before he could open his mouth to cry out, she yanked her pistol from her waistband and jammed it against his temple.

"Not a fucking word," she hissed.

The man gritted his teeth against the pain and fear. His face reddened as she threatened to twist his arm out of the socket. Lucky for him, Conor was soon at her side. He stuck the wide suppressor against the back of the man's head.

"Easy now, son," Conor said. "You're getting to your feet and coming with us. If you cooperate, you won't be harmed. If you try to raise an alarm, they'll find your body in the weeds tomorrow. In pieces."

The man nodded, wide-eyed, lips curled back.

"Ease up, Barb," Conor whispered. "Don't break him."

She did as instructed and they got the man to his feet.

Barb and Conor walked behind their prisoner, each holding the fabric of his jacket and pressing a weapon against him. With the man unable to see in the darkness, Conor guided him. Hopefully the man understood that his options were limited and didn't try to make a break for it. Conor wasn't interested in killing him yet.

With their night vision gear they had an advantage. It would be difficult for the other group to pursue them through the night but that wasn't how he wanted this to go down. This was about information. It was about finding Jason's wife.

Near the spot where their horses were tied, they set the man down in the tall grass. Conor held him at gunpoint while Barb slipped back into her tactical gear. With no visible lights, their prisoner could only make out the faintest outline of his attackers against the night sky.

On the other hand, Conor could see his prisoner pretty well. He could see the expressions and the range of emotion that played across the man's face. He could see the fear. The indecision. Conor let him wait in silence for an uncomfortable period. It would cause his panic to escalate.

While he waited, Conor prepared for his first question. It would set the tone, giving him insight into the man's resistance and hostility. It was this first question that would help him figure out if the prisoner was going to die immediately or live a little longer.

"What your name?" Conor asked.

"Furillo," the man replied with no hesitation at all.

That was good, he'd come out right with it. He wasn't oppositional and he made no threats of retaliation. "What are you doing here, Furillo?"

"We're just passing through. We ran out of fuel and had to abandon our vehicles a few miles up the road. We lucked up and traded for some horses so we're hoping to get back on the road soon. Some of them are trying to decide if it's better to go now or wait until spring."

The man sounded completely sincere. Everything he said matched up with what Conor had learned from Wayne on the day they traded horses at Johnny Jacks' house. Of course, it could have all been a well-rehearsed lie. A cover story.

"Where did you get the horses?" Conor asked.

"We traded for them. We got them fair and square from some local guy named Johnny. He had more horses than he needed and was glad to get rid of them. He seemed to be happy with the supplies we traded him."

"Where did those supplies you traded come from originally?" Conor asked.

The man shrugged. "Some of it was stuff we brought with us. Some of it was stuff we found coming down from Detroit."

"Did you steal it?" Conor accused. "Did you rob people?"

"No sir," the man replied with an offended tone. "Some of it we found in abandoned vehicles or houses on the way down but we never robbed anyone."

Conor stepped closer and put the cold ring of his suppressor against the man's forehead. "You feel that, son?"

"Yes sir."

"Do know what it is?"

"I have a pretty good idea," the man replied tentatively. "A gun barrel?"

"That's right, my boy. It's there because I want to impress upon you the importance of this next question. There could be life or death consequences to your answer. You understand me?"

"I do."

"Have you been back to Johnny's house since that day you traded for horses? Did you go back there today?"

"No," Furillo replied. Again, he sounded sincere.

Men could be good liars, Conor knew. He'd lived under a cover story of one kind or another since he was a kid.

"Are you certain about that? Maybe you weren't able to get all the horses you wanted? Maybe you decided you'd just go back and steal some more? Maybe your people needed some beef? That what happened?"

"Hell no!"

"Keep your fucking voice down," Conor hissed. "If anyone wakes up you'll be the first to die but you damn sure won't be the last."

"That's not how we do things, mister. I mean, we've all had to do things we weren't proud of to survive. I bet you have too. But we didn't steal any horses. None of us went back to that house."

"I hear what you're saying," Conor breathed. "Let me take it one step further. This next question is important. It's really the crux of why I'm here so I want you to think carefully before you answer. That girl of mine, the one who kicked your ass, is good with blades. If we're not satisfied that you're telling the truth, you're going to find out just how dangerous she can be with a piece of sharp steel."

Barb drew her knife, the blade hissing as it scraped against leather on its way out of the sheath. She placed it against the man's neck. She felt him flinch.

"I suggest you don't even cough," she said in a whisper that absolutely terrified the prisoner.

Conor cleared his throat. "I was at Johnny's house today. Johnny and his son were both shot. His dear wife is dead and his daughter in law is missing. It was a brutal scene and left me a little upset. These were people I liked and that's a short list. I'm looking for the people who did it. Are your people responsible?"

Perhaps out of reflex the man attempted to shake his head in denial but the movement caused Barb's knife to poke him in the neck. He flinched again. "No!" the man insisted. "Wayne liked that old man too. He would've never done anything to hurt them."

"You better not be lying to me, son. Bleeding to death in the weeds on a cold, lonely night is a miserable way to die."

"I'm not!" The man's voice quavered with the certainty that his life would soon end.

Conor got close to the man's ear and whispered. "If I find out you lied to me, I'm going tie you up and slit your belly. I'll drag you across the road to the edge of the Dismal River over there. The pickerel, the catfish, and the snapping turtles will feast on your innards while you're still alive."

"I'm not lying," the man insisted.

"Barb, I need to get something from my saddlebags. You have him?"

Barb let out a low laugh. "Completely."

With the aid of his NVD, Conor dug into his saddlebags and came out with a pouch and a hard case. "We're going back to your camp now."

"What are you going to do to us?" Furillo asked.

"I need to talk to Wayne," Conor said.

"He's going to be pissed about this."

"I'm pissed too," Conor said. "He can fucking get in line."

They walked to the fire hall, the only sounds that of the river and of feet scraping on the road. In the parking lot, at the edge of the firelight, Conor halted.

"Keep him here a second. If he struggles, kill him. If shit gets hairy, kill him."

Conor went to a distant vehicle, a Toyota Celica, parked about a hundred feet from the fire hall. He planted a device on the metal body of the car, then flipped a switch. An LED on the small box flashed red four times and then went dark. He worked his way closer to the fire hall, planting another device on the van Furillo had been stationed in, then placing a final one on the rolling steel door of the fire hall. When he was done, he raised his weapon to the ready and backed away from the building, receding into the dark.

When he reached Barb, he put his gun back on Furillo. "Go inside. Get Wayne. Tell him I need to speak to him. No funny shit."

"You're not going to shoot me if I walk away are you?" Furillo asked.

"I'm more likely to shoot you if you *don't* get moving."

Furillo jogged across the parking lot, bending down to pick up the weapon he lost in his scuffle with Barb. He threw a look back over his shoulder, angered again by his recalling of the indignity, then moved forward until he reached the door to the fire hall. He twisted the handle and entered slowly.

"Barb, you move up into the brush where you have a view of what's going on. I want you up high. If you see anything wonky you let me know. If people come streaming out the back and try to circle us let me know. If they try to rush me, drop some three-round bursts onto the asphalt between me and them. If things go nuts and we get separated, we meet back at the horses. If it's not safe to wait on me there, fall back to Johnny's house and we'll rendezvous there."

"Got it." Barb clambered up the bank to the right and tried to find a vantage point where she could see both the front and back of the fire hall.

Conor looked for a good position for himself. He noticed that to make more room inside the fire hall, Wayne and his men had rolled one of the pumper trucks from a garage bay. They pushed it well clear of the building. He took a position by the front of it. He would be visible to Wayne when the man came outside but he could take cover behind the massive engine block if things went south.

It was a few minutes before Wayne appeared. He opened the door cautiously then stepped into the opening. He stared out into the darkness, looking for Conor. The only light was the dwindling flame from the fire barrel and it didn't travel far.

Conor stepped clear of the pumper truck and threw up a hand. "Over here!"

"What the fuck is this all about?" Wayne demanded.

"I hope you don't mind but I had ask your boy there some questions. I need to put the same questions to *you* before I leave."

"That's assuming we let you leave. You attacked my guard."

Conor erupted into a musical laugh the rolled boldly across the parking lot and into the night. "Nobody got hurt. I think he's just a little burned that he got rolled up and disarmed by a girl. He shouldn't feel bad. I doubt there's a man in there that could go toe-to-toe with her."

"We'll see about that," Wayne said. "We don't like being ordered around. We don't like people showing up in the middle of the night and making demands."

Conor shook his head. "I hate to do this but let's get it out of the way first so we can quit the shit-talking." He reached into his pocket and pulled out a device, holding it into the air. "I'm not sure you can see this all the way over there but it's a universal TV remote. They make these for the dumbasses that lose their television remotes all the time. It's a simple but versatile piece of equipment. This particular one has five buttons at the top. Those buttons are made for surround sound, DVD players, CD players, or other pieces of equipment. What you might not know is that you can assign other more interesting things to those same buttons if you know how."

"I'm in awe," Wayne said, his voice flat, sarcastic.

Conor laughed again. "You're a cheeky bastard, Wayne. Why don't we see what's behind button number one?"

Conor pushed the first button and the most distant of his explosive charges detonated. There was a loud pop, the shattering of glass, and debris rained down on the parking lot. Conor had his eyes closed and the tube of his NVD cupped in his palm to shield them from the flash.

"Maybe you'll find that to be a little more impressive than my lesson on remote controls."

Wayne looked pissed but he bit his tongue. He didn't want to provoke Conor into more pyrotechnics.

"I've found that a display like that speaks louder than words. All I'll add is that I've got more of those little devices tucked around your building there. Just for my own safety. If you decide to get shifty on me, I might have to pop them off so I can make my getaway. If it comes to that, I'll flatten your building and everyone in it."

"So you disappear in a cloud of smoke just like a genie," Wayne said. "That what you are? A damn genie?"

"I'm here on business. Like I told your boy Furillo, I found Johnny Jacks and his son shot up. They're both severely injured. Johnny's wife is dead and his daughter-in-law is missing. I'd like to know what happened. I'm here because, I have to admit, I wondered if you might've decided you needed a few more horses than you could pay for."

"You don't know me! You don't know my people! You've got no reason to think that we would do something like that." Wayne moved out from the doorway of the building and into the parking lot. He wasn't close enough to present a threat to Conor but his outrage emboldened him.

"On the contrary, I've got a good reason to be here asking you this question. I saw you there trading with the man. You're strangers to the area. You are the likely suspects. You still haven't answered my question, either. Did you go back to Johnny Jacks' house?"

"No dammit! I liked the old man. I wouldn't have done anything to hurt him or his family. They seemed like decent folks. Like grandparents or something."

Conor considered the man's statement for a long moment before responding. "I believe you, Wayne. You have to understand my suspicion, right?"

In the green glow of his goggles, Conor could see Wayne shrug and throw his hands up. "I guess. Fucking strangers. Always get the blame for whatever happens in a town. Like the gypsies or the carnies."

Conor took a few steps away from the safety of the truck. "You ever decide if you folks are staying or moving on?"

"Harkening back to our earlier conversation at Johnny's house, is this where the sheriff tries to run us out of town? Is this where you tell us that we're not welcome here?"

"Not at all. I have my hands full right now. But if you stay, I'd rather work with you than against you."

Wayne gave a dismissive laugh. "If this is where we get all touchy-feely, hug, and all that bullshit, I'll throw my cards on the table. We've got nothing to hide here. Honestly, I'd rather my group lay in some firewood and stay put for the winter."

Conor walked toward Wayne. He lowered his gun and extended a hand, walking into the circle of light where he was clearly visible to the other man. "Then let's call a truce. Are you willing to shake hands on it?"

"I'm afraid to say no. You're the one with the guns," Wayne said. "But, yeah, I'll accept your truce."

The two men shook hands.

"I'm sorry about rousting you out of bed," Conor said. "As you can see, I'm loyal to those I call a friend. I need to find out what happened to Johnny's daughter-in-law. If she's alive, I'm taking her back to her family. Either way, the men who took her are all going to die a shitty death. I'll see to that."

"If you need more men we might be able to help you. The old man was good to us and I'd be glad to return the favor."

"Then if you don't mind, I'll just retrieve my explosives and be on my way. I've places to go and men to kill."

Wayne raised both hands. "Don't let me hold you back."

18

Before they approached Johnny Jacks' house, Conor pulled a radio from a pouch and hailed the folks inside. Seconds later Shannon responded.

"You're clear to approach. I promise not to open fire on you."

Barb wondered if that was a sincere promise or some weak attempt at a joke.

Conor was dying to ask after Johnny and Jason but he didn't want to have that discussion on the radio. To do so would broadcast to anyone listening that the men were injured and their property vulnerable. It may also invite some bunch of miscreants to come and attempt to rob Conor and his group.

The pair did not want to leave their horses where they couldn't see them but the animals had a long night. They needed shelter and a little comfort, just the same as Barb and Conor did. They rode them to the barn and put them in clean stalls, took the tack from them, and found a place for it in the barn.

The slipped quilted turnouts over the horses to keep them warm while they cooled down from their exertion. Barb climbed up into the loft and was able to scrape together a couple of buckets of hay that had come loose from bales over the years. Conor filled two water buckets from the gravity-fed trough to the side of the barn and hung those in the stalls. Only when their horses were settled in for the night did the pair walk across the cold, dark yard to Johnny's house.

"I'm getting ready to knock on the door," Conor said into the radio. He absolutely did not want to startle an armed young woman. She could have been rock solid and cool under fire but he didn't have enough experience with her to know that for certain.

When he knocked, Shannon was waiting just the other side of the door and opened it, ushering the pair inside. They banged their way in, gear rattling from hands, shoulders, and necks. Shannon helped relieve them of some of it and placed it along the wall, out of the path of traffic.

"How are the patients?" Conor asked.

"The old man hasn't regained consciousness but Dad thinks he has the bleeding under control. He stitched him up and has a tube draining his wounds, and put him on fluids and antibiotics. Now it's just a matter of watching and waiting. "

"What about Jason?"

"Dad's pretty certain he has a concussion. He's been unconscious most of the time but he woke up a little when he was throwing up. He was confused and started fighting because he didn't know who we were. We convinced him we were here to help him but he keeps trying to get out of here. He keeps saying "Hell Creek" or something like that. It's hard to understand him because his mouth is so messed up. Dad had to give him some pain medication. He's awake now but he's staring at the wall in a daze. The only way Dad got him to settle down was to tell him you'd be back soon."

Conor nodded, scratching his chin. "I need to see him."

"Where's Hell Creek?" Barb asked.

"It's where the church is that I went to with Johnny and Jason. It's where I went to make a recruiting effort."

"You think that's where they took the girl?" Barb asked

"I have no idea," Conor said. "There's more to Hell Creek than just the church. All we know at this point is who *doesn't* have her."

"That's if you choose to believe those people at the fire hall," Barb said. "Maybe we should have demanded to look around inside."

"I believed him."

Barb yawned. "I'm too tired to argue about it."

Conor put a hand on her shoulder. "Why don't you find a place to crash? I have a feeling we'll be back on the road in the morning. You'll need all the rest you can get."

"What about you?"

"Don't worry about me. I'm going to try to talk to Jason a second and then I'm going to find a place to nod off."

Barb nodded, staggering off with her gear to find an empty room.

"I can help you get settled," Shannon said, picking Barb's pack up from the floor.

Barb took it back from her. She didn't do it viciously but with enough attitude to let Shannon know her efforts were not required.

Shannon released it and stepped back. "Sorry," she replied, her voice holding more sarcasm than apology.

Barb wandered off through the house, using a flashlight to navigate.

"Why doesn't she like me?" Shannon asked. "Are we intruding?"

"No, you're not intruding," Conor replied. "And I'm not certain that Barb even dislikes you. She just has a certain *way* about her. It takes some getting used to."

"If you say so."

"Trust me. I'm her dad and she treats me the same way most of the time." Conor patted Shannon on the shoulder and headed back to Johnny's bedroom.

The room was lit by a battery-powered lantern. Conor was glad to see that Shannon had followed through on covering the windows to prevent any light from escaping and drawing attention. Doc Marty wore a headlamp to provide him with task lighting. He looked as tired as Conor felt.

"I hope you're the relief shift," Doc Marty commented when he saw Conor.

Before Conor could reply, Jason swung his head from the wall and focused intently on the new arrival. Though the dried blood had been cleaned from his face, the young man looked even worse than he had in the moments after they'd found him. The swelling and bruising were in full bloom. In his fury, he looked like the battered but defiant loser of a mixed martial arts championship bout. Even through the pain meds, there was a determined fire in those eyes.

Conor took a seat on the edge of Jason's mattress. The young man tried sitting up but struggled. Conor noticed bandaged fingers and a greasy film on the young man's face, likely some type of topical medication. Several dark, spidery patches on Jason's face were actually lines of stitches.

"I think there's a broken rib or two," Doc Marty said, coming to Jason's side and putting a hand on his shoulder. "That's why he's having trouble sitting up."

"Sam?" It was a desperate mumble from Jason, a plea.

Conor hadn't known her name until that moment. "You stay down, lad," Conor said. "We've been out looking for your wife. For Sam."

Jason shot Conor a hopeful glance. Conor responded with a shake of his head.

"She was taken, right?" Conor asked. "Did you see her? Was she injured or shot?"

Jason shook his head vigorously, then winced at the movement, easing a hand up to touch his damaged face.

"We went to find those men who bought your horses," Conor said. "I wanted to make sure they weren't the ones who'd done this. I didn't know who it might have been. With you both unconscious we had nothing to go on."

Frustration flared on Jason's face. "Hell. Creek," he annunciated carefully and with much pain.

"Where we went to the church? The soup kitchen?"

Jason nodded slowly.

"You got a look at them? You recognized them?"

Another nod.

"Was it...the minister? The folks from the church? Did they take Sam?"

"Nooo," Jason groaned, obviously impatient and aggravated at his inability to communicate effectively.

"Who?"

Jason hesitated. Conor realized the young man was trying to figure out a way to explain it using the least words possible because of the pain. Conor waited patiently. Finally, Jason took a deep breath.

"Big. Bowl. People."

Awareness hit Conor like a stick to the head. His eyes flew to Jason's. "Those assholes in the soup line? The ones with the big bowls?"

Jason gave a pained nod.

"Dammit!" Conor shot to his feet. "That's what happens when you leave folks like that alive. I wanted to kill them then but I was trying to win points with the minister. Those guys either followed us back or figured out where you lived."

Jason nodded.

Conor smacked his palm on his forehead. "We wasted the entire fucking night chasing down the wrong bastards."

"You didn't know," Doc Marty said. "It sounds like you made the reasonable assumption based on the information you had at the time. You can try again tomorrow."

"Going. Now," Jason hissed, trying again to sit up in the bed.

Conor put a firm hand on his shoulder. "I understand how you feel. I was the same way when my daughter was missing but do you think you're up for hours in a saddle? You think you're up for a fight or do you think you might hold me back from doing things the way they need done?"

The look in Jason's eyes was defiant. He was ready in spirit, but only in spirit. Tears poured and his mouth curled into a tortured, jagged sob.

"We will get her back," Conor assured him. "I'm leaving right now."

"You just got here," Doc Marty said. "Don't you think you need a break? A few hours of sleep at least? You're not optimal."

Conor spun on Doc. "How do I sleep? Tell me that. How do I sleep knowing that I failed this girl? This family?"

"You didn't fail them," Doc Marty said. "We already went down this road. You acted on the intelligence you had, which is all of any of us can do."

"Now I'm acting on the latest intelligence," Conor said. He jabbed a finger toward the bed. "Make sure he doesn't get out of that bed and try to follow me. If he moves, sedate him."

Conor wasn't even sure Doc Marty had the drugs for that but he figured Jason didn't know either and might take the threat seriously. The injured man eased back in the bed but looked far from settled.

Doc Marty followed Conor back to the kitchen. Shannon was sitting at the table wearily drinking a cup of hot herbal tea.

"Can you keep an eye on Jason?" Doc Marty asked his daughter. "I'm afraid he might try to get out of bed. Yell if he does."

Shannon stood and complied with a tired smile.

"She seems like a good girl," Conor said. "She doesn't complain and she's not afraid of diving right in. She'll do fine with whatever the world throws at her."

"She *is* a good girl," Doc Marty replied. "She's a better kid than I ever deserved. Are you taking Barb?"

"She's probably asleep," Conor said. "I'm hoping to leave her be. She needs her rest."

"You need *your* rest," Doc countered. "Hell, we all need some rest."

Conor dug a foil packet from a pouch on his plate carrier. He held it up to Doc.

"What's that? Dextroamphetamine?"

"Modafinil."

"I hate running on chemicals," Doc Marty said, shaking his head. "It's a nasty fucking feeling."

"I hate letting people die."

"Are you going somewhere without me?"

Conor and Doc Marty spun at the voice to find Barb standing in the door, her gear still on, a pissed look on her face.

"You need your rest," Conor said.

"I think you and the doc already chewed that fat, as the expression goes. I'm *not* staying behind." Her tone made it clear that there would be no arguing.

"I'm not giving you any speed," Conor said. "If you go it's because you have enough juice left for it."

Barb pushed by Conor and slung open the back door. "If you need pills to go on the op, maybe your old ass should stay home and leave it to me. There's a nice recliner in the den there. But if you're going, let's go now." She slipped out the door, the gear on her shoulders banging off both door frames as she struggled through the opening.

Doc Marty chuckled softly.

"What?" Conor asked.

"I thought your daughter was kind of a firecracker. She's more like a claymore."

"Yep. It's a constant struggle to make sure I have the dangerous side pointed toward the enemy. Sometimes it spins around the wrong way and there's collateral damage." Conor tore open the foil pack and took the Modafinil, tossing the empty pack onto the kitchen table. He shouldered his gear and tore off after his daughter.

19

The only place Conor knew to start was the church. Their horses had not even had time to cool off, only to drink and eat a little, so they didn't push them too hard. While both Conor and Barb had the same headstrong nature and would have preferred to gallop off into the night as they had earlier, they needed to save their horses. They might need an extra burst of speed or energy later and they didn't want their horses so spent they couldn't perform.

They'd even discussed riding the two horses Doc Marty and Shannon had ridden, but those weren't *their* horses. Even though the Maguires were fairly new to riding, they'd built a relationship with this pair of animals and felt rider and horse were learning each other. On a mission as critical as this one, they didn't want to risk a new horse they knew little about.

By the time the riders reached the mouth of Hell Creek, the sky was lightening enough that they could stow their night vision. They blinked at the hazy morning, so different outside of the green glow of the goggles. It was foggy, the mist of the river bottom trapped in the constricted valley and rising until it rolled over the summits like an overfilled bucket. Had this been summer, the birds would have already started in on their morning songs as they collected breakfast. This late in the year, there were fewer around. Somewhere, a solitary crow cawed. Herons stalked the shallows of the creek with a movement slow as time itself.

Before they even reached the church, the pair smelled the hearty aroma of soup mixed with the smell of river and silty banks. It was a curious, provocative smell that reminded both riders they hadn't eaten in some time.

"They're cooking already?" Barb asked. "Tad early for soup, if you ask me."

"They said it was a never-ending pot of soup. Maybe it literally stays on the fire all the time."

Barb curled her lip. "That's kind of nasty. If that's really the case, they're probably cooking a never-ending stew of bugs, dust, and bacteria."

"They're saving lives."

Though the heavy shod feet of the horses made a clatter in the quietness of the foggy morning, Conor made no effort to mute their progress by moving off into the grass. If there were people at the church, perhaps a guard with occasional soup-stirring duties, Conor did not want to startle him. Scared people made bad decisions. When they came within sight of the church, they found a group of folks standing around a fire. A different group, smaller, was standing closer to the road with a motley assortment of firearms leveled at the riders. The sound of approaching horses had definitely caught their attention.

"Do we kill them?" Barb whispered. "I take the left half, you take the right. We work our way toward the middle."

With a half-dozen weapons trained on them from a distance of less than fifty feet, Conor could only shoot his daughter a stern look. Was she that confident in her skills or did it completely piss her off to be on this end of a gun barrel?

"Relax. These are the people we came to see."

"I'm not the one you need to be asking to relax," Barb replied.

"Is Pastor White about?" Conor asked. "My name is Conor. I was here the other day with Johnny Jacks. I was here when those greedy bastards...excuse me...*undesirables* tried to go through the soup line with the big pots."

The men, wearing a mixture of hunting clothes and work clothes, did not lower their guns. "He's in the church," one of the men responded. "He likes to start his day alone with the Lord."

"I'm not here to harm you folks. I'm a friend. Your guns are making my daughter here a little nervous. Think you might be able to lower them? We'll stay where we're at until the pastor gets out here and we'll keep our hands where you can see them. No sudden moves."

There was some discussion among the men. "Fair enough," one eventually said and each man lowered his weapon to the ground. Conor noticed they still maintained a grip that would allow them to raise and shoot if needed. That was smart technique considering the circumstances.

"I can take them now," Barb whispered. "Maybe all of them."

"I'm going to put you in time-out if you don't relax," Conor said. "Save your killing for the people who deserve it."

After a few minutes, with no sign of the pastor, Conor called across to the group of men. "How long do the pastor's morning prayers usually take?"

The men looked at one another before someone took the initiative to reply. "Sometimes it's a half-hour. Sometimes it's a couple of hours. Reckon it just depends on what they got to say to each other."

Barb shot Conor an impatient look. "We can't sit here all morning. You know it's best to hit a target early. Especially if it's a bunch of druggies. They're used to sleeping late. We can bust in, get the girl, and shoot the vermin in their beds."

Conor sighed at Barb's enthusiasm. He vividly recalled a moment when his wife was pregnant with Barb. He told his wife that he wanted a feisty little girl who acted just like him. His wife laughed and told him to be careful what he wished for. That conversation replayed in his head, and he understood that his daughter was both exactly what he asked for and acted just like him. It made her well-suited for this world but sometimes made it difficult for her during more conventional times, like when a flirtatious young man was as likely to get placed in a choke hold as to get a smile back.

"I hate to impose," Conor said, "but would it be possible that someone might retrieve Pastor White for me? It's imperative I speak to him as soon as possible."

"Where's the fire?" one of the men replied, smiling at his own wit.

"Johnny Jacks' home was attacked yesterday. His wife is dead and he was shot up pretty bad. His son was beaten nearly to death and his daughter-in-law is missing. My daughter and I were out all night looking for her but didn't have anything to go on. When we got back to Johnny's house, his son told us that the men who attacked them were the same folks he saw trying to go through your line with the big bowls."

The men exchanged glances and conferred. There was some arguing. Some men appeared to feel adamantly that the pastor should not be bothered despite the gravity of whatever Earthly situation was taking place. Others seemed to think that the pastor would want to know. Finally, a man trotted away from the group, running toward the church.

"We'll fetch him," a man called.

"Thanks," Conor replied.

In a few moments the man returned with the pastor, who was also wearing the type of high visibility work clothes used by miners and gas workers, with fluorescent panels and bold reflective stripes. The pastor approached the riders and finally seemed to recognize Conor. When he did, his face softened, though he did not smile.

"They told me Johnny Jacks' home was attacked."

Conor nodded.

The pastor shook his head, his clouding face indicating that the news left him unsettled. "How about you all come over here to the shelter and tell me about it."

"We need to be on the road," Barb said. "Why can't we just get the information we need? We've wasted enough time sitting here already."

"You can tie your horses off to that tree over there," Pastor White said, pointing to a tree near the church, ignoring Barb and her comment.

Conor shot her a glance and saw her body flexing. "That's one!" she whispered.

"Easy now," Conor said.

He wouldn't have been surprised to see her stand in the saddle and spring off onto the pastor's back. Being ignored and disrespected was not something that sat well with Barb. Conor held a hand up to her, indicating she should relax. They needed to do this in accordance with local custom. They need to join the chief of the tribe around his fire.

Barb reluctantly did as Conor wanted. Her expression reflected her displeasure at what she felt was a waste of valuable time. They tied off their horses and walked with the pastor to the picnic shelter. A fire was going in a cinderblock grill. The never-ending pot of soup was warming off to the side and several folks stood there warming their hands and bodies in the cold, damp morning.

When they joined the group, the pastor explained who Conor was. He didn't recognize many of the faces, other than the woman named Betty who'd been ladling the soup on his prior visit. They took a seat at a picnic table away from the group.

"What happened at Johnny's?" the pastor asked.

Conor explained what he and Doc Marty had been doing in the area yesterday, putting up signs as part of a recruiting effort. He explained how they'd found Johnny and his family, but that they'd been unable to find his daughter-in-law. He told them how he'd made the incorrect assumption that the attack was likely the work of the group he'd seen Johnny trading with.

When he explained who Jason revealed as being the real attackers, there was a flurry of chatter and exchanged glances. Betty, the soup-server, seemed hardest hit by that news. Conor looked at Pastor White with confusion.

"Her daughter runs with that trash," he explained. "She lives with them but she wasn't here for that escapade with the soup. She doesn't like to be around her mother and those of us who knew her as a little girl. She feels guilty at what she's become. Her mother didn't raise her to be like that. Her church family didn't raise her to be like that."

Barb couldn't handle it any longer. "We need to know where to find them," she snapped. "The longer we sit here, the longer she's in the hands of those people. We don't know what's happening to her. You know the things they could be doing. We need to get her back."

The pastor listened without acknowledging or looking at Barb. It irked her but she kept her mouth shut. Finally, he nodded. "They live about four miles from here. Got an old run-down house ain't fit for a cat to live in. That boy with the mouth, Clark, owns the house. He got it when his granny passed away. It's on the main road. There's a big old swimming pool in the front yard and a white Mercedes SUV with all the windows broke out of it."

Barb stood up abruptly, glaring at the pastor. "Anything else we need to know? Family trees? Regional history? This is taking too long."

The pastor still refused to look at her, his eyes on the worn surface of the old picnic table. "You just settle yourself down, little missy, and let the grownups talk. I ain't even sure why you're here. This is a matter for men."

"That's two!" Barb said, holding two fingers up in front of Pastor White's face.

Conor's head sagged and he shook his head. He could only do so much. The pastor was digging his own grave here.

"What's that supposed to mean?" the pastor asked.

Barb leaned forward, resting both palms on the picnic table. She was directly in front of the pastor but he still didn't meet her eye. When he refused to look up, she took his face in her hand and forcibly raised it to her. "If you hear me saying 'that's three,' I promise it will be the last thing you hear for a while."

It was said so low that no one beyond their table could have heard it. Still, Conor looked around and every eye was on them. This could turn ugly in an instant. Hell, it was already ugly. It could turn into an outright brawl and any chance of recruiting this group to be a western lookout for the community would be lost.

Pastor White's hand shot up to Barb's wrist and he squeezed so hard his knuckles grew white. He was trying to pull her hand away from him but was encountering her powerful strength firsthand.

Conor couldn't let him hurt his daughter. Sure, she would insist that she could protect herself, but he couldn't just stand here and watch this. He cleared his throat loudly. Both Barb and the pastor flicked their eyes in his direction and met Conor's disapproving frown. The two slowly released their grip on each other, their eyes locking again, attempting to finish without words what had nearly gone physical.

Barb spun on her heel and went back to her horse. She was done with this.

"I think I need to go with you," Pastor White said.

Conor chuckled while shaking his head. "There's a whole lot of reasons why that is not a good idea."

"I intend to bring Betty's daughter home to her," Pastor White said. "I want to make sure she ain't hurt in the violence that you two likely bring with you. I ain't disapproving of it, I know it's necessary sometimes. But that girl was once part of this church and I feel an obligation to offer her another chance."

"Suit yourself," Conor said. "Only you though. I can't be responsible for all those untrained men of yours running around with guns."

"That won't rest easy with them but they'll accept my decision. I'll leave the fighting to you two. I'm sure you're more than capable of handling it without me."

Conor cleared his throat, seeking a delicate way to broach the subject. "Speaking of fighting, I'm not here to question your beliefs or your attitudes, but you best watch yourself around my daughter. I sense you have a certain attitude about women that's not sitting well with her. She's not one to be trifled with. You treat her with respect or she'll stab you to death with one of your own ribs."

The pastor shrugged but didn't react to the comment.

Conor stood. “We leave out of here in five minutes.”

“Can we make it ten?” the pastor asked. “I need to speak with some folks.”

Conor left, shaking his head, and calling back over his shoulder. “Three minutes. My second offer will never be as good as the first.”

The pastor’s men swarmed upon him, wanting answers as to what had transpired. The man disentangled himself from the picnic table, stretching as he got to his feet. “I’m going for a short ride with these folks. You might pray for us. We’ll need it.”

20

Even though an hour had passed since Bryan gave his men permission to raid and loot the town, gunshots rang out. Bryan hadn't known what to expect. He listened from the bridge for a long time, the world darkening to night, isolating each man in his own pocket of obscurity. From his men came whoops and war cries, cheers of victory. From the victims and the vanquished came cries, screams, and utterances of despair.

Bryan had no desire to run from house to house participating in the melee. This was something he gave his men. It was an offering to them, an effort to buy their cooperation and to bond them as a group. He knew they would do horrific things, things he hadn't allowed at Douthat Farms. That responsibility would be on him. The blood would be on his hands.

Seeking a place of calm and quiet, he walked down the main street, turning a blind eye to the carnage he'd unleashed. Eventually, he found what seemed to be the stateliest house on Main Street. It was brick, in the federal style, with antique shutters expertly painted in a dark green. The majestic double entry doors were painted a bold red and had brass handles worn smooth beneath hundreds of hands.

Bryan tried the door and found it locked. He let out a long exhale and looked down at his filthy boots planted on the worn brick steps. Then, prompted by some mysterious inspiration, he raised a hand and knocked politely on the door. He lowered his hand back to his side and waited a long time. He was eventually rewarded with the pleasing creak and pop only made by worn wooden floors.

From within, there was a rattle and the clank of a substantial iron bolt being drawn back. The door opened about a foot and a face appeared in the opening. It was a woman, her skin loose as if she'd been fleshy in her prime but now grew sallow from a lack of food. She appeared to be in her early seventies, her curly hair swirling around her head in a wild mane. It was deep black on the ends but a crisp white closer to her head. He was certain she was the kind of woman bothered by that fact each time she looked in the mirror.

“Yes?" she asked, her voice low, proper.

Bryan studied her. "Do you have a fire tonight?"

She looked at him with indecision and a degree of well-warranted fear. She had no inkling of how to respond except with the truth. "Yes, I do."

"May I sit by it?"

The woman hesitated a long time. She didn't know what to do but she also didn't know how to turn him away. As she explored his eyes she no doubt evaluated the consequences of her decision, of a refusal. It occurred to her that, if he wanted to, he could merely push the door and he would be inside. In the end she granted his request, stepping aside and swinging the door open. She offered no welcome or hospitality, just stepped aside as if she had no way to refuse him, knowing she may well have invited her own death upon her.

Bryan did not express any appreciation. He did not wipe his dirty boots upon the rug left there for that very purpose, nor did he offer to take them off. Inside, her house was immaculate even in the apocalypse. It was well decorated with lavish art and antiques. The floors were highly polished antique oak, strewn with Oriental and Persian rugs. Once he was inside the foyer, she shut and locked the door behind him. Acceptance of this single visitor was not an act of surrender.

"Are you alone?" he asked.

"Yes."

The interior was lit with candles and lamps, a manner of lighting which was likely period correct for the home. It was easy to visualize it that way, newly completed and being proudly displayed to guests by the warm light of oil lamps. Bryan moved forward on his self-guided tour. He examined her belongings, picking up objects of curiosity and turning them in his hands.

On the left was a large room. He squinted into the shadowy interior and found it to be a library. He plucked the flashlight from the pocket of his jacket and flicked it around the room. There was an extensive collection, the shelves covering all the walls and running to the ceiling. It was a mix of old and new, a reader's library. There were sets with matched bindings and gilded titles.

Though he felt a strong pull of books and wanted to stop, Bryan knew he might spend hours in there and he felt too weary to pursue that interest. Like an old dog with tired bones, he sought the warmth and reassurance of a good fire. He found the fireplace in a formal parlor decorated with historic furniture and ornate stained-glass lamps.

The only light came from the fireplace itself and candles in ornate brass holders. A tall leather wing-backed chair sat close to the fire with a matching stool in front of it. Bryan didn't think this was where she had been sitting because there was a book and a blanket on the sofa. Without asking permission, he settled himself into the worn chair and felt a burden lift from him.

The woman stared at him, not retaking her seat, perhaps not sure what to do with herself. Should she sit down? Should she run screaming for the back door? Should she grab the revolver tucked between the cushions of the couch, right beside where she'd been sitting when his knock came?

"This was *his* chair wasn't it?" He was referring to the man he sensed had once sat in this chair.

She nodded.

Bryan put his feet on the stool, feeling for the first time like he should probably remove his boots but he was too weary. Perhaps as fatigued as he'd ever been. He laid back in the chair, rested his eyes, and basked in the fire warming his face. The next thing he knew, he was asleep.

BRYAN WOKE UP FEELING WELL-RESTED. The feeling was unusual enough in the current state of things that he could not recall the last time he woke up with such a profound feeling of relaxed contentment. He opened his eyes and looked in the direction of the windows. It was daylight. He's slept through the night.

He experienced a moment of startled comprehension, remembering where he was, and that he was not alone. He whipped his head to the right and found the old woman, apparently the sole resident of the house, still staring at him exactly as she had when he fell asleep nearly twelve hours ago.

He regarded her curiously, uncertain as to why she was still there. He wasn't aware if anyone had seen him come into this house or not. If she had killed him, it was unlikely anyone would even have noticed. She could have easily escaped. Even though she was an older woman and did not have his strength, he had been completely vulnerable in his deep sleep. Just like in the game of Clue, she could have picked up the fireplace poker and bashed his head to pulp.

For some reason, she hadn't.

Had she sat there and stared at him all night long, just like he was staring back at her now? Had she moved at all? What had she thought about? Had she considered killing him or trying to escape? Perhaps she was too dignified to stoop to murder. Perhaps she was a true Southern gentlewoman, naturally possessing the comportment and dignity to which he strived.

Bryan stood and stretched. The woman watched him like a mouse watching a cat. Her eyes moved down to his waist. Bryan followed her gaze and saw she was staring at his holstered sidearm. He put his hand on it and straightened his belt which had twisted slightly in the night. He looked around and saw his rifle still leaning against the arm of the chair. He picked it up and checked the chamber. Then the safety.

Across the parlor, the elderly woman sat mesmerized by him, her expression a mixture of fear, questioning, and acceptance. Or maybe it was none of those things at all. Maybe the things that passed through her mind, which had likely seen twice as much time on this Earth as his, were things which he was not even capable of pondering.

He leaned over toward her and delicately plucked her cool hand from where it lay on her thigh. She offered no resistance, made no effort to withdraw her hand. It was so lifeless that it might have been a cool fleshy glove or even a dismembered hand he picked up in the street. He held the hand before him.

"Thank you," he said with a curt nod. Then he bent over and kissed the back of her hand.

He met her eyes one more time before lowering the hand and replacing it on her leg. He backed away and retraced steps he barely remembered through the house, to the front door. He paused with his hand on the polished brass of the interior knob.

"You may want to lock up behind me," he called over his shoulder.

He did not wait for a response but slipped out the door. There, he entered a cold morning filled with harsh, brilliant sunlight that would no doubt cast a glaring and judgmental light on the activities of the night. He skipped down the brick steps and turned right, immediately screeching to a halt when he found himself standing with both feet in a thick puddle of black blood. It appeared to originate from the nearly exsanguinated corpse of a young woman who lay on her side, her ear pressed to the ground as if she were listening for the approach of heavy artillery. Her hair fanned out delicately, the ends glued to the ground with her own blood. Her eyes were open as if she were looking at Bryan, as if she were wondering why he'd let this happen to her.

He had no answers for her. He found his impetus and stepped over her body as if she were merely a downed log on the trail. Even in her expired state, she nearly got her revenge when he slipped in the thick slime of her blood and almost fell onto the spiked railing of a knee-high iron fence. The irony of it was not lost on him as he imagined dying before the lifeless, impassive scrutiny of this young woman. Although he hadn't intended for people to die last night, it was an inescapable collateral consequence of his decisions.

That's just a fancy way of admitting it's your fault, he reminded himself. *Or trying to distance yourself from the fact it's your fault.*

The smell of wood smoke hit his nostrils and he instantly salivated, hoping the cook had coffee and breakfast going. Then he remembered that part of his justification for last night's atrocities was the death of the cook and the loss of the wagon that held their food. At the end of the block he found that the wood smoke came from the smoldering ruins of a real estate office.

His men were gathered on the bridge, in the very spot he'd delivered his emotional address. It was the very spot where he'd loosed his men like furious and wrathful hounds upon the unsuspecting and undeserving remnants of the townspeople. One of the men tossed him a plastic bag of leathery scraps.

Bryan opened the top and sniffed at it. "Jerky?" he asked.

"Deer jerky," the man replied. "Damn good too."

Chewing on the jerky and surveying the wrecked town, Bryan felt for the first time like a general on a campaign. Sure, he'd done bad things and made tough decisions, but last night still seemed necessary, as if only by going too far, by going *past* the line, could they learn where the line lay.

They had found that line last night. Not just Bryan but all of them. He wasn't certain yet if this was all his men or not, but the men standing there in the cold with him had undoubtedly walked up to the edge of that line and spat over it. They were scratched and bruised, their clothes torn and splattered in the blood of the vanquished. They had a motley assortment of luggage, pillowcases, and totes packed with the cans, boxes, and jars of food. They had guns, gear, sleeping bags, and tents. For all the things they lost with the wagon, they found more to replace it.

"Let's get those horses saddled, boys," Bryan said. "Somebody track down the stragglers."

"You found your missing men. You know they ain't coming back now," Zach said. "Where do you go from here?"

Bryan swallowed a chunk of the deer jerky, feeling like he was gnawing on the tongue of a shriveled leather boot. He gestured at one of the men and they tossed him a water bottle, essential for getting the jerky all the way down to his stomach. When his throat was clear, he replied, "We're going to figure out who did this and track them to their lair. Then we will kill each and every one of them."

21

Most of the world was still sleeping when Conor, Barb, and Pastor White rode through the river mist to the home where they suspected Jason's wife might be held. The pastor was riding behind Conor. For now that might buy him a little safety.

Barb was still simmering. She had little tolerance for being disrespected. In different circumstances, with fewer witnesses, the pastor may have found his head lopped off for his attitude.

Conor's focus was on saving Jason's wife. Barb and the pastor would have to settle their own accounts when this was done.

Over the few miles of paved road between the church and their objective, the pastor spoke of those who lived in the houses they passed and what fates had befallen them. It was much like travelling with Johnny Jacks. Some woodstoves were already stoked back to life from their overnight lows, chugging white smoke out of rusty pipes or masonry chimneys. Other chimneys puffed thick black smoke and emitted the sulfurous stench of coal fires.

"That's it yanner," Pastor White said in the deep Appalachian contraction for "over yonder." *Yanner* rhymed with *manner* and was only found in the secluded pockets where the language had not been corrupted. Speech like that brought a smile to Conor's face, reminding him of home.

The house the pastor was pointing at was an older style home dating from the forties or fifties. The siding was locally-milled clapboards thick with white paint that almost, but not quite, covered the coarse, unplaned texture of the wood. The windows were double-hung with both paint and glazing peeling away. A lack of maintenance allowed the surrounding jungle to encroach on the home. Thick vines found purchase on the wood siding and spent the warmer months working to engulf it.

An odd luxury that seemed displaced among the bushy weeds and debris, was an above-ground swimming pool in the front yard. It had not been covered for winter and Conor could only imagine the rank soup it held, abundant with rotting leaves, soggy bugs, dead birds, and rotting mice. Properly cared for it could have served as a water supply or a storage pond for fish. In its current state all it stored was stink and disease.

There were no lights inside, but that was typical of many homes. There was a chimney, though nothing rose from it, which was less than typical. The morning temperatures had to be in the thirties. Maybe they'd let their fire burn out or maybe they were just too lazy to keep a supply of wood on hand.

Conor indicated they should move out of sight of the house and tie off the horses.

"What's your plan?" the pastor asked as they dismounted.

"You stay with the horses," Conor said. "Barb will take cover behind the pool and provide backup for me."

"While you knock on the door?"

Conor looked at Pastor White and found he was serious. "Yeah, I'll knock with my boot when I kick the bastard in. I won't give them time to organize. This is a raid, not a social call."

"If that's what you think is best," the pastor said.

"It is what's best," Barb said. "You tend to the horses and leave the fighting to us."

"I've got no problem doing the job best suited for me," the pastor said, "though I will not be spoken down to by a woman. By a wicked and insolent child who has not been taught her place in the world."

It was unlikely the pastor even saw the blow that got him. It was a lightning-fast side kick what Barb launched with such fluid efficiency that her boot was contacting the pastor's jaw and dropping him on his ass before his brain even registered the attack. He was out cold.

"That's *three*," Barb said.

Conor shook his head. "Did you have to go and do that?"

Barb considered, then replied, "Yes. Yes I did."

Conor dropped to his knees and checked the man. "He's out. Jaw may be broke."

"Serves him right," Barb said. "Maybe it will limit the amount of stupid words that fall out of his face."

"How am I supposed to explain that to his people? They worship this man. They'll want your head on a stick."

"Tell them to bring it."

"I'll say no such thing. You realize that this totally screws any chance of forming a strategic relationship with these people?"

Barb shrugged. "We don't need assholes on the team." She winked at Conor. "Other than present company, of course."

Conor got to his feet, mumbling about bad timing and parental failures. Barb ignored him. They dragged the pastor away from the horses. No need to let him get trampled. He was injured enough already.

"Let's do this," Conor said.

Barb nodded. She was ready.

Each checked his own weapons and then they checked each other. They fully expected this to go ugly and violent, so weapons checks were not just a formality. This was insurance against dumb mistakes.

"Ready?" Conor asked.

Barb nodded.

"I'll cover you from the weeds while you get in position behind the pool. When you're ready, give me a signal. I'll join you at the pool, then hit concealment at that big doghouse before rushing the door."

"That's a big doghouse. You think there's a big dog in it?" Barb asked.

"No idea. I can't imagine these people feeding a dog when they're too lazy to build a fire. I'd be more inclined to think they either ate the dog or set it loose to fend for itself."

Barb didn't look certain about the whole dog situation but crouched low and moved across the yard. It was maybe fifteen yards to her position and she closed the distance quickly. The pool was four feet high and too wide to see around. She moved to the side, as far as she dared, until she was able to see one corner of the house. It didn't allow her to see the front door yet but she was close enough that she could get eyes on it quickly if she heard any movement.

When she was in position, Conor followed in her tracks, crouching low and trotting across the yard. He flattened himself against the pool, then pointed to the doghouse near the edge of the porch.

Conor moved again, slower this time, focusing on his ability to return fire rather than speed. The doghouse was a crude affair of scrap wood with a shingle roof. From its size, it could have held a Rottweiler or German Shepard. It was plenty tall enough to hide Conor from the house. One he was behind it, he leaned out and stared in the direction of the house, watching for any signs of life. His next step would be to charge the door and, using the momentum from his approach, shatter the door, jamb, or lock.

He plotted his movement, figuring how many steps it would take and where each foot would go. He figured which foot to start with and where that would put him after climbing the three steps. Then he noticed the rusty chain coiled on the ground in front of him and leading into the doghouse. It was thicker than would be required for most dogs. At least any dogs of normal size. He traced the chain with his eye and found one end attached to a wooden support post holding up the porch. The other end led into the doghouse.

Damn, Conor thought. *Maybe there is a dog.*

If he hadn't woken the dog by now, then he likely would when he ran by the front of its house. His only hope was to do it so quickly that no one in the house had a chance to react to the barking dog. He stayed put for a moment, breathing deeply and gathering his thoughts. He glanced back at Barb, who was watching him. Waiting. He nodded at her and prepared to launch himself into the shit.

Then the voice came.

"Who's out there?" someone whispered from inside the doghouse.

Conor was so startled he lost his balance and toppled over on his ass. He landed with his gun levelled in at the doghouse. He had enough restraint, enough training, to not overreact.

"Show yourself!" he demanded, his voice a harsh whisper. "Do it now!"

There was the rattle of chains, the thump of a body brushing against the interior of the doghouse, and a moment later a dirty hand emerged from the mouth of the doghouse. Conor was looking at it from the side and could only see the hand, not the owner.

"Both hands!"

"I need them to crawl out," came the desperate response.

"Hold them both out and don't move," Conor said. He flattened himself against the side of the doghouse and then rolled toward the front of it, coming to rest with his weapon aimed into the dark opening. Inside was a thin young woman, framed in the arched opening to the doghouse. She was dirty, dressed only in jeans and a flannel shirt. No jacket, no shoes, no socks. Conor hadn't seen Jason's wife, Sam, except in pictures hung on Johnny's wall, but he thought this was her. He pulled his aim off.

"My name is Conor. I'm a friend of Jason's. Are you Sam?"

She nodded desperately, her mouth contorting and her eyes filling with tears.

"He's okay," Conor offered, sensing her question. "He's a little banged up but he'll live."

"What about his parents?"

Conor hesitated. "We can talk about that when we're safely out of here. How are you locked up, Sam?"

She reached for her neck and touched a rusty padlock, raising her head to show it to Conor. "They have this chain locked around my neck."

Conor could see they'd wrapped the chain securely around her neck and padlocked it beneath her chin. They hadn't left enough slack to pull it off over her head. Unless he could find bolt cutters, he'd need the key. "Which one has the key?"

"A red-haired guy. I don't know his name."

"Are you hurt?"

Sam shook her head. "Cold. Very cold."

Conor waved to Barb and she came jogging over. She had no idea what was going on but had been watching with interest, ready to shoot if things went hinky.

"Barb, this is Jason's wife, Sam. Sam, this is my daughter Barb. She won't let anything happen to you. You come around the back side of this house and stay beside Barb. I'll be back with the key in a few."

"They have guns," Sam warned.

Conor winked. "They'll need them."

He broke into a run, leapt the steps, and kicked the door just above the lock. The flimsy casting of the discount store lock broke into four pieces and folded like a politician's promise. Conor found himself in a cramped living room with mildewed carpet and clutter scattered from one end to the other.

A red-haired man with a scraggly beard was stretched out on a filthy couch and bobbed up sleepily. His mouth gawped open and he appeared to have trouble focusing. He quickly realized it didn't matter what was in front of him. If they were kicking in the door it couldn't be good. He flipped to his side and reached for a shotgun on the coffee table. He barely had a finger hooked into the trigger guard before Conor unzipped him with a burst of suppressed gunfire.

The red-haired guy flopped violently before laying still beneath a blood-spattered wall. Conor turned away from him, touched a remote switch on the foregrip of his weapon, and activated a light. The harsh flow of LED light illuminated a hallway ahead of him. No sooner had he cast a spotlight than someone staggered out to fill it. This time it was a man Conor recognized from the incident at the soup line. He was prepared to order the man to drop his weapon but things happened too fast.

The man was blinded by the weapon light but raised a handgun anyway. Conor squeezed the trigger and pumped two bursts into the man. He staggered, firing a wild shot into the wall as his dying brain issued faulty signals to his muscles. The man's fall coincided with the eruption of a scream from the bedroom he'd just left.

Conor stepped forward, ready to swing in the door of the bedroom, and secure the screaming woman. Three steps down the hall, still several from the doorway, a woman dived from the bedroom, landing on the body and fumbling for the pistol.

"*NO*!" Conor bellowed but there was no indication she'd even heard his command.

Her hands wrapped around the grip of the pistol, determined to avenge her man. She yanked it up and swept it toward Conor. There was no time for anything but life-preserving action. He nailed the trigger, spotting the woman's gun flying into the air as she jerked backward. She fell against the wall, her neck at an awkward angle, her eyes open and accusing.

Conor cleared the room the two had come from and was preparing to go across the hall to a closed door, when he heard a scream from behind it. He considered throwing open the door, then flattening himself against an adjacent wall, but those thin old walls offered no protection. He was better off charging inside and throwing the occupants off guard.

He closed the twelve feet in three steps, a fourth kicking open the door with a loud crunch. His weapon was up, ready to fire, with the red circle of his optic landing dead-center on a young woman's face. She threw her hands up and screamed before she was jerked violently in front of a different man. He was bearded, with long hair and bad skin. He had a shiny nickel-plated revolved in one hand but instead of pointing it at Conor, he placed it against the girl's temple.

"Drop it!" the man yelled at Conor. "Put down the gun or I kill her."

Conor's thumb eased the selector switch from three-shot burst to single shot with only a barely perceptible *click*.

"I'll do it!" the man yelled. "Drop your shit."

Conor flicked his short-barreled rifle a hair to the left, the circular reticle of his optic covering a grapefruit-sized region in the center of the young man's face, and squeezed the trigger. The suppressed gunshot flared in the dark room. The man's mouth flew open but the scream came from the woman. Conor shot again, sending the man reeling backward into the wall. He left a starburst of blood and brain matter, his head smearing it as he leisurely sagged down the wall.

The girl dropped to her knees. Conor stood over her, gun levelled. "How many more are there?"

She was in shock, staring at the sunken puddle of gore in her friend's face. Blood filled and overran it, streaking his neck and face. She reached out to touch him, to stroke his face, but could not find a part not already splattered with his blood.

"Are there more?" Conor demanded, raising his voice and nudging her with his foot.

She looked at him and shook her head. "That's all." Her voice was unnaturally calm, disconnected from the violence and chaos of her surroundings.

Conor let his rifle hang from its sling while he flex-cuffed the girl. "I'm checking the rest of the house. You move, you try anything, and you'll end up like the rest of them."

Conor searched the closets and under the bed, then went through the rest of the house until he was satisfied it was empty. It was a small house, built in a day when closets were shallow affairs only intended to hold a few meager changes of clothing. There were few places where one might hide. There wasn't much to be found in the house except for dirty clothing, garbage, and objects that looked so out of place he assumed them to be stolen. When he was done, he returned to the young woman. He slipped the heavy Donnie Dunn knife from its sheath and cut the cuffs loose.

"Pastor White came with us. You know him?"

The girl nodded. "My mama goes to his church."

"We came for the girl you all kidnapped but we're taking you back to your mother. How could you hang with trash like this, robbing and killing decent folks? How could you let them treat a girl like that, chaining her like a dog out in the cold?"

The girl looked back at him, her eyes wide with surprise. "They didn't treat me much better than that. What was I supposed to say?"

"You could have left."

"And go where? Back to Pastor White's church? They ain't just like regular people going to church on Sunday. Those people live and breathe that church. It's all they do. It's like some crazy cult you see in the movies."

Conor shrugged. "You can stay or you can go. It's nothing to me. Like I said, I came for the girl. She'll be needing shoes, a jacket, and a blanket. You get them while I search for the keys to that chain."

"Tim," she said. "The guy on the couch. He had them."

Conor set off in that direction, finding the keys in the blood-soaked pocket of the red-haired dead guy. "Got the stuff I asked for?" Conor yelled back through the house.

The girl came struggling up the hallway, her arms laden with a sleeping bag, a pink fleece jacket, and a fashionable pair of slip-on fur boots.

"Take them outside," Conor said.

The girl did as instructed. When she was gone, Conor made a cursory pass through the house. He found a vile pillowcase with a greasy head print on it and dumped what ammunition he found inside it. He cleared any handguns he found and dumped them in his loot sack. He piled the hunting rifles he found into a clear spot in the living room. He'd leave those for the pastor's folks. They could bury the dead if they were so inclined and confiscate the rifles for their troubles.

Conor took two shotguns and a low-end AR-15 that he could use for parts, sticking them in the sack and knotting the open end around the protruding barrels. He left the decrepit house and found Barb supervising while the young woman helped Sam get dressed. Pastor White watched from the safety of the road, tenderly probing his damaged jaw and looking even more embittered than he'd looked just before Barb knocked his ass out.

Conor slung the sack of gear over his shoulder, descended the porch, and joined his daughter. "Where are the horses you stole?" he said to Sister Betty's daughter.

"Around back. There's an old barn."

Conor warily circled the house and returned several minutes later with a half-dozen horses who were still saddled.

"You ain't taking all of them, are you?" the girl asked. "How are we getting back to the church?"

"It's not far. You can walk," Conor said. He shot Barb a look. "Besides, I don't want to have to take Pastor White back to his church and fight off his congregation. When they see his condition they're liable to attack us."

"I'm not scared of them. We can take them," Barb insisted.

"We don't need to *take* them," Conor said. "We need them alive and securing this valley."

Barb frowned. "You may have a problem there. Could be some hard feelings over the broken jaw. You might have to try again later."

Conor gave his daughter a withering stare as she expressed exactly what he'd been trying to tell her. There would be hard feelings. Of course he would have to wait now. Neither of those were good things.

"Looting the dead?" came a slightly-garbled comment from the approaching pastor. "Are the ghoul and his daughter plucking trinkets from the corpses? Can't say I'm surprised."

Conor was preparing an answer when Barb spun on the man. "You haven't had enough of me yet? You want to taste my boot again? I can be a nasty bitch, preacher. Trust me, you don't want to see how nasty."

Conor intervened to try to keep things from getting ugly again. "There are guns in the living room, pastor. You and your people are welcome to those. You can bury the dead or burn the house, makes no difference to me. You'll have to walk back to the church. We're returning these horses to their owner."

"Suits me fine," Pastor White said. "I prefer not to ride alongside Satan's minions, anyway. I've had my fill of the 'justice' you and your foul daughter dispense upon the land."

Barb whipped out a knife and took a step toward the pastor. "That's four," she hissed. "Nobody has ever got to four."

"*Barb*!"

She spun toward her father, her eyes alight with a simmering fury.

"Help Sam. Take the horses," Conor said. "Saddle up."

Barb sheathed her knife and reluctantly took Sam by the arm, leading her away. When she passed Pastor White, Barb shouldered him out of the way and burned him with a look that might haunt the pastor for years to come.

Conor stepped over to Pastor White and leaned close. "I tried to stay out of the fuss between you and my daughter. She can be hot-headed, especially when she's being disrespected."

"She—"

"No," Conor said, interrupting the man. "You don't talk to her or about her ever again. You ever refer to her by any unflattering term or in any demeaning manner again and you'll suffer. I'll cut out your tongue and blind you. You'll be forever dependent on the charity and goodwill of others. You won't be able to manipulate with your tongue, and you won't be able to cast judgment with your eyes."

"I'm not scared of you," the pastor slurred with some difficulty.

Conor shrugged as if the comment was immaterial. "Then you'll sit easier for the cutting." The two men stared at each other for a long moment before the pastor looked away, turning his broken jaw up at Conor.

Conor left the pastor with Sister Betty's daughter and took the reins of his horse from Barb. "We'll cross the river and keep it between us and the church," he said. "Maybe they won't notice our passing."

Barb merely nodded at him, apparently having said all she cared to say. Sam sat on her own horse, looking frail and exhausted. Conor swung into his saddle and they rode off.

It would be some time before they crossed paths with Pastor White again. Sister Betty was so overjoyed at the return of her daughter that it helped soothe some of the Pastor's anger over his injuries. When the more hot-headed men of his congregation were ready to ride off in pursuit of Barb and Conor, determined to settle the score, the pastor dissuaded them.

"You'll all die," he warned them. "If you leave, you won't return. Your bodies will not be found and your bones will never have a Christian burial. Let it be. If we're to work with this man or smite him, only time will tell."

22

It was late morning when Conor, Barb, and Sam reached Johnny's house again. This time the mission had been a success. Instead of heading to the barn to care for the horses first, they rode directly toward the house after announcing themselves on the radio from a safe distance.

"We got her," Conor stated, answering the question before it was even asked.

Sam slid off her horse and hit the ground running. She was under a full head of steam when her husband stepped onto the porch, Shannon and Doc Marty behind him. Jason pulled away from their supportive hands and stumbled down the steps. Conor could tell that stiffness was setting in from the beating he'd taken. He was moving slower, more carefully, but when he hit the ground he started running toward his wife. His arms were thrown out, his battered face contorted with both relief at his wife's return and grief at all else that had taken place. He ran like a hurt child, knowing that the faster he traveled, the faster the hurt would stop.

When Sam and Jason met, they slowed, each afraid of hurting the other. Hands hovered tenderly around faces. They came together with a heartbreaking delicacy, finding a gradual confidence that they could increase the intensity of their embrace without killing each other.

Conor and Barb had stopped to watch, not wanting to intrude on the reunion.

"Kind of gets to you a little, doesn't it?" Conor said to his daughter.

Barb rolled her eyes. "You've seen one Lifetime movie, you've seen them all."

Conor gestured at Jason and Sam. "Where's your heart, my child? Tell me, can you not appreciate the emotion of that? The discovery that the person you loved more than anything had been returned to you from a certain grave?"

"You're being a bit dramatic, aren't you?"

"You're being a bit cold," Conor replied. "Is that chest of yours hollow? Are you like the Grinch with some little bitty kitten-sized heart in there?"

"You told me once that the heart is the most useless chunk of gristle in a human carcass."

"I did?"

"Yep."

"I must have been in an especially shitty mood that day."

Barb nudged her horse and peeled off toward the barn. "I'm too tired to stand around for another of your *where did I go wrong* speeches. Let's lose the horses and catch some sleep."

"Roger that," Conor agreed, falling in behind her. The stimulant he'd taken earlier was starting to wear off. Had he still been in the shit, he could have taken more but it seemed pointless now. He just had to stow his horse and carry his crap inside. Surely he could manage that.

Inside the barn, he and Barb worked in silence, too tired to talk anymore. With the adrenaline ebbing, they were dead on their feet. While Barb fed the horses, Conor cleared their weapons, emptying chambers and making sure there were full mags inserted. When everything was done, they piled their gear on their bodies—Go Bags, weapons, armor, NVDs with helmets, everything—and slogged out of the barn.

Shannon and Doc Marty were coming toward them and took some of their burden.

"I cleaned Jason's mom up and wrapped her in a sheet," Doc Marty said. "I laid her out on that long coffee table until we could bury her. Jason and Sam are paying their respects now."

"I'll help you dig the hole," Conor said, "but I've got to have me some shut-eye first. I'm so tired I could puke."

"God, I hate that feeling," Doc Marty said.

"The sooner we get to the house, the sooner we can get to sleep," Barb announced, determined to avoid any conversation that delayed her getting to sleep. "So quit mucking about."

Taking the lead, she charged off toward the house. Shannon ran and caught up with her since she was carrying part of Barb's gear.

"How'd it go?" the doc asked.

"We got Sam back."

"I noticed as much," Doc Marty said. "Was it that easy?"

"I killed three men, one woman, released a second prisoner, and Barb broke a pastor's jaw."

Doc Marty nodded. "That's more along the lines of what I expected to hear. Was it hairy?"

Conor shook his head. "No worse than any other door you kick in. You just never know what's on the other side of it. The preacher business was the worst."

"How'd that even happen?"

"After what Jason said about who took his wife, we went to the church and asked if anyone knew where to find those folks. They did but the pastor insisted on going with us to bring home the daughter of one Sister Betty, a member of his congregation. I'm not sure the daughter was a prisoner but she was definitely a subordinate. One of the men I killed tried to use her as a human shield."

"How'd that work for him?"

"It didn't."

"So how did the pastor get his jaw broken?"

"He seemed to have an attitude about women. It didn't sit well with Barb so the two of them kept butting heads. She gave him three chances and he failed to grasp the gravity of the situation."

"So he's wearing his lower jaw as a hat now?"

"Pretty much."

"She that good?"

"She's bloody dangerous," Conor admitted. "I started her in martial arts at four years old. She can grapple with anyone. She's like one of those Gracie's in Brazilian Jujitsu. You think you've got them under control and the next thing you know you're tapping out and hoping to God there's no permanent damage."

"Good to know."

Conor gave Doc Marty the side-eye. "Why? You planning on pissing her off too?"

"Absolutely not," the doc replied. "But Shannon needs that kind of training. She's got the basics. The Foreign Service trainings designed to keep Americans safe abroad, a little street safety and self-defense stuff designed for young women. Nothing serious."

"Barb can teach her," Conor said. "You ask her tonight and she'll have Shannon working out tomorrow."

"Good. I'll do that."

The two men stopped and finished their conversation on the porch, trying to give Sam and Jason some quiet time to deal with the loss of his mother.

"Before we go in, what's the plan here?" Doc Marty asked.

"What's Johnny's condition?"

Doc shrugged. "He'll make it. Eventually. He'll be down for a while. He'll need meds and monitoring."

"You think Jason and Sam can do it?"

"With a little instruction, yes. I'd probably want to check on him once a day for a few days, then start cutting back."

"We can talk about it when I wake up," Conor said. "But how about you plan on staying here another day? Shannon, Barb, and I will return to the compound. One of us will come escort you home the day after tomorrow."

"Escort?" Doc Marty replied with a look of disgust. "You think I need an escort?"

"Until I see you in action yes," Conor said. "You may be too rusty to fight. I don't know. You kind of proved your worth today, despite not being a real doctor." Conor let that hang in the air, wanting to get the maximum sting out of his insult, then he opened the door and went inside.

As soon as the door was open, soft crying filtered outside.

"Not a real doctor," Doc Marty grumbled. "I am too."

23

At night, the compound on the top of Jewell Ridge could be a spooky place. Ragus had never been there alone before. The place was so ridiculously big, with its acreage and array of buildings, that he was often working away from Conor and Barb, although he always knew they were there somewhere. Now there was no one there but him. He didn't even know where the other folks were exactly. It was the most alone he'd felt since moving onto the property.

He'd been left with no specific instructions other than to keep an eye on the place and to not go outside the fence. Ragus knew that a routine would distract him from boredom and from the spooked feeling he had. He could never tell Barb about the feeling. She wouldn't understand. She'd make fun of him and probably go out of her way to scare him when he least expected it. She was like that sometimes, a cold-hearted and mean-natured person. He'd overlooked those qualities earlier when he was so enamored with her, partly because they seemed inextricably tied to the qualities he most admired in her: her strength, her determination, and her ability to make decisions under pressure.

With Shannon in the picture, so sweet and kind, the contrast made it difficult to imagine why he'd pursue Barb over Shannon. The only risk he could imagine in falling in love with Shannon was a broken heart. With Barb, one risked not only a broken heart but perhaps a broken arm, leg, or ribs as well. Shannon was normal. She was like the girls he'd gone to school with, though much more cultured and well-travelled. She was predictable and he understood her.

Barb, not so much.

Barb was like no one he'd ever met before. He'd only won her over in the most superficial way by pursuing her when she'd been kidnapped and helping lead Conor to her. He was still uncertain if he'd actually won her over or if she simply gave in and agreed to tolerate him since he'd risked his life for her. There was a lot of ground between tolerance and affection. Ragus wasn't sure where he stood on that long, desolate stretch of ground.

After Conor had so hastily fled with the girls earlier, Ragus had geared up in what Conor called his *load-out*. It was the collection of gear that was for his exclusive use when they were outside the walls. Besides a Go Bag, there was a ridiculously heavy plate carrier that slipped over his head and held armor. When he'd pointed out that Conor's seemed lighter, Conor told him that his own armor was ceramic and the armor in Ragus' vest was thick steel.

"That carrier can't be comfortable to wear all day," Ragus said.

"Ever worn a bullet?" Conor had asked.

Point made.

The plate carrier had a variety of pouches for ammo and a few tools. There was a flashlight, batteries, and a multi-tool. Besides the plate carrier, Ragus had a pistol belt with a holster, a knife, a water bottle, and magazine pouches. All the gear, combined with camo clothing and his own assigned weapons, had gone a long way toward making Ragus feel like he was part of the team.

While being outside, moving around in the dark, was spooky, Ragus preferred it over sitting inside and worrying about what was out there. He didn't have night vision on a helmet like Barb and Conor but he did have a night vision rifle scope. Within the presumed safety of the compound, Ragus was wearing a headlamp to help him navigate. He also had a much more powerful LED flashlight on his vest if he needed a spotlight. He hated to wear a headlamp because Barb and Conor had both drilled into him that wearing any sort of light at night only provided an illuminated target for your enemy, but he didn't see a choice. There were a lot of things to fall over or fall off at the compound and all of them hurt.

Despite the size of the property Conor owned, they mostly stayed on the same twenty acres. That was the area where the coal company's offices, workshops, parking, and helipad had been located. The twenty acres was fenced with eight foot high chain link fence with barbed wire on the top. The coal company had installed the fence to keep locals from wandering onto the property to steal copper, tools, and equipment. It wouldn't keep out a determined trespasser but it sent a message that you were entering restricted space. In educating Ragus about life on the compound, Conor pointed to the fence and summed it up with a simple statement: they climb the wire, we open fire.

If Ragus took his time patrolling, checking that the fences were intact and all the buildings were secure, a circumnavigation of the property took him about forty-five minutes. He intentionally dawdled at points along his route, turning off his headlamp and sitting in the dark to listen for noises. There were always noises. With most of the leaves gone from the trees, sounds carried for great distances. Located high on the mountain, you would once have been able to hear cars on the distant roads and the twenty-four hour clamor of heavy equipment from coal mining operations. Now the night sounds were more subtle. The scampering of a rat. The crack of a limb as a larger animal moved in the shadowy forest. It was the movement of the compound's livestock as it shifted in its bedding or got up to wander.

Ragus felt proud of himself upon the completion of his first circuit. He felt braver than he expected, never once feeling as if he was being crept up upon by some imaginary monster or being stalked by a bear. In fact, he never experienced any fear at all. The only emotion he could recall was pure wonderment at how the sky opened up above him and how the deep silence of the world folded around him.

He returned to the living quarters, hanging all his gear by the door for quick access. He made a sandwich, realizing he'd missed dinner because of the way the evening had been disrupted by the events at Johnny Jacks' house. He made a wrap of goat, cheese, olives, and pickles. He went to the living room area and put in a movie Conor recently made him watch. It was called *Billy Jack* and was about a mixed-blood Native American trying to find peace on the reservation after the Vietnam War. The movie was one of Conor's favorites and he couldn't watch it without making Ragus watch some particular scenes over and over. Ragus had to admit that there was something satisfying about the movie, watching bad people get what was coming to them.

When he finished his sandwich, Ragus made sure to clean up his mess. He'd once had the habit of leaving his dirty plates and empty cups on the end tables but Barb broke him of that. Every time she picked up one of his dirty dishes, she clouted him on the head.

Ragus would shield himself and scowl at her. "I was going to get that when I got up," he'd say.

"It's a bad habit," she'd reply. "Don't leave messes."

Through her power of negative reinforcement she'd nearly broken him of ever leaving a mess anywhere. It wasn't like he was a pig or anything, but she and Conor were two of the most organized people he'd ever seen in his life. It went way beyond the way normal people lived. At first he'd thought there was something wrong with them. Gradually, Conor made him understand that it was related to the type of work he did. Not the machine shop work but the *actual* work. Loose ends and sloppiness got you killed. Fastidiousness, attention to detail, and never letting down your guard kept you alive.

Being that he wanted to remain alive, Ragus felt there may be some benefit in adopting the habits of those around him. Besides the small stuff, like cleaning up his messes, Ragus was training to be a better shot and learning some of the basics of fighting tactics, like how to work together as a team. As much as he hated getting his ass handed to him by Barb, he'd also been allowing her to teach him some of the fighting techniques she used. He had to admit she wasn't just good, she was scary good. He'd never been aware, due to the sheltered nature of his life, that there were so many people out there with the ability to kill you bare-handed. There were, though, and she was one of them.

After returning from the kitchen, Ragus added a log to the fire and settled back into his movie. He checked his watch. He would wait one hour and then make another sweep of the compound. It was still early in the evening. His plan was to patrol for one hour then break for one hour up until midnight. After midnight, he would do two patrols with two hours in between them.

He was pretty confident they wouldn't have any trouble at the compound. They never had before. By rumor, reputation, or frequency of gunfire, people understood to avoid the place. Anyone who went by on the road usually kept moving. Still, it was the first time he'd been left alone with such responsibility and he wanted to demonstrate the he could handle it.

~

When bedtime finally came, he didn't sleep well. It wasn't fear or the weight of the responsibility as much as it was the feeling of aloneness. For some reason, that sense of aloneness pushed thoughts and emotions onto him that he'd successfully kept at bay since moving onto the compound. The last year of his life replayed through his head, an inescapable loop that he already knew the ending to. He saw the lows of going to high school and dealing with their stupid crap while his mom was sick. Then there were the highs of becoming a wrestler and finding something he was good at that simultaneously helped exorcise the demons created by the stress of his mom's illness.

When the terror attacks came, Ragus thought it was one of the worst things that could happen but he was wrong. The world around him and his mother slowly went quiet and dark. There was no more school, no more wrestling, no more friends, and no more support. It was just him watching her die slowly in their crappy home stuck on the side of a remote mountain.

Looking back, he didn't know how he survived it. Many times he wished he was dead and no longer having to watch his mother suffer. When she finally passed, he thought the pain of that would finally kill him but it didn't. Now it seemed so long ago that the memories might belong to someone else, like something remembered from a book or movie.

He'd gotten stronger since her passing. While his past and the memory of his mother still battered him like a typhoon, he finally felt anchored again. He felt able to resist the buffeting of those waves of sadness and bottomless grief. He felt like he could survive despite what the world threw at him. Certainly he understood that part of his newfound resilience was due to the support of Conor and Barb, but not all of it. Part of it was him changing and growing.

He checked his watch. It was 5 AM. He'd gotten back in from his last patrol an hour ago and there'd been nothing going on out there. If he'd been keeping a log it would have simply stated *cold and dark*. Even at this early hour, the light outside was changing enough that he felt a need to get up and get started with his day. He'd fed the fire each time he awoke but probably needed to again. Ashes needed to be taken out, animals needed to be fed, and the ice broken up on their water if it had frozen last night. There were too many things needed doing to just lay in bed.

He made a cup of strong black tea, a drink he'd developed a fondness for. He'd slept in his clothes, not wanting to be caught unprepared. He was standing in his sock feet drinking tea in the kitchen when he heard a goat start bellowing.

"I'll feed you in a minute," Ragus muttered. "Bossy goat."

When the goat persisted, Ragus went to the window and looked out but couldn't see anything. Conor had made ballistic shields for any windows exposed to the outside perimeter of the compound. The shields were heavy steel but stood off from the window about eight inches so that some light made its way inside, though they did restrict the view.

Ragus slipped his boots on, then his coat, and stepped out onto the porch. He heard the faint rattle of chain link, as if the gate were being touched. Or opened.

Or *breached*.

He slipped back inside the house, quickly throwing on the rest of his gear. He slipped out the door and circled the office building. There was a dozer there expressly for the purpose of providing a ballistic barricade. Ragus could get behind it and watch what was taking place at the gate. It could be Conor and Barb returning. It could even be Shannon and Doc Marty. It could also be someone he didn't know at all, deciding it was time to climb this gate and see what goodies were on the other side.

The dozer was a John Deere 450, thick, old steel with few of the creature comforts found on modern machines. The machine was angled in such a way that Ragus could get on the ground and look around the blade. Conor assured him that no one with standard weaponry was going to put a round through that heavy blade.

Peering over the top, he saw two men at the gate. They were bundled up in warm hunting gear and both held rifles. Whatever their mission, it couldn't be good, and they had no business reaching this side of the gate. One man appeared to be nearly stuck, trying to squeeze himself through the point where the rolling gate was chained to a steel post.

"It's no good," the other man said. "You can't get through there."

"What the hell am I supposed to do?"

"Maybe you should just keep yelling like I told you. If this guy is as mean as they say, he might not like you crossing his fence. He locked it for a reason."

The stuck man disengaged himself and pulled back from the gate.

"I been yelling and nobody answered. I ain't going to stand here all day and scream my head off like a damn fool."

"What do you want?" Ragus bellowed, trying to make his voice deeper, more intimidating that normal.

Both men jerked in surprise.

"Don't move! I've got a gun on you!" Ragus ordered. "Are you seriously trying to break in here? Don't you know who you're messing with?"

"We're not breaking in," said the man who was at that moment extricating himself from the gate.

"I just watched you pull yourself out of the fence. What were you trying to do?"

"I've been screaming my head off out here for about fifteen minutes," the man countered. "Nobody came outside."

The men couldn't fully see Ragus with most of his body concealed. Apparently they could tell enough from what they did see and from his voice. What they saw disappointed them.

"Don't tell me you're the Mad Mick," the gate crasher said. "You're just a kid."

"I'm not the Mad Mick, I work for him. This is his place. I can give him a message."

"Where is he?" asked the other man.

"I don't think that's any of your business," Ragus replied. "Why are you asking?"

"Listen kid, we're just here to deliver a message. We've seen all the signs about this area being protected by the Mad Mick. We've heard the stories. Are they true?"

"They're true."

The two men looked at each other, perhaps finding confirmation that coming here had been the right thing to do. "We were on a hunting trip. Buddy of ours had some horses and we took out north along the highway. We ran into some folks on an ATV who were headed south. They warned us there was an army coming our way."

"An army?" Ragus echoed.

"I know. It sounds crazy. We didn't believe it either, but we ran into them the next day. There were probably a hundred riders."

"They could just be refugees," Ragus said. "Maybe they're fleeing south because of the weather."

The gate crasher shook his head. "Rumor is they destroyed a whole town where the highway crosses the river. Said it was revenge for something that happened there."

"On the Greenbrier River?"

"That's the place. Destroyed the town. Looted it and killed folks. Those guys on the ATV said they're looting their way south."

"You think they're headed here?"

The man shrugged. "I don't know for sure but the thought scares the crap out of me. I got family here. I thought the Mad Mick might want to check it out. Unless those signs were just a bunch of BS."

"They're not BS," Ragus said. "I'll let him know."

"You better let him know fast," the man said. "They may not be more than a day or two behind us. We rode all night to get here."

"I'll pass it on. For future reference, don't ever try to get through that fence. That's an automatic death penalty."

The man who'd attempted to get through the fence swallowed hard. His buddy swatted him on the arm in an "I told you so" gesture. The men were off without a word.

Ragus watched until they were gone. Then he waited longer to make sure they weren't doubling back. For the entire time he laid there on the cold ground, huddled behind that dozer blade, he thought about what the men had said. There was only one town where the highway crossed the Greenbrier River. It was the same town where Conor had caught up with the men who kidnapped Barb. It was where the battle took place and where Conor exacted his revenge. Could this be related? Could the army these men were referring to have ties to the men Conor killed?

When he'd waited for a half-hour, he got up, stretched his stiff body, and went inside for breakfast. He ended up eating oatmeal. He'd never been a fan of it but Conor assured him that its finest quality was that it stuck to your ribs, which was kind of what Ragus imagined it doing as he ate it, pasting itself to his insides. He stared off lost in thought, eating robotically, trying to figure out what he should do.

Should he go and see what the men were talking about or should he wait for Conor to return? He knew the route and he had a horse this time. He also had explicit instructions from Conor, and he wasn't sure he wanted to ignore those. If the army was that close, he might have a little time to wait and see if Conor got back. But not much.

24

The last two days of riding reminded Bryan of being very sick with fever, bouncing in and out of consciousness, unsure what was a dream and what was reality. He had very lucid moments of clarity that he could recall in vivid detail. Other times he was only vaguely aware of people trying to talk to him and of being so lost in thought that he could not muster a response. He hoped they didn't think he was nuts, and saw him as a determined leader completely immersed in trying to make important command decisions.

One of the moments he remembered with great clarity was ordering his army down an on-ramp to expand their ranks with local conscriptions. His recruiting speech had evolved over time. While still talking about their great and noble mission to build an estate, he focused more and more on appealing to each person's individual greed. He pointed out how a group of this size had more opportunities to line their pockets than each of them as an individual might. There was a strength in numbers that was beyond the sum of their parts. He spoke about how his group was actively going out and seizing fortune rather than sitting at home foraging and living off scraps. When describing life in his army, he conveniently left out any details on how robbery, murder, and enslavement might be required.

Regardless of how motivational and inspiring his speech was, regardless of how the audience seemed to be responding, the grand finale of the performance was always the same. The men were stood in a straight line and Bryan worked his way down the line asking each man if he would join or not. It was his Shining Path technique. It never failed to amaze him how that first guy always mustered the bravado and defiance to say no. After those first few "no" responses were dealt with in the customary manner, a bullet to the face, the refusal rate declined drastically. It put a smile on Bryan's face to see it in action.

Still, he asked each man the question rather than just rounding them up en masse. If there was ever an issue later, Bryan wanted to be able to point out that each man had come willingly, that each man had accepted his invitation. In this clear vignette of memory, rising from the fog of his mind like a shark's fin rising above water, Bryan had about fifteen men lined up. They all had some type of familial bond, were related in some way. Brothers, uncles, in-laws, or some sort of kinship. Under armed guard, their wives and small children watched from a distance.

When the first man refused to join, as expected, Bryan dropped him with a gunshot. There was an audible gasp, choked sobs, and the other men clenched their fists, wanting to act but unable to do so without risking death to themselves or their families. The second man's eyes were filled with tears but his mouth screwed up in defiance. Rage and hatred seethed from him like a bad smell.

"Will you join us, my friend?" Bryan asked.

The struggle was evident, as if everything within the man was conspiring to prevent his agreement. Everything inside him knew it was wrong to join and that it would lead him down the road of participating in acts he wanted no part of. Yet, not only did he not want to die, he especially did not want to die here in front of people that loved him. He did not want that memory etched in their brain. If he survived, he might one day make his way back to them. If he died here and now, it was over and there would never be a reunion.

"I will," the man replied. Bryan was already moving to the next man in line when another word escaped his lips. "But..."

Bryan stopped in his tracks, cocking his head to the side like a puppy trying to understand someone speaking to him. He backed up a step. "Excuse me? Did you have something to add?"

The man shook his head, regretting that he'd been too weak, unable to control himself. Regretting that the word had escaped his mouth like a snake poking its head from beneath a rock. "No sir. Nothing. I'm sorry."

Bryan studied the man closely. His pistol was raised dramatically into the air, as if he were prepared to signal the start of a street race. "No, you clearly have something to say and I want to hear it. It's written all over your face. What's your name, man?"

All eyes were on the man. No one spoke and no one moved. The only sound was a babbling creek beyond the road and the occasional sound of a bird lingering into the cool weather.

"Phil."

"Phil, do you have something more to say? You seem determined to add something to your statement. I'd like to hear it because I'd hate to be accused of stifling your rights. You got free speech, use it. Tell me what's so important that you just have to say it, even at the risk of death."

The fear Phil experienced when Bryan backed up to confront him was suddenly pushed beneath the surface by a surge of anger. "I said I *will* come with you *but* I will also enjoy seeing what the Mad Mick does with you when he finds you."

Bryan raised an eyebrow. He needed to address this insolence. He lowered his gun to his side, perhaps growing tired of holding it aloft or perhaps simply forgetting about it as he was distracted by a new piece of information, a shiny trinket in a world of mud and filth.

Phil raised a hand and the sudden gesture resulted in Bryan's army turning all their guns on him. Even Bryan stepped back in reaction to Phil's movement, raising his pistol to point it at the man in front of him. Phil opened his palms in a non-threatening gesture, then folded all his fingers inward except for one. He extended his arm and with that finger, pointing at a thick sycamore growing nearby. In the thin bark, two letters were carved by the bold strokes of an ax. The straight lines merged to form a pair of "M"s.

Bryan stepped back from the line of men and approached the tree. He touched the deep marks as if conducting a forensic examination. "Let me guess. MM stands for the Mad Mick?"

"Yes," said Phil.

Bryan strolled casually back to the line of men, holstering his pistol, and stopping in front of Phil again. "Who is this Mad Mick?"

"He came through here a couple of weeks back," Phil replied. "The story is that his daughter was kidnapped by an army of slavers and he went after her. They say he killed every single one of the kidnappers. With my own two eyes, I saw him riding through here with a boy and a big group of women. They stopped here at this creek to water their horses. While he was here, he carved that symbol in the tree."

Bryan looked at the symbol again, the mark of the Mad Mick, and returned his gaze to Phil. "Why?"

"Why what?" Phil asked.

"Why did he carve that symbol in that tree?"

"I didn't talk to him personally but he told some folks that the mark right there, *that very mark*, is the line. Beyond that line is his territory."

"He runs it?"

Phil shook his head.

"What then?"

"He protects the people. Once you get past this point, those marks are everywhere. They're carved in trees, painted on the road, and spray-painted on the highway signs."

Bryan nodded, vaguely unsettled by the confirmation that he was on the correct track. It was what he'd wanted this whole time, to find out what happened to his men and rain vengeance down upon whoever attacked them. This was not what he'd expected to find. He always thought he'd find out that it was a determined family with a lot of sons. Maybe Top Cat and Lester had kidnapped the wrong woman and the men of her family hunted them down like dogs and took their women back. This was different.

One man? It couldn't be true. It was likely a hastily-formed campaign of disinformation. It was psychological warfare. What likely lay behind the façade of this Mad Mick character was a man like Bryan himself. Probably a teacher, professor, or history buff using some technique from an ancient empire.

But Bryan would not be out-*historied*. The past was his realm. Its stories and techniques were his toolbox. He smiled at Phil. "Thanks for sharing that information. I get the feeling that I could have gone down this whole line of sad sacks and no one would have had the balls to tell me what you just did. You are to be admired for your forthrightness."

The look on Phil's face was a look of smug satisfaction. The problem was it also revealed the obvious fact that he couldn't wait for Bryan to get what was coming to him. It irritated Bryan, and he so hated irritation.

"I'm not fond of old sayings," Bryan said. "I particularly hate people that throw them up in your face at every opportunity, like you're supposed to base your life decisions on unattributed and undocumented drivel."

The look of satisfaction faded from Phil's face and was replaced with confusion. That made Bryan feel a little better.

"I'm sorry, that was clearly above your head. I'm referring to the old saying to not shoot the messenger. I *do* shoot the messenger," Bryan clarified, pulling his pistol and tapping two quick rounds into Phil's face.

Bryan enjoyed the sounds of shock that rose from the people around him. He loved having that affect on people. The power made him surge with vitality. Had he known earlier in his life that killing men gave him such a charge, he may well have turned out differently. He might have become a hit man or a serial killer.

He moved down the line and smiled at the next man in line. "Will you join us?"

~

WHEN THEY WERE BACK on the road their number had grown by eleven men. Eleven men able to understand that failure to go along with Bryan meant a sudden and irreparable end to their existence. Those men were under the careful watch of Zach, undergoing their orientation to the way this army operated. They all looked terrified, which was exactly what Bryan wanted. It was the best possible reaction they could have. A man who came aboard without a little fear and trepidation likely had his own agenda and would be trouble.

After learning about the Mad Mick, learning that he was crossing into the Mad Mick's territory, Bryan faded in and out again. He rode alone, sometimes talking to himself. Lecturing in front of a class had helped him solidify his thoughts as a professor. Now there was no class, but that did not mean that he could not speak his thoughts aloud when the desire hit him.

For much of this journey, both revenge and the desire to return to Douthat Farms had played back and forth as being his primary objective. He wanted both things to happen. They'd lost so much there. Returning to the shell of his operation at Douthat would be like living in the shadow of a monument to his failure. Each day he would stare loss and defeat in the eye. As had crossed his mind at several points in this journey already, perhaps starting anew was the right thing.

After he got his revenge.

It was one thing to travel south in pursuit of the mere suspicion that his men might have been killed. It was another to find the actual scene of their demise. To find verbal confirmation from locals that his party had been caught and killed was the icing on the cake. There was no mystery surrounding their fate any longer. He knew what happened, where it happened, and who did it.

He had a name. The Mad Mick. He couldn't be sure if it was actually a name, a nickname, or a title. Perhaps in the new world it didn't matter. Maybe it was no different than him taking Douthat State Park and making it Douthat Farms. Maybe it was no different than remaking himself in the semblance of Thomas Jefferson. Maybe this was how things were now. You could be who you wanted if you had the strength to force your vision on enough people. If you could force enough people to call you the king then you became the king.

That indecision, that vacillation between whether this was a campaign of war or a resettlement mission, weakened him, he finally decided. There needed to be a singular mission with a singular goal. It was easier to think that way now that he had a more concrete vision of his enemy. He had an actual target. From this point forward, this was a campaign of war. Once he had defeated his enemy, once he had laid waste to the lands that this Mad Mick so arrogantly claimed as his own, he could focus on what to do next.

Now that Bryan knew what the MM meant, he saw it everywhere. It was indeed sprayed on highway signs and abandoned cars, hacked into trees, painted on the windows of gas stations and restaurants. The scale of the promotional effort was impressive. While the proliferation of the symbol told him nothing about the size of the Mad Mick's army or how effective they might be in combat, it did indicate they had some level of support among the locals. Surely the Mad Mick himself couldn't be making all these symbols. There had to be some local folks participating as well.

The idea that the Mad Mick had local support dawning on him, Bryan felt a shiver of uncertainty for the first time. It was almost as if he felt he were being watched. He knew what it was; it was the realization that he was in the Mick's territory. Somewhere within the area he was travelling was this man who had killed his team. Somewhere within this area was the man he would have to kill before he could move on with his life.

25

"I didn't know what to do," Ragus said when Conor, Barb, and Shannon returned to the compound.

Conor smiled at the boy. "You knew exactly what to do. You knew to stay here until I returned. It may not have been what you wanted to do, and I appreciate you doing the right thing instead of giving in to what you wanted."

Barb rolled her eyes. "Big honking deal. He can follow directions. Hell, a *goat* can follow directions. Patting him on the back for that is like giving him a participation trophy."

Conor looked at his daughter. "Would you have stayed or would you have gone to check out the men's information?"

"Oh, I'd have probably gone," she said without hesitation.

"I thought so," Conor said. He turned back to Ragus. "Thanks for not being like Barb."

Emboldened by the compliment, Ragus could not resist doing something so childish he could not remember the last time he'd done it. He stuck his tongue out at Barb. Seeing the expression on her face, he immediately knew it was a mistake.

Barb sprang over the coffee table and caught Ragus by the foot as he tried to escape over the back of the couch. She pulled him to the floor and had him in an ankle lock before he even understood what was happening. Shannon, sitting peacefully on the couch, drinking a cup of hot tea, lurched back in surprise.

"You hurt him and you'll carry him on your back until he heals," Conor warned.

Barb released the stunned Ragus. He'd been so taken by surprise that he hadn't even had the opportunity to tap out.

"Be glad I went for the submission," Barb said. "The other option was to shorten that tongue so you couldn't stick it out again. Trust me, you don't want to experience that."

It made Ragus wonder for a moment if she'd actually cut someone's tongue off before. He didn't want to ask.

Conor sorted the two of them out, helping them to their feet. "We don't have time for this. Sit your arses down and listen to me."

Ragus took a seat beside Shannon. She leaned over and patted him on the arm. "Are you okay?" she asked.

Ragus nodded, embarrassed by the attention. He couldn't help but look over at Barb. She was choking back a laugh.

"Yeah, Ragus, are you okay?" she teased.

He gave her a harsh look but kept his tongue in his mouth this time.

"Barb, are you paying attention?" Conor asked.

She nodded.

"Get your patrol load-out ready to go," he said. "Medium-range rifle. Gear for a night or two in the field."

"Got it," she said.

"What about me?" Ragus asked.

"Doc Marty is expecting someone to show up and escort him home tomorrow. I'd rather he not try to get back here on his own. He's got his own set of skills but he's at his best in the city. The hills are not his area of operations."

"What about me?" Shannon asked.

Conor was pleased that she asked. It showed that she saw herself as part of the team and expected to carry her own weight. "You're with Ragus. You need to learn the area. You guys go together to get your dad."

"Okay."

"This is a strict out-and-back mission, Ragus," Conor advised. "No sightseeing. I want you guys to go straight there and come straight back. I don't like leaving the compound unattended if I don't have to. You hear me?"

Ragus nodded.

"That's not an answer."

"Yes, I understand," Ragus assured him. "What should Shannon take?"

"Shannon, we don't leave the walls of this compound without basic patrol gear. You never know when you're going to get stuck outside for a day or two. Do you have a Go Bag?"

"Yes," Shannon replied.

"Ragus will go through it with you and make sure you have all the gear you need for this area. You'll probably want an M4 with a low-power scope or red dot optic. Your dad said you could shoot but I'll ask you. Can you shoot?"

"Yes. Dad wanted me to be able to defend myself if his cover was ever compromised and they came for us. I'm proficient with nearly everything you might come across."

"Of course you are," Barb snipped.

Conor shot her a look. "Problem?"

"Just with wasting time," she replied.

"Then get your gear together while I finish with these two."

"You're just going to leave them here together?" Barb asked.

All eyes turned to her questioningly.

"That a problem?"

Barb gestured at Shannon and Ragus. "They're clearly *interested* in each other. You think they'll be focusing on security?"

"Barb!" Shannon said. It was the first time she'd responded to any of the snippy and sarcastic comments. "We're just friends."

Barb opened her eyes wide. "Oh...*friends*. Excuse me."

"What the hell is this about, Barb?" Ragus asked. "You can't stand me most of the time. Why would you even care if it was true? And I'm not saying that it is." He shot Shannon a look to make it clear he wasn't jumping to conclusions.

"You're jealous!" Shannon said, the truth suddenly dawning on her.

It was completely the wrong thing to say. Barb erupted with an even greater viciousness than she'd displayed when attacking Ragus earlier. She launched herself toward the younger girl. There was none of the playfulness there'd been earlier when she was trying to teach Ragus a lesson. This was Barb unleashed.

Though Conor was not as quick as Barb, he did manage to hook a hand in the back of her belt as she flung herself past him. He got to his feet and hauled her backward while she cussed, spat, and snarled like a wildcat. Ragus had shielded Shannon with his arm, ready to throw himself between them.

Conor slung his daughter into the hallway. "I don't know what the hell has gotten into you. Get your gear on now. Don't look at Shannon and don't speak to Shannon until you're ready to apologize."

"I'm sorry," Shannon told Conor when he returned to the couch.

Conor held up a hand. "You have nothing to apologize for. It's best you get out of here until she cools off. You two go back to your cabin and let Ragus go through your Go Bag with you. We'll be out of here in fifteen minutes. Ragus, keep the fire burning and take Shannon on perimeter patrols with you. Plan on heading out of here by 8 AM tomorrow. It will take you a couple of hours to get over to Johnny Jacks' place."

"Got it," Ragus said.

~

IN A HALF-HOUR, Conor and Barb were walking their horses down the paved mountain road. They'd try to make better time when they hit flat ground but the shod horses didn't corner well on these roads if they were moving too fast. Added into the mix was the fact they had been forced to go with unfamiliar horses. The horses they were used to riding needed a break after the experience with Johnny Jacks' family. They were sore, tired, and risked injury if they kept pushing them.

"So what was that all about?" Conor asked. "I've never seen you like that."

"I don't want to talk about it," Barb said. She'd been sullen since the incident, not speaking unless she had to, and not meeting Conor's eye.

"We have to talk about it. We're out doing dangerous shit and we can't risk having that tension between us. You and I don't have anyone else in the world. If something is bothering you, it's bothering me."

"Or maybe you're just bored and don't have anything else to talk about."

"Nonsense. I'm serious. If I didn't know any better, I'd think that Shannon was right. You did seem jealous."

Barb flushed a deep red. "I'm tired of talking about Shannon," she mumbled. "I'm tired of looking at Shannon. When are we getting shed of that pair?"

"You know the answer to that," Conor said. "It could be a while."

"Great."

"Look, Barb, I will be the first to tell you that I don't know a lot about women. I have very little understanding of the female mind. I was young when I married your mother and young when I lost her. By the time I was finally old enough to get my head out of my ass, it was just you and me. So I apologize for failing you in that respect. Hell, for that reason alone I thought you might enjoy having another woman around. I thought you might be wanting more girl time. I thought the two of you might bond."

"If I want girl time, I hang out with JoAnn," Barb said.

They rode in silence for a while before Conor picked the conversation up again. "There was a time when I thought you and Ragus might hit if off."

Barb sighed. "Can't let it go, can you? The idea that he and I might spawn little Conors for your herd."

"You know he was crazy about you. He risked his life to save you.

He did things he never thought he was capable of, all because he was enamored with you. But a guy can only take so much of bashing his head against the wall. You never reciprocated at all. You treated him like a kid and gave him the impression that you weren't interested in him."

"Are you done?" Barb asked.

"I'm not sure yet," Conor replied. "My point is that if you are jealous, if you feel like you blew it, you got no one to blame but yourself. None of this is Shannon's doing."

"I haven't thought about it much," Barb said. "I don't know how I feel about him. It's not something I've spent any time dwelling on."

"Ah," Conor said.

Barb cut him a look. "What's that supposed to mean?"

"Maybe it's not that you *want* him," Conor said. "Maybe it's just that you don't want anyone else to have him. Maybe you're pissed off that your puppy dog started following someone else around."

"That what you think of your daughter?" Barb asked.

"Don't act all offended with me," Conor said. "I'm not buying that for a second. No one in this world knows you better than I do. And I'm certainly not one to judge. The morality in this family has always been slightly skewed. What's right for us, may not be right for others."

"What's right for us might be wrong," Barb shot back.

Conor shrugged. "I live with that reality every day. There was a point when violence went from simply being our family legacy, inherited from my father and grandfather, to being my legacy too. It happened when I built my first bomb and used it on another person. Not everyone can live with the weight of that. I can. I sense you can too. It may be a flaw in our personalities that allows us to do so. Perhaps we're sociopaths. I'm okay with it."

"That's a lot to think about," Barb said.

"I've had a lot of time to process it," Conor said.

"I'll need more time to think about that and all the other things on my mind. I can't do it with you rattling on in my ear. How about we just shut up for now?"

"Good enough."

Before long, Conor began humming *Mo Ghile Mear*, an old Irish ballad. As the humming reached a fervor, he burst into song.

"I think I preferred the interrogation to this torture," Barb mumbled.

26

After learning of the existence of this character who called himself the Mad Mick, Bryan felt like he was being bombarded with the MM symbols every time he turned his head. They were everywhere he looked and each angered him a little more than the last. It was an arrogant taunt, rubbing it in his face that his men were dead and his farming enterprise destroyed. The anger made him erratic in his thinking and Bryan's interactions with locals turned from violent recruitment to equally violent interrogation.

He had over seventy soldiers in his army now. Here in the Mad Mick's territory he was afraid to do any more recruitment. While the loyalty of troops recruited under duress was never a sure thing, he would be even less comfortable with troops recruited from within the Mad Mick's backyard. His standing army was as much of a force as he would have for his mission to find this Mad Mick. Perhaps when this task was accomplished, when the Mad Mick was dead, Bryan could once again seek to increase the size of his workforce, finding more people with hands-on skills and strong backs for the work of building their new estate. His current army had but one task now, and surely they were of an adequate size and skill-level to accomplish it.

This Mad Mick was only one man, after all.

At a mid-nineteenth century farmhouse outside of Bluefield, Virginia, Bryan halted his force on the road. It was a sprawling brick structure likely built by a gentleman landowner who had done quite well for himself. Bryan knew that brick like this was made at a local kiln of local clay, possibly with the kiln or town's name stamped on the bottom of the brick. There were various barns, all painted a matching white, and masonry siloes with round tin roofs. He wasn't there to appreciate the architecture though. That was his old life as a history professor, before he became whatever he was now.

From the road he could see five men of various ages watching another skin a small deer. The deer hung upside down from an oak tree many times older than the house. If they had a notion to do so, it would have taken several of the men just to encircle their arms around the base of the tree. The five men, likely just back from a hunting trip, were probably armed. Bryan waved to his men, gesturing toward the deer skinners.

"Forward ho!"

One of his men opened a galvanized cattle gate separating the farm from the road and the procession moved up the gravel drive toward the house. The men working the deer spoke among themselves and cast nervous glances toward the group, uncertain as to what to do. One of the men dispatched someone smaller than him, perhaps a child, back to the house. He then took up a lever-action rifle from its rest against the tree and faced Bryan's army.

"That's far enough," he called when perhaps fifty feet separated them. He leveled the rifle on Bryan, riding front and center of the group.

Bryan raised a hand to halt the procession behind him. He regarded the gun-wielding man with an easy smile that was entirely inappropriate to the situation. It could have meant many things—that Bryan was comfortable with the odds, that he didn't fear the gun pointed at him, or that he was completely out of touch with the reality of events transpiring around him.

The history professor within Bryan could not help but notice that the deer hung from a crude iron gambrel that was probably forged here on this very farm. Imprecise hooks twisted beneath the tendons of the deer's back legs. Rusty chains connected those hooks to a spreader bar stout enough to hold a hog or small steer. How much meat had hung from those hooks over the years? Bryan could not help but wonder.

"Excuse me, friend, but I was hoping I might bother you with a question," Bryan began.

The man shifted uncomfortably, as if the situation was already deviating from the script that played out in his head. He looked back to his companions and found no help there. They were as scared, as confused as he was, by the sudden appearance of this army, like nothing else they'd seen since the world went dark. The oldest of them, the deer skinner, stood with his bloody wrists folded onto his hips, the fur-encrusted knife gripped loosely in his hand. It was a stance that would appear feminine on men of today but was frequently seen among men born of a generation long gone, men who spent more time walking, standing, or hunkering.

When he received no response, Bryan held up a hand in contrition. "Sorry, didn't mean to put you on the spot. I acknowledge it was a might abrupt of me to simply ride up to your home and head straight to the business at hand. I realize it's important we don't forego manners and decorum in this time of chaos and scarcity. Shall we start with names? My name is Bryan."

Bryan continued to smile, fixing the man with an expectant stare that begged a response.

"Gabriel," the man replied cautiously, as if even offering such a scant detail could provide Bryan with the ammunition to bring about their ruination.

With the odd smile still plastered across his face, Bryan nodded. "Good, good!" he said, as if they'd spanned a social hurdle. "Nice to make your acquaintance, Gabriel. Now that we're friends, can I ask that you please avert your rifle from me? I find it makes the conversation a little awkward."

"It's not awkward from this end," said Gabriel. "Matter of fact, I'm a mite more comfortable this way." His speech had the unrushed pacing of a farmer.

The smile finally left Bryan's face, leaving an ugly and cruel mask in its absence. He sighed heavily and called back to his men. "Gentlemen?"

Seventy-two rifles raised in Gabriel's direction, their movement creating a disconcerting mechanical murmur, a battle rattle that no one wished to be on the wrong end of. Gabriel's eyes grew wide.

"I'm sure you can see what I meant, right?" Bryan said. "A bit unsettling isn't it?"

Gabriel nodded but did not lower the gun. "I can see your point."

"Unfortunately, your failure to comply with my request in a timely manner has made it difficult to proceed in a congenial and gentlemanly manner. I'm afraid now I'll have to ask you to drop your weapon completely. Maybe just lean it against that tree there if you prefer to be gentle with it."

"And you'll drop yours?" Gabriel asked.

Bryan laughed and shook his head. "No, no, my friend. Our guns will remain pointed at you and your party until the conclusion of our dealings. Whatever that conclusion may be." That last bit Bryan added with a hint of menace, with a prediction of dark consequences.

Gabriel did not lower his gun. Perhaps he did not scare easily either, finding himself not intimidated by the odds. He stood boldly and unwavering, displaying no more fear than a man driving a raccoon from his garbage. Perhaps he knew that to toss aside his weapon was also to toss aside any chance for survival.

"Are you familiar with the blues of Robert Pete Williams?" Bryan asked. "I'm fond of his song *Parchman Farm*."

Gabriel had struggled to follow the intention of the stranger's fancy words throughout the entire conversation, and this tangent lost him entirely. He raised a quizzical eyebrow. Unfortunately that would be the last expression Gabriel willfully made. From somewhere in Bryan's group, the trucker Zach pulled the trigger on the Marlin .45-70 he'd taken to carrying. There was a deafening boom and a hole the size of a coffee cup opened up in Gabriel's chest. The next expression

Gabriel made, one of awe and confusion, was purely the result of facial muscles slackening in death.

The men to each side of Gabriel flinched at the shot but were simultaneously frozen to the ground in fear. Their eyes locked on Bryan, a collective with only one question between them—would they be the next to die?

Bryan surveyed the remaining men with a serious expression. "That whole question about Robert Pete Williams was just a trick, you see. He is a damn fine musician but the question was a signal to my man back there to go ahead and shoot because I could see diplomacy was failing here. It would be to your benefit to recognize from this point forward that I am no longer proceeding as a friendly visitor to your farm. We are not neighbors bullshitting through the windows of our pickup trucks about hay or whatever other damn things you talk about. I am the pissed-off leader of an invading army demanding answers. Respect and cooperation is expected."

The old deer skinner dropped his knife to the ground and wiped his face with a bloody wrist. He was crying. "Dammit, why'd you have to go and do that? We'll tell you anything you want to know. We wasn't bothering nobody. Been keeping to ourselves."

Bryan shrugged dramatically, producing an exaggerated hunching of his shoulders. "I felt a need to make a bold statement. To emphasize the seriousness of our discourse. You picking up what I'm putting down?"

The man frowned in frustration and gestured at Bryan's army with an angry sweep of his gory hand. "You got a hundred men pointing guns at us. You think we're not going to take you seriously?"

"Whatever mistakes you made earlier in our relationship, I don't think you'll repeat them."

The crying man gawped at Bryan. "Then ask what you're wanting to ask and get the hell out of here. Leave us alone."

"Very well then," Bryan replied. "Where do I find a man called the Mad Mick?"

"Who?" the man replied, confusion on his face. He looked back over his shoulder, curious as to whether the name rang a bell with anyone else.

"The. Mad. Mick," Bryan repeated. "Allegedly, he killed a number of my men and came through here with a group of women." With that bit of information disclosed, Bryan saw the dawning of awareness flare up in the remaining faces.

"Oh, that feller," the deer skinner said. "He's the one been putting that double-M all over the place."

Bryan nodded. "That would be him apparently. What can you tell me about him?"

The deer skinner looked to his associates for confirmation, then looked back at Bryan. "Not a damn thing, really."

Bryan screwed his mouth up in frustration. "That's it?"

Sensing his life was suddenly in danger from this erratic madman, the old skinner held up both hands as if that might ward off any flying bullets. "We know he's real. We weren't sure at first but we heard the story firsthand from the family of one of the kidnapped women. He's real, alright."

"Then where might we find him?"

The man shook his head. "Southwest of here is the rumor. He ain't local to us. We'd know if he was."

"You have nothing more to add?"

The skinner looked around, then back to Bryan. "No."

Bryan nodded, a grim expression of dissatisfaction evident on his face. Was he going to have to stop at every house and repeat this process until he got a firm answer? He hoped not. He made eye contact with Zach, who'd assumed the role of his de facto lieutenant in the absence of Lester and Top Cat.

"Kill these men. Burn their house with everyone inside it. Take the deer."

Zach nodded. Bryan continued staring at him until Zach met his eye.

"You can do it right?" Bryan asked. It was the first time he'd asked such a thing of Zach. The man appeared to have had no trouble shooting the armed man a few minutes ago but this was a different thing entirely. This was mass murder. This was the kind of thing that would be seen as a war crime even in the ugliest of wars.

"Leave me a half-dozen men," Zach said. "I want to check the farm for supplies first. We'll catch up with you at the next camp. That work?"

"Pick your men. We'll see you tonight," Bryan replied, spinning his horse with a tight rein and galloping off.

Zach picked the crew of truckers he'd been stranded with and a few of the others he felt he could trust. They held the deer hunters at gunpoint while the rest of Bryan's army turned slow as a cruise ship in a tight harbor. Bryan was already back to the road and, once turned, his army galloped off after him.

"Don't kill us, mister," begged the old skinner. "We got women and young'uns in that house."

Zach walked his horse closer to the man, his gun still on him. "I think you understand the seriousness of this situation. Am I right?"

The old man nodded.

"I'm going to give you one minute to run to that house and get your folks out. You better run like the devil is trying to pinch your ass. Once you're out, you all keep running and don't stop. I'm going to hold your buddies right here to make sure you don't come out shooting. You comprende?"

The man's response came in the form of launching into an awkward run toward the house. It wasn't pretty but it covered ground. Zach looked to the remaining men. "When he gets out, I'm going to start shooting. I need my boss to think you're all dead. Then I'm going to burn your house. He'll be looking for the smoke."

"It's all we got," one of the men pleaded. "You burn it, we die."

Zach leveled the lever-action rifle on him. "You don't listen, you're going to die anyway."

"They're out," Carrie, the female trucker said. "Running like a scalded dog."

"Your turn, boys," Zach said. He fired a shot into the ground, then another as fast as he could work the rifle. The rounds impacting the ground flung dirt but there was no one left to be sprayed by it. All the men were now making haste across the muddy stubble of a cornfield behind the house.

"You fellows fire a few, too," Zach called to the rest of his party. "I'm going to check out the house."

It took them about fifteen minutes to perform a hasty looting of the farmhouse. Upon completion, they gathered back in the yard where one of the men remained to guard the horses and ensure that the displaced homeowners made no attempt to circle back around. Each had a pillow case or two of items they felt held some value or benefit to the group.

"Spark it up, boys," Zach said.

"You think we could just burn the barn instead?" Carrie asked. "It would smoke as much as the house and these poor son-of-a-bitches would have some place to come back to."

Zach shook his head. "If we were to ride back in this direction and Bryan see this house still standing, he'd kill us on the spot for not following orders."

"You're right," Carrie acknowledged.

"Burn it down!" Zach called out.

One of the men lit a glass kerosene lamp, then tossed it through an open door. The lamp shattered, spilling a carpet of flaming oil across smooth pine floorboards. In minutes, the old wood structure that lay beneath the handmade bricks was fully engulfed. Zach and his men had to back up several times, first because of the growing heat and, later, because of the risk of one of the tall brick walls collapsing onto them.

"I ain't got to tell you all that word of what we did here better not make it back to Bryan. Are we clear?" Zach said. He looked at each in his group, seeking confirmation that they held an alliance between them. "You all know he's kindly high-strung. He'll kill all of us if he gets wind of this."

"He's an asshole," Carrie muttered.

Zach cocked his head in agreement. "I'll give you that but until we find a different asshole with a different plan this is all we got. Now let's get that deer down and get back on the road."

27

Their first day's ride took Barb and Conor past the roadside barbecue joint that held memories for both of them. Barb remembered being locked there in an old garage with the other women who'd been kidnapped with her. Conor's memories were of finding the man that Ragus had tied up there and left for him.

Barb hadn't wanted to stay there at first but Conor told her it looked like it might rain in the night. They'd be better off staying under a real roof than stretched out under a tiny tarp in the woods. In the end she conceded, telling herself that she was returning to this place as a victor, not as a victim. The men who'd brought her here the first time were dead now and she'd played a part in dispatching them.

They slept on long dining tables in warm sleeping bags. The place was a wreck but it still beat sleeping out in the weather. In the morning they had a quick breakfast of protein bars that looked like old cookie dough and tasted like damp cardboard. They were back on the road as the horizon lightened and color returned to a murky world.

It took them around two hours to make it to the town of Tazewell, Virginia. Neither had spent much time in the town. The four-lane highway passed by it, so if they were travelling, sometimes they'd stop here to fill up on fuel or grab a snack. The highway wound through farmland and stayed to the north of the town. There were few houses visible from the road and they saw no foot traffic. It was better that way.

They were passing the last exit to the little town that was once on the edge of the frontier when Conor reined his horse to a stop. Barb's horse took another couple of steps before she stopped too.

"What?" she asked.

"Fresh horse poop."

"So what?"

"We didn't meet anyone coming toward us."

"Maybe whoever this belongs to is on the road ahead of us going in the same direction we are."

Conor was quiet, listening, thinking. He searched his gut to see if it pulled him in either direction. "It makes me wonder if we should ride down this exit and have a look around in the town itself."

Barb turned her horse. "If you say so."

They angled down what would have been the onramp to the highway back in the days when there were cars on the road and rules that governed them. They were halfway down the ramp when they heard a distant gunshot. Both riders stopped.

"Could have been a hunter," Barb pointed out.

"Could have been."

They started riding down the ramp again when there was a flurry of gunshots in the distance. Several dozens rounds were fired.

"Different guns. Different calibers. Sounds like a gunfight," Conor surmised.

He took the lead and Barb followed him into a dense cluster of underbrush. They sat their horses for a while, waiting to see if anyone was following them or saw them go into the woods. When no one came, Conor dismounted and tied his horse off with a short lead.

"Take the gear?" Barb asked.

"Definitely," Conor said. "These horses can make a racket with their snorting and chewing. If they draw any attention I don't want to lose my gear."

Barb dismounted, tied her horse off, unstrapped her pack, and threw it over her shoulders. She double-checked the chamber of her weapons and Conor did the same.

"Take the lead, father dear."

Conor gave his daughter a slight bow and waded out of the woods. He kept to the edge of the tree line, perhaps fifty feet onto the shoulder of the road. There were no houses anywhere close to them now but they could see some in the distance. More houses, more people, more danger.

"Utmost caution, Barb."

"Roger that."

28

"I've always wanted to visit this town," Bryan said as he led his army past an antique iron sign that said *Welcome To Tazewell.*

"Why's that?" Zach asked. He and Carrie had been riding alongside Bryan since getting off the highway.

"It was originally named Jeffersonville back in 1800," Bryan said. "Named after one of the greatest men of his time or any other, Thomas Jefferson."

"I didn't know that," Carrie said.

Bryan frowned at her. "I wouldn't expect that you would. It's an obscure bit of historical trivia."

Carrie bit her tongue but gave Zach a look when Bryan turned away from her. Bryan was a dick. He had no respect for women at all. She wanted to teach him some respect but hadn't yet had the opportunity to do so, although she swore the time would come. She wanted to deliver him an old-fashioned ass kicking.

Bryan regarded the old brick houses and the stately rural mansions. Many of the historic structures of the town still stood. Locals had done their best to preserve what they could.

"Jefferson is a personal hero of mine. In fact, I strive to model myself after him. As far as this town goes, a hundred or so years later they renamed it to Tazewell, a much less dignified name if you ask me. At the time, it was the smallest town in America to have an electric street car. As far as I know, that was their only claim to fame."

"You know your history," Zach said.

"Can't remember if I told you or not, but I was once a history professor in a different life," Bryan said.

"You mentioned it. Or someone did."

Bryan nodded, paying little attention to the conversation as his eyes roved from building to building. "I love these old towns."

"Someone else does too," Carrie said, pointing toward a colonial era brick church.

The double-M symbol of the Mad Mick was painted upon the handmade bricks in garish six-foot high letters.

Bryan's lips tightened. "Damnit!" He nudged his horse into a trot, stopping in front of a historical marker that indicated the church was built in 1783. A modest house of more recent construction stood at the edge of the property. Smoke curled from a chimney of dark brick.

Bryan rode to a house with a sign in the yard indicating it was the parsonage for the adjacent church, slid from the back of his horse, and tied it off to a wrought iron fence. He stalked up a sidewalk of brick pavers and banged on a solid white door with antique hardware.

A pleasant man with a shock of bushy white hair opened the door and smiled at his guest. "Good afternoon. Can I help you?"

Staring at the man, not understanding how he could fail to grasp the source of his rage, Bryan shot out a hand and grabbed the man by his hair. He yanked him violently from the doorway, the man losing his glasses in the process. He staggered in his sock feet, trying to keep up with the way he was being tugged and jerked about, trying to get a hand up to lessen the pressure on his hair.

When Bryan had him in the middle of the yard, a point at which they had a clear view of the side of the church, he slung the elderly man to the ground and gestured at the large letters. "How could you allow this blasphemy?"

The old man rose carefully to an elbow, trying to smooth his hair back in place, and squinting to see what Bryan was raving about.

Bryan rolled his eyes the minister's failure to comprehend. "The letters! The damn letters!"

"Oh," the man said, understanding dawning on him. "I didn't allow that. Someone did it of their own accord without my knowledge or permission. I haven't attempted to remove it, because I see nothing particularly blasphemous about it. One might even take the mark as a gesture intended to show the church and its people are protected. While the mark has no religious significance, I see it as being similar to the story of the Passover in the bible."

"I don't give a damn if it's a church or not!" Bryan bellowed, his face red and his eyes fiery. "It's a significant historical building now serving as little more than a billboard advertising some murdering madman."

The minister tried to get up, bracing a hand on the ground, but Bryan kicked it out from under him, sending him sprawling.

"Is everything okay?" came a voice from the house.

Bryan spun in that direction and found a grandmotherly lady, likely the minister's wife, standing at the door. She was distraught but too fearful to come outside. Bryan drew his gun and levelled it at her. "Back in the house, lady!"

She did as she was told, receding back inside like inhaled smoke. Bryan went to the minister and hovered over him, his pistol still in his hand. "What do you know about this Mad Mick?"

The minister seemed confused in his distress. "Why, very little actually. My parishioners have told me that he rescued some kidnapped women and is forming some type of militia to organize folks. That's all I know. To the best of my knowledge, I've never laid eyes on the man."

"Who in this town would know something?" Bryan demanded.

The old ministered hemmed and hawed. Bryan couldn't tell if he genuinely knew nothing or if he was just playing dumb. It was time to turn up the stakes. He pointed his gun at the minister's face.

"I will kill you," Bryan hissed.

In the face of threats, the minister seemed to find some strength. He stared at Bryan with a deep resolve. "You can physically assault me but I will not be bullied. If it's my time, then I will walk joyfully into the arms of the Lord."

29

Barb and Conor moved house to house with practiced precision, running along alleys and climbing fences. If anyone saw them, they were too scared to react. The town was laid out in the organic and meandering manner often found in old towns. Over time, these towns never expanded as much as they evolved, streets popping up where they were needed and where it became most convenient for people to travel.

The pair were several streets away from the church when they first heard angry yelling. Barb was the first to hear it. She made a clucking sound to get his attention and waved him in the direction of the yelling. They cut through a gravel alley, staying to one side. They moved through private yards, hoping there were no residents ready to shoot at them out of fear or a desire to rob them of their possessions.

They cut around a mansion dating back to the Civil War, with towering columns and tall windows. It was surrounded by brick sidewalks and a retaining wall with iron spikes inset to prevent loafers from passing the day there. What had once been a world-class garden designed by a botanist of some note was now an over-grown thicket indistinguishable from the surrounding woods. Barb and Conor found the overgrowth useful for concealing their movement. Eventually, they found a vantage point where they were looking down off a slight knoll and over a vast mob of riders and pack horses.

"What the hell is he going on about?" Conor hissed. "Is it a shakedown?"

"I believe you have a fan," Barb whispered. She pointed at the large double-M symbol on the wall of the church.

"You think that's why he's so angry?"

"Could be. This has to be the army the hunter was referring to, but how do they know the significance of the symbol?"

"I don't know, but I can't let him keep beating that old man."

"The odds suck," Barb whispered. "If we open fire on him this is going to get real hot, real fast. Bullets will be flying everywhere and we don't know the area."

"Then I'll just break up their little party," Conor said. He opened a pouch on his plate carrier and retrieved two grenades. "I'm going to throw a flash bang and pop smoke. We'll dump a few rounds over their head and then change positions."

"You think that's going to save the old man?" Barb asked.

"There may not be any way to save that old man. Maybe in the chaos, we can separate the guy doing the yelling from his people and ask him a few questions."

"You think he's the leader?"

Conor shrugged. "We'll find out." He pulled the pin on a smoke grenade, compliments of his boss Ricardo, and tossed it toward the rear of the mob. As smoke began hissing out, voices rose in the crowd. "Get ready to fire."

Conor waited until there was enough smoke wafting around to conceal him, then pulled the pin on the concussion grenade and tossed it in the same direction as the smoke. There was a boom and the sound of horses panicking. Riders were shouting to each other.

"Now!" Conor hissed.

Barb moved clear of Conor and started popping off rounds. Shooting above the smoke, she shattered several high windows in the church and rounds rang off the brick walls. Another smoke grenade sailed over her head, Conor deciding they needed a little more concealment.

"Let's roll," he said, patting her on the back as he passed her on the right.

Barb fell in step behind him and they moved across the yard, over the retaining wall, and down to street level. The smoke and concussion grenade sent most of the riders away from them, hurrying further into town. Others could still be heard moving around in the chaos, shouting to each other, trying to find their way to safety.

Conor yanked two more grenades from pouches on his chest. He tossed one and there was the hiss of more spewing smoke. He tossed a second flash-bang toward the stragglers, wanting to encourage their movement in the other direction.

"There!" Barb said, pointing to a white-haired man staggering out of the smoke.

Conor ran toward him while Barb took a position near a tree and provided cover.

"Where is the man who was yelling at you?" Conor asked.

The minister looked traumatized, but Conor needed to know.

The man raised a wavering finger, pointing east. Conor couldn't tell if the old man knew what he was talking about or not. Perhaps he was just telling Conor something to make him go away and leave him alone.

"Get inside!" Conor told him, steering him toward the nearest structure, unsure if it was the man's house or not. "Barb, let's go."

They moved as a team, weapons at high ready. There were fewer voices. The epicenter of the chaos, the bulk of the men, were elsewhere now, likely regathering themselves outside of the thinning smoke.

A man staggered out of the smoke, a pistol raised in their direction. Conor was still trying to figure out if he was the man they were looking for when Barb pulled the trigger. A suppressed double-tap caught the man in the sternum and neck. He spun, spraying blood like a bad brake line.

Conor looked at his daughter with a *what the hell* look.

"Not him," Barb called, taking a hand off her rifle to gesture ahead of them. "There."

At ten o'clock to his position, Conor could see a man trying to mount a spooked horse. This was the guy. The horse was circling, trying to free itself. The man held a rein tight, trying to get a foot into the stirrup. He was cursing and threatening the horse. Forty feet separated him from Conor and his daughter.

The smoke was thinning, moving in the direction of town, carried away by a slight breeze. It still hid them from the larger mass of riders but barely obscured them from this man. Had his back not been turned, had he not been distracted by his problems with the horse, they would have been looking right at each other.

"Can you choke him out?" Conor hissed. "You're faster than me."

Conor knew how to put a man's lights out better than most but he could not close that distance as fast as Barb. Before he even finished the sentence, Barb had dropped her pack, handed off her rifle, and was sprinting across the distance. Conor scanned their surroundings, watching for anyone that might see what was happening. By the time he got his eyes back on the man, Barb was clinging to his back, her arms cutting off the flow of blood to his brain. He fought her for a moment, then staggered. A moment later, her hold was all that kept his head from hitting the ground.

Barb took her gear back from Conor. He transferred his own rifle to his off-hand and grabbed the fallen man by the hood of his parka. Using it as a drag handle, he started moving, trying to put some distance between them and the mob. It was exhausting even though the parka reduced the friction. It was like dragging a dead deer from the woods. Each step pumped Conor's quadriceps and jacked up his heart rate.

They made it roughly the distance of a city block before Conor was huffing and puffing.

"There." Barb was pointing at a stone dairy. It was a type of masonry root cellar that people in these old homes would have used to keep milk and vegetables cool before refrigeration came along.

Conor started off in that direction and Barb passed him by. She planted a foot in the door and the screw holding the hasp in place flew in all directions, then popped a white chemlite and tossed it inside. After propping her gun against the wall, she helped Conor drag the man over the concrete threshold. Once inside, she closed the door carefully.

Sagged against the wall, Conor sucked wind.

"Need to work on that cardio, *grandpa*," Barb said.

Conor wiped a sleeve across his forehead, acknowledging with his eyes that she was probably right but unable to get enough air to comment. He nodded toward their prisoner and, again, Barb knew exactly what to do. She rolled the man onto his stomach, quickly secured his wrists and ankles behind his back with a pair of zip ties, then rolled him over onto his back.

She pulled her water bottle from a black Maxpedition pouch on her belt. The bottle had been wrapped several times with duct tape. There was nothing wrong with the bottle, it just provided a convenient place to store a few wraps of the tape. She pulled off a two-foot strip and wrapped it over the man's eyes. It wasn't like he could call the cops if he got out of here alive but their appearances were information that he didn't necessarily need to have.

She was less than delicate with her application of the tape. As she was firmly patting the tape into place, the man began to stir. She looked around at Conor to make sure he was aware of this fact. Conor was still flattened against the wall with a water bottle in his hand but he appeared to have recovered from the exertion of the long drag. Not satisfied that the tape was sufficient, she spotted a moldy burlap sack on a shelf, shook the mouse droppings out of it, and bagged Bryan's head.

"We don't have much time, Dad. They'll probably be looking for him."

Conor replaced the water bottle on his belt. He crouched at the man's side and took the meat of his bicep into his hand, applying as much force as he could. He couldn't see the man's eyes open because of the tape and the hood but the move had the desired effect. The man was awake now.

"What do you want?" the downed man croaked.

"Initially, I was trying to keep you from beating that poor defenseless old man to death. Now I want to know who the hell you are and why you've brought an army into my territory."

The man was silent, a macabre, hooded figure in the pale artificial light of the chemlite. "Your territory?" he finally said. "That's kind of ironic. I was beating that old bastard because I wanted to know where I could find the Mad Mick. Are *you* the Mad Mick?"

"The one and only," Conor replied.

The bound man chuckled. "You're the reason I'm here. You're the reason I've left a trail of dead for over a hundred miles."

Barb and Conor exchanged glances.

"If you were a hundred miles away, why did you bother coming to look for me?" Conor asked. "Why didn't you just stay wherever the hell you were and leave well enough alone?"

"Because I have a score to settle with you," the man hissed. "It took me a while to figure out what happened but I know now you're the reason my men never made it back. You're the reason I didn't have enough labor to keep my farm going. You're the reason I lost it all."

As the awareness hit Barb that this was the man responsible for her kidnapping, she couldn't contain herself. She lashed out and stomped the man on the groin. "And I'll be the fucking reason your nuts will swell up like grapefruits."

The reaction was instant. Bryan grunted and rolled onto his side, contorting from the pain. He retched and threw up. Rather than finding a sense of satisfaction in the man's discomfort, Barb only grew angrier. She lashed out with a foot again, kicking him in the kidneys. Bryan arched backward.

Before Conor could stop her, Barb whipped a wicked blade from her belt and sat on Bryan's chest. She stuck the knife to his throat, smiling when comprehension dawned on him. She yanked the hood off his head, forced a thumb under the tape, and shoved it upward. One wide, terrified eyeball screwed around to find her.

"You see me, asshole?"

Bryan didn't nod, knowing any movement would force the knife into his flesh.

"I was one of those women your people kidnapped. My dad came after me and, together, we killed every damn one of your men. We didn't leave a single of those fuckers alive. And you know what else? We're going to do the same thing to this bunch. The only question is whether you die now or you die with the rest of them."

Conor leaned forward and yanked the tape back down over Bryan's eye. When Barb looked at him quizzically, Conor crooked a finger at her. He made sure the coast was clear and then led her outside, closing the dairy door behind them.

"We kill him now, then we have to track down each and every one of his men individually. I think it would be better to let him go. He'll be so pissed he'll come after us."

"You don't think he'll turn tail and run?"

Conor shook his head. "No way. His vanity won't allow it. He'll come. We'll let him lead his men into a trap and we'll get all of them. No one escapes."

Barb sighed. "It's hard to let him go. We could end this today."

"That just ends it for you," Conor said, "not for everyone. If we want it to end for everyone, we let him go now and take our revenge later. Think strategically."

"Fine. But I'm giving him a parting gift."

Conor looked suspicious. "Nothing that impairs his movement. I don't want him having to go home and heal before he attacks."

Barb didn't reply but pushed open the door. Before Conor could follow her inside, he heard the sound of three solid blows.

"What did you do, girl?" he asked.

"We needed him unconscious anyway," Barb replied. "We couldn't leave him here tied up. He needs to be able to find his way back to his men."

"I might have had more questions for him, Barb."

"You should have spoken up."

"Guess so."

Barb peeled the tape off Bryan's head, grinning when some of his hair came with it. She rolled him over and cut the zip ties loose with her knife. When she sheathed the knife, she drew a permanent marker from a pouch on her gear. Conor insisted markers be part of their load-out so they could leave messages if they needed to. She used her sleeve to roughly scrub off Bryan's forehead and then wrote a message there in big bold letters. Satisfied, she tucked the marker back in her vest.

"What's it say?" Conor asked, unable to make it out in the dim light.

"I wear pink panties."

Conor shook his head. "Now if I had done that, you'd give me a lecture on how immature I was."

"You are immature," Barb replied.

Conor couldn't hold back a smile. "How long do you think he'll wear that before someone tells him?"

Barb slipped into her pack and put a fresh magazine into her rifle. "Depends on how much of an asshole he is, I guess. Let's go."

They dragged the limp body out into the light, then slipped off toward their horses.

30

While Barb and Conor were skulking around Tazewell, chasing down Bryan Padowicz, Ragus and Shannon were riding over the mountain to Johnny Jacks' house to escort Doc Marty home. Ragus considered leaving Shannon at the compound but she wasn't having it. She was up for an adventure and for seeing the country. She had no interest in sitting around the compound staring at goats.

The day was cool but sunny, even making the leafless and barren terrain interesting to look at.

"It reminds me of hiking in Italy," Shannon commented.

Ragus raised an eyebrow at her. "I wouldn't know."

"Never been to Italy?"

"Never been hiking either."

"It's just walking," Shannon replied, "with more of an emphasis on enjoying the scenery."

"I've done plenty of walking," Ragus said. "Usually just to get from one place to another."

Shannon asked lots of questions about the area and Ragus played tour guide, passing on what little information he had about this side of the mountain. He shared place names, family names, and stories about feuds. He talked about farms, coal mines, and mountain people in general.

"It has to be hard growing up here," Shannon said. "All that isolation."

"Not if you don't know any different," Ragus said. "It's just normal."

"But isn't it boring?"

Ragus considered. "Sometimes. Don't you ever get bored?"

"I guess. But I think I'd really be bored here."

"I guess it's what you get used to."

Despite their differences, Ragus found he enjoyed talking to Shannon. It was much more relaxing than talking to Barb. With Barb, he had to be constantly on guard. She was always turning the things you said against you or challenging statements you made. She wasn't a person you could hold a normal conversation with. It was more like verbal jousting. Every exchange was confrontational, like a test. She was as dominant in conversation as she was in combat, and that meant talking with her wasn't much more fun than fighting with her. It also meant he was usually on the losing end.

Talking with Shannon, on the other hand, was enjoyable. It was a type of relaxed, mature conversation he'd never experienced in his life. As much as he enjoyed it, he couldn't help but remember there was a point where it would end. Shannon and the Doc weren't here to stay forever. At some point this would all end and they'd go home. He'd be left with Barb again, no peace and no mercy. It wasn't something he wanted to dwell on.

"You okay?" Shannon asked.

"I'm fine," Ragus said, shooting her a quick, forced smile.

"You just kind of trailed off there," Shannon said. "One minute we were talking and the next you were staring off into the distance."

"No reason. Just thinking."

Shannon stared at him curiously but let it rest. Soon the conversation began to flow again and they lost themselves in it until they arrived at Johnny's driveway.

"We're here," Shannon announced.

Ragus was almost sad the ride was over. It was the best time he could remember having in a long time. Perhaps ever.

Shannon trotted her horse up the driveway with Ragus bringing up the rear. Though he'd made an attempt to maintain some level of awareness as he travelled, it hit him that he'd probably not paid as much attention as he should have. The fact that he'd been lost in the conversation meant he'd surrendered some of his situational awareness. Someone could have been lying in wait for them. They could have walked right into a trap. The risks, the dangers, were everywhere. Conor had drilled that into him. So had Barb. Apparently, it all went out the window with a pretty smile. He would have to do better next time. This was a different world with different rules.

Doc Marty was standing on the porch when they arrived. Shannon jumped from her horse and ran to hug him.

"You're a sight for sore eyes," Doc Marty said. "Did I miss anything?"

"Lots," Shannon said.

Doc glanced at Ragus, looking for further explanation.

"Just another day in doomsday," Ragus said.

Shannon released her dad. "When Conor, Barb, and I got back to the compound, some people had come by and told Ragus there were men headed south. Bad men. Some kind of army, looting and killing. Conor and Barb went out to do some recon. They left us behind to escort you home."

"Conor apparently thinks I've gone soft," Doc Marty said. "I just need to get my gear together and we can get out of here."

"How are the patients?" Shannon asked.

"Jason will be fine. He's still sore but his injuries aren't life-threatening. I think we saved Johnny, but there's always a possibility infection could set in. I left Jason and his wife with instructions for Johnny's care. They know to come get me if his temp goes up and won't respond to medications. He'll be down for a while."

"That's good," Ragus said. "Do you need some help?"

"Probably," Doc Marty said. "I've got crap scattered out all over the place. Some of it I'm going to leave for them to use until Johnny's better but most goes back with us."

Ragus climbed down from his horse and tied the pair of horses to the porch post. "Your horse ready?"

Doc Marty shook his head. "I don't have a clue how to saddle one of those things. I'd probably just get myself hurt."

Ragus laughed. "I'm not the best at it myself but I'll take care of it."

"Thanks," Doc Marty replied. "I'll get Shannon to help me gather my stuff inside."

"Back in a few," Ragus said, heading toward the barn with his rifle slung over his shoulder.

"How was the ride over?" Doc asked Shannon as they headed inside the house.

"It was great, considering the circumstances. It's beautiful here and Ragus told me all about it."

Ragus smiled as he heard their conversation trail off. Maybe she'd enjoyed the ride as much as he had. Maybe she liked him as much as he liked her. *Stop it*, he told himself. *You keep thinking like that and you're just going to get yourself hurt.*

At the barn he slid open the rolling door and looked for the familiar horse, Bacon. Conor thought its coloring reminded him of a strip of bacon and Conor's mind was never more than one degree off the topic of food. Especially bacon, biscuits, and sweet tea, preferably from Bojangles.

"Hey, Bacon," Ragus said.

The horse perked its ears. Ragus found Bacon's tack hanging outside his stall, with the exception of the saddle. It sat on a specially-outfitted sawhorse designed for that purpose, the saddle blanket folded neatly on top of it. Ragus swung open the gate and went inside with the bridle. In short order he had the bridle in place and led the horse out of the stall. He tied it off to a ring mounted on a post in preparation for saddling it.

He threw the blanket across the horse's back, talking to it all the while. He straightened the blanket, then heaved the saddle into place.

He hooked the stirrup over the saddle horn to keep it out of the way while he strapped the saddle on. When it was done, he dropped the stirrup and stroked the horse. He'd never had any experience with horses until recently and the damn things were growing on him. They seemed to have all the best features of a dog, with the added bonus of being able to haul you around from place to place. If the world ever went back to normal, horses would be one of the things he missed.

Ragus untied the reins from the ring on the wall, slung his rifle over his shoulder, and led the horse across the barn. It followed him out the door but began to act funny as he was preparing to roll the heavy door shut.

"What is it, Bacon?" Ragus asked.

The horse jerked its head, flaring its nostrils. Then a distant horse reacted with a whinny, apparently smelling Bacon. Ragus looked toward the house, expecting to find the noise coming from the pair of horses he and Shannon rode over. Instead, he found two horses that appeared to be completely ignoring them. Then there was another whinny, and this time Ragus didn't think it came from the direction of the house. He scanned around him, then found the source.

Riders.

They were at the road and there were a lot of them. Maybe twenty to twenty-five of them, and they weren't passing by. They were spilling through Johnny's gate and headed straight toward the house.

Shit!

Ragus turned the horse and smacked it on the butt to send it back into the barn. He rolled the door back shut, hoping it would keep the animal contained, then took off at a run. Johnny's driveway was long but probably not long enough that he'd beat them. The horses carrying those men were at a trot. Ragus had to do better than that. He pumped his arms and ran for all he was worth. His rifle bounced loose from his shoulder and he held it one-handed, more intent on being fast than being ready to return fire.

His eyes flickered between the approaching men and the house. He was in the open. If they saw him and decided to shoot, he could do nothing but eat dirt and hope their shots went over his head. Halfway there, he heard a loud voice from the driveway. He looked and saw a man pointing at him. They'd seen him.

He ran even harder.

"Shannon! Marty!" he yelled.

They couldn't hear him.

He was closing on the house, but so were the riders. Despite his best effort, they were going to get there around the same time, them hitting the front door just as he hit the back.

"Shannon!"

Then he saw her, coming out the back door with a stack of Marty's gear in her hands.

"*Shannon*!" he yelled.

She looked at him, confused, then saw the look on his face and got scared.

"Riders! Out front!" he gasped.

Shannon dropped the gear and grabbed her rifle from her horse. "Dad!"

Ragus was maybe thirty yards away now and knew the riders had to be arriving at the front. He tried to raise his rifle to a more combat-ready position but his body was jolting too much.

Calm down, he urged himself. *One step at a time.*

At the house, Ragus leapt for the back porch. His momentum, combined with his spent legs, made him misjudge the leap. He didn't get high enough and he wiped out, catching feet on the lip of the porch and hitting hard on his side and his knees. His rifle went skittering across the porch and bounced off the house.

Sensing he had no time to spare, Ragus rolled to his knees and crawled for the door, scooping up his rifle as he moved. He got to his feet and shoved his way through the screen door. He got a hand on the back door, slamming it shut and locking it. He was breathing too hard to form words, so he just stood there sucking air and watching. People were scurrying around—Doc Marty, Shannon, Jason, and Sam. Everyone had rifles and ammo. They were taking firing positions.

"Hello in the house!" came a voice from outside.

Ragus groaned. He wished Conor was here. As much as she frustrated him sometimes, he would even take Barb at this point. She would know what to do. She would find a way out of this. He had no clue what to do. He hoped someone else would start giving orders because that was the only way they were going to survive this.

Fortunately, Doc Marty seemed comfortable jumping into that role. He was telling people where to go and what to do. He had them sliding furniture around to provide some level of ballistic protection if this went hot. He seemed completely at home in the stress of the situation. It made sense; he came from a similar background as Conor. They'd been in the shit before and survived. He'd follow Doc Marty's lead.

"Hellooooooooo!" repeated the voice.

Doc Marty moved to a window and flicked a curtain back, glimpsing outside. "You got a lot of men out there," he said to Jason.

"We can take them," Jason whispered, straining to muster some bravado while still finding it painful to talk.

"First question is do we *need* to take them out? If bullets start flying, everyone loses," Doc said. "Grab a look. See if these folks look familiar to you at all."

Jason edged toward the window and took a glimpse out the forest green curtains. They were made of some obsolete pilled fabric that old women seemed to favor for curtains. Jason squinted and shook his head as if trying to clear it.

"Well?" Doc Marty asked.

"I think I might know them. Maybe," Jason said. "My vision is still a little fuzzy but I think it's the men who bought the horses off us."

"The men Conor assumed had attacked your family?" Doc asked.

Jason nodded. "The very same."

"Let's you and I go talk to them," Doc said. "Shannon and Ragus, if this gets weird and I start firing, you shoot into the group. Look for anyone with a rifle raised in this direction and take them out but do not fire a shot unless I've already done so. Got it?"

Shannon and Ragus, both wide-eyed with fear, could only nod in agreement.

"I'm depending on you," Doc said. "Jason, you ready?"

Jason nodded.

"Then let's do this."

"What if they're here to steal horses?" Jason asked, stopping abruptly.

"We deal with this one problem at a time. And we make sure there actually is a problem before we get all bent out of shape."

Jason nodded again, breathing hard. "Okay."

Doc Marty unlocked the door and went outside first. He had a rifle cradled in his arms. It was a non-threatening position but he could whip it into firing position and on target in the blink of an eye. Jason came out behind him, standing to his right, a step back. He also had a gun in his arms, but appeared considerably more nervous than Doc Marty.

Across from them was the entourage that had purchased horses from his dad a few days earlier, led by the man named Wayne. He man nodded at Jason. "Morning."

Jason nodded and mumbled a greeting.

"Morning. You'll have to excuse Jason, there. His jaw is broken and he can't do much talking," Doc Marty spoke up. "I don't think we've met. Folks call me Doc Marty."

Wayne nodded in Doc's direction. "I'm Wayne. You really a doctor?"

"He's a dentist," Jason said in a low voice, without thinking.

Doc Marty frowned and gave Jason a look. Was he actually having to go down that road again? He'd saved this guy's father and he was still having to prove he knew what he was doing.

Perhaps Jason sensed he'd strayed into sensitive territory because he rushed to cover his tracks. "But he's a good doctor anyway," Jason added, struggling to speak loudly enough that Wayne could hear him. "I didn't mean to make it sound like he wasn't a real doctor or anything. He did a good job of patching me and my dad up."

Doc Marty shook his head. When were people going to get over the whole dentist thing? He really was a doctor. Dentists *were* doctors.

"That's why we're here," Wayne said. "I just wanted to check up on your dad. Make sure you were okay and see if there was anything we could do for you."

That threw Jason off guard a bit. He'd thought the appearance of these men meant trouble, that perhaps when Wayne heard that Johnny and Jason were injured, he got the idea he could come steal the rest of their horses. That didn't appear to be the case. "We appreciate that. It's a hard time."

"I hope you don't mind me asking, but were you able to bury your mother?" Wayne asked. "We'd be glad to pitch in if you need help with a grave. I brought a few men with me."

Jason was again taken aback. "Seriously, I appreciate that. We took care of it already."

Wayne nodded. "Animals need fed? Any fences down? Anything we can do for you at all?"

Doc Marty was watching the whole thing with a skeptical eye. It required diplomacy to question a man's motives without offending him, but sometimes it had to be done. "If you don't mind me saying so, we expected the worst when we saw you guys coming. Visitors don't always bring good news these days. I'm surprised you guys are so motivated to help out someone you barely know."

As tactfully as possible, Doc had laid it out on the table. Although he wasn't demanding an explanation, he'd created a situation where it would be difficult for them not to explain themselves. He looked at them expectantly, letting the silence pressure Wayne.

"We didn't intend to stay over the winter," Wayne said. "We planned to keep moving south until we reached our destination. We had to get out of the north but I don't think we're going to be able to get where we wanted to go. We talked about it and decided to winter here. The way I was raised, that means being a good neighbor to folks. Helping where help is needed."

"I hope you're sincere about that," Doc Marty said, knowing that it rang a little harsh. "It's better to have neighbors you can depend on."

Jason had his hand pressed against his jaw, an indication he'd probably overdone it and couldn't muster a response. Wayne picked up on it.

"We'll be going then. Please let your dad know we're praying for him. If there's anything we can do, just send someone. We're down at the fire hall. That crazy Irish bastard and his daughter know where to find us."

Doc Marty couldn't help but smile. If he had a nickel for every time someone referred to Conor in a similar fashion he'd be a millionaire.

Jason gave a wave and disappeared back in the house. Doc Marty stood on the porch while Wayne turned his group and headed back down the driveway. Only when the whole group had disappeared from sight did Doc Marty head inside.

"You think they're telling the truth?" Ragus asked.

"No way to know yet," Doc Marty replied.

"Maybe they planned on attacking but hesitated when they found us here," Shannon said.

"That's a possibility," Doc Marty said. "Time will tell."

"We still leaving?" Ragus asked.

Doc nodded. "You get my horse and we'll head out."

Ragus took off back to the barn to retrieve the horse a second time.

"Keep a close watch on your dad," Doc Marty told Jason and Sam. "I'll be back day after tomorrow, if not sooner. If for any reason you need me, I'll be at Conor's place."

Jason nodded. Sam ran to the Doc and wrapped her arms around him. "Thank you!"

Doc Marty smiled. "You're more than welcome." He gathered the last of his gear and headed out the door.

31

When Bryan first awoke, face down in the dirt, he thought he was hung over. It was the only reference point he had for feeling so damn bad. He ached from head to toe. Then he recalled how he ended up this way. He had been abducted and beaten by this Mad Mick character and his psychotic daughter. He put his hands beneath him like he was doing a push-up, rolling himself over onto his back. There were so many various pains it was difficult to even isolate what might be injured. His mouth felt dry and...odd. He wondered if perhaps something had been beaten loose. Had they cut his tongue out and it was dried blood he was feeling? He opened his mouth, stuck his fingers inside, and found something thin and soggy. He pinched it between his fingers and pulled it out, raising it to his eyes.

It was a business card.

Bryan shaded his eyes and squinted at it, the late afternoon sun shooting daggers into his throbbing head. The card read *Conor Maguire, Master Machinist and Fabricator, Jewell Ridge, Virginia*. There was no street address and no phone number. That was kind of odd for a business card. Maybe it meant that everyone knew where this Conor Maguire lived. Maybe Jewell Ridge was so small that it wasn't difficult to locate his shop. Either way, Bryan now had a name and a location for the man who had become the bane of his existence.

Bryan flipped the card over to make sure there was no further information on the back. What he found was a message scrawled in permanent marker: *Turn around and go back if you know what's good for you.*

Bryan frowned and tasted his now empty mouth. Perhaps whatever ink was in that permanent marker was responsible for the weird chemical taste and numbness in his mouth. How absurd it would be to survive this far into the apocalypse but perish from permanent marker poisoning.

He sat up and took stock of himself. His neck and face were sore and he felt like he had some bruises from rough treatment. Nothing permanent, if the marker ink didn't kill him. He got to his feet and brushed off. He shaded his eyes and looked around, searching for his men. He didn't see anyone but he could hear yelling in the distance.

It was his name being called. His men were looking for him.

Bryan tucked the business card into a shirt pocket and staggered off in the direction of the yelling. He didn't recognize where he was but it turned out that his attackers had not dragged him very far. In minutes he could see the church again and his men combing the area for any sign of him. He threw up a hand and called to them. His voice came out weaker than normal, a coarse croak that made him clear his throat and try again

On his second attempt they heard him. The men called to each other and came running in his direction.

"You okay?" Zach asked when he reached his side.

Bryan nodded, trying to pull himself together and look like a leader despite what had happened to him. "How long have I been gone?"

Zach looked to the other men for confirmation then back to Bryan. "Twenty, twenty-five minutes tops."

Bryan furrowed his brow. "Really?" It seemed longer. Like hours or even a day later.

Zach nodded. "What happened?"

"If he was being truthful, I ran into the Mad Mick."

The growing crowd of men murmured and looked at each other. This was unexpected. Bryan had met the Mad Mick and lived to tell about it?

“My memory is a little hazy. They roughed me up pretty bad,” Bryan said. “I remember trying to mount my horse in the smoke and the chaos and I heard something behind me. I spun around and found two attackers. Not wanting to give them a chance to strike first, I pounced on them. I gave them a pretty good scrapping but in the end there were two of them and they overpowered me. They tied me up and dragged me off for a brutal interrogation. I was lucky to escape with my life. All I remember after that is waking up in the grass."

As he spoke, Bryan looked in the faces of the men surrounding him. They were engaged in his story but also bore strange looks on their faces. He caught some pointing at his face, who dropped their hands when his eyes met theirs.

Bryan waved Michael over to him with a crooked finger. Although Michael was not one of his closest associates, he was from the original Douthat Farms group, and the man had always been straight with him.

“What the fuck is going on?” he asked Michael with a low voice.

Michael hunched his shoulders. “I’m not sure what you’re talking about.”

“The men are not meeting my eyes. They’re looking at me funny. Am I bleeding?”

Michael looked terrified.

“Now you’re doing it too.”

Michael stuttered, trying to find a response but Bryan shoved him back into the crowd of men. “Zach!”

Zach was at the front of the crowed and stepped closer.

“What the hell is going on that everyone is looking at me like I’m biting the heads off chickens? Is there something wrong with me? Somebody better be telling me something.”

Zach didn’t react.

“Damnit, I’ll show him,” Carrie said, stepping out of the crowd. She dropped her daypack off her shoulder, fished out a hand mirror about the size of a pack of cigarettes, and held it up to Bryan’s face.

“What am I supposed to do with that?” he asked.

“Your face,” Carrie said.

Bryan leaned forward, his eyes going from Carrie’s down to the mirror. There was utter silence in the crowd. Bryan saw lettering on his forehead.

I wear pink panties.

He rubbed his sleeve furiously against his forehead. When he stopped, the letters were still there. This would take more than elbow grease. Then he noticed everyone watching him.

“Get the hell out of here!” he screamed, his eyes bulging and his face blushing as red as a tomato.

Carrie and Zach remained, Carrie still holding the mirror. "So the Mad Mick lives here?" Carrie asked.

"Some place called Jewell Ridge,” Bryan said, scrubbing at his forehead. “We need to find out where that is."

"How can you be so sure that’s where he lives?" Carrie asked.

Bryan reached into his pocket and withdrew the sodden business card. He handed it over to Zach, who shook it once or twice carefully reading it. He passed it to Carrie.

"He left a calling card? That's one cocky bastard,” Zach said.

"Or maybe it’s just one dumb bastard," Carrie remarked.

"I need a drink of water. See if there’s any alcohol wipes in a first aid kit somewhere. Maybe that will take off this marker," Bryan said. "You guys bang on some doors and see if you can find out where Jewell Ridge is."

Carrie gave Bryan a water bottle and offered him the mirror. Bryan took it, then found a bench on the sidewalk and planted himself there. By the time he'd finished the bottle, Zach was back at his side with the information he’d requested.

"Take Route 460 to a place called Claypool Hill. When you pass the McDonald's, you turn right and head in that direction. First town we come to, we stop and ask for further directions. Nobody could tell us the rest of the directions."

"Did you demonstrate our thanks?"

Zach nodded. "Of course. We looted their house but we left them alive."

"Good enough. Like proper gentlemen. Now let's get out of this godforsaken town and find a place to camp for the night."

"Already on that," Zach said. "The county fairground is a couple miles away. It's right beside the highway. We can camp there for the night and we'll be ready to go in the morning."

"Come across anything appetizing for dinner?" Bryan asked. "My ordeal has left me famished."

"Six chickens and a pig," Carrie said. "We found them while we were looking for you. They're already lashed to a horse."

"Where's my horse?" Bryan asked.

"Tied up to a parking meter on Main Street," Zach said.

Bryan stood, wavered unsteadily, and hands shot out to right him. "I think I need to get settled and take it easy for the evening. I'm feeling a little unsteady."

"Nice plate of pork chops and ribs might take care of that," Carrie said. "Let's get you to that horse."

Bryan raised his bangs and leaned toward Carrie and Zach. "Did I get it all? Is it gone?"

"You can't even tell it was there," Zach said.

Bryan handed the mirror back to Carrie and walked off.

Carrie shot Zach a look. "Liar."

32

When the chain-link gate at Conor's compound rolled open, Ragus shot awake and looked at his watch. It was a little after 4:30 AM. He'd spent the night by the stove in Conor's living room, too anxious to lay down in his bed. Shannon and Doc Marty had hung around in the living room with him until nearly midnight, then headed off to their own quarters.

Ragus took his rifle from its hook, unbolted the door, and stepped out onto the porch, illuminating the area with a tactical spotlight to make certain of who was coming in the gate. He spotted Barb and Conor leading their horses across the compound. Both man and beast looked exhausted.

"Get that fecking light out of my face before I shove it down your pie-hole," Barb complained.

"What did you find out?" Ragus asked, leaving the spotlight on, but averting it from Barb and Conor.

"Give me a second to attend to these horses. We pushed them hard. Then we can talk about what we found."

The noise had reached the guest quarters and woke Shannon and Doc Marty. They came out dressed and wearing headlamps. "Anything we can do, Conor?" Doc Marty asked.

"Negative on that. Give me a second to help Barb with these horses and I'll be right in."

Barb waved him off. "I've got the horses, Dad. You better go in and tell them the scoop before they all wet their pants."

Ragus frowned at the condescending smugness. It was the thing that he liked least about Barb. On the other hand, the way she talked and acted was such an integral part of Barb that he couldn't imagine ever changing her. It only reaffirmed to him that his previous obsession with her had simply been a phase. Perhaps it was vulnerability motivated by his loss and desperation, yet after having met someone like Shannon, he was more certain than ever that the abrasive Barb was not what he wanted in a woman. Shannon made him feel capable, funny, and worthwhile. Barb made him feel like a bumbling nobody, and who wanted to feel like that?

Conor grabbed his pack from his horse so Barb wouldn't have to carry all the gear when she came inside. He trudged to his quarters, a weary and exhausted warrior. He handed his pack off to Ragus so he could clear his weapons before going inside. Ragus admired the proficiency with which he did so. It was smooth, polished, and practiced. Ragus could only hope that one day he could handle weapons with the same ease. It was a skill he wanted to have.

Ragus held the door open and Conor went to stow his gear, hanging his backpack in its proper place in the ready room. After some rest, Conor would go through it to replace any gear expended or damaged on the mission. The weapon he had taken was wiped down and stowed in its space on the rack. The battle belt was hung on its own hook. After his nap, when he restocked his pack, he would check the battle belt with the same thoroughness.

Everything had to be in its proper place. If they were attacked in the middle of the night or if some other situation took place that required grabbing gear in a hurry, Conor wanted to be able to lay a hand on things in total darkness. He never wanted to have to search for critical gear. It should always be in the same place and ready to go when he picked it up. That was how he lived. That was how he survived.

"I've got to fix me a bite to eat," Conor said. "I can't think over top of this empty stomach. Every time I say something I hear an echo in that void that used to be me belly."

"I got that," Shannon said. "We had some leftovers. I'll throw something together for you. You sit down."

Conor barely had the energy to muster an entertaining comment. He nodded appreciably in her direction. "Thank you." He sagged to the couch, exhausted.

"I'm assuming you rode all night?" Doc Marty asked.

Conor gave a nod that widened into a yawn. "We don't have a lot of time. There really is an army coming. I'd say we have a day or two at the most."

"Really?" Ragus asked. "An army?"

"An avenging army would be more accurate. It turns out those guys that stole Barb and the other women had a boss. He's pissed off because we killed all those men of his. I spoke to him in person and I don't think he's going to let bygones be bygones."

"You spoke to him?" Doc Marty asked.

Conor nodded, too tired to embellish the gesture with unnecessary words.

"How did you get him to sit down and talk?" Ragus asked. "How exactly did that come about?"

Doc Marty gave a knowing laugh. "Under duress, I would assume."

"Exactly. We choked him out and zip tied him," Conor said.

Ragus had envisioned a meeting arranged in the middle of the street, like gunfighters in a western, or the two of them meeting face to face in the middle of a battlefield. The last thing he'd imagined was a kidnapping and interrogation. It showed him that he still had a lot to learn about the family sheltering him.

"How many men?" Doc Marty asked, jumping straight into strategy.

"They were scattered all over the damn place and constantly on the move. It was hard to get an accurate count but I think somewhere in the neighborhood of eighty to one hundred would be a fair assumption."

"Eighty to a hundred armed men!" Ragus said, suddenly less confident about their abilities.

"That's a handful of men, even if they're untrained," Doc Marty said.

"Agreed," Conor said. "I've got to catch some shut eye before I fall ass over teakettle. In the morning we need to beef up our numbers pronto."

"We've been handing out flyers. You think that's enough?" Ragus asked. "You think people are going to be ready to join us? It's one thing to agree when you're safe but it's an entirely different thing to volunteer when you know there will be gunfire."

"Anyone who lives in this area should have a vested interest in us prevailing," said Conor. "If we lose, they lose. They could all end up slaves."

"And we couldn't?" Shannon asked, setting a plate with a flat-bread sandwich next to Conor. "I made one for Barb too."

"Thank you," Conor said. "I don't think we'll end up slaves. I'll fight to the death to make sure that doesn't happen."

"Those guys that you thought had attacked Johnny Jacks' family came to check on him while I was there," Doc Marty said. "There were nearly two dozen of them. They said if there was anything they could do to let them know. They decided to stay on through the winter and they wanted to be good neighbors. Maybe this is when you cash in that chip."

"There's more of them back at their camp. A lot of women and kids. I'm sure they don't want them ending up in the wrong hands." Conor yawned again and rubbed his eyes. "I need to get some rest. Don't know when the next opportunity will be."

"We've all slept," Doc Marty said. "Is there anything we can do while you're out?"

Conor thought, his brain struggling to process clearly through exhausted pathways. "Maybe one of you could go alert those folks you were just talking about. They're staying in the firehouse, like you were heading to West Virginia from Johnny Jacks' house. Might be a good idea to stop by Johnny's house, too, and let them know the score."

"I can do that," Ragus said.

"You sure you're up for that, lad?" Conor asked. "You'll need to keep your wits about you. Head on a swivel and all that."

"I got it," Ragus said confidently.

"The lad seems a little green, Conor," Doc Marty said. "You sure he can do this?"

Conor regarded his young friend. "I'm sure I need to let him try."

"Good enough," Doc Marty said. "Shannon and I will work on squaring away our gear. We still have some goodies packed up that may come in handy."

Conor finished his sandwich and pressed up off the couch. "I'm going to bed. Ragus, be careful. Safety first."

"Roger that," Ragus said, hoping it made him sound more skilled and proficient than he actually felt.

About that time, Barb shoved her way through the door, her arms laden with gear. She dropped it by the door with a heavy thud. "As Dad is fond of saying, I'm so hungry I could eat the southbound end of a northbound mule."

"I made you a sandwich if you want it," Shannon offered.

Barb pursed her lips, staring at the other girl. "You spit in it?"

"No! Of course not."

"Sprinkle poison on it?"

"You're being ridiculous," Shannon said, offended. "I wouldn't do anything like that."

Barb reached out and snatched the plate from Shannon's hands. "Then I'll eat it. Just had to ask." She gave the exasperated Shannon a wicked smile.

"She'll grow on you," Ragus said. "Or not."

Barb paused in her chewing. "I can kick your ass, Ragus, and not even drop this sandwich."

"Please, Barb, this isn't the time," Ragus said. "I need to get out of here. I'll see you guys later." He headed down the hall, to his room, to grab a few pieces of gear for his Go Bag.

"Where's he going?" Barb asked.

Neither Shannon nor Doc Marty responded to her.

"Excuse me?" Barb growled. "I'm talking and somebody should be answering."

"He's going to see if he can recruit some men to come help in the fight. Your dad asked him to do it," Shannon said, her tone implying that she wasn't certain whether it was even any of Barb's business or not.

Barb's eyes grew wide. "By himself? He'll get killed. Or lost. Or some shit like that."

"Your dad seemed confident he could do it," Doc Marty said.

"Yeah, well, Dad's cornbread isn't done in the middle. He's hardly a sound decision maker in the best of times and he's sleep-deprived right now."

"Your dad is one of the best in this business of ours," Doc Marty fired back. "The fact that he's still alive when so many men want him dead is a testament to something."

"I'm not attacking my dad," Barb said slowly, venom oozing from each word. "You can be certain he has no bigger protector in this world than I. In fact, when he expressed concern about your arrival here I was ready to put a bullet in your head and claim it happened in transit. I don't know what happened between you and him in Helsinki, but when I find out, you better hope it's not something that makes me lose my shit. When that happens, things get ugly."

"Out of respect for your father, I'm ending this conversation," Doc Marty said. "I apologize if I've angered his *child*."

The way he emphasized child hit Barb like a splash of acid. She wanted nothing more than to jump on the man and kill him with her bare hands. The only thing that stopped her was, without Conor to break it up, this would be a fight to the death. Shannon would likely try to intervene and she'd have to kill her too. She knew how her father would feel about that. He would disapprove. That, and only that, saved two lives.

Ragus entered the room wearing his patrol clothing, his plate carrier, and his Go Bag. Walking into the room, the tension was immediately noticeable, like stepping into the smell of burnt popcorn. He paused halfway to the door. "What did I miss?"

Shannon and Doc Marty looked at Barb, which told Ragus all he needed to know. Barb ignored all of them, her attention focused on Ragus.

"I'm going with you," she said.

"You need sleep in case this turns into a battle."

"I'll be fine," she said. "You, on the other hand, will not be."

Ragus opened the door and shot Barb a last look. "You're not invited. You're not welcome this time." He eased on out, banging his rifle and pack on the doorframe as he squeezed through.

Barb stared at the door, her face turning a brilliant red as if it had been intentionally slammed in her face. She coolly tossed her half-eaten sandwich onto the coffee table. "I'm about done being disrespected in my own home." She turned on her heels, went to her bedroom, and slammed the door behind her.

Shannon looked nervously at her father.

He shrugged as if it were routine. "Lots of big personalities in this line of work. Lots of attitudes. You get used to it."

She looked doubtfully toward Barb's room. She wasn't sure if she would ever get used to it. She wasn't even sure she wanted to.

33

Ragus wasn't at his most comfortable on the back of a horse but he was getting better with every ride. He rode the horse he was most experienced with and pushed it to the limits of his abilities. The ride down the back side of the mountain was a long series of switchbacks. Miles and miles of them. In some places, where the mountain wasn't nearly vertical, there were trails connecting the switchbacks made by game, logging roads, or off road vehicles. The trails, when passable, allowed him to take a more direct route down the mountain. It seemed to him that this route ended up cutting the distance in half.

Once at the bottom of the mountain he pushed his horse to a gallop, staying on the grassy shoulder where the horse felt more confident. He rode straight for Johnny Jacks' house, wanting to give his horse the opportunity to drink and rest for a moment.

He rode up the driveway, waving his hat in his hand, and announcing himself. Jason came outside and waved back to him. He pushed the horse back to a gallop and closed the distance between him and the house.

"What's up?" Jason called. "I wasn't expecting anyone until Doc Marty came back to check on Dad."

"There's trouble," Ragus said. "An army headed this way."

"*The* army?" Jason asked.

Ragus shook his head. "An army of bad men. Let me get this horse a drink and I'll tell you about it." They led the horse around the corner of the house and tied it off near a trough filled by the gutters.

They went around to the front of the house and sat on the porch while Ragus filled Jason in on the entire story. Jason didn't interrupt, stoically absorbing the information until Ragus reached the end.

"I'll help," Jason said.

"I don't think that's why I came over here," Ragus said. "I think they expected you to stay with your family. They wanted me to recruit those men who offered to help your dad."

"Your family has gone out of their way to help me," Jason said. "I believe in returning favors. Sam can stay with Dad. She's a good shot and more than capable of keeping an eye on things."

"They'll appreciate that. Every armed man improves the odds."

"How about I go inside and break this to Sam? You stay out here and give me a minute. I'll need to get some gear together. Then I'll go with you to the fire hall. Those guys have never seen you before. They might be more receptive to a familiar face."

"Okay."

"There's a curry comb right there," Jason said, pointing it out. "You take care of your horse and I'll be outside by the time you're done."

~

TRUE TO HIS WORD, Jason was back out by the time Ragus was finishing up with a much happier horse. He had a pack slung across his back, a handgun holstered on his belt, and a rifle cradled in his arms.

"Let's go saddle a horse," Jason said.

They headed around to the barn and Jason saddled his own mount with an efficiency of movement that Ragus took note of. It was like Conor with his weapons. There were so many things he wanted to get better at. Minutes after reaching the barn, they were galloping back down the driveway.

"How did Sam take it?"

"She's sad. Worried. But she understands. She knows it's what has to be done."

Ragus nodded. There were a lot of things in the world he didn't understand the nuances of. Most things, in fact. With great certainty, he knew that the intricacies of how husbands and wives negotiated such matters were light years beyond his comprehension. He'd never seen such things modeled in his own life having spent most of his childhood in a single-parent home.

"I appreciate you coming, Jason." It was all Ragus knew to say.

They rode hard. Ragus let Jason pull ahead. He was a more experienced horseman and understood better which lines were more easily travelled by horse. With Ragus, it was a combination of guesswork and dumb luck. Jason was a lifelong horseman and his expertise allowed them to ride faster. He was always on the lookout for hazards that Ragus simply didn't have the experience to recognize.

When they closed on the fire hall, Jason extended an arm to his side, a gesture similar to the hand signals used by bicyclists. They slowed their horses to a walk.

"The fire hall is just ahead," Jason said. "Probably best we don't ride up on it like it's a raid. Too many nervous people with guns. I don't want to get killed before the fight even starts."

Ragus fell in step behind Jason. They eased up to the fire hall and stopped in front of it, staying on the road.

"Helloooooo," Jason called. When there was no answer, he called again. "Hellloooooooooo!"

"We heard you," came a voice from behind the riders.

Ragus spun in his saddle, startled by the sudden voice.

"Easy there," the man said. "No fast movements."

"You with Wayne in the fire hall?" Jason asked.

The man had a thick red beard and wore a grubby wool hunting jacket. "How do you know Wayne?"

"Some of your men were at my house. Yesterday maybe? Hard to keep track of days anymore. Wayne said if I ever need anything to just ask. I'm here to ask."

The man lowered his gun, withdrawing a family band radio from his pocket. "Wayne?"

It took a moment for a response to crackle from the radio. "*Yeah*?"

"I got a couple of riders out here. Johnny Jacks' son is one of them. They want to talk to you."

"*I'll be right out*."

The bearded guy kept his distance, remaining vigilant but not threatening. In a few minutes, Wayne came out the front door of the fire hall with two other men. He waved Ragus and Jason over.

"What brings you to our neighborhood?" Wayne asked, his manner congenial.

"Trouble," Jason said. "You can either take this as a warning or a recruitment visit."

The smile eroded from Wayne's face. "That sounds serious."

"There were some men came through here a few weeks ago," Ragus said. "They kidnapped a lot of women and killed several people. They took my friend Conor's daughter and we went after them. He caught them north of here and they got the short end of the stick."

"So now they've come back with more men?" Wayne asked.

Ragus shook his head. "Ain't none of those men coming back. He killed every one of them."

Wayne raised an eyebrow at that. "How many men are you talking about?"

"The kidnappers?"

"Yeah."

"Maybe two dozen."

"And Conor, the one they call the Mad Mick, killed them all?"

"Well, his daughter helped."

Addressing one of this companions, Wayne said, "I knew there was something about that guy."

"The point is that those men Conor killed had a boss," Jason said.

"Their boss is headed in this direction. They're estimating as many as a hundred men."

"Shit!" Wayne said.

"We honestly don't know how far they're coming," Ragus said. "We know they're determined to take Conor out. They want his head on a stick."

Wayne scratched his head, then asked, "How can we help?"

"You told me if I needed any help to let you know," Jason said.

Wayne nodded. "I did."

"I came to see if you'd be interested in joining the fight. Conor's a dangerous man but the odds are against us. We need all the men we can get."

Wayne didn't respond, taking some time to roll the idea around in his head.

"You aren't obligated," Ragus said. "We'll understand if you say no."

"I ain't said no yet," Wayne said.

"I will say that they killed dozens of men on their way down here. The women they took were meant to be used for slave labor on their farm," Ragus told him. "That's what the men told them. If they do beat us and they come for you, you all better pack your shit and run. There won't be any peace with them around. Your families will never be safe."

"That's a lot to think about," Wayne said. "How long do we have?"

"Best guess is tomorrow or the next day," Ragus said.

"Can I have time to talk to my people?"

"Absolutely," Jason said. "We're going to head back. If you want to help, bring your men over the mountain tomorrow. You'll see an office on the top of the ridge surrounded by fence. We'll leave instructions on the fence as to where to find us."

"If you come, come ready to fight," Ragus said. "Guns, ammo, food, knives, flashlights, hunting clothes, whatever you got."

"Will do. Either way, I wish you boys luck." Wayne strode forward and shook their hands.

Jason and Ragus turned their horses and sped away. It was

already midday and they had a mountain to cross. By the time they got there, it was likely Conor would be up and pulling together a plan. They anticipated a long night that might stretch into several long days. Whatever battle they were preparing to engage in, it had already begun.

34

That same evening, Bryan's army passed the McDonald's at Claypool Hill and turned onto Route 460 toward Richlands, Virginia. The McDonald's was looted and partially burned, empty Happy Meal boxes and French fry containers strewn around the parking lot. Bryan couldn't imagine what people expected to find beyond sugar packets and straws. The food would have been gone quickly and what wasn't eaten would have spoiled without electricity.

They passed a home improvement store, the parking lot also littered with trash, but with smoke curling from an improvised stovepipe. Clearly there were people there, although Bryan didn't feel like engaging them at the moment. Any force big enough to keep that store might be a pain in the ass to deal with and he couldn't afford to lose any men the moment. They had enough food from their efforts in Tazewell to get them through the night and morning. The only thing they needed at the moment was information. Specifically, how to find the residence of one Conor Maguire, aka The Mad Mick, reputed to live in some area called Jewell Ridge.

They got off the first exit and began looking for someone that might be able to provide them that information. They wanted easy pickings, someone vulnerable and easily intimidated. That someone turned out to be an old man with a shopping cart, scouring through refuse piles for anything that met the esoteric threshold at which he assigned value. The man had a pronounced limp and the cart appeared to serve both as an aide in walking and as a container for loot.

The sound of the many horseshoes clattering off the pavement reached the man long before the riders were close to him. The town wasn't big. Both a river and a railroad ran through it. Squat brick buildings lined the main street. The sound of hooves echoed off a post office, a beauty salon, a school, and a funeral home. The old man stopped what he was doing and watched their approach, squinting through his glasses. When the lead rider, Bryan, was closer, the old man threw up a hand in a friendly greeting.

"Hallloooo," he called, a long drawn-out greeting from a man obviously proficient and practiced at greeting folks.

Bryan tipped his hat to him. "Good afternoon, kind sir."

The old man smiled. "Kind sir? I've been called many, many things in my life but never that."

Bryan quickly became aggravated when dealing with "local color," those folks with expansive personalities and a humorous saying to match every situation. This was one of those folks, the guy that everyone was delighted to run into in the post office, the grocery store, or the doctor's office because he had gossip or a funny story to share.

The annoyance Bryan already felt with the man, even so early in the conversation, made him want to pull his gun and rid the world of some "local color" but that would not further his mission. This was exactly the kind of man he needed to talk to. Someone who had been around forever. Someone who knew the name of every hill, holler, and podunk community.

"What's your name, old timer?"

"Jessie," the old man replied, his possum grin pasted in place.

"How long have you lived around these parts?" Bryan asked.

"All my life."

Bryan sighed. "How long has that been?"

"Well…all my life." The man was still grinning, amused with himself.

Bryan's mouth stretched tight, struggling to remain patient. "Could you provide that figure as a numerical value? Use of your fingers and toes to assist you in calculating this is acceptable."

The remark stung Jessie, who's smiled faded, darkening his face. "I'm not sure I like you."

Bryan's first thought was to tell the man how much he didn't like him either, and to explain it great detail. He would then demonstrate his dislike in a physical manner, promptly killing old Jessie and tossing his body in the rusty shopping cart. Yet he needed to refrain. Jessie was the bird in the hand. If Jessie could provide the information he needed, it would be better to get it from him than have to find someone else.

"I apologize," Bryan said, forcing himself to utter the words he so disliked using. "I've had a rough couple of weeks. I'm very stressed and am subject to a lot of responsibility. People are depending on me. I failed some of those people and don't want to fail any more of them. You can understand that, right? With the mantle of leadership comes a great burden."

"Wouldn't know nothing about leadership, mantles, or any of that. Burdens I know a fair bit about."

"Let's try again," Bryan said. "The reason I was asking you how long you lived her is that I'm trying to locate a place called Jewell Ridge. Do you know where I might find it?"

"Of course I know Jewell Ridge. I've lived here all my life."

"How do I find it?"

"You don't," Jessie said. "You don't want to go there."

Bryan forced a smile so hard the tiny muscles within his cheeks trembled with the effort. "If I didn't want to go there, I wouldn't be asking."

Jessie shuddered, as if even hearing the name gave him a chill. "Still, you don't want to go there."

"How about you let me decide where I want to go?" Bryan asked. There was a dangerous undercurrent to his voice that would have scared anyone who knew him. It was the tone that often served as a prelude to violent deeds. It was the timbre of voice that was often the last thing men heard before their blood spilled onto the ground.

"Mister, if I let you go up there and something happens to you, it's just the same as if I killed you myself. You think I want that hanging over my head for the rest of my life?"

"Jessie, if you *don't* tell me where Jewell Ridge is, you will be able to count the number of minutes remaining in your life on a single hand. Do you understand what I'm saying?"

Jessie frowned. "Yeah, I get it but I'm an old man and you ain't the boss of me. I don't care if you kill me or not. I'm right with my maker and my plot is paid for. If I had my burial suit on I'd be ready to go this second."

This was exactly what Bryan was afraid of. Escalate the situation too fast with old people and they didn't care if you killed them or not. They got all stubborn and shut down on you.

With great effort, Bryan said, "How about we back this up a little bit?"

"Like rewinding on the VCR?" Jessie asked.

"Exactly."

"Okay."

"What would it take for you to tell me where to find Jewell Ridge?"

Jessie scratched his chin in thought. "Got any Little Debbie cakes?"

Bryan stared at the old man. "Little Debbie cakes?"

Jessie grinned. "Any kind, but Oatmeal Crème Pies and Fudge Rounds are my favorites."

Unable to muster an argument, mentally weary, Bryan spun his horse to face his army. "Does anyone have any Little Debbie cakes?"

Not a hand rose, nor did anyone call out.

"If I find that any of you have one and are holding out on me, I will have you killed in a slow and degrading manner!"

A man in the back by the name of Groves rode forward. He was reluctant and moved slowly, begrudgingly. It made Bryan wonder.

He'd never had one of these Little Debbie cakes before, but what kind of dark enchantment did they cast over a man that this entire negotiation hinged on one man's desire for of these precious cakes and another's unwillingness to give one up?

Groves handed over two Oatmeal Crème Pies without meeting Bryan's eye. Bryan was certain he saw a tear running down the man's cheek. He took the two snack cakes and turned back to Jessie. He found the man to be almost at his side, practically salivating. Bryan extended his arm and Jessie reached for the cakes.

Bryan snatched them back. "That little piece of information first."

Jessie's eyes were glazed with lust for the tiny cakes. "Get back on the highway. Go down another exit. Turn right and follow the signs."

Bryan handed the cakes down and the old man grabbed them from him. He tucked one in a jacket pocket and tore into the other, shoving it in his mouth with greedy bites. Bryan was certain that if he looked back at his riders he would find Groves sobbing.

Zach rode up alongside Bryan. "You want me to kill him?"

"No. He's been enough bother already. Let's be gone and be done with him." Before he rode off, something occurred to him and he turned back to Jessie, now licking the wrapper of the snack cake he'd devoured. "What's so dangerous about Jewell Ridge?"

"Why, the Mad Mick, of course," Jessie said. "He looks after folks in these parts and he'll not take to you riding up there on his mountain with this mess of people."

Bryan swept an arm back toward his army. "You don't think we can take him?"

Jessie began to cackle like a madman. His cackle rose to wild laughter. He threw the dripping wrapper into his shopping cart and returned to pushing it down the street, his laughter turning into a chorus as it echoed around them.

For the first time, Bryan began to feel a little uneasy.

35

Conor got about four hours of sleep. When consciousness first tugged at him, there was no rolling over and ignoring it. He sprang from the bed fully-dressed, his mind already racing. There was a lot to do and he had no idea how long they had to perform all the tasks that needed to be done.

He slipped on his boots and went into the living room. A burst of warmth from the woodstove hit him in the face. Barb was already up, her personal weapons laid out in front of her. She was double-checking everything. There were times you wanted to be ready for anything because there was a chance things might get serious, but this was beyond that. This was the day when you *knew* shit was going to get serious. People were going to get killed. Little details like weapons and gear maintenance went a long way toward making sure you weren't one of the poor suckers taking a bullet.

"Ragus back yet?" Conor asked.

"Ragus who?" Barb replied without even looking up from the rifle she was attending to. She was still pissed over the way he'd treated her earlier.

"I don't have time for your tantrums today, Barb. Having to ask you twice wastes time we might need later. You can get your head in the game or go to your room and sulk like a spoiled child until this thing is over with. I need to be able to depend on you. Can I or can I not?"

Barb slammed the bolt release on an M4 and the bolt shot home with a solid *thunk*. "You can." She was gritting her teeth, choking down the fusillade of smartass comments she wanted to unleash.

"That goes for dealing with everyone else too, Barb. Be professional or stay home."

"I got it the first time," she hissed. "Lecture over."

"I decide when the lecture is over!" Conor bellowed, raising his voice to his daughter, something he rarely did. "You go into the shit with this attitude and it may blind you to something that gets you killed. I'm not joking. Clear your head or stay home."

Barb looked up at her dad and met his eye. "I got it, Dad. Seriously."

"Good. We'll speak no more of it then."

"Ragus isn't back yet. Doc Marty and Shannon are going through their own gear. They've apparently got a whole lot more gear in that shipping container than we've seen so far."

"Doc always has tricks up his sleeve," Conor said. "It's the nature of the job." He went into the kitchen and poured a cup of cold coffee, sucking it down with a grimace.

"You could have heated that, you know."

"I know," Conor said, rinsing the mug and placing it back on the countertop. "I need the caffeine, not the comfort." He returned to the living room.

"So what's the plan?"

"I'm going to split us into two teams. You and Shannon will work together. Doc and I together. Can you deal with that?"

"No issues," Barb replied.

"Good. I want you on horseback with your full load-out and all the ammo you can carry while still moving effectively. No ridiculous loads that may slow your horse. Same for Shannon. Make sure all the armor is in your plate carrier—front, back, and sides. No shortcuts to save weight. You'll take radios. They may not be able to reach back to here but hopefully as we all get closer to each other they'll allow us to coordinate operations."

"What about Ragus? What if he's not back when we leave?"

"We lock this place up like Fort Knox and leave him a note. He has a key to get any gear he didn't take with him. We'll leave him a radio and he can alert us when he reaches the area of operations."

"What's our mission?"

"The overall mission is to decimate this army. You and Shannon will alert the neighbors as you head off the ridge. Be careful— folks are jumpy. You two may seem less threatening than me and Doc."

Barb started to make some remark about her dad's less than cuddly nature but bit her tongue. It wasn't the time.

"Tell everyone that we need to stop this army before it gets here. Make sure they know it's the kidnappers that took you and the other women. Tell them to gather at the base of the ridge. They should wear their hunting camo, and come armed and ready to fight."

"What do Shannon and I do once we've made it down the mountain?"

"I want you to keep a low profile but try to find the enemy and keep them under surveillance. Once I'm within radio range, part of your job is to keep us informed of their movements."

"So I'm basically sitting this one out on the sidelines? You think you can't trust me anymore so you're taking me out of the fight?"

Conor shook his head. "Not at all. If you think it's safe, you can leave Shannon and join us. Communicate your moves first. If bullets are flying we need to know where people are. This is not the time to show up unannounced."

"Got it. When do we go?"

"I'll talk to Doc and Shannon. Be ready to go within an hour. There's enough daylight that you should be able to make your way down the mountain and get in position tonight. Plan on spending the night, so pack accordingly. Sleeping gear, tarp, clothing for the weather, and rations."

Barb wasted no time. She got to her feet, gathered her pile of gear, and headed to her bedroom. Conor stepped outside into a breezy afternoon. The temperature was probably in the mid-forties with the wind chill knocking a little off that. It would be a cooler night. Perhaps down into the twenties with frost. A cold night for anyone out camping without a fire but it couldn't be helped.

He found Shannon and Doc Marty standing outside the conex box surrounded by a wall of gear. "Building a fort?"

"Just making sure I've got all the goodies where I can get to them. We packed in kind of hurry. Ricardo's men were also shoving things in here that we didn't have the opportunity to discuss. Things he thought we might need. I've found several decent surprises."

"Like what?"

Shannon pointed to a stack of hard plastic Pelican cases. Conor picked up one around the size of a briefcase but a little thicker. He flipped the latches, opened the lid, and found thirty-two grenades nestled in the black foam lining.

"Jeez, that's a pleasant surprise."

"There's several," Doc Marty said. "Smokes, frags, concussion, and CS riot control grenades."

Conor laughed. "Nice."

"There's more but I haven't had time to check through it all."

"I need to run you guys through the plan and make sure you're cool with it. Time is short. We need to get people into position."

Conor ran through the details, as he'd done with Barb. Conor could tell that Doc Marty was apprehensive about his daughter having any role in a potential engagement.

"I think it's safer to have her out there working with us than to leave her behind by herself. We can't even maintain radio contact with the compound while we're in the valley," Conor said. "We put her in an observation post above the fray and that's probably the safest place to be."

"You sure putting me somewhere alone with Barb is the safest place to be?" Shannon asked, seeming wholly unconvinced. "I'm not sure the enemy I need to worry about is the one I'll be observing. It may be the one sitting behind me."

"I've dealt with that," Conor said. "I give you my word that she will behave professionally. She understands the consequences."

Shannon nodded but still appeared to harbor doubts. "If you say so."

"When are the girls leaving?" Doc Marty asked.

Conor looked at his watch. "I need them on horseback in forty-five minutes."

"We need to get on the stick then, Shannon," Doc said to his daughter. "We'll get you geared up and I want to go over a few things with you."

"Okay."

"You up for this?"

"I'll be fine, Dad."

"I'll leave you two alone," Conor said. "Doc, figure we'll pull out an hour behind them. I have more to get ready. We'll be taking two pack horses."

Doc Marty gestured at the piles around him. "What kind of goodies should I bring?"

"Your preferred flavor of rifle, overnight patrol gear, shitload of ammo, and some of those grenades. I think I have the rest covered unless you have any goodies in there you haven't mentioned."

"There might be. We didn't get through all of it. There's probably not enough time before we have to leave."

"Bring the case of grenades. After you get Shannon ready, prep your own gear, and take it to the barn. I've got some surprises of my own to pack up."

"I enjoy your surprises," Doc Marty said.

"I enjoy yours less so," Conor said, both men knowing he was referring to the debacle in Helsinki.

Doc Marty looked at Conor seriously. "Aren't you ever going to get over that?"

"No," Conor replied. "Not until I get even."

Conor returned to his quarters leaving a concerned-looking Doc Marty behind.

36

Bryan and his army settled for the evening on the high school football field. Most of his men were able to find indoor accommodations in the high school. The building had been a shelter in the immediate aftermath of the terror attacks but had been abandoned when the organizations running the shelter had no longer been able to provide food or water. The building was ransacked by those who had stayed in the shelters, but it was tolerable. Bryan's folks had stayed in worse and it damn sure beat sleeping on the cold ground.

The horses were turned out onto the football field, which provided fenced grazing. Zach set up a watch schedule to keep two men on the horses all night. The good news for the sentries was that the entire field could be watched from the announcer's booth. It provided both an observation post and a position from which they could fire at anyone dumb enough to try to steal their horses. It beat the hell out of walking the perimeter all night.

Cooks set to work preparing a meal before darkness fell. The school cafeteria still had some large institutional size pots in the kitchen. One man cleaned the pot, another built a fire and a platform of cinderblocks to hold it. Other men rode to the river and brought back jugs of water. When the water came to a boil, the cooks added the spoils of the last day's travel, some jars of home-canned tomatoes and green beans, along with some potatoes, carrots, and onions found in a basement in Tazewell.

They added the meat of a rabbit shot on the highway and that of a cat found skulking around behind the high school. The addition of the cat to the stew pot was not discussed beyond the cabal of the two cooks, nervous to assure that they had enough food for everyone. Once skinned, the cat looked pretty darn similar to the rabbit. They disposed of the incriminating cat hide in a school locker, hoping no one opened it.

"Can Carrie and I speak to you in private?" Zach asked Bryan. All the assignments had been given out and the ad hoc camp was bustling with activity.

"Can we do it in the library? I want to see if they have anything interesting," said Bryan. "I need a good book to read. The burden of command is weighing heavy and I need distraction."

"Sure," Zach said.

They walked down long dark halls filled with trash and debris. All carried flashlights, for watching where they stepped and for scavenging anything useful. They passed a trophy case broken into for seemingly no other reason than to destroy the trophies. Zach wondered if it was the result of some long-standing vendetta carried out by someone from another school. An intercom speaker had been snapped off the wall and dangled by a thin strand of wire.

The office area had received special attention. Apparently, harboring many bad memories, those unable to move past childhood grudges had vented their frustration on this particular area of the building. The glass windows had been shattered by tossed furniture. The teacher mailboxes had been turned over. Stacks of charred paper records lay in the floor, the shameful evidence of an unskilled arsonist. Pictures of old principals hung from the wall, the target of a violent baseball bat attack. Old men smiled from behind shattered glass and warped frames.

They found the library on the second floor. The most visible characteristic of the room was that whole shelves of books were missing.

"Must be a book lover remaining in the town somewhere," Bryan said. "Some solitary man of letters on a mission to preserve the classics."

Zach and Carrie had no comment on that, just looking at each other as they often did during Bryan's rambling diatribes. Bryan perused what remained like an entranced customer finding the best used book store in the world. He strolled the shelves, touching thick institutional bindings, and scanning titles. He remembered most of them as being the same books that graced the shelves of his own high school library a lifetime ago.

"Such a burden," he whispered.

"What?" Carrie asked.

"Books," Bryan said. "We invest so much in them as readers. Our hopes, our dreams, our aspirations. They get us through hard times. They stave off emotional collapse. Sometimes they become reservoirs for parts and pieces of our *self*. Because of that, we don't want to let them go. To sell them, to give them away, to lose them, would be to lose something essential, some part of us that we fear we couldn't live without. At the same time, they can be like anchors. You ever move a houseful of books?"

"No," Zach said. "I prefer audiobooks. Not much storage room in my truck."

"I prefer magazines," Carrie said.

"Moving a houseful of books can be a brutal and exhausting experience, but what do you do? It's like those cultures where people burn the hair removed in a haircut because they don't want to leave it for a witch to use against them. I couldn't leave a book. I would feel like I was abandoning something vital to me."

"Where are your books now?" Zach asked, knowing Bryan obviously must have books somewhere to be so enamored of them.

"Douthat Farm. Hopefully stored in a manner that they'll remain safe until I can retrieve them."

"I hope we make it back there," Carrie said. "Sounds like you had a good thing going."

Bryan looked at her with a look of both incredulity and disgust. "Of course we'll make it back there."

"That's right, Carrie," Zach said, attempting to smooth things over. "When we're done here, we'll be heading back there. I can't wait to see the place myself. It sounds amazing."

Bryan didn't respond, torn between his inner fugue state and the feeling that they were patronizing him. "What did you want to talk to me about?"

"Let's have a seat," Zach suggested, ushering them to a dusty oak table.

They sat down in the hard chairs. There was an old book on the table, a battered copy of *The Gypsy Caravan* by Howard Pease. Bryan opened it and examined the pages. He'd read it as a child.

"I didn't want to mention this in front of the other men but I think we should split up into two groups," Zach said. "I don't want to walk into a trap."

Bryan focused on the man in front of him. "You're concerned that might be the case?"

"He did seem to be baiting you," Zach said.

Bryan huffed at the suggestion. "I think the Mad Mick believes his own legend. He likely expected we would turn tail and run at discovering who we were dealing with. He'll be surprised we are pursuing him. If we follow his trail, we'll catch him off guard. I think we have the numbers. This shouldn't even be a challenge."

Carrie cleared her throat, struggling to find a way to word the question that wouldn't offend Bryan. "The rumors are this man is a skilled fighter. Does that not concern you at all?"

"I suspect it's all a campaign of disinformation. I doubt there's anything of substance to this man at all. He's likely some hillbilly who read too many thrillers and thinks he's a superhero. I think we can dispel the myth pretty quickly. Once we do so, I intend to hang his body in some prominent place so that everyone will soon know that the Mad Mick was nothing but a smoke screen behind which some pathetic mountain man was hiding. We will pull down the curtain on Oz to reveal the buffoon behind the controls."

"I'm not questioning your judgment here, but in my opinion, this all came together a little too neat. The fact he left you a business card makes me wonder if he expects you to come to him," Zach said. "Have you thought at all about a plan of attack?"

"Of course," Bryan said.

"What is it?" Zach asked.

"First, I find your tone dangerously close to being insubordinate, but I'll answer your question anyway as I've come to think of us as colleagues of sorts. I'll remind you to remember who is in charge here."

"Sir, I asked to speak to you in private because I did not want, in any way, to create the appearance that I was questioning your leadership. We are here because I respect you and want to aid in the success of *our* mission," Zach said.

"Very well then," Bryan replied. "You should be well aware that I am a student of history and historical warfare. Part of my mission here is not just to prevail, but to discredit and perhaps even embarrass this Mad Mick."

"How do you intend to do that?"

"I intend to teach him about gentlemen's warfare," Bryan replied. "We march to his residence in a single body with a massive show of force. We call him out upon the battlefield. I hurl a few insults, to which I suspect he will respond by hurling some back. Then we kill him and drag his body to a public intersection where it will hang until the buzzards and crows carry off the last remnants of him."

Several things hit Zach like a landslide at that very moment. One was the realization that Bryan was, at least, delusional, and at worst, completely mad. It was apparent in the complete confidence and resignation with which he stated his plan, as well as being visible in the dark, flat pools of his eyes. Zach also realized that to go with Bryan was to walk into certain death. It was no different than the English troops marching into battle during the Revolutionary War only to be devastated by the ungentlemanly guerilla tactics of their opponents.

For his own safety, it was essential that Zach get his friends out of that force. There was also the possibility that Zach could outmaneuver the Mad Mick. If this Mad Mick was basing his strategy on a frontal attack by Bryan, perhaps he wouldn't expect Zach to sneak up from the rear. Zach's success hinged on presenting Bryan with a plan that would still allow him the glory he so desperately desired.

"Can I present a suggestion without offending you?" Zach asked.

Bryan nodded. "Certainly."

"When do you plan on launching your attack against the Mad Mick?"

"Tomorrow. If we locate him promptly," Bryan replied. "If it takes us all day to find him, then we'll hunker down for another night and attack the following day."

"If I could get a team out of here tonight, we could approach Jewell Ridge from the back side. I was checking the map in the school office and there's a way to do it, through some place called Pilgrim's Knob. We could move in from the back and hide out until you guys attack. If the Mick tries to retreat, we drive him back forward. If he attacks you, we jump into the fight from there. I don't think he'll be expecting that."

Bryan considered the idea for several uncomfortable minutes. His eyes wandered around the room, his brain processing in the background, running scenarios. "Okay."

"Okay?"

"On the condition that you not forget who's running this show. You only move when I move. If I'm not there yet, you wait. You do not engage the Mick until I'm there. This is not just about winning. It's also about crushing and demoralizing a legend. Don't forget that."

"You fine with us leaving tonight?"

"Yes. You can take eight men, and your personal gear."

"I don't think you'll regret this," Zach said.

"Let me remind you that if you double-cross me, if you head

home instead of doing what you told me, I'll track you down and kill you."

Zach and Carrie both nodded.

"Let's get to it then," Bryan said, shoving his chair back and getting to his feet.

They exited the library and headed down the hall they hadn't yet explored. Shortly, the reek of sewage hit their noses and the mystery of the missing books was solved. They hadn't been rescued by a devoted reader. Their pages had been ripped out to use as toilet paper. Discarded bindings lay in a stack outside the doors to the restrooms. Loose pages carpeted the floor, covered in dirty footprints.

Bryan clutched the Howard Pease book tightly. "Fucking animals."

37

Conor and Doc Marty hadn't even made it halfway down the ridge before they began running into clusters of armed locals mobilized by Barb's warning. The first group they rode up on was initially startled at Conor's approach but cheered when they recognized them. Conor wrangled his horse to a stop beside the two men and the teenage boy that made up the party.

"Hope you fellas are coming to help out."

The men nodded enthusiastically. "You got three generations here, buddy. We heard about what happened to those girls who were kidnapped. We don't want to see it happen again. We want to help."

Conor nodded and smiled. "Did my daughter tell you where to meet up?"

"At the community center," the boy said.

Conor smiled at him and nodded. "That's right, son. I hate to ask this of you but it might mean working through the night. If we can get some proper traps in place we may be able to reduce their numbers without putting any of our men at risk. Some good booby-traps will even the odds."

The men on the road looked at each other and conducted an entirely wordless conversation in their glances. "We probably got a good two hour walk ahead of us," the elder of the trio said to Conor. "Don't remember because it's been years since I had to walk out of here. Probably since I was a teenager determined to walk into town for some pretty young thing. But we'll get there and we'll do what we can."

Conor thanked the men and rode off with a wave. Over the course of the ride they met several more groups, varying in size, but all bearing the same determination to protect their community. Conor made certain each knew where to assemble.

"I'm impressed," Doc Marty said. "For such a contrary and unlikeable bastard you've done well to bring these folks together. Is this because you're such an upstanding member of the community? You sit with the elderly and host Easter egg hunts at your compound?"

Conor laughed. "I think it's a combination of things. They've probably heard the embellished Mick stories we've been passing around and I think it's made them confident that I can get them through this. It's a tightknit community and I'm sure the group of women I brought back have extended family among these men. They've probably heard what those women went through on the road and don't want it to happen to the women in their family. If those women told any stories about the final battle that probably made an impression as well. It was a little over-the-top, even for me."

"A little excessive?" Doc Marty mocked. "*You*?"

Conor shrugged. "It happens. Sometimes things get personal. You have a daughter—you think her kidnapping wouldn't be personal to you? Wouldn't justify a few excesses?"

"I see your point. It would become very personal."

It was dark when Conor and Doc Marty reached the community center between the base of the ridge and the town where Bryan's men were holed up for the night. Conor could see a few flashlights and lanterns, men gathered and talking in low voices. Conor hailed them and introduced himself before anyone got twitchy with a firearm.

With the men here and the men still on the mountain, that gave him somewhere around two dozen fighters. Then there was his own party—Barb, Doc Marty and Shannon, and Ragus—which added a handful more. Conor dismounted and searched around in the load on his pack horse. He came out with a large bag of brown beans.

"If you dig around in the community center kitchen you should be able to find a big pot. Gather some water in the creek and start heating it. Make sure it reaches a boil and stays there for a few minutes. These beans will take a little while to cook but we have a night of work ahead of us. These beans will fill some bellies when we're done. He tossed them to one of the men, then reached back into the saddle bag again, coming out with a healthy chunk of salt bacon. "I assume you men know what to do with this?"

The man who'd caught the beans grinned. There probably wasn't a man for thirty miles in any direction who didn't know how to cook soup beans.

"Cooking beans ain't going to take all of us," said one of the men. "You got anything else?"

"You know where the highway department shop is?" Conor asked the man.

He nodded toward town. "About a mile and half that way."

"That's the place. I need five or six of you to go down there. Stay alert, don't make a lot of noise, and don't draw a lot of attention. If you see a group of men on horseback, don't engage them. Turn around and get back here. If you can make it, I need you to get into the shop and find an ax, a couple of shovels, and every steel drum lid you can find. Got it?"

"Ax, shovels, barrel lids," the man repeated.

"That's it," Conor confirmed.

The man gathered a few of his buddies and they peeled away, heading toward town at a hurried walk. That left three men who were not engaged in the cooking operation.

"You men up for a job?" Conor asked.

They nodded eagerly.

"You know that barn down the road with the antique metal signs on it?"

One of the men nodded. "Got antique tractors and such."

"That's it. Besides those signs, there's also an old two-man crosscut saw fastened to the side of that barn. I need you to bring it back here. If the owner of the barn is home, tell him what we're doing and why we need it. Don't take no for an answer. If he's interested in saving his family, recruit him."

Happy to have a mission, something to calm the nerves that frayed during periods of waiting, the men took off. Conor spotted one man sitting on his knees, carefully assembling a teepee of kindling for the cooking fire. "You guys will probably have some time on your hands while you're cooking. You see that shed across the road?"

The man raised his head and squinted against the darkness. He could make out the vague outline of what had once been someone's old car shed. "I see it. Barely."

"Tear the roof and siding panels off of it. It doesn't matter if they're in good condition or not. The easiest way to do it is to get a long pole, maybe an old two by four, and bang the panels off from the inside. Stack all the metal panels you can get over here at the community center."

"Got it," the man said.

Conor was impressed with everyone's enthusiasm and eagerness to participate. Even if they lacked fighting skills, eagerness and the willingness to listen would take them a long way.

"With all the assignments handed out, we done for the night?" Doc Marty asked.

Conor shook his head. "Not at all. We have our own list, my boy."

38

"There's somebody on the move," Shannon said, breaking what had been a long silence.

"Where?" Barb asked.

"My two o'clock."

Barb adjusted her position to better see what Shannon was describing. The girls had quietly searched the town until they heard the sound of penned horses. They located them on the high school football field and quickly determined that the high school itself was serving as the temporary quarters for the approaching army. The girls figured out the best way to observe the football field and the immediate area was from a cliff on the other side of the four-lane highway where the rocks had been blasted away to make room for the road, leaving a sheer rock wall several stories high.

Fortunately, a crude trail led to the top of the cliff, likely made by stoners who wanted to lay out of high school and get high. From this perch they could smoke pot and laugh at the poor saps still having to suffer through a day of school.

The girls were lying at about thirty degrees to each other, both of then scanning with binoculars in a manner that allowed them to cover the entire vista before them. They had a plastic tarp beneath them to keep from getting wet and each was burrowed deep into a zero-degree sleeping bag. During long periods of inactivity, such as keeping an enemy under observation, it was nearly impossible to keep warm without layering up.

"I've got multiple folks on the move, headlamps and flashlights," Barb confirmed when she saw the activity Shannon noted a moment ago.

"You think the entire force is heading out?" Shannon asked. "Are they making their move?"

"I don't think so," Barb replied. "There's still a lot of folks back at the high school sitting around campfires. Let's just keep an eye on the movers. Could be a patrol or a scavenging party."

"If you've got them, I'm going back to scanning my zones. I don't want us both to get so dialed in on those folks that we miss something else."

"Got it," Barb said.

Shannon got her eyes back on the high school. With no lights, her observations were limited to what she could see in the firelight or tracking the movements of men with lights. "You're right about the rest of the army. No one seems to be getting ready for anything but bedtime."

"Shannon, these guys on the move seem intent to get somewhere."

"How can you be sure of that?"

"I'm not, but they're not acting like scavengers. There's no wandering around and searching. There's no disappearing into houses. They're making a beeline for some place."

"Maybe they're headed toward your dad's place. You think they got directions from someone? Maybe they kidnapped someone local and they're forcing them to act as a guide."

"I don't think that's it," Barb said. "I'm not sure where they're going, but it's nowhere close to the direction of the compound."

"Then I guess the next question is how badly do we need to know where they're going," Shannon said. "Is that critical intelligence?"

" I don't particularly like the idea of them wandering around out there without eyes on them. Whatever they're up to, I want to know about it."

"If we weren't in the early steps of launching an operation against them, it wouldn't matter," Shannon said. "With circumstances being what they are, I agree with you. We need to know what they're up to. One of us needs to stay on them."

"Maybe the best plan is for me to tail them," Barb said. "I know the area well enough that I can reorient myself if I get turned around. You stay here and keep an eye on the larger force. Listen for my dad on the radio. I'll take my radio and try to communicate my moves back to you. Don't flip out if you lose me. Radio reception is pretty shitty around here."

"Sounds like a plan," Shannon said. She laid down her high-powered binoculars. In the dark, she could only see the vaguest outline of the other girl. "Barb, I know we've had our differences but be very, very careful out there."

Barb hesitated, wondering what she should say. She sensed the girl's sincerity. "Those differences are personal, Shannon. This is work. You'll find that I'm much more careful and meticulous about my work."

Shannon could not help but notice that Barb said their differences *are* personal instead of *were* personal. It was acknowledgement that the differences still existed and were not yet relegated to the past. She didn't know how to respond to that even though she felt she needed to.

Barb felt like she should say something else. That she should issue warnings to Shannon about the noises she could expect to hear in the night. About how she should be careful in which direction she went if she had to flee the observation post in a hurry. She found it hard to add any words to those she'd already sent out into the world. Her father talked a lot, joked a lot, and rambled on sometimes. She was not like that at all. Her words were sparse, stark in contrast to the silence and seriousness she carried with her. She was not good at idle conversation or heartfelt exchanges. For her, words were about communicating. Or cutting.

In the deep, cold silence, by feel alone, Barb packed her sleeping bag and her gear. When everything was in its proper place, she backed away from the edge of the cliff and located the trail that would take her down the mountain. With the mountain between her and the town, she felt comfortable turning on the red bulb of her headlamp. In the eerie glow, she double-timed it, jogging down the hill to her horse, anxious to pick up the trail of the breakaway team.

39

The sky was changing hue, the sun an hour from rising, when all of Conor's troops gathered again at the community center. To a man, they looked like they'd fought a war already. They were tired, dirty, blistered, and hungry. The look in their eyes was the glazed exhaustion of troops returning to their camp after a particularly ugly battle. In this case, they hadn't fought the battle yet, they'd only decorated for the party. Now it was time to wait on the guests.

"Eat up," Conor said, "then grab a quick nap. I've got sentries posted along the road so we'll have warning if anyone shows up. Sleep ready to jump up and fight if you have to. That means shoes on, weapons at hand, and gear beside you. In two hours, I'll wake you, hand out assignments, and brief you on the battle plan. I want to thank you for everything you've done, for having the courage to show up to protect your community."

The men voiced their assents, yet with considerably less enthusiasm that they had earlier. Conor understood, knowing these men were speaking from their weariness and not from their hearts. They were not men used to being pushed to this level. In Conor's line of work, Ricardo had inserted him into different military schools or trainings. Conor would become just another nameless guy that everyone assumed was a spook, or something worse. No one talked to him, no one asked his name. Ricardo wanted him to learn some of the critical skills that the military and special units trained for.

Conor wasn't up to the level of some of those men in strength and physical assets but he gave it his all. He learned how to think, fight, and function when totally exhausted. He learned how to do the same things when cold, hungry, or overheated. Like anything else, there were tricks to it and that was part of what training taught you. The other thing it taught you was about your limits.

Everybody thought they knew their limits, but they didn't. That limit was usually just an arbitrary line placed where they imagined it should be. The actual limit wasn't where you got tired, thirsty, or your body cramped. The limit wasn't where your feet ached and turned into a solid blister. The limit wasn't where your shoes turned pink from blood and darkness began creeping into the sides of your vision.

The real limit was where your mind ran out of tricks. Where it couldn't fool your body into functioning any longer. Where your body wouldn't respond to commands, pleas, pain, or desperation. Everyone needed to know that point. It was something they needed to understand about themselves.

What did it feel like before muscles failed? What were the warning signs you were going to pass out? How did you know if heat stroke or heat exhaustion was on your heels? How long could you *personally* go without eating or drinking and still make sound decisions?

Those limits were different for everyone and Conor knew his. Barb knew hers; he'd made certain it was part of her training. These men in front of him—this brave, determined community militia—were about to learn theirs.

40

The first attempt to wake Bryan Padowicz was made right as Conor's own men were stretching out to catch some sleep.

"Sir," Michael said, shaking him. "The sun will be up soon. Shouldn't we be getting ready?"

Bryan had been sleeping well and was angry at being awakened. He frowned and mumbled.

"Sir?"

"Dammit, we're gentlemen not guerillas!" he spat. "Don't wake me up again. We'll fight this battle in daylight, not skulk around the shadows like peasant soldiers."

Michael retreated from the room and told the men assembled in the hall what Bryan said. While they were all disappointed, clearly not thinking this was the correct decision, they didn't know what else to do. They knew how Bryan was. If he said to leave him alone, that was what he wanted.

Sometimes having his sleep disturbed made it difficult for Bryan to find slumber again but that wasn't the case this time. He fell into a deep sleep again. He dreamed, perhaps because of memories stirred up by sleeping in a high school, that he'd never become a college professor. Instead, he taught high school history and was miserable. His students didn't listen, he had no money, and his wife hated him.

He awoke around 10 AM. The room was cold but the sun was high in the sky. He looked around in confusion, uncertain as to why he was still in bed at this late hour. Then he recalled what had happened.

"Damnit!" he grumbled, unzipping and extricating himself from his sleeping bag.

He pulled on his shoes and crammed any loose gear into his pack. He took a moment to get himself together, wanting to appear calm and collected before his troops. It was part of the persona of leadership, of command. When he felt ready, he opened the door to the principal's office and stalked out into the hall. It was empty.

Having a vague recollection of how he got to the office last night, he wound his way to the back door, toward the athletic field where they'd corralled the horses. He walked fast, the sound of his steps echoing through empty tile hallways. When he shoved his way out the heavy steel doors and into the bright sunlight, he found his army waiting on him, all wearing sullen and disapproving expressions. Even minus the team Zach took with him, it was a formidable group and the focus of their stares was withering. He felt like an ant squirming beneath a magnifying glass on a sunny day.

"Mount up!" he commanded, anxious to divert their attention somewhere besides him. He owed them no explanation. He was in charge here. Had they not bigger concerns, he'd teach them some discipline for their insolent looks. "Where's my fucking horse?"

One of the men, already mounted, rode forward with Bryan's horse and handed the reins off to him. Bryan secured his own gear and checked his weapons before climbing onto the horse, making sure everything was ready for whatever lay ahead of them.

"Make ready your weapons, men! Make certain there's a round in the chamber and that you have additional ammunition available to you. The rules of engagement are that you only shoot on my command. Are we clear?"

Bryan received a disjointed and staggered chorus of understanding. It was not the bold, enthusiastic response he'd hoped for, though perhaps his expectations were too high. While he may feel like Napoleon marching into battle, his troops were not a polished fighting machine. In the canon of edged weapons, they were rusty pocket knives, not swords. He had to hope that their numbers let them prevail. If it came to skill and determination, they would face an uphill battle.

Having stolen a local map from the school, Bryan took a moment to get his bearings and overlay the map upon the reality before him. He turned it a few times, took a reading from an antique brass military compass, and nodded. He folded the map and tucked it into his jacket.

"This way, men!" he called, turning his horse in the high school parking lot and heading toward Main Street.

Bryan was riding at the head of the pack when he heard the sound of hooves breaking pace and rushing to catch up with him. "What is it?" he asked when a man pulled alongside him.

The man extended a hand containing a clear plastic bag of jerky.

Bryan took it, realizing that he was hungry and probably needed his strength for the day ahead of him. "Get back in formation," he told the man. This was not a theatre where gratitude was expressed or even expected any more.

It took the entourage nearly thirty minutes to make the ride across town and find the road that led in the direction of Jewell Ridge. Once they were on that road, the town and its concentration of people fell away quickly. Houses no longer sat side by side. With the exception of the occasional trailer park, there were few clusters of dwellings. No people were visible at all, having either abandoned this area or having the good sense to stay hidden.

The mountain grew steeper to either side. The valley narrowed until there was only space for the road and the creek that wove alongside it. Houses and mobile homes were stuck on ledges where the mountains allowed it. In other places, the hills to either side were so steep as to consist of only rocks, roots, and trees growing sideways. Dried kudzu vines overlaid it all, like a straw-colored net struggling to hold everything in its proper place. In the summer, the green vine looked like it was attempting to consume everything—houses, trees, power lines, cars.

The land was too inhospitable, Bryan thought. This was not the kind of place where he would want to reincarnate Douthat Farms. He would either have to return to Douthat or get outside these infernal peaks to someplace where the land opened up and let you breathe. Someplace normal and populated with normal people.

His reverie was interrupted at an abrupt twist in the road. He turned the corner to find a gigantic oak laying across the road. It must have been six feet in circumference at the base and was tall enough that it wholly blocked the road with its maze of thick, abundant branches.

"We'll never move that," said the man who'd brought him the jerky.

Bryan couldn't remember his name— Greg or Craig—something like that.

"It was cut on purpose, too," Jerky Man said, pointing up the hill to the white stump and the pile of fresh sawdust.

"Can we pull it out of the way with the horses?" Bryan asked.

"Pull it where?" Jerky Man asked. "It's too big. Even if we could swing it around, it would still block the entire road."

"Find a way around," Bryan ordered.

"Sir," another of the men spoke up, "a lot of these houses below the road have bridges over to them. If we go back to that last house we can cross the creek there. It looks like there's a trail alongside the creek. It probably leads to a house beyond this tree. If those folks have a bridge, we can get back on the road there. Won't have to fool with trying to move this tree at all."

Bryan smiled. "Good thinking. You might be in line for a field promotion."

"Should I go see if we can get through that way?"

"Go ahead," Bryan said. "Take a couple of men with you. If you make it this far on the other side of the creek, I'll bring the main body of the men."

The man took off, recruiting riders to join him as he went.

"Take a break!" Bryan called to the rest of the men.

41

"I have men at Position One," Conor said into his radio. They'd maintained radio silence up until this point. Although the men coming for them weren't military, he wanted to discourage idle chatter that might be overheard or prevent the transmission of critical information among their own group.

From their vantage point on the hill above the road, Conor and Doc Marty watched the army ride by them. They wouldn't get far because his men had sawn down that big oak. He hoped they were smart enough to back up and try another bridge. He'd counted on it.

"*Conor*?" came a voice on the radio. It was young and female.

Doc Marty raised his own radio. "Shannon?"

"*It's me, Dad.*"

"Are you okay, baby?"

"*I'm fine. When the army started moving I fell in behind them.*"

"Keep a safe distance," Conor warned. "Barb with you?"

"*I am at a safe distance, not on the main road. Barb isn't with me anymore. A team peeled off last night and separated from the main group. She's following them.*"

That concerned Conor. Barb was plenty capable but he didn't like the idea of her being out there alone.

"No word from her?" Conor asked.

"*She told me she would radio in when she could,*" Shannon said. "*I haven't heard anything.*"

"Any idea where that other party was headed?"

"*We don't think they were scavengers. They seemed to be headed somewhere and she wanted to find out where. She said it wasn't toward your place.*"

"We got movement," Doc Marty said, pointing to the road below them. "They found the tree."

"We've got to run, Shannon. Stay safe and stay out of sight. Don't hesitate to request help if you need it."

"*Roger that.*"

Doc Marty lay on his stomach staring through a spotting scope. "Seven men returning."

Conor raised his binoculars. "Got them."

"They're pausing at the bridge."

"Cross it," Conor whispered, urging them on. "You know it's the only way."

The lead man, the one who'd so brilliantly offered up this solution, tried to follow the trail with his eyes, trying to figure out if crossing this bridge would allow them to get past the tree. He paid little attention to the bridge itself, constructed of wooden beams, its disused surface strewn with leaves and debris.

"Let's go!" he told the others. "I can't see enough of the trail from here."

He spurred his horse, anxious to perform this mission expeditiously and get in Bryan's good graces. Another rider fell in alongside him and two behind them, the bridge only wide enough to cross in pairs.

High above the riders, Conor smiled. "Got you."

With the purloined cross-cut saw, a team of men had cut the oak across the road in their overnight labors. That same team had then gone to the wooden bridge below them, cutting a large opening into the center of the bridge and covering it with thin metal roofing. After scattering some leaves, dirt, and gravels over the tin, it was indistinguishable from any other bridge on the road.

Except for the fact that this one would not bear weight.

The first two riders were nearly halfway across when the forelegs of their horses stepped on the roofing and it gave way. Both horses fell forward. It was not as elegant as dropping straight through a trap door in the movies. One horse fell forward and plunged through the opening to the creek. Due to the angle of its body, its rider struck his head on one of the bridge timbers as he fell. His forehead was crushed inward and he died instantly.

The horse to the right went down on its side, landing on an exposed timber. The rider's leg was pinned between the bridge and the horse, snapping at thigh level. The man screamed, his agony further increased as the horse writhed and tried to regain its footing. It could not, only succeeding in shoving its injured rider off the side and then falling on top of him. The water was only a few inches deep but it lay nearly eight feet below the bridge. Fortunately for the horse, its life was spared when the body it landed on cushioned its fall.

One of the horses in the second row was startled by the cries and desperation of the injured horses. It reared and staggered on its hind legs, one of those steps going over the side and spilling horse and rider into the creek. This horse too landed upon its rider, crushing the man from skull to groin and staining the water with his blood.

The rest of the procession managed to get off the bridge without loss of life. The main body of Bryan's army heard the distressed cries of the horses and the shouts of the men and came back to them, shocked at what they saw.

Bryan wove his way through the gawking men to reach the head of the crowd.

"What the hell happened?" he asked, directed at anyone who might have an answer.

"The bridge was a trap," a scrawny, scared kid replied. "It fell through with them."

Bryan had to bite his tongue to restrain himself. He wanted to scream and curse but it would not instill faith in his men. He needed them to move forward with him and they wouldn't do that if they thought he was losing it.

"Abandon the bridge," Bryan said. "We go through the creek. You'll have to lead your horses but I think they can make it."

"That water is cold," one of the men complained. He was bean-pole thin.

Bryan stared at him, uncertain if the man's weight was a lifelong condition or a result of the deprivation he'd experienced since the collapse.

"You can go first," Bryan said.

"If I get my shoes wet, they'll take forever to dry," the man complained.

Bryan pulled his .45 automatic and pointed it at the man's head. "My offer for you to go first was not me being polite!" Bryan bellowed, his face reddening and spittle flying. "It was a command. Now do it!"

The man climbed down from his horse and stepped off the shoulder of the road. The horse was reluctant and it took a combination of tugging and coaxing to make him cooperate. Once they'd managed to make their way down the slope, the man hesitantly stuck a foot in the water like a cat dabbing a paw at a puddle.

He shot Bryan a quick, spiteful look. Bryan tightened his grip on the pistol and was nearly provoked into shooting the man. *Troop strength*, he reminded himself. *I need him.*

"Aw, to hell with it," the man muttered, plunging forward into the creek, and tugging at his horse.

At the opposite bank, the man had to lean forward, tugging at roots and weeds to pull himself up. The horse required several powerful lunges to make it to the top. Proud of himself, the skinny man held the reins of his horse aloft and took a bow. As he straightened back up he took a step, preparing to mount his horse. Then he sank to his waist, an agonizing scream erupting from his mouth.

"Damn," Doc Marty whispered to Conor, watching from the hillside. "Fucking brutal."

"*Help me*!" the skinny man cried.

Bryan was wide-eyed with panic, his horse scuttling from the sound of terror. He fought to control it. "Someone help him! Get across that bridge!"

One of the men climbed off his horse and walked tentatively across the bridge, testing each step to see it would hold him. Progress seemed painfully slow but he was across in less than a minute, running to the aid of the injured man. Then he was down too, one leg sinking into the ground knee deep. His body pitched forward, a round steel disc encircling his leg, jagged teeth embedded in his flesh.

"What the hell?" someone yelled.

Another man started across the bridge, trying to stay within the footprints of the first, hoping to render aid to both of his screaming companions. Once across, he went to the closest man, the one trapped around the leg, and found that he couldn't remove the steel circle without inflicting more pain. He moved to the second man, finding that the skinny man had sunk to his midsection within the hacked up drum lid. Wedge-shaped barbs of the thin steel were buried in his flesh.

The man there to render aid had no clue what do. Any attempt to remove the barrel lids from their bodies only inflicted more pain. He turned to make his way back to the bridge. Three steps into his escape, he hit a drum lid too, sinking his calf through the jagged steel and falling to the ground.

"Position One, men down," Conor said into his radio. "Position Two, men down. Good job, boys."

"What's happening down there?" Doc Marty said. "I didn't see you all set that up. I was helping saw down the tree."

"Drum lids. Take an ax and cut wedges into them like you're cutting a pie. It's like a plastic cup lid from a fast food place. You stick a straw through the opening and those little flaps of plastic push inward. In this case, they're made of steel and dig into the flesh."

"That's nasty," Doc Marty said. "It's an easy shot with a rifle. Should we finish them off?"

Conor shook his head. "We need to stop them but we also need to leave a few alive to tell the story of what happened. That story becomes part of the legend that will help protect us in the future."

Doc Marty smiled. "The legend of the Mad Mick?"

"That's right."

Below them, more men were attempting to cross the bridge and render aid, stepping carefully, tapping their rifles on the ground to listen for steel. Some were reaching the injured and finding it difficult to help them. The easiest solution would have been if they had some way to cut the edge of the drum lid and unwrap them from the victim, but they had nothing capable of cutting through steel that thick.

"Two of you can stay to care for the wounded!" Bryan bellowed. "The rest of us are going to go back and climb over that tree!"

"Two men?" an injured man asked. "What can two men do for us?"

"They can euthanize you if you become a pain in the ass!" Bryan snapped.

The rest of Bryan's men returned to the tree.

"Tie off your horses. The rest of us are moving forward on foot," Bryan told his men.

A lot of questioning looks were going back and forth. For some of these men, the prospect of walking was no more pleasant than the prospect of moving forward against an enemy who clearly had no compunction against maiming and cruelly injuring them.

"That was not a question," Bryan said. "That was an order."

Men began responding, reluctantly climbing from their horses and tying them off to anything they could find. Men shouldered their gear and weapons. Bryan led the way, climbing and ducking through the maze of branches like a child on the monkey bars.

Far above them, Conor watched. "I expected more to go AWOL by this point. I thought for sure those barrel lids would have more of a psychological affect."

Doc Marty shrugged. "This guy has a hold on them. They're obviously scared."

The pair followed the men with their optics, watching them tie off their horses and move single file to the massive tree. Then Conor smiled. He saw that one flicker of hesitation and he knew he had them.

Maybe two-thirds of the men were beyond the tree and hiking up the road when one man at the end of the line, waiting his turn to climb through, simply turned tail and ran. It created some kind of instinctual reaction and more men fell in behind him, running to their freedom. They saw the writing on the wall and wanted no part of the story.

"Those are the smart ones," Conor said. He keyed his radio. "Moving to Position Three."

42

Barb was pissed at herself. She had little tolerance for failure and even less tolerance for her own failures. She'd stayed on Zach and his men for hours, stalking them through the night, but it was incredibly difficult to follow men in the darkness. She had the benefit of top-notch night vision equipment but it was still difficult going. She had to stay far enough back that the group wouldn't hear her horse. That distance turned out to be just enough that she lost them at a remote intersection of two gravel roads and never found them again.

She rode to a high ridge and searched the night for their lights but never caught any. Maybe they stopped to bed down for the night and turned them off. Maybe they'd heard her, despite her best efforts, and were hiding to lose her. Either way, she'd lost them. She spent all night trying to find their trail but the hard gravel road gave up no clues.

She was both disgusted and exhausted, but she didn't feel comfortable bedding down in the woods during daylight. Using her GPS, she found a gas well road that would take her roughly back in the direction of Jewell Ridge. She guessed it might be a two-hour ride. She would ride toward the compound, catch the road, then find her dad. Maybe there was still time for her to get in the fight. She had skin in this game. It would be the conclusion to something that started when she was abducted from her friend Joann's house. There was no way she was missing it.

She rode hard, pushing her horse and her riding ability to the limits. She took shortcuts, trying to work the contours and topography of the land to avoid getting stuck in steep valleys or at the base of cliffs.

When she reached the compound, she didn't slow but began working her radio. For nearly a mile she heard nothing in the earpiece, then out of nowhere, she heard her dad's voice. He was handing out instructions and calmly directing people where he needed them.

She keyed the microphone. "Dad!"

"Barb?"

"It's me. I'm about a mile past the compound, coming down the road."

"Stop where you are," Conor instructed. *"I don't want to give up our position on the radio. I'll send Ragus for you. Tether your horse in the woods and start walking the road in this direction. Over."*

"Roger that, Dad. Over and out." Barb steered the horse into the woods and tied him off on a long lead. She was relieved to have found the group. Not so much for the comfort of their presence, but because she didn't want to miss any of the action. Although there were a lot of questions she'd wanted to ask, they would have to wait. She needed to find out if they'd heard from Shannon. It was all stuff she could ask Ragus when they crossed paths.

She jogged back to the road and turned down the ridge.

43

Zach had not lost Barb through stealth or cunning, but through his own difficulty navigating the confusing mountain terrain. He'd learned the hard way that it was often impossible to tell what was a private gas well road owned by an energy company and what was a public road. They looked indistinguishable and often neither was marked in any way. Whoever maintained these roads seemed to have the attitude that if you were on this mountain you should know where you were going.

By sheer accident, he'd led his group onto a gas well road, missing the turn they should have taken. That wrong turn was enough to allow them to escape Barb's tracking. Once Zach noticed his mistake and found the correct road, his team travelled until the wee hours of early morning, finally bedding down in the woods for a few hours sleep.

Once they awoke, stiff and cold as corpses, they choked down a quick breakfast of questionable jerky and got on the road. After an hour's ride in a cold fog, they hit the community of Hell Creek and were finally certain they'd navigated to the correct spot.

"According to the map, we'll be on Jewell Ridge in a few hours," Zach said. "My guess is this Mad Mick character won't expect anyone to sneak up behind him. This could be what tips the scales in our favor. If Bryan screws up the attack, maybe we can save it."

Carrie flipped the hood of her green Carhartt off the top of her head and scowled. "I'm not sure why we're even doing this. We could just as easily have gone the other way and put some distance between us and this crazy asshole."

"The Mad Mick?" Zach asked.

"No, *Bryan*. I'm not sure coming with him was such a great idea. It seemed like a good idea at the time but I'm kind of soured on it at this point."

Zach shrugged. "I agree he's a few sockets short of a set but a better opportunity hasn't come along yet. If one presents itself, maybe we jump ship. Until now, he's kept us fed and I've been pretty comfortable."

"I'm not comfortable. I'm cold and I'm tired of sleeping on the ground. I had a decent bed in the sleeper of a truck back at the rest area. I was out of the weather."

"Things will get better. We just caught this guy in the middle of waging war. Once they're done with that, they have a place with cabins, greenhouses, and solar power. I've heard all about it and not just from Bryan. It's real."

Carrie looked uncertain.

"What?" Zach asked, seeing there was something still bothering her.

"I don't get this whole *battle* thing he's so obsessed with now. I know there's times you have to kill folks, but big battles with a lot of shooting seems like a senseless risk to me. I only like to go into fights I know I'm going to win."

"You think we're not going to win this one?"

"I don't know," she replied. That's the whole problem." She flipped her hood back in place, signaling an end to the conversation.

They rode on in silence. To one side of the road, a broad river of greenish-brown water rolled along. Zach thought it looked like good fishing water. He wished for a fishing pole and the time to stop to use it. Even cold weather fishing would be better than no fishing and he couldn't remember the last time he'd gone.

The scent of wood smoke was in the air, a sure sign folks were alive and hiding behind locked doors in the houses they passed. It made the group a little uneasy, as if there were crosshairs tracking them as they plodded by unlit windows. They went unchallenged, either unnoticed or deemed unworthy of attention.

At an intersection just past Hell Creek, they met a group of riders roughly double them in size. Two of the men were ahead of the group, intently studying a map. In the obscurity of the dense fog, both groups were startled by the sudden appearance of the other, the river masking the sound of hooves until they were upon each other. No one had time to ready weapons prior to the encounter and to do so at this point might inflame the situation beyond salvage. At this close range, men would die for certain. Perhaps all of them would die, leaving behind a mystery for a future traveler to puzzle over, wondering why so many shot-up bodies lay in one place.

Zach nodded at the man with the map but did not make eye contact, did not still his horse. "Excuse us. We're just passing through. Didn't mean to startle you folks."

Wayne nodded in response, a reaction unseen since the man was not looking at him. His mind was racing. Jason Jacks and that boy who'd come to see them at the fire hall warned there was an army approaching. He said they needed help. After discussing it with their families, they'd agreed to send a party to aid in the defense of the community. It was, in fact, this very group that was on their way to lend support to the Mad Mick, as soon as they could confirm which road led to the top of Jewell Ridge. This was not their country. They had a county map from the wall of the fire hall but no compass. The lack of signage in the sparse country was not helping matters.

Something inside Wayne was sending up alarms. The other group didn't seem like they belonged here. Wayne could say this with a degree of certainty because his group didn't belong there either. There was a similarity in the manner both groups related to their environment that was telling. They seemed alien, uncertain in the surroundings in a way the locals did not.

Was this other group also coming to lend support to the Mad Mick? Perhaps they were just outliers who'd been recruited, as Wayne and his people had, to help in this fight?

"Y'all take care," Zach said, and his group continued on their way.

Wayne was wracking his brain, trying to figure out some way to determine if these guys were friend or foe. As the last rider moved past him, he blurted out a question. It was all he could think to do and he needed some way to delay them until he could make the call. "You guys from around here?"

Zach paused, the riders behind him coming to a staggered stop. He didn't turn around to address the man speaking to him. His back stiffened, as if he'd thought they were in the clear and now their fate was uncertain. "Why do you ask, friend?"

"We're new here. Just trying to make sense of this map. Ain't many signs around this damn place."

Zach was slow to respond, weighing the value, and the consequence, of each word that might come from his mouth. "Afraid we can't help you there. Don't know anything about this area either."

"Then where you going?" Wayne asked. "You seem to be on your way somewhere, which is a mite curious since you don't seem to know the area any better than I do." The entire time he was speaking, Wayne was drawing his pistol. It was a Glock and, unlike in the movies, there was no sound required to train it on a target. No safety, no hammer click, no random and senseless sounds, just silent death creeping from a holster.

Detecting their leader's actions, the rest of Wayne's sizeable group all moved to ready their weapons as quietly as possible. Wayne saw Zach tilt his head to the side as if stretching his neck, perhaps just reacting to the hair standing up on the back of his neck.

Zach spun his horse, drawing and shooting wildly into Wayne's group. The rest of Zach's party, not anticipating his move, was behind the eight-ball, still trying to figure out just what the hell happened. They caught on fast, pulling their weapons and jumping into the fray.

Wayne's group was not so hesitant. Their guns were out by the time Zach fired and they opened up at his shot, instantly dropping two of his party. Their horses side-stepped in terror, trampling their riders and eliciting a scream from the one who was still alive.

Jumping to the ground, Zach tried to keep his horse between him and the larger force spraying rounds of all calibers in his direction. Unscathed by the flying bullets, Carrie bolted and ran, kicking her horse to top speed. She was done. This was her resignation.

Then Wayne was off his horse, moving and firing. He'd served in Afghanistan and knew a little about shit kicking off with no warning. He shouted orders to his men, trying to get them to take cover. Zach took advantage of those slow to react or heed Wayne's warning. He fired into areas of human density, striking several folks more out of luck than accuracy.

The ditch at the intersection was the closest thing to a foxhole and Wayne went for it, shoving any of his nearby folks in that direction. They may twist an ankle from the fall but at least they'd live to complain about it. Standing around in the open was certainly going to get them killed.

Another pair of Zach's riders must have been lured by Carrie's defection. In tandem, they bolted up the road, coats flapping as they dug their heels into their horses and slapped at them with their reins. Wayne grabbed a scoped hunting rifle from another of the men in the ditch, a bolt-action .308, and checked the chamber to confirm there was a round ready to go.

He proned-out in the grass by the ditch while his men laid down cover fire. At about one hundred and fifty yards, he put a round in the back of the first man, sending him slumping off the side of the running horse. Wayne jacked another round into the chamber and lay the crosshairs on the next rider. He was a little past two hundred yards now, a reasonable shot with a good rifle, and Wayne pulled the trigger. The man flinched, stiffened, and rolled off the back of his horse.

"How many left?" Wayne asked.

"Two!" one of his men said.

With a more precise weapon in his hands now, Wayne turned on the men pinned down across from them, between the road and the river. Zach had changed magazines and raised his head up enough to return fire at Wayne's men. Wayne caught the top of his head in the scope picture, the rifle boomed, and Zach's head erupted in a red mist.

There was a scream from that side of the road. It came from the last remaining man. Then Wayne heard a splash. He jumped to his feet, rifle shouldered, and moved toward Zach's firing position. Zach's last man was floating on his belly in the two-foot deep water, letting the frigid current carry him away as he desperately paddled with his arms.

"I think you can hit him," a voice said from behind Wayne.

Wayne didn't see the speaker, focusing so intently on man in the crosshairs of the scope, but he pulled off, raising the rifle and flipping the safety on.

"Why didn't you shoot him?"

"He'll probably die of hypothermia, soaked in this weather. No use wasting a good bullet on him." Wayne turned back to his group. "We lose anybody?"

"One dead and two wounded. Neither of the wounded are serious but they're out of the fight," replied a man named Chance.

Wayne saw men in his group gathered around a body on the ground and he went over to see who'd been killed. "Shit!" It was his friend Larry. They'd worked for the same construction company back before this whole mess happened.

"At least he didn't have family," Chance said. "It's a small consolation, but I'd hate to have to go back and tell a family that someone wasn't coming home."

"That was a gamble we all took when we came out here," Wayne said. "Put his body on a horse. Bandage the wounded. Collect all the horses, gear, and shit belonging to the dead men and roll their bodies into the river. The wounded, if they're fit to ride, can go back to the fire hall and take the gear we collect."

"We should probably leave one man to help," Chance said. "If they come under attack they'll need someone who can fight."

Wayne nodded. "Find a volunteer. The rest of us need to get back on the road."

In two minutes, they were riding in the direction that Zach and his men had been headed, hoping the dead men had a little better navigational intel than they did.

44

Position Three was an extended straight stretch of road between two switchbacks. Towering poplars and oaks lined the road, completely shading it in summer and turning it into a gloomy tunnel of foliage. Those trees stood like stark sentinels menacing Bryan's terrified army. They'd been bold and confident up until the incident at the bridge. They'd never suffered defeat before. Even the attack at Tazewell, when Conor and Barb kidnapped Bryan for a short time, didn't affect most of the men. They thought their force was invincible, their leader unstoppable.

Bryan was extremely angry when he realized they had deserters who'd abandoned them at the tree. Despite struggling to maintain appearances so it wouldn't demoralize the rest of the troops, he couldn't restrain himself completely. He cursed and ranted until he felt well enough to move forward. If he ever came across any of those deserters again, they would die a slow and agonizing death.

The road before them angled upward, cut into the mountain with no shoulder on either side and no guardrail to stop an inattentive driver from plunging to disaster. It happened a couple of times a year with cars and about once a year with a semi-truck driver whose GPS indicated this was a short cut. If you met a vehicle coming the other way, you held your breath and crept by each other, the driver on the outside edge praying their wheels stayed on the pavement.

Used to riding horses, the effort of climbing wore on the men. Their legs ached and burned from the effort, their lungs screaming for air. All of them suspected they had a lot farther to go, but the manner in which the road curved around the mountain prevented them from seeing how far. It could be one mile or it could be five. Their physical suffering further demoralized them. They were afraid to complain but it was likely that most in Bryan's army wished they'd thought to desert with the others.

The road was scattered with debris. Damp leaves formed a woven and matted carpet that added additional effort to each step. Twigs and fallen branches lay buried in the leaves, offering hidden hazards that caused stumbles and falls. With each minute of struggle, their frustration increased. Then a man hit the first tripwire.

He wasn't even aware that he ran into it. Fishing line ran across the road between two eyehooks, then fifty feet back to a short length of white PVC pipe taped to a tree and buried in leaves. The pipe was slightly larger in diameter than the fragmentation grenades Doc Marty had brought. When the pin was pulled from each grenade, Conor slid the grenade back into the PVC pipe and it held the spoon, or safety lever, in place, preventing the grenade from being triggered. That was, until the tripwire pulled the grenade from the pipe and the spoon went flying off into the leaves, triggering an explosion near the end of Bryan's formation.

BOOM!

Two men dropped and more screamed, rolling on the ground and clutching at wounds on their bodies. The explosion at the back of the line pushed the rest of the group forward. Despite their exhaustion, men ran wildly, staggering uphill through the leaves. Even Bryan didn't know what else to do but join them. He ran as blindly as the rest of them.

One of the running men snagged the second tripwire, pulling another grenade from its pipe sleeve, and detonating a second explosion.

BOOM!

The explosion toward the end of the line pushed the men again, urging them forward. Gasping, they plunged headlong up the hill, sucking air, trying to fuel starved muscles. They staggered, wide-eyed and open-mouthed, in sheer panic.

BOOM!

A third tripwire. A third explosion. More men dropped.

The frantic procession reached a switchback. "Stop, dammit!" Bryan screamed, fighting to gain control of his own breathing. "Stop running...let's think...a second."

The men found it hard to think. Adrenaline surged through their bodies. Many of them were wounded, blood soaking their clothes. Behind them, on the stretch of road they'd just travelled, lay a dozen or more of their screaming companions, wounded to the point that they could not stand up and flee.

"He's just trying to scare you!" Bryan screamed. "Stop a minute and let's figure this out!"

From higher on the ridge, Conor watched the chaos unfold. He keyed his microphone. "Position Three is a go. Repeat. Position Three is a go."

On the uphill side of the road, nearly forty men silently raised from concealed positions behind fallen logs. Among them was Conor, Barb, Doc Marty, Ragus, and Jason, along with most of the volunteers who'd come to participate in the defense of their community. They were a gritty and unwavering force.

"Fire!" Conor bellowed.

At the sound of his voice, all of Bryan's men, eyes wide with panic, turned to face the woods. Gunfire erupted and men began falling. There were screams as men launched themselves in all directions, tripping over collapsed friends, scrambling for the minimal cover available.

Thinking a little faster than his companions, Bryan dove over the shoulder of the road like a man hurdling from a burning building. On the steep mountain, his dive resulted in a vertical drop of nearly twelve feet. He hit hard, his breath leaving him, and then he was rolling out of control. He lost his rifle, unaware even of where it sailed off to. He slammed into a rock at high speed, his backpack all that prevented him from breaking his spine.

Behind him, above him, shots rang out. There were more screams.

"Kill or capture all of them," Conor said into his radio. "We can't leave any of them loose in the community. If in doubt, shoot."

Leaping to his feet, Bryan attempted to run down the mountainside but tripped over a branch and went down on his chest. He slid in the soggy leaves, barreling face-first down the mountainside like a kid on a sled. The ride ended abruptly at the base of a poplar. Bryan wrenched his head to the side just in time, his shoulder catching the brunt of the force, wracking his entire body with agony. He cried out and rolled onto his back, cradling his arm and trying to clear his thoughts.

He listened for a moment, thinking he may have gotten away. If no one saw him, he could slip away if he kept quiet and moved cautiously. He looked up and it took him a moment to find the road he'd jumped from. Everything looked identical in these hardwood forests. It all blended together. There was a face at the edge of the road. A woman. She was looking right at him as she leapt over the edge in pursuit.

"Barb!" Conor yelled, launching himself from his position and tearing off after her. They were supposed to stay together.

Barb didn't hesitate at Conor's yell, tracking the fleeing Bryan with laser intensity. She knew who he was, knew he was the man responsible for all of this, and knew it wasn't over until he was dead.

She was much more capable of controlling her descent. She practically skied down the slope on the soles of her feet, one hand dragging behind to steady herself, the other clutching a short rifle. When her slide arrested, she popped off two shots at Bryan but he managed to scuttle behind a tree like a rat in a spotlight.

He started down the mountain again, trying to keep trees between him and the female terminator intent on killing him. With his focus directed behind him, he missed the fact that the road had turned through another switchback and was now directly below him again. He fell off the high shoulder, dropping nearly straight down onto jagged chunks of slate and shale, then rolling into the road. Besides the paralyzing shock of pain at the fall, his hands were now shredded and bleeding.

He staggered to his feet, then began running down the road. It was smoother and easier to travel. He could hear the shuffle of damp leaves on the mountain above him. The girl was still after him and perhaps there were more behind her. He couldn't tell and he didn't have time to stop. It hit him that he'd never be able to outrun anyone on the road. His muscles were too spent, his body too battered. He leaped over the low shoulder again, figuring it was faster to roll down to the next point where the road crossed below him.

It was the same story but hurt worse because he knew what was coming. Rolling, sliding, bouncing off trees like a pinball, and slamming against rocks. He cried out when the pain was too much. He'd learned though. He was watching for the road this time and stopped himself before he dropped from the high shoulder, clutching a branch with bleeding hands at the last moment. He eased himself down, his feet sliding in the loose shale, then he was back on the road and running again.

A quick glance over his shoulder told him that he'd kept the distance between them but she was still coming. He could also hear a man's voice now, yelling at the girl to wait on him. Bryan didn't think she'd wait. She was relentless. She was an unstoppable machine with a level of determination and fitness for which he was no match.

Then he saw the tree laying across the road and nearly cried with relief. Beyond it were horses. He practically dove through the maze of branches, feeling them tug and tear at his clothing. He could hear the slap of boots on pavement behind him, knew the girl was closing on him. She fired at him as she ran but her movement sent the shots wild. They sang off nearby branches, launching bark and dirt onto him.

He burst from the far side of the tree and grabbed the nearest horse, yanking the reins loose. He struggled to pull himself into the saddle, yelling with the effort. The men he'd left there to help with the wounded were on alert from the shooting but didn't know if it was friend or foe. Seeing their leader on the run, their hearts sank.

"Where you going?" one asked. "What happened?"

Bryan ignored them, kicking the horse hard and urging it desperately forward. He threw a quick glance behind him and saw the girl was nearly through the tree. She dropped, resting the rifle on a branch, and lined up a shot. Bryan flattened himself against the horse and yanked the rein hard, forcing the horse to veer to the side.

Three shots rang out in less than a second. Bryan heard the rounds whistle by him like angry bees but none connected. He couldn't help but smile. Maybe he was going to make it. More gunfire rang out behind him. Had his men taken out the woman?

He soon realized this wasn't the case. He heard the clatter of hooves behind him and his fear shot through the roof. There appeared to be no stopping this woman. He was certain she was gaining on him. How long before she got a clear shot? How long before a chunk of hot lead ripped through his back, shredding vital organs, and spilling his precious blood?

Ahead of him he saw a young woman on the road walking directly toward him. She had a rifle in her hands, carried across her body. She appeared to be trying to figure out who he was. When she caught his eye, something gave him away. She had the answer to her question and she raised the rifle in his direction, lining up her shot.

He couldn't let it end like this, not when freedom was at hand. Thirty yards separated them and he ducked his head behind his horse, banking on the likelihood that this young girl would hesitate to fire on the horse. He was right; she held her fire. The clatter of hooves was getting nearer. An idea came to him, an act of desperation, and he went for it.

It was all he had.

As his horse closed in on the girl, he leapt from its back and onto her. She went down hard, her rifle clattering away toward the shoulder. She screamed and fought hard as Bryan swung around behind her, trying to shield himself from Barb. He pulled the tiny backup pistol from inside his coat, jamming it to the girl's head as the other woman rode up on them. She reined her horse and came to a stop, her rifle aimed right at him.

"You'll hit her," Bryan said, his voice cracking, his mouth dry from sucking air. "You try to shoot me and you'll hit her."

"You assume that will stop me," Barb said. "You okay, Shannon?"

"Not really," Shannon replied, her voice straining against the arm wrapped around her throat.

"Put down your gun!" Bryan bellowed in a croaking scream that was barely human.

There was the sound of more hooves and then Conor was there too. He swung off his horse, his gun also levelled at Bryan.

"Let the girl go," Conor said in a firm voice. "You don't have a chance."

Bryan's eyebrows raised at the Irish accent. "It's you! The Mad Mick himself!"

"It is," Conor admitted. "Now let her go."

"Get back on your horses and let me go," Bryan said, jerking Shannon with his arm as he said it. "If you don't, I'll kill her."

"And you'll still die," Barb said. "Just slower."

Bryan swung the pistol toward Barb. "Then maybe you die too!"

Shannon took advantage of Bryan moving the pistol away from her head. She whipped the knife from her plate carrier and plunged it into Bryan's knee. He screamed as she doubled over hard, like she was doing a sit-up. Shannon's movement pulled Bryan forward with her, exposing the crown of his head.

Barb fired and Shannon felt Bryan's body jerk at the impact. Warm blood poured down her neck and back, running beneath her clothes. She squealed and threw herself to the side. Conor put another round in Bryan for good measure, then retrieved the small pistol, cleared it, and shoved it in his thigh pocket.

Barb extended a hand to Shannon and helped her to her feet. Shannon extended her arms to her sides, grossed out and feeling contaminated.

"I'll check on the others," Conor said. "Can you help clean her up?"

Barb nodded, made her rifle safe, and shifted the sling to her side. She was helping Shannon doff her body armor when Conor mounted the stolen horse and rode back toward the downed tree. The men caring for the wounded at the booby trapped bridge were all dead or gone. Barb had taken care of them before pursuing Bryan, too busy to fool with taking prisoners.

He left the horse at the tree, climbed back through the maze of branches and stopped to speak into his radio. "Position Three, what's the status?"

Doc Marty replied in a moment. "*Seven prisoners. The rest either dead or getting that way*."

"Roger that," Conor replied. "What about our people?"

"*No casualties. One sprained ankle and one broken wrist. Both from falls*."

"March those prisoners down here so we can find a place to secure them," Conor said. "It's time to lick our wounds, grab a meal, and get some rest. We can deal with this mess tomorrow."

"*Anyone heard from Shannon*?" Doc Marty asked. "*She's not answering her radio*."

"Had eyes on her a moment ago," Conor replied. "She's fit as a fiddle."

45

The men from Wayne's group missed the fight, delayed by their encounter with Zach's group, but they'd been close enough to hear the gunshots. Conor agreed that the men Wayne had encountered were likely part of this enemy force. Intercepting them before they joined the fight had probably saved lives.

Better rested than Conor's group, they offered to assist with watching the prisoners overnight. Those who had been captured were stuck in a windowless brick hut the phone company used to house switchgear. Some within the community wanted to kill all of the prisoners in a public execution. Conor discouraged it.

"We've killed enough of them to make it clear to everyone that we tolerate no foolishness," he said. "If we release these men with a warning never to come back, I think they'll spread the word far and wide that we are not to be trifled with. The story of what we've done will travel farther with living men than with dead men."

In the end, the people agreed, and the next day a party escorted the unarmed men back to the highway. They turned them loose with no horses, no weapons, and no food. The only thing they received was the gift of their lives and a warning to never return.

As for the dead of Bryan's army, there were too many to waste the effort of individual graves. Ragus mentioned the subterranean foundation of a house that had burned to the ground. The open foundation hole was around four feet deep and filled with the ashes and debris of the fire. The bodies were taken there on horses and stacked respectfully on the earthen floor of the basement. Everyone able to shovel took a turn heaving dirt into the foundation hole. While it took three hours, it was faster than individual graves. No words were spoken over them since no one in the community, despite their deeply-held religious beliefs, felt like blessing the men who'd come to kill or enslave them.

Before everyone went their separate ways and returned home, Conor took advantage of the gathering to remind people that incidents like this were why they needed to have security for their community. He saw on their faces that they understood.

"There's a role for all of you, despite any physical limitations. It's your skill level and your knowledge we need to grow. If I offer to train you folks, will you come?" he asked.

It was mostly nods around the assembled faces.

"Then expect I'll come calling," Conor said. "I'll give it a week or two so you can rest up."

"You can start with us," Wayne offered. "We're pretty isolated over there. My group and the Jacks family are about all you have in that back valley."

"Except for a pissed off preacher," Barb piped up.

Conor shot her a look, then went back to Wayne. "Sounds good, my friend. I'll swing by in a few days to get things started."

There were tired waves as the group broke up. People pulled off, heading back up the ridge and to their homes. From the way they talked among themselves, Conor could see that they were more than neighbors now. They had indeed transformed themselves into a loose militia.

~

THINGS STILL SEEMED STRAINED between Ragus, Barb, and Shannon. It was evident even to Doc Marty and Conor, who discussed it on their first full day back at the compound. They were sitting on the porch drinking coffee Doc Marty had brought in his shipping container. Ricardo had included twenty pounds for Conor. It wasn't an indefinite supply but would fuel many early mornings and late nights.

"I'm sorry if our presence here is causing conflict," Doc Marty said. "I thought it might be a little intrusive and I was okay with that, but I don't want to cause personal rifts."

"You seemed to have fewer concerns about that in Helsinki," Conor noted.

"I know that. I owe you for that, for putting us up, and for saving my daughter."

"You don't owe me for saving her but you do owe me for putting up with you and for Helsinki."

"How can I make that up to you? Just tell me and I'll do it. I'm tired of living with this over my head. Tired of sleeping behind a locked door in a booby trapped room because I'm afraid I'll wake up to your grinning face hovering above me."

"You sleep with booby traps?" Conor asked. "Good to know."

Doc Marty sighed and waved his arms in frustration. "I'm serious. I want this done and out of the way. Shit is too serious right now to constantly be worrying about that."

"It didn't stop you from coming here, did it?"

"I did that for Shannon. I didn't think I had a choice."

Conor considered for a moment. "The offer is this and it's non-negotiable. There's one offer and one only. You stay here until this mess is over. You stay as our doctor. I don't care if Ricardo finds better accommodations or you get a better offer. You stay. Deal?"

Doc Marty screwed up his face in consideration, then stuck out his hand to shake on it. "Deal."

Conor took his hand and the men faced off to shake on it. As they did, Conor clamped onto Doc's hand and pulled him in for a head-butt. Doc Marty went staggering backwards, falling on his ass. Addled, he rubbed his forehead.

"Damnit, Conor!"

"I pulled the blow," Conor said. "Didn't want a doctor with a concussion."

"I thought we had a deal."

"We do. That was part of it."

"You could have mentioned that part," Doc Marty mumbled, pushing up to a seated position. "I might have thought about it a little longer."

Just then, Shannon, Barb, and Ragus came piling out the door. Shannon ran to her dad's side. Ragus and Barb stared in confusion, trying to figure out what happened.

"It's fine," Conor assured them. "We made a deal. Doc Marty is going to stay on as our personal physician until this mess is over."

"Did you have to hit him?" Shannon said, a furious scowl on her face.

"He said he wanted to clear the air over the matter in Helsinki," Conor said. "This seemed the best way to do that. Consider it part of the handshake."

"I'm tired of hearing about Helsinki!" Shannon yelled at both men. "Just what the hell happened over there that neither of you can move past?"

Conor gestured at Doc Marty. "You tell them."

Doc Marty hesitated.

"Dad!" Shannon said. "Tell me or I'm not speaking to you for a long time. I've had it with this."

When Doc Marty wasn't forthcoming, Conor spilled it. "He stole me bloody teeth."

Everyone looked at Conor in shock, then at Doc Marty with a tinge of disgust.

"What?" Shannon asked.

"He. Stole. Me. Bloody. Teeth," Conor repeated.

"How do you steal someone's teeth while they're still alive?" Barb asked.

"We were on an operation," Doc Marty said. "Planting false forensic evidence. We'd kidnapped this Russian. If his organization knew he was kidnapped, they would have changed all their protocols in response. We thought it was better that they think he was dead. Then they wouldn't feel a need to change anything."

Ragus and Shannon helped Doc Marty up, putting him in a porch chair. He swiped his hair from his face and touched his tender forehead before continuing.

"I'd been provided with a set of his dental records and a bag of loose teeth that matched them. Conor and I stole a body from the morgue that was an approximate match for our man. I was supposed to pull all the corpse's teeth and rebuild them to match the guy we kidnapped. Turned out I was a few teeth short."

"We were under a time crunch," Conor interjected. "We had to get the work done and burn the body. We figured police would find it, match the teeth, and everyone would think the guy was dead. We had some ether we'd used to knock out the guy working at the morgue. The next thing I know, the Doc slips a rag over my mouth. I'm trying to fight him off but I pass right out. I wake up in the back of a van a few hours later and half my fecking mouth is gone."

"I only took six teeth," Doc Marty grumbled. "I had to or the operation was a failure. We were in too deep to let that happen. Your teeth saved the day and the company paid to fix them."

"That's not the point," Conor said. "The point is that we were partners and you don't steal your partner's teeth."

"That sounds like a reasonable rule," Barb said.

"No shit," Conor agreed. "But we're over it now. It's out in the open, I've given you a cracking good headache, and we can move past it."

"Are you sure?" Shannon said. "I don't want to hear it dredged up again."

"If he doesn't mention it, I won't," Conor promised.

"Dad?" Shannon prompted.

"I won't either," Doc Marty said.

"Should we shake on it?" Conor said, an evil grin on his face.

Doc Marty looked at him like he was nuts, then got to his feet. "I need a pain pill. My head is killing me." He wandered off toward his quarters, Shannon helping him along.

"And you won't need those booby traps anymore!" Conor yelled after him. "I won't be paying you a visit."

"That'll be the day," Doc Marty grumbled.

Conor laughed and slung an arm around Barb. He noticed Ragus to his other side and drew him in too. "Weird family, aren't we?"

He looked to each side, noticing they were both looking at him like they just couldn't understand him.

"I'll take that as a yes."

ABOUT THE AUTHOR

Franklin Horton lives and writes in the mountains of Southwestern Virginia. He is the author of the bestselling post-apocalyptic series *The Borrowed World* and *Locker Nine*, as well as the thriller *Random Acts*. You can follow him on his website at franklinhorton.com and sign up for his newsletter with updates, book recommendations, and discounts.

ALSO BY FRANKLIN HORTON

The Borrowed World Series

The Borrowed World

Ashes of the Unspeakable

Legion of Despair

No Time For Mourning

Valley of Vengeance

Switched On

The Locker Nine Series

Locker Nine

Grace Under Fire

The Mad Mick Series

The Mad Mick

Stand-Alone Novels

Random Acts

51324272R00176

Made in the USA
Columbia, SC
16 February 2019